W9-BNV-989

The Paris Key

Center Point
Large Print

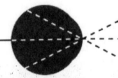

**This Large Print Book carries the
Seal of Approval of N.A.V.H.**

The
Paris Key

Juliet Blackwell

CENTER POINT LARGE PRINT
THORNDIKE, MAINE

This Center Point Large Print edition
is published in the year 2016 by arrangement with
New American Library, an imprint of Penguin Publishing
Group, a division of Penguin Random House LLC.

The text of this Large Print edition is unabridged.
In other aspects, this book may vary
from the original edition.
Printed in the United States of America
on permanent paper.
Set in 16-point Times New Roman type.

ISBN: 978-1-62899-818-4

Library of Congress Cataloging-in-Publication Data

Names: Blackwell, Juliet.
Title: The Paris key / Juliet Blackwell.
Description: Center Point Large Print edition. | Thorndike, Maine :
Center Point Large Print, 2016. | ©2015
Identifiers: LCCN 2015037599 | ISBN 9781628998184
    (hardcover : alk. paper)
Subjects: LCSH: Women—France—Paris—Fiction. | Life change
events—Fiction. | Family secrets—Fiction. | Large type books. |
Domestic fiction.
Classification: LCC PS3602.L32578 P37 2016 | DDC 813/.6—dc23
LC record available at http://lccn.loc.gov/2015037599

To Sophie
"Get 'er done."

Acknowledgments

Many thanks are due to my wonderful editor, Kerry Donovan, who shares my love of Paris and encouraged me to write a standalone novel set in that incomparable city. To my incredible agent, Jim McCarthy: Thank you for having my back and for your unstinting enthusiasm—I can't wait to see where we go next!

And most of all, to the incomparable City of Lights, and to those who make me feel so welcome in France: the staff of the charming Hôtel Saint-Paul le Marais, my home away from home. *Merci beaucoup à* Madame Michèle Stauffenegger; Marie-Louise, Marie-Pierre, *et* Jean Michel Dartevel; Philippe Berrard and Catherine Dargaud of Haut Bana Winery; Olivier Daridon *et tout la famille*; Remy and Genevieve Bonnet of Bonnet-Huteau Vignerons; Francis Unique and his beautiful family; Liliane and Corrine Garde of Château Haut-Goujon; Marie Claude and David Chauveau of the Domaine de Beausejour; and Daniel Hecquet of Le Logis des Ségur. Special thanks also to *la famille* LaCroix, and to Marc-Antoine Stauffenegger, his guitar, and his entire family for unforgettable summer nights of wine and song. And speaking of wine and song . . . thanks to Aux Trois Mailletz cabaret, which we never seem to manage to leave before the sun comes up, no matter how we try.

To Carolyn Lawes, sister and friend, unfailing support, and muse. Words aren't adequate to express what you mean to me, and to my writing. And what is a writer without a writer's circle? Many, many thanks to Rachael Herron, Sophie Littlefield, Mysti Berry, Victoria Laurie, Gigi Pandian, Nicole Peeler, Adrienne Miller, Martha White, Lynn Coddington, and Lisa Hughey. I can't believe I get to rub shoulders with such talented, beautiful, funny, smart women.

To Maddee James and Jen Forbus with Xuni Designs—thank you for the beauty, and the friendship. And to my chosen family: Bee Enos, Anna Cabrera, Mary Grae, Susan Baker, Kendall Moalem, Bruce Nikolai, Shay Demetrius, Suzanne Chan, Pamela Groves, Jan Strout, Wanda Klor, Cathy Romero, Chris Logan, and Brian Casey. And to the entire Mira Vista Social Club, especially Sara Paul, Dan Krewson, and Oscar and his crew. There could be no better neighbors.

Thanks to Jordan H. for allowing me to follow him around while he picked locks. I'm still not much good at it, but I have a newfound appreciation for how hard it is! And to Glenview Lock and Key for their generosity to our elderly neighbors through the Rebuilding Together project—and to putting up with my incessant questions. To Karen Smyers, Jungian therapist and anthropologist extraordinaire, for the analysis of Fitcher's Bird and discussions of sand tables and dream therapy. And to the Basque Library of the University of Nevada, Reno.

Much gratitude to Amy Vaudreuil for tracking down the source of the Victor Hugo quote used in the epigraph, which was taken from his notes on the city of Paris rather than from one of his novels. It was driving me crazy!

To Robert Lawes, whose strength and indomitable spirit continues to amaze and inspire me. This past year has been something of a rough road, but you've tackled it like the motorcycle-riding, downhill-skiing, jet-piloting former Marine you are. To my sister Susan Lawes, who taught me an early love of reading, and who remains a tireless cheerleader for my writing.

To my son Sergio Roberto, who has become a loving, deeply thoughtful man who works hard for what he believes in. Thank you for making me, always and ever, an exceedingly proud mama.

And finally, many special thanks to Eric Paul Stauffenegger, for his editing of the French in this book . . . and for so very much more than that: Thank you for welcoming me to your native country, and into your heart. *Merci pour l'amour et la joie et la amitié. Et le vin! Encore et toujours . . .*

The Paris Key

He who contemplates the depths of Paris is seized with vertigo. Nothing is more fantastic. Nothing is more tragic. Nothing is more sublime.

—VICTOR HUGO

Paris is always a good idea.

—AUDREY HEPBURN IN *Sabrina*

Chapter One

Her uncle Dave always used to say, "Remember the locksmiths' code, Genevieve. Never reveal the secrets you find behind locked doors, and never—ever!—abuse the power to open a lock."

Genevieve pondered this morsel of advice while Jason, her soon-to-be-ex-husband, spoke.

Uncle Dave had been on her mind a lot lately. For one thing, she kept dreaming about kneeling before a locked door, hearing his ever-patient voice in her ear as she tried repeatedly (and unsuccessfully) to pick the lock. For another, her uncle's recent death had left her with a hollow feeling: sorrow mixed with regret.

Dave's passing also left his Parisian locksmith shop unattended.

"I've never met a person as locked down as you are," Jason was saying as he leaned back against the stainless-steel Sub-Zero refrigerator (wide enough for party platters) that cost as much as Genevieve made in a month. His stance was belligerent—hands on hips, gym-toned chest thrust forward—but his liquid blue eyes conveyed contrition mixed, annoyingly, with a touch of self-conscious pity. "How can you even *think* of moving to Paris while we're in the middle of this? There are papers to sign, and lawyers to meet with."

"Sounds like the perfect time to leave the country," she said, "you have to admit."

"Be reasonable, Genie."

She winced. Yet another reason to move to Paris: The French knew how to pronounce her name. *Genevieve.* Not Jenny or Genie or even Jen-a-*veev,* but *Zhohn-vee-ev.* Was it any wonder her marriage hadn't worked out? That's what she got for marrying a man who couldn't—or wouldn't—say her name properly. But he wasn't the only one; even her best friend, Mary, called her by her surname: Martin.

All things considered, Genevieve decided, it was her mother's fault. They weren't French, after all. Her mother had spent a few weeks visiting her brother in Paris the year before Genevieve was born; a framed photo had rested on her bureau: Angela and Dave, him smiling and goateed, her with wind-whipped hair. The two of them were bookended by gargoyles high atop the Cathedral of Notre-Dame, the city laid out in the background. But was that one trip abroad reason enough for her parents to saddle their daughter with such a hard-to-pronounce name?

"It's not as though I planned my uncle's death," Genevieve said, consciously trying to accede to Jason's wishes, to be reasonable. "Someone needs to go tend to things."

"He has a daughter, doesn't he? Let her take care of it."

"Catharine doesn't know the first thing about locks."

"And you do, don't you? Sometimes I think that's all you care about."

Out of habit, she reached up to play with the rusty key that had hung on a copper chain around her neck ever since her mother's untimely death, when Genevieve was fourteen. To modern eyes it looked nothing at all like a key. More like a hunk of rusted metal.

Around here, often, this key put people in mind of the Oakland hills conflagration, the wildfire that ate through hundreds of splendid homes and claimed twenty-five souls. In the smoldering aftermath, heartbroken owners went back to sift through the rubble, collecting items from their former homes that they would later incorporate into shrines: twisted slabs of glass, slumped shards of metal, half-burned albums with a few miraculously intact photographs of Grandma.

And keys: some twisted and charred, others still jingling in pockets, ready to open doors that no longer existed.

Years later, having rebuilt with better, treeless views of San Francisco, homeowners displayed these fragments of their old lives in niches, or hung them by fishing line from pieces of gray driftwood. While sipping cocktails they would retell the story: the unseasonably warm day, the shifting winds, the panicked warnings to evacuate.

They would speak of wrangling cats and grabbing heirlooms and locating passports; of fleeing down the snakelike turns of hillside roads, a wall of black smoke at their backs. They would think, but not say aloud, that it was unfair that their beautiful homes should have blazed in the inferno while the rest of Oakland—much of it due for a good burning—had remained intact.

The key Genevieve wore around her neck had nothing at all to do with the Oakland hills fire, but she let her neighbors assume it did. It was easier that way. All she had to say was "the fire," and people nodded and looked away. They treated her with hushed tones, allowed her to avoid their eyes.

"Genie, are you even listening to me?"

"Tell you what," Genevieve said. "I'll make this easy: All I want is a ticket to Paris and enough money to take over my uncle's locksmith shop. You can keep the rest."

Suspicion clouded Jason's beautiful eyes.

Genevieve had always thought herself smarter than her husband, her mind able to make quick logical leaps that evaded him. Still, he was much more successful than she. Jason was in software sales. He wooed his clients with truffles made from organic free-trade cocoa, hand rolled in powdered sugar by single mothers at a women's collective in Berkeley. Jason felt virtuous when he bought these chocolates, the clients felt good about eating them, and, fueled by sugar and caffeine, they placed software orders in record numbers. "It's a win-win," was one of Jason's favorite phrases, and he lived by that credo. But then, fate had been kind to him: Tall and well built, with light brown hair and blue eyes, he worked out religiously, dressed fashionably, and had a knack for remembering names. Nothing in Jason's experience had suggested that life was anything other than a series of mutually beneficial relationships. Win-win.

What business had someone like Genevieve, she wondered for the hundredth time, had marrying a lighthearted optimist?

A thick sludge covered the bottom of her coffee cup. A freebie from a fund-raiser luncheon, the mug was the perfect size and weight, and she relished the way the palm of her hand cradled it, telegraphing the warmth of its contents to her blood in the mornings. Because although their house was expensive, it was old and drafty and always cold, built in a stand of redwoods on a hill overlooking Oakland and the San Francisco Bay. On a clear day an astute viewer might catch a glimpse of the Golden Gate Bridge, an earthy shade of Tuscan red gleaming in the sunshine. But clear days were rare. The house was engulfed by fog most mornings and by clouds most afternoons, and the soaring trees reached up into the haze and dripped dew onto the roof, the water tap-tap-

tapping in a steady cadence that Genevieve found pleasant but Jason did not.

Genevieve knew Jason would have preferred to toss her old chipped mug into the trash in favor of the creamy bisque coffee set he had bought in a tiny Italian boutique in San Francisco's North Beach not long after they married and moved into the house with the blue door. "It's called Bianco de Bianco," Jason had said, showing off the ceramics to their guests as they lingered over after-dinner coffee. "You mean 'white'?" Mary had asked in her signature dry tone. Genevieve had snorted; then, in penance, had remarked upon the set's simple, refined beauty. That was back when she had been careful to protect her husband's feelings, his pride. Not anymore.

Clearly this marriage is no longer mutually beneficial. Genevieve wondered whether the woman Jason had been seeing, Quiana, found their affair a win-win.

"Are you serious?" Jason asked, looking at Genevieve out of the corner of his eye. "All you want is a locksmith shop?"

"Maybe I'll take this cup, too."

She could almost make out the sound of wheels grinding as Jason considered her offer, searching for the catch. "How much are we talking? What's a locksmith shop in Paris worth?"

Priceless. "I'm not sure. I'll need to speak with my cousin Catharine and figure out the details.

For the moment, I just want the plane ticket."

"Genie . . ." Jason's voice dropped, becoming gentle, earnest. "What in the world are you going to do in Paris? You're a copy editor, not a locksmith."

"Suddenly you're a fan of my copyediting?"

"At least it's a real job. Locksmithing is a . . . a dream. A childhood memory."

His words sent Genevieve's mind tripping over the memory of all the locks she had mastered at her uncle's side: the double-ball padlock and dimple devices she practiced on until she was ready for Schlage's side pin. She could hear their soft clicks and whirs in her mind, drowning out Jason's words.

"Genie . . . you don't have to do this. We could see a marriage counselor, work things out. How many times do I have to say it? It was a mistake. I'm *sorry*. It didn't mean anything; it just happened. . . ." He trailed off, shook his handsome head. Remembered what his life coach told him about being a man and taking responsibility. "No, that's not right. No excuses. I'm so sorry I hurt you, Genie."

Genevieve continued searching the contents of her coffee cup without responding.

Here was the truth: *Deep down she didn't care.* She was using Jason's affair as a reason to demand the separation, but it was the very fact that she couldn't get herself to care that made her realize they should divorce. When they first met, she had been dazzled by Jason's straightforward, sunny disposition; now she found it stifling, exhausting. Unbearable. Jason was not a bad man. He needed something from his partner that Genevieve could not give; must he be condemned for that? And yet, publicly, she *did* place the blame on him, citing his affair, feigning heartbreak, taking the easy way out. Allowing people to make assumptions, just as they did about the key she wore around her neck.

She reached up to brush her fingers along the rusty talisman, warm from her skin.

Genevieve had found the key while cleaning out her mother's lingerie drawer, not long after she died. It had been swathed in Bubble Wrap, in an airmail package.

With it was a note written in a spidery, all-caps scrawl: *YOU HOLD THE KEY.*

It was postmarked Paris.

Chapter Two

1997

The uncle she had never met picked her up at Charles de Gaulle Airport, which she learned the locals called Roissy. They drove toward Paris in the smallest car Genevieve had ever seen, past hulking blocks of cement buildings that made up dismal housing projects and industrial sites. At long last they exited the thruway and began inching through thick traffic in the streets of Paris. Ominous skies were drizzling more than raining: a sluggish, lugubrious wetting. Parisians hunched over in their coats and boots, collars turned up, wielding umbrellas like weapons on the crowded sidewalks.

Everything, from the darkening sky to the balconied buildings to the trash in the street, was some dreary shade of gray. Why did people speak of this city with such adoration? Her mother always used to refer to Paris as "the City of Lights," her voice taking on a rare reverential tone when she spoke of it.

"How was your trip?" asked Uncle Dave as they drove.

Genevieve shrugged in response, not wanting to look at him.

Dave was an old man, Genevieve had realized with a shock when she first set eyes on her uncle in the airport. He had a full head of white hair and a Don Quixote–style goatee, and he walked with a limp. At more than twenty years her mother's senior, Dave seemed more grandfather than uncle. According to family lore, a teenaged Dave had come to Paris to help rebuild after World War II, fell in love with a Frenchwoman named Pasquale, married, and never returned.

At the airport, he had stood outside of customs

holding up a hand-lettered sign, black ink on bright red paper: GENEVIEVE MARTIN, WELCOME!

Her Air France escort, who had been tasked with making sure Genevieve didn't somehow become lost on the nonstop flight from San Francisco, was an elegant, slender blonde who filled out her uniform perfectly and called Genevieve "sweetheart" in English with a lilting, melodic accent. Genevieve had hated her on sight and throughout the twelve-hour journey answered her gracious condescension with sneers and eye rolls.

Upon spying Dave's sign the flight attendant gave Genevieve's uncle a frosty nod and handed her charge over to him without a word, disappearing behind doors clearly marked: DÉFENSE D'ENTRER. No admittance.

Despite her attempts to alienate the attendant throughout the flight, Genevieve felt a pang of abandonment as she watched the woman go. Glancing up at the smiling old man with the sign, Genevieve thought, *He could be anyone*. He had shown no documentation, after all. And he didn't look much like the old photo on her mom's bureau. What if he was some creepy French child molester who'd read her name on a list somewhere and decided to pick up an "unaccompanied minor" to do awful things, the kinds of crimes spoken of in whispers?

Genevieve wished her brother, Nick, were here, or her dad. Uncle Dave had invited them all to come; Genevieve had overheard his boisterous voice on speakerphone, declaring that Paris could cure heartache. Her father and brother claimed they were too busy with the farm, but they booked a flight for Genevieve, whether she wanted to go or not. Probably glad to be rid of her, she thought.

"Did you eat on the plane?" Dave asked as they drove.

Genevieve shrugged again. Still, she was relieved he spoke English. She hadn't been entirely sure he would but had been too embarrassed to ask. Her mother, Angela, had told stories about her Parisian brother over the years, and Genevieve had a vague sense that he might be the reason she was saddled with a name that was so difficult to spell, but she hadn't really put all the pieces together. But now she realized that, like her mother, Dave had been born and raised in Mississippi. He even spoke with a slight drawl, reminding her of home. Of her mom.

Her *dead* mom.

She felt the hot prickle of tears behind her eyes. Threatening, humiliating. Genevieve had come up with a trick to keep them at bay: She bit her tongue and imagined peppermint candy, the red-striped disks she used to steal from her neighbor's candy dish. The metallic tang of blood let her know she'd bit too hard. Not for the first time.

"Well, I hope you're hungry," Dave continued, unfazed by her sullen silence. "Because Pasquale's a great little cook. One thing about living in France, you eat well. Hey—you like croissants?"

She shrugged again.

"You tellin' me you've never had a croissant for breakfast? How about a *pain au chocolat*? No? Why, you're in for a treat, darlin'."

"We eat whole grain at home."

"Oh, well, that's commendable. But a genuine Parisian *pain au chocolat* . . ." He trailed off with a chuckle and a shake of his head.

"Is it breakfast time?" Genevieve asked.

"Oh no, it's almost suppertime. The croissants will be for tomorrow morning. We'll take a walk, see the neighborhood. You'll love it."

She gazed out the foggy window. It was rush hour and the streets were jammed; pedestrians made swifter progress than the cars.

"This corner might not look like much," Dave said as they sat immobilized, watching as the light turned red for the second time, "but this is where the Bastille used to be."

"What's the Bast-ee?" she asked, curious in spite of herself.

"You haven't heard of Bastille Day? It's sort of like Fourth of July, but here it's *le quatorze juillet*, the fourteenth of July."

"Independence day?" Genevieve wasn't great at history. Had France been a colony?

"Not an independence day like in the States . . . but sort of. The Bastille was an old prison that

26

stood right there." As he pointed, Genevieve studied the crookedness of his finger, the gnarled blue veins and ugly brown spots that covered the back of his hand. She tried to reconcile his rheumy eyes and sagging cheeks with old family photos. Dave had been a teenager when he first came to Paris: dashing and romantic, with dark hair and a goatee. More than fifty years ago. He had lied about his age, insisted on enlisting. It was the tail end of the war, but they still needed fresh, uninjured boys. "See that sign over there?"

Genevieve searched but saw nothing more than gray shopfronts, a restaurant, and a bar. Spindly-looking chairs were tilted forward to lean against tiny café tables, glistening in the rain. A clutch of commuters waited for the bus, huddled under a bright yellow awning that looked garish in the otherwise monochromatic cityscape.

"On the corner of the building, there," Dave said as the light changed and they finally moved on. "Not that interesting, I suppose, in any case. But here's a good skill to learn: In Paris the signs are usually found on the corners of buildings, not on poles like in the States. So if you're looking for a street sign, look for a plaque on a building. And sometimes you'll learn a little bit about history, instead. Almost by accident."

They pulled behind a sea of cars at the next light. The lanes seemed to be mere suggestions, with cars straddling the painted lines willy-nilly.

Ahead, a pair of drivers vied for position and began to argue, the taxi driver opening his door to half stand with one foot out, one foot in, the other yelling through his open window. The cabdriver made a series of hand gestures that, though foreign to her, left no doubt as to their meaning. Genevieve took note for future reference.

The gesturer won the spot and nosed his taxi into the lane.

"So, anyway," continued Dave, "round about 1789 the French people got tired of the abuse they suffered at the hands of the aristocrats, and stormed the Bastille to release the prisoners."

Now interested, Genevieve twisted in her seat, looking behind them to see any traces of such a place.

"We can walk by there one day when we're out sightseeing, if you want," said Uncle Dave. "But like I said, there's not much to see anymore. You'd probably like the Eiffel Tower more."

"I went to a prison once," Genevieve said.

"Did you, now? Did the judge throw the book at you?"

"I mean, just to visit. With my mom."

Genevieve had been in the fourth grade. There was a rally planned to protest the imminent execution of a condemned prisoner at San Quentin, the hulking state prison on the shore of the San Francisco Bay. Genevieve had begged and pleaded with her mother to be allowed to go. Angela had hesitated, pointing out that it was Sunday, a school night. But Genevieve's father had encouraged the outing. "She's not too young to understand injustice," Jim had said, making Genevieve wonder why he never joined Angela at such protests.

On the way, they sang her mother's favorite childhood song: *"I love you, a bushel and a peck, and it beats me all to heck, how I'll never tend the farm. . . ."*

But once they arrived, things turned grim. The crowd milled around, chanting, witnessing, crying, or praying for a man none of them had ever met. The musty wool blanket scratched Genevieve's neck when her mother wrapped it tight around her shoulders to ward off the chill blowing across the bay. Well-dressed television reporters checked their lip gloss and applied hairspray; bulky news vans bristling with antennae were parked in driveways rented from the locals; cameramen hoisted their equipment on their shoulders and scanned the crowds, looking for a good shot. A few reporters were interviewing random protestors, but most were waiting, as they all were, for something to happen: for the governor to issue a reprieve or for the executioners to act.

Genevieve had gazed through the gates at the well-lit, Art Deco façade of the massive penal structure, her mind conjuring lurid images of what went on inside those walls.

She knew she was supposed to care about the man who was about to die, but what caught her imagination was the town itself. It had an ice-cream parlor and a post office and sat right on the water, little clapboard houses inhabited mostly by prison staff and their families. A sweet little main street, like a movie set . . . but what about their monstrous neighbor at the end of the lane? How did the residents manage to drift off to sleep? Did they shrink from imagined faces in their windows? Did they wonder if this was the night a convict might scale the walls, jimmy the lock, sneak in to exact a grisly revenge?

It made Genevieve shiver to think of that face in the window.

Angela had gathered the prickly blanket tighter around Genevieve's ears and pulled her daughter to her side, wrapping her arm around her.

The back of her mother's arm looked like melted ice cream, its skin puckered and shiny, yet to Genevieve the scars were familiar and comforting. She liked to run her finger over the strange surface; it felt slippery and hard, like plastic, so different from regular flesh. Whenever she asked her mother what had happened, Angela would say only that there had been an accident. If Genevieve pushed for an answer, Angela would reply, with a rare edge to her voice, that life was complicated and it was impolite to stare.

Genevieve had craned her neck to study her

mother's face in the hazy yellow glow of the streetlamps. Angela was pretty (thick auburn hair, chocolate brown eyes, even features) and Genevieve noticed how some of the dads would linger at the school gates to talk with her. But Angela never responded, rarely smiling, always holding herself apart; "aloof" was the word Genevieve once heard someone use to describe her mother. She had looked it up in the dictionary, but to Genevieve it didn't describe Angela. Angela was too good for them, was the problem.

But then Angela had looked stricken, tormented by the stranger's imminent death.

"Do you know him?" Genevieve asked, embarrassed that she hadn't thought to ask earlier.

Angela looked down at her, an uncomprehending look on her face. "What?"

"Do you know the man they're going to execute?" Genevieve clarified.

"No, baby," said Angela. "I just . . . I just think it's wrong to kill."

"No matter what?"

"No matter what."

"Even if it's self-defense?"

Genevieve would have thought it impossible, but the sorrow on her mother's face seemed to intensify, her brown eyes gleaming with unshed tears.

"Like, I mean, if someone was trying to kill you," Genevieve hurried to explain, not wanting her mother to think she was an ogre, that she thought it was okay to kill. "Then it would be okay to do it to them first, right?"

Angela nodded slowly, looking back toward the prison. When she spoke, her voice was hushed. "Yes, I suppose self-defense is a different matter altogether. Hush, now, baby; let's remember why we're here."

Genevieve fell silent. The cold salt air stung her cheeks, and her stomach growled. But she didn't complain. She knew she was supposed to feel sad for the man, but the truth was she hoped there would be more protests, that this would become a regular mother-daughter event. It felt special, grown-up, even magical to be outside in the middle of the night, stars sparkling overhead.

No reprieve was granted. At 12:13 a.m. an announcement was made: The man had been put to death. A few protestors lingered, gathering in prayer circles or making statements to the press, but most shuffled back to their cars in silence.

Angela had driven them home, her cheeks wet with tears. It was only as they were nearing the farm that Genevieve realized she didn't know what the man had done to earn his death sentence. The sad, distracted look on her mother's face kept her from asking.

She was sorry, now, that she hadn't. There were

so many things she wished she had asked her mother when she had the chance.

"What had they done, the prisoners in the Bast-ee?" Genevieve asked her uncle.

"Offended the king in some way. They were political prisoners."

"Were there a lot of them?"

"Good question!" Dave chuckled and shook his head. "Actually, turns out there were only seven prisoners in the Bastille at the time, but it was a symbolic victory. And never underestimate the power of a symbolic victory. Now, see that river, right there? That's the famous Seine."

The river was a black expanse in the rapidly fading light. A series of small bridges lit by ornate streetlamps straddled the water, leading to yet more bleak buildings on the other side.

"And here we are, home at last," Dave said as he turned onto a tiny street with cobblestone sidewalks.

Genevieve looked up just in time to catch sight of a small plaque on the side of a building. Craning her neck, she made out white letters against a faded blue background.

"Village Saint-Paul?" she read.

"Village Saint-Paul," Dave repeated with the French pronunciation. "One of the oldest neighborhoods in all of Paris. Full of nooks and crannies, little lanes and courtyards with no cars allowed, just the occasional bicycle. We're known as the antiques district, people come from all over to shop, and we have a few big outdoor antique fairs every year."

"Oh."

Dave looked at her with amusement. "You don't like antiques?"

She shrugged.

"I'll tell you a secret," he said in a whisper. "I don't care much about them, either. Not antiques per se, anyway. But I do love antique keys and the old houses they belong to."

Dave stopped the car in the middle of the street, killed the engine, and got out, circling around to get her suitcase and bag out of the trunk. Genevieve followed suit. It made her nervous that they were blocking the way, but there weren't any other cars on this narrow side street. In fact, there seemed to be no life at all.

"This is it," he said proudly, gesturing toward a storefront. The lights in the shop were out, so all she saw was a display window in the anemic glow of a streetlamp that barely cut through the cool mist of the evening. A wooden sign over the window read: UNDER LOCK AND KEY.

"It's in English." The one thing Genevieve had been prepared for upon her arrival in France was not to be able to understand anything.

"Yep, I keep meaning to come up with a better French name but never quite got around to it."

"Do people here speak English?"

Dave chuckled. "Not so's you'd notice. The younger folks more than the older ones. But I went with the English saying because the French word for locks, *serrures*, was hard for an old country boy like me to pronounce. And besides, after the war Americans were pretty popular around here."

Genevieve tried to remember why. She knew the U.S. had been involved in World War II, but she was fuzzy on the details. The Gulf War, Vietnam, Korea, the world wars . . . the dates and details bobbed aimlessly in her head, sticking around only long enough to carry her through whatever test she was taking. Ancient history.

"We helped liberate France from the Nazis," Dave explained. "Now, can you carry this heavy bag all by yourself?"

She nodded, grabbing her suitcase and hoisting it as best she could. The little wheels on the bag wouldn't roll on the uneven stones. Dave limped as he led the way into the alcove. *Maybe everyone had scars by the time they grew old,* Genevieve thought.

He unlocked the little shop and waved her through the door.

The locksmith shop was petite, more like a large walk-in closet than a proper store. Its dusty shelves were jammed with locks and keys, door-knobs and doorknockers, decorative hinges and shutter hardware. Small wooden barrels held bolts and screws and other metal tools. It smelled of pipe tobacco and some sort of oil, like a car mechanic's garage.

One wall was festooned with clocks: cuckoo clocks, painted clocks, clocks with no numbers, clocks in the shape of the sun. Their frenetic ticking filled the otherwise silent space.

"Let me introduce you to your *tante* Pasquale— that's 'aunt Pasquale' in French—and to your cousin Catharine, and then I'll run and park the car. Let me tell you, Genevieve, parking in Paris is not for the faint of heart. But your old uncle Dave has a few tricks up his sleeve."

He gave her a wink and opened a small door behind the old-fashioned brass cash register.

"*Bienvenue chez nous*," he said. "Welcome home."

Chapter Three

Mary insisted on taking Genevieve to the airport, located many miles to the south of San Francisco, in the city of Burlingame.

"Those bags are too heavy to schlep on BART," Mary said. "Besides, I feel like Paris will swallow you up and I'll never see you again."

"That's not true. And anyway, it's only a flight away. You should come visit."

"Maybe," she answered with a shrug. Mary was

nervous about driving on the bridge, so she kept her eyes fixed on the span, her hands wrapped so tightly around the wheel, her knuckles were white. Still, when Genevieve offered to drive, she declined, citing the need to practice.

This had always intrigued Genevieve: Mary was fearless about so much of life, but occasionally some small thing, some everyday function—like signing up for health insurance or driving on the bridge—threw her for a loop.

Mary was an artist. Like Genevieve, she had been on her own from a very young age. Probably that was why they'd gravitated to each other in the crowded coffeehouse where they'd met; Mary asked to share the table, and after trading a few snarky comments about the oddly bewhiskered hipsters surrounding them, they recognized kindred souls. Unlike Genevieve, however, Mary had a straightforward way of saying what she needed and wanted and thought, without subterfuge.

The airport was a series of long lines and overly personal security inspections, but Genevieve barely noticed, buoyed as she was by the prospect of imminent freedom. Her seatmate on the plane was a young Greek man, flying to Paris on business. He was dark and handsome, and despite his nice gray suit and sleek leather briefcase, he smelled like the beach: warm sunshine on bare skin, mixed with exotic spices. After perfunctory hellos, she brought out her book and he put in earbuds and closed his eyes.

The moment the airplane reached altitude, an exquisite blond flight attendant came by, offering flutes of champagne to everyone of legal drinking age. Upon first glance Genevieve had an irrational thought: Could this be the same woman who had escorted her to Paris so many years ago?

No, of course not; far too much time had passed. This was simply what so many Frenchwomen looked like: slender, elegant, gracious—a flurry of adjectives came to mind, not one of which described Genevieve.

Genevieve thought of herself as ordinary, clumsy, even evasive. She had inherited her mother's thick auburn hair and deep brown eyes, but otherwise she felt run-of-the-mill, slightly shorter than average. Thirty-three years old, unhappy, and on the verge of divorce. It dawned on her, only then, that she was almost the same age her mother had been when Angela went to visit her brother in the Village Saint-Paul, a last hurrah before Genevieve was born.

Was she unconsciously retracing her mother's footsteps? That sounded like something Jason would propose, now that he was in therapy. Probably his life coach would suggest that Genevieve had never gotten over her mother's death and that she was running away in search of answers.

No kidding, she thought. Could anyone who hadn't lost a parent early truly understand the extent of the loss? Was it even worth trying to explain?

Angela's death was the brutal dividing line in Genevieve's life: First she had a mother, and then she didn't. The course of the devastation was swift, with only a few weeks from initial detection of the disease to her death. Not even long enough for extended family to be notified and called to her bedside. Her husband and children were still in denial when Angela's remains were whisked away, leaving them stunned and mortified, awkwardly shuffling through their days, tending to the animals, not talking. Angela hadn't wanted a memorial service; instead, she requested that her husband and children sprinkle her ashes at the base of the dusty old sycamore tree, the one that shaded the turkey shed. Nick suggested they plant a rosebush in her memory, but Angela had laughed and said no, that if the bush died it would be like her leaving yet again. *"The sycamore's a better bet,"* she'd said with a smile. *"Nothing will kill that thing. And I'll be perfect fertilizer."*

Three weeks after Angela's death Genevieve experienced the fresh new hell of Mother's Day. During school Genevieve was allowed to read in the library while her classmates made cards, but she couldn't avoid the fund-raisers selling carnation posies. See's Candies, the local florist, even the grocery store . . . she had felt inundated at every turn by the push to celebrate the mother who had abandoned her by dying, who had left her with a yawning void in her life, a need that ran so deep and dark that Genevieve feared she would never reach the bottom, no matter how far she dared dive into the abyss.

Yet another good reason to move to France, Genevieve thought. *No Mother's Day.*

Or . . . was there? Had they, too, been infected with this Hallmark holiday? Sometimes it snuck up without warning, like in her senior year of high school, when her father took her to Philadelphia for college tours of Penn and Drexel. Jim saw it as an opportunity to teach his daughter a little about history, insisting on shepherding her to see the Liberty Bell and Independence Hall. While walking downtown they spied a plaque dedicated to Anne Jarvis, who had begun the tradition of Mother's Day as a tribute to her own mother, and who then lobbied for it to become a national holiday.

"Screw Mother's Day," Genevieve had muttered under her breath, and Jim, her sad, stoic, somber father, who normally admonished her to watch her language, for once seemed to understand his rebellious daughter.

He nodded thoughtfully and said, *"I'm with you, kid."*

• • •

A flight attendant came by and offered more champagne. Champagne in economy class: You had to love the French. But with the second glass, a gnawing uncertainty took root in Genevieve's belly.

Ever since hearing about her uncle's passing and Catharine's suggestion that Genevieve take over his shop, Genevieve had been absolutely sure of what she wanted. Her mind had remained focused on escape, the safe passage away from her current life that Paris seemed to offer. But . . . who was she to think she could make a new life *anywhere,* much less in Paris? She had already begun the paperwork to request permission to work as a foreign national, but the officials at the Consulat de France had warned her it would be a grueling, time-consuming process.

And even if she succeeded in that, she would have to figure out how to become certified as a locksmith to maintain the business. Genevieve still practiced opening old thrift-store locks while watching TV many evenings, but locksmithing involved more than just picking locks. She didn't even speak French, just a few scattered phrases remembered from childhood, a couple of long-ago courses at college, plus the little bit she convinced herself she could learn online. She had planned to continue to study on the plane, but of course a few hours of intensive language acquisition would not be enough to do the trick. How was she supposed to operate a business in a foreign land, in a foreign *language?*

And the only souls she knew in France were her *tante* Pasquale, who was, according to her cousin Catharine's infrequent e-mails, now beset by dementia; and of course Catharine herself, who had always been a tad strange.

"I don't really like the French," Mary had said with characteristic forthrightness when Genevieve told her she was moving to Paris.

"How many French people do you know?"

"None," she said with a shrug. "But still."

Mary was one of the things Genevieve would miss about the U.S. Most of her other friends were conditional: old school friends or work friends or couples friends. Even though Jason was the one who had had the affair, he was keeping the majority of their mutual acquaintances in the separation. With her blessing.

She pulled out her notebook—a pretty one she'd bought for the trip, wrapped in faux red leather and embossed with what looked like ancient scribblings—and began a list. Blue ink on heavy white sketch paper. *I will miss:*

1. Mary
2. Convenience stores open twenty-four hours
3. Mexican food
4. Redwood trees

Her pen hovered above the paper. What else?

Her father had passed away last year. Her brother, Nick? Not really. Not if she was being honest. He was still working the family farm in Petaluma, which was newly chic because trendy, upscale restaurants adored his organic specialties, not only vegetables but things like homemade free-range pork sausage. Nick's wife was an earnest, well-put-together woman who spoke to the farm animals in baby talk and commuted to a nondescript job in San Francisco's financial district that paid a good salary, with benefits. They traded occasional phone calls, and there were dinners at Christmas and birthdays, but otherwise they rarely spoke or visited.

Surely there were other things Genevieve would miss. People didn't just leave their native land without regret. It wasn't as though she was fleeing war or famine.

After a long moment, she added one more item to her list: *The Golden Gate Bridge*. Then she put away the notebook and opened the computer to continue her French lessons. As the hours ticked by, dinner was served—good food served with free wine, this being a French airline—and Genevieve started two different novels but found herself dissatisfied with each; worked on the *New York Times* crossword puzzle until she was stumped by the name of the German mathematician who invented set theory; then turned back to her French-language page.

The foreign words—most of which contained far too many vowels—started to blur and bob. She closed her computer to save the battery, shut her eyes, and fell asleep envisioning the Paris that she had visited so many years before.

The pilot's voice came over the loudspeaker: They had begun their descent into Paris.

Chapter Four

Angela, 1983

She is a terrible person.

It doesn't matter how many times Dave tries to assure her that, no, this isn't so; Angela knows the truth.

Perhaps this is why, no matter how she tries, she can't draw a single deep breath. She awakens gasping, night after night, feeling as though she is suffocating.

So she has left her husband, and worse, so very much worse, her son. She left her little boy, Nicholas. Tricky Nicky, they call him, but it is a misleading nickname (Nick name!) because the truth is, he isn't tricky at all. He is honest and straightforward and kind: a good boy with an even temper. Like his father, he is quiet and hardworking and eager to please.

Angela has left behind his sticky hands and clinging arms and the warm, solid weight of him when he sits on her lap, which he does every rare moment he catches her sitting down. She has left behind the terrible burden of the trust in the big brown pools of his eyes, the pure love that shines from his open countenance.

Nicholas is just entering the second grade but already he is helping his father on the farm. Already he is preaching to other children about the benefits of organic vegetables, the importance of appreciating the simple happiness of a pig in the wallow when the sun is setting, the dusty elegance of the sycamore trees, the magic of the "fairy circles" that the baby redwoods create when their mother dies.

Already he understands the importance of the farm not just as a living, but as a vocation.

The farm. Somehow in all the time when Angela was fighting her way out of rural Mississippi, landing a scholarship to college, where she rallied and marched for civil rights and social justice—everything from voting rights to banning the bomb to ending apartheid—she had never imagined herself ending up on a farm. She had grown up on something very closely approximating that, but when Jim talked about going back to the land in such romantic, sweeping terms, she hadn't fully realized what his talk about food-as-politics signified. It meant mornings spent feeding livestock that stank of musk and damp. Days in the punishing sun tending to aphid-infested broccoli and pulling Japanese beetles off the spinach. Evenings spent haggling over endless paperwork, trying to get their farm officially certified as organic. Their future and their son's future dependent on whether it rained too much or not enough, whether the blight or the insects or the drought would deal them a deathblow. It meant never, ever taking a vacation because the farm must be tended to at all times.

It is a good life. She is very lucky. Everyone tells her so.

Still, the farm is as relentless and unforgiving as a child. Its demands are more or less outrageous at different points in the season, but they are always there. Forever in the back of your mind, even when you manage a day trip to San Francisco with girlfriends or a rare evening out with your husband.

If only she could breathe.

It had gotten so bad Angela tried confiding in her mother, of all people. But she laughed at Angela, her words coming over the telephone line, cutting and bitter, saying it's not so easy to run away from real life, is it, missy? Reminding her that she had tried to escape her rural background, even honeymooning in la-di-da Paris, but oh, how the mighty do fall. And telling her to do her duty, take care of her husband and child, and stop whining.

Complaining is the number one sin. Angela knows that. Accept your situation, count your blessings, get back to work. Stop whining.

And Angela will go back. Of course she will. She just needs a little break, just a brief respite. To remember how to breathe. She will go back to Jim and Nicholas and things will be just as they were. Among other things, she has to attend to the canning; she imagines the peaches are almost ready, and when they come, they come with a vengeance, the tree's drooping arms finally letting go its heavy fruit like the rush of falling marbles in one of Nicky's favorite games.

She will go back and she and Nicholas will watch silly reruns of *I Love Lucy* together over organic cornmeal-crust vegetarian pizza, and Jim will fret about the state of the broccoli, and everything will be just as it was, as it always has been.

What she wouldn't give for one deep breath, the air streaming fully into her lungs, that exquisitely sweet feeling of expansion. Of life. Even the radio seems to mock her. In one of the year's most popular songs, the Police keep singing: "Every breath you take . . ."

"Look at everything we've built here," Jim had said. *"The crop's looking good this year. And the*

turkeys are on track for Thanksgiving sales. We're surrounded by beauty, living the dream. What more could you want?"

She had no answer for him. Most of her old friends from school had landed regular jobs with stock options and dental plans and benefit packages and lived in tract homes in the suburbs. Imagining swapping her life with theirs makes her feel just as tired, just as breathless.

Perhaps she is experiencing nothing more exotic than an early-onset midlife crisis, like she'd read about just the other day while in line at the grocery store, right after Nicholas—good, obedient Tricky Nicky—refused the candy she offered him, since she wanted to indulge in a Snickers bar herself. She knew she was a bad mother for trying to tempt him. In theory, she and Jim didn't believe in processed sugar, though truth to tell, Angela couldn't give a damn from time to time. Let the poor kid have some fun before he had to start thinking about things like fat-free diets and processed sugar and preservatives.

"Here, have a *pain au chocolat*. The best in the city. Then you can tell old Dave what's going on in that pretty little head of yours."

His tone is light, but Angela knows Dave's heart is breaking for her. She knows he is appalled that she has left her husband and son behind, but he can't know what it's like, that life. The oppressiveness of it; all encompassing, heavy, energy sapping, like the full, wet heat of an August afternoon in Mississippi. When they were kids they had no air-conditioning; at night their mother would place wet sheets on top of them so they could sleep in the still, hot air. Angela remembers that feeling: every inch of her skin damp and feverish, yearning for a breeze, for relief.

She wishes she could tell Dave what is wrong. She wishes she knew herself. Since arriving in Paris she has been sleeping fourteen hours a day, waking only when Pasquale or Dave drags her from bed, insisting she shower and sit at the table. She has no interest in food or conversation, no interest in anything. She wants nothingness.

"Did Jim . . . ? Did he hit you?" had been Dave's first question, before they even got on the thruway from the airport. The natural query of a protective older brother, a brother old enough to be her father. There are snapshots, faded by now to yellow and blue, of Dave visiting from France, always with a young Angela astride his wide shoulders. So many photos that Dave once joked that he used to have a strange sort of growth on his back, but he'd had it removed when Angela was five so she could go to kindergarten without him.

Now he asks again: "Did Jim do something to hurt you?"

"No, Jim would never hurt me," Angela answers with a firm shake of her head. Her auburn hair gleams in the light streaming through the café windows; her hands shake as she brings the coffee to her lips. The cup is tiny, holding a café au lait about half the size of one typically served in the States. The *pain au chocolat*, on the other hand, is easily twice the size of the typical American concoction. It is bigger than her hand, the hand still wearing the simple gold band Jim had placed upon it ten years ago, only six months after they had met at a peace rally in Washington, DC.

She bites into the pastry. It is huge, yet unlike most overlarge things, it does not lack in taste. The flaky layers are soaked in rich French butter, chewy and crumbly at the same time. The chocolate is soft and creamy, a dark and sensuous experiment in cocoa.

Angela's eyes flutter closed as she loses herself to the sensual experience of caffeine and chocolate and butter, a memory of the last time she visited Dave, with Jim on their honeymoon.

"Did he have an affair?" Dave asks.

Angela understands why her brother is persisting. In his mind, it makes no sense. Dave adores his wife and always has; he forsook his country for hers, falling in love with Paris just as he did with Pasquale. In Dave's mind, you built a life upon everyday pleasures, reveling in time spent with family and friends. He had been a neighborhood locksmith for more than thirty years, packing his little black bag and walking or bicycling all over

Paris, happily letting people into their houses, opening old boxes and safes, installing safety equipment. He probably owns keys to half the homes and businesses in the city, and yet there is no question of trust with a man like Dave.

In the middle of the day he would take a leisurely lunch at a café with a friend, and at night he would return to a lavish dinner prepared by the apparently ever-patient and pleasant Pasquale, often shared with extended family; on weekends he played *pétanque* with his friends in the Jardin des Tuileries. It is a good life, a steady life.

What about Pasquale? Angela wonders. Does Pasquale ever wish to simply turn and walk away from her husband and child? To leave the cloying embrace of her big extended family, the ones who drop in for dinner, asking for help with child care and finding jobs and making rent?

"No, no affair," Angela answers simply.

Dave gazes at her across the table, and she knows he wants her to say whatever it is she needs to say. But she has nothing for him. After so many years of tamping them down, swallowing her words whole, she doesn't know how to explain the things that she is feeling.

"I'll go back," Angela finally utters with as much conviction as she can summon. "I'm going back soon. I just . . . I just needed a little breathing room."

"Ah yes, of course," says Dave, and Angela sees

relief in his blue eyes. "Just a little vacation in the City of Lights, and you'll be back to your old self!"

The *pain au chocolat* sits heavy in her gut; the coffee churns.

She is suffocating.

She is gasping for breath.

She is a terrible person.

Chapter Five

Catharine had been full of apologies to Genevieve for not being in Paris to greet her "little American cousin" at the airport, but Genevieve was just as glad. She liked the idea of taking an anonymous cab for the long ride into the city, experiencing the trip in silence, by herself. She wanted to be free to let the memories flood her mind, to sate her nostalgia, untainted by the presence of another, by the need for catching up or innocuous questions about the flight.

Still, Genevieve hadn't anticipated the effects of lack of sleep and the overwhelming, awkward strangeness of arriving, alone and unable to speak the language, in a foreign city.

Her eyes were gritty and sore. Every part of her felt sticky with the funk of travel.

Upon disembarking from the airplane, she found herself unaccountably irritated that all the signs were in French. Embarrassment washed over her when she couldn't figure out which line to stand in for immigration, and when it was finally her turn at the kiosk she had a panicked moment when she couldn't locate her passport. By the time Genevieve made her way to baggage claim, found her bags, and wandered through customs, she began to feel famished: a deep, sickly hunger.

She emerged from the air-conditioned terminal into an unseasonably warm and muggy day under overcast skies. Her leggings stuck to her skin; her jacket was far too warm, but she couldn't take it off—one arm was holding her purse and her carry-on; the other was pulling her suitcase, which was so heavy she'd had to pay an exorbitant overage charge at check-in in San Francisco.

She fought the urge to calculate what time it "really" was (middle of the night? dawn?), reminding herself instead that this was it: Paris was the new reality.

Paris. Where she didn't speak the language and knew almost no one.

By the time Genevieve made it to the taxi stand she was covered in a sheen of perspiration and wondered if she smelled as bad as she feared. She could feel a drop of sweat rolling down the center of her back. She had practiced a few lines in French and made a token stab at negotiating the cost of the trip into Paris with the supervisor at the taxi stand, but who was she kidding? At this point she would pay a small ransom to be dropped off in the Village Saint-Paul.

All she wanted was to hide and regroup. To drop her luggage and peel off her clothes and take a shower. To pull herself together, far from chicly dressed strangers speaking their lyrical, unintelligible language.

The cabdriver was North African, and French appeared to be his second language as well, so there was no attempt at small talk as they zoomed down the thruway in the blessedly air-conditioned cab. As her clamminess subsided, Genevieve looked out the window and started to relax. This is what she had remembered: ugly gray blocks of apartments and factories. She could be on the outskirts of Detroit, she thought, happiness suddenly bubbling up. The ordinariness of this approach to Paris seemed almost ludicrous, hiding as it did such a spectacular city. Like a winning sweepstakes ticket presented in a ripped and stained manila envelope, the kind usually tossed directly into the recycling.

Once they escaped the thruway and made their way through thick city traffic to the Village Saint-Paul, Genevieve started to feel fluttery with excitement. She had an inkling of imminent victory, not unlike the feeling of being close to defeating a frustrating lock.

True, she didn't speak the language. And she

hardly knew a soul in France. As Jason had tried his best to convince her, moving to Paris was a foolish, impulsive thing to do.

Still. The last time Genevieve felt this kind of excitement was when she found out her husband had slept with another woman.

That sounded terrible. She knew it did.

And of course it had been wrenching, devastating, painful. She could still recall the nausea, the otherworldly sensation of the world falling away beneath her feet, like being on the Santa Cruz Big Dipper roller coaster with her brother when she was a kid: that queasy, thrilling rush as the cars whooshed down the first tall hill and you weren't sure whether you were about to throw up or were having fun or just wanted everything to stop so you could get off.

But the truth was, Jason's infidelity had cracked open the dark, cramped cell that her marriage had become.

It was a glimmer of hope: her way out.

A new start.

Chapter Six

The cobblestones were uneven beneath her feet, making the suitcase impossible to roll, and the air seemed even muggier than at the airport. But Genevieve was elated to see the neighborhood looked exactly as she remembered from the last time she was here, when she was fourteen.

Nothing had changed.

Of course it hadn't. Given the scale of French history, nineteen years was a blink of an eye, the passing of a dust mote, a single tick of a clock.

The rue Saint-Paul, main street of the fairy-tale-like Village Saint-Paul, dated back to the medieval period. Its minuscule antiques shops, art galleries, and restaurants looked nearly as ancient. The city of Paris was founded by the Romans; Notre-Dame itself was built upon the stone remnants of a Roman temple dedicated to Jupiter. There were catacombs below her feet, still in use, dug centuries before Europeans would ever set foot on what was later dubbed California.

And unlike in America, Genevieve thought, people here would never bulldoze a centuries-old building to construct a 7-Eleven, even if such a convenience store were bound to make a fortune in a place where many shops—even in the capital city—were closed on Sundays and holidays, and in the middle of the day for the long lunch-hour *sieste*.

The big sign on the front of the building still declared: UNDER LOCK AND KEY; DAVE MACKENZIE, PROPRIÉTAIRE. And under it, in French:

SERRURIER: OUVERTURE PORTES BLINDÉES, DÉPANNAGE SERRURE, REFAIRE DES COPIES DES CLÉS, TARIFS COMPÉTITIFS.

As ever, the big bay window displayed ancient keys—not unlike the one she wore around her neck—as well as metal lock plates and padlocks, from the antique to the new. A thick layer of dust muted and unified the inventory.

For a delicious moment Genevieve was tempted to try picking the lock on the shop door, just to see if she could. But there were half a dozen people milling about rue Saint-Paul, window-shopping and ducking in and out of antiques stores. It wouldn't do to get arrested for breaking and entering on her first day in Paris. So instead she used the key Catharine had sent her in the mail.

She pushed the door wide, stepped in, and paused.

This. This was what Genevieve had wanted. Ever since she'd learned of Dave's passing, ever since Catharine had urged her to come to Paris, ever since she'd found the e-mails and confronted Jason about his affair with Quiana and realized her marriage was over. Ever since then, Genevieve had wanted to return to this place. Alone. All by herself. To breathe in the mingled aromas of stale pipe smoke and rusty metal and the oil Dave used to maintain his instruments.

As a fourteen-year-old all she had seen were the old keys and locks, the charmingly antiquated world of the locksmith.

But now, Genevieve recognized the contemporary tools of the trade: A relatively new machine for cutting keys sat on the back counter next to a rotating stand full of metal blanks (she remembered Dave teaching her to grind the keys by hand first, then with the machine); on one side wall, new hardware in molded plastic cases—dead bolts, hinges, padlocks—hung from hooks in regimented rows. These concessions to modern life were limited, however: Catharine had warned Genevieve that there was no Internet at the house, nothing more technologically sophisticated than an old broadcast TV, a record player, and plenty of LPs.

Genevieve didn't even have a cell phone she could use here. It was like being cast back into the 1950s.

The shop shelves cradled a jumble of dusty door hardware, from locks and bolts to knockers and hinges and shutter stops. Many of the shutter stops were molded to look like flowers or what Genevieve, as a girl, thought were little Dutch people. As she picked one up now, feeling its solid weight in her hand, she realized why: Their old-fashioned hats made them look like characters out of a children's book. Door knockers featured ornate scrollwork or took the form of hands holding balls, or fanciful fish; the old metal was spotted with rust or covered in layers of chipped paint; multiple colors peeked through, hinting at other times, other lives, other fashions.

Genevieve slid open the "special" drawer. It was full of ancient keys, many of which, like her necklace, bore little resemblance to keys today. She smiled as she picked up a black iron ring, from which jangled a dozen different skeleton keys: She remembered her uncle explaining that this was a Victorian-era thief's ring. Dave had always intended to write a book about such historic hardware.

"Complete with photos, Genevieve. What do you think? C'est super, n'est-ce pas? I am going to call it Love Laughs at Locksmiths. *Or maybe* The Paris Key, *because really, Paris is the key to happiness! What do you think?"*

More than a dozen clocks crowded the back wall of the shop, a few with their shoulders touching, as though trying to edge one another out. Their hands marched through the hours, filling the compact space with their frenetic ticktocking. Only two indicated anything approximating the current time; Genevieve remembered how the three Bavarian cuckoo clocks used to make their raucous announcements at random moments throughout the day.

"They are as accurate with time as you are, old man!" Tante Pasquale would say.

"Ah, but there's always time for a kiss, old woman," Dave would respond, nuzzling her neck and making her laugh.

Genevieve heard their laughing voices, ghost-like, as real as the ticking of the clocks that surrounded her. They seemed as much a part of the building as the smell of pipe tobacco and the occasional whiffs of damp emanating from the plaster-covered stone walls. Had Pasquale and Dave left bits of themselves here, gossamer traces of their love lodged in the crevices of the tile floors, in the grain of the oak beams overhead?

More likely it was simply jet lag, the other-worldly, out-of-time sensations that resulted from international travel.

Genevieve hesitated, steeling herself for a moment before finally unlocking the little door at the back of the shop. It opened directly onto Dave and Pasquale's *salon*—their living room.

The apartment was smaller than she remembered. A cramped, old-style Parisian haunt made up of a main room, a kitchen, and two bedrooms. The toilet was in its own tiny closet (not even large enough for a sink) off the hallway; the shower was in a small room attached to the master bedroom. Throughout, the floor was tiled, decorated with a muted design of terra-cotta, ochre, and green; the finish was matte, unlike any tiles she'd seen in the U.S. Threadbare rugs warmed the bedrooms, but otherwise the bare floor made sweeping easy.

The beamed ceilings were at least ten feet tall, and the lace-curtained casement windows were embellished with flower boxes, their contents now long dead.

The windows and front door, trimmed in a chalky green paint, opened onto one of a series of interconnected cobblestone courtyards: the heart of the Village Saint-Paul. Ivy-covered walls, tiny wrought-iron balconies with colorful flowers spilling over the edges, spindly tables and chairs set outside for morning coffee. Two old bicycles leaned up against a stone pillar, as though awaiting riders.

It was as charming as she remembered, a picture-postcard neighborhood.

The apartment itself was crammed with the collection of a lifetime. Clearly, no one had gone through the clutter since Dave's death and Pasquale's relocation. Seeing it now brought home the grim, quotidian logistics of death and dying, of boxing things up and selling things off. Genevieve remembered coming upon her father as he was cleaning out her mother's closet: He was sitting on the bed, tears in his eyes. Jim didn't say anything (he never said very much) as Genevieve took the pink negligee from his calloused farmer's hands and folded it on top of the pile in the big black plastic garbage bag, then continued until all that remained were empty hangers. Nick joined them, wordlessly taking down shoe boxes full of family photos and old letters, the bag of half-finished knitting projects, the fancy maroon satin heels none of them remembered ever seeing her wear.

Poor Catharine had been saddled with dealing with her father's death, alone. And now she was watching her mother slip away as well.

A small, never-to-be-given-voice part of Genevieve was glad she'd gotten the whole "parents' dying" thing out of the way already. Now, at least, the dread of loss no longer loomed over her. Her father's passing last year had been a long, drawn-out battle with congestive heart failure, but to be fair, her brother, Nick, had taken the brunt of those doctor visits and hospital stays.

Jason had been exceedingly kind through the whole ordeal. He'd played the devoted husband to perfection, and Genevieve had been grateful to have his easygoing presence by her side to support her through her father's final days and the memorial service.

Later she would discover that this was when Jason had started sleeping with Quiana.

But she had been blissfully ignorant of his infidelity at the time. And when her mother passed she'd had her father, however silent, and her brother, however annoying. But at least they had shared the sorrow. And when she came to spend the summer in Paris, of course, she'd had Uncle Dave and Aunt Pasquale, who had mourned with her and held her and shown her she wasn't alone.

Catharine had no one.

On the other hand, Genevieve thought as she opened the windows to air out the stuffy apartment, Catharine had grown up in the Village Saint-Paul. Surely she had friends, and there were plenty of relatives on her mother's side of the family. Right now she was visiting her godmother in Provence, so she wasn't alone. Or so Genevieve hoped.

Not for the first time, Genevieve admonished herself for not remaining closer to her Parisian family. She had been furious, and hurt, when Dave had put her on the plane, sending her back to California, when all she wanted was to stay with them, in the village. Every birthday she received a card signed by all of them, and every Christmas a present. But as a teenager she had refused to write in return, holding her resentment close to her chest, a shield over her heart.

Once she became an adult she had tried to make amends, sending cards and letters and calling on birthdays and holidays. But it wasn't enough. Not nearly enough.

Draped over the arm of the old floral couch was one of Pasquale's unfinished needlework projects: a scene of a swan-studded lake in front of a château. Genevieve picked up Dave's old silver-inlaid pipe, turned it around in her hands.

Put it down, watching it rock for a moment before falling onto its side. She trailed her fingers along the hurricane glass of a gas lantern, which, she remembered, Dave always kept handy; the village was so ancient and insular that many residents didn't have regular plumbing until the 1970s, and the power was still erratic.

She opened an old walnut armoire chock-full of bottles of all sizes and shapes: This was the cabinet of tinctures and liqueurs made by grandfathers from the herbs collected on certain mountains, in very special valleys. Genevieve inspected a few of the yellowing handwritten labels, remembering Uncle Dave flinging the doors wide, waggling his eyebrows, and saying: *"Let's see what we have here. . . . This eau-de-vie will fix that stomachache"*—or headache or backache—*"in a heartbeat!"*

Genevieve had come home to the last place she could remember being happy . . . but at the same time she was a stranger, an intruder, a person out of time here.

A creeping dissatisfaction nibbled at the edges of her heart.

Not yet, she thought. *Give me just a little bit longer.* A little bit longer in the bubble of forgetting the present and remembering the past, of feeling that elusive, intangible anticipation of happiness.

"In AA they say that there's no such thing as

a geographical cure," Mary declared when Genevieve talked about running away to Paris.

Intellectually, Genevieve knew this was true. She might well be lugging her unhappiness with her to another country, packing it up in her suitcase right alongside dental floss and underwear. But in her heart she refused to accept this possibility. The idea of escape was too enticing.

"Oscar Wilde wrote that when good Americans die, they go to Paris," Genevieve had replied.

"Okay . . . not sure what to make of that. But anyway, you're not *dead,* Martin. You're just getting divorced."

There were a lot of people who claimed to be happy. Or content, at least. Jason found fulfillment in making money and putting together win-win solutions to business deals. Some folks seemed most satisfied when they were stirring up trouble, like the people with whom Genevieve had mingled at the death-penalty protests with her mother, all those years ago. And Berkeley types touted the wisdom of the Buddha, preaching that once a person no longer *wanted* anything, she would no longer face disappointment. But didn't that seem like a cop-out? A sour-grapes approach, as in, "I didn't want it anyway"?

Her brother, Nick, appeared content. Whenever Genevieve visited, he would take her for a tour of the farm, show her how well the kale was doing now that he'd found a natural way to keep the aphids at bay, exhibit the impressive girth of his pumpkins and the deep hues of the carrots, which he grew in the traditional orange variety as well as red and purple and yellow, a veritable rainbow coalition of root vegetables.

Nick told her that happiness was an attitude, an approach to life. That you had to *choose* it.

Could it really be that simple? Could one simply *choose* to find fulfillment in kale?

Genevieve picked up a sparkling goblet from a set sitting on the chipped tile kitchen counter. It was small and decorated with cut-glass diamonds that formed geometric flowers. She weighed its heft in her palm. The glass was cool and slick, thick and sturdy. Perhaps her imagination was running away with her, perhaps her mind was jet-lag muddled, but she thought she remembered these goblets: old-fashioned, smaller and bulkier than the sleek stemware she was used to, the ones into which Jason would pour his exorbitant Napa Valley cabernets, proclaiming with false modesty that "you wouldn't believe how much it costs, but one sip, you know it's worth it," even though to Genevieve it never seemed truly worth it, never seemed much better than the inexpensive Bordeaux she liked to buy from the grocery store, if only to watch Jason squirm when she placed it on the rack beside his precious *Wine Spectator*–ranked bottles.

Over the old gas stove, soot marks marred the wall and ceiling. A copper *couscoussier* with its verdigris patina sat atop a burner; the top was used to steam couscous and vegetables while meats stewed below. When Pasquale lived here the whole apartment always held the aroma of food: roast chicken, *tomates provençales*, *haricots verts*.

And spices and chocolate and fresh bread.

A dozen mismatched but sturdy wooden chairs surrounded a heavy farm table, too large for the available space, so long it extended into the living area. The table appeared to be waiting for a large family, and though Pasquale and Dave had only one child, Genevieve remembered lavish Sunday dinners with family and friends crowded around, children sitting on laps, dogs awaiting dropped tidbits. The lamb on the table, the steaming tagine—an intricately painted ceramic bowl with a conical hat—full of fragrant couscous and braised vegetables. The water with a dash of wine, pale pink in the cut-glass goblets that made her feel like a princess.

Genevieve remembered asking Tante Pasquale why the refrigerator was so tiny, the size of a "dorm fridge" college students might use to chill a few six packs of beer.

"In your country they are, what do you say? Énormes!"

"Enormous," Genevieve had corrected her.

"Yes, enormous. Because the people, they shop only one time a week. Here we shop every day."

"Why?"

"So the food is fresh, you see? We must buy the baguettes every day, so they are fresh. This will be your job while you are with us, to buy the baguettes."

At the thought of those meals, Genevieve's mouth began to water. What time was it? None of the many clocks were reliable. She didn't have a watch, and she didn't want to even turn on her cell phone for fear of exorbitant international rates.

Would restaurants be open? But . . . she couldn't face Paris. Not yet. Not until she'd had a shower and gotten herself together.

Atop the table sat a fruit bowl on a doily, and a picnic basket. The only other item was a note, a full-sized sheet of heavy linen paper, snow-white against the dark wood of the table.

It was from Catharine:

Chère Cousine Geneviève,

Bienvenue à Paris!

I am so sorry I am not here to give you welcome as I should. I am in the South of France with my godmother's family—I am sorry you come to Paris in January, so cold and rainy! I have made the beds in our old room with fresh linges (I forget how you say that), and have asked a neighbor to leave you a little food and wine because I think you are hungry. Look in the frigo! Please enjoy—comme chez toi!

I know my father would be very happy to know you are here, looking after his shop. I will not be surprised if he comes to you in your dreams to tell you so. Do not forget to note your dreams! I will interpret them for you when I return.

I am very pleased and excited to see my little cousin. It has been too many years.

I wish you good sleep and bon appétit!

In the *frigo*—fridge—were three generous wedges of cheese under a glass dome. Two bottles of wine, one white, one rosé, chilling. Genevieve unwrapped a package of wax paper to reveal a thick slab of country pâté; another bundle held thinly sliced ham. There was a container of cornichons, a tiny round jar of Dijon mustard, and a fat stick of yellow butter on a small blue dish.

Two bottles of red wine, a fresh baguette, a bar of chocolate, and a tin of foie gras were nestled together in the picnic basket.

With the exception of the two perfect pears that scented the kitchen, these were all foods Genevieve habitually denied herself. But here people ate such things without shame. And managed to look fabulous while doing so.

Genevieve fell, more than sat, in one of the wooden chairs.

It was outrageous, what she had done. *Who does something like this? Who moves to Paris on a whim?* Her heart hammered in her chest and she couldn't catch her breath. She felt woozy. Was she having a panic attack?

But then she heard Mary's voice in her head: *"You're not* dead*, Martin."*

No, she was very much alive. And she had a choice to make. She could get back on a plane and go home like a sensible person, before anyone had even noticed she'd gone.

Or she could open a bottle of wine.

Chapter Seven

The rosé was dry and crisp and perfect.

The baguette was ambrosia: crispy on the outside, chewy on the inside. What *was* it about bread in France? Like the French version of butter, it seemed to bear little relation to the item of the same name back home. Genevieve sliced a wedge of pâté, topped it with a cornichon, and made a little sandwich. Another glass of wine, a bit of cheese: P'tit Basque, tangy Roquefort, a stinky and delicious washed-rind Brie. Even the pear seemed better than the ones she was used to: the perfect combination of tangy and sweet, the juice running down her arm as she ate.

Sated, Genevieve could barely keep her eyes open.

She made her way down the hall and fell into the twin bed she had slept in as a girl, in the bedroom she had shared with Catharine. It was a small room full of old books, comics, and two four-poster twin beds; nothing fancy. But the sheets were cool and smelled of lavender.

Genevieve let out a long sigh, gazing at the cracks in the plaster overhead and remembering making pictures from their spidery lines as she lay awake, crying for her mother, hiding her sobs in her wet pillow, listening to her cousin's heavy, steady breathing.

Soon she fell asleep and dreamed of a locked room.

Genevieve kneels before the door. Her lifting finger is sore. Her knees ache. Tears of frustration sting the backs of her eyes. She keeps dropping the pin stack.

The pick slips, nicking her finger. A fat drop of blackish red appears.

Uncle Dave stands behind her, coaching her, his words patient and encouraging.

You can do it, *he says.*

I can't, *she replies, though the truth is she's not sure she wants to. What lies behind the door?*

Haven't you ever read the fable of Bluebeard? *she demands of her uncle, only half joking.* Some doors are not meant to be opened.

Dave just laughs. See it with your inner eye, Genevieve; feel it. Do you see the pin stack?

Apply a bit of torsion with the wrench—just a little—and lift with the pick. When the pins are aligned, the plug will rotate, ever so slightly.

Finally, finally, *the plug begins to turn.*

Feel it? *Dave asks.* Now repeat, nice and slow. Don't forget to breathe . . . and when all the stacks have been lifted, the plug is free to turn, and voilà!

Genevieve rides a surge of victory, relishing the sense of release and relief that comes with defeating a lock.

She reaches up. Her fingers close around the knob. The brass is cold and hard in her palm, unyielding. But when she tries to turn the doorknob, it doesn't budge. It is still locked. Frustration floods through her, poison rushing through her veins. She rattles the knob like a rookie.

Again. *Dave's voice is coaxing, eternally patient.* Try again. Will you let yourself be defeated by a silly old lock, of all things?

She closes her eyes, takes a deep breath, forces herself to try again. She inserts the pick, concentrates on seeing the pin stack in her mind, drawing a mental map, feeling the pins aligning . . .

Genevieve heard a buzzer and awoke with a start.

Whenever the shop-door buzzer rang, the teenage Genevieve would run to see whom it was. "*Vite, vite!* Hurry!" Uncle Dave would boom, laughing, while Pasquale would chastise him in rapid French. *"Allons-y*! Let's go!"

Someone was ringing the shop buzzer, over and over again.

Heart pounding, Genevieve took a moment to register where she was. The cracks in the tall ceiling overhead, the bookshelves lining every wall, *Star Trek* paraphernalia, the matching four-poster twin beds.

Paris. Dave and Pasquale's house.

The buzzer rang again.

Genevieve stumbled out of the bedroom, down the short hall, across the salon, to the door to the shop. The brass knob was cool and slick under her hand. She hesitated, but the knob turned easily.

An impossibly old man stood outside, hands cupping the window, his rheumy eyes trying to peer within the shop.

Upon spying Genevieve he held up one gnarled hand in greeting and grinned to display crooked yellow teeth. He was wearing a beret, a scarf, and a black overcoat; he leaned on a cane. If only he were cradling a baguette, he could have been featured on a poster as Traditional Old Frenchman.

Genevieve swore under her breath and tried to gather her wits.

She had stumbled to the door half-asleep, not even stopping to check her reflection in the mirror. She hadn't showered since she left San Francisco . . . how long ago?

Her mind cast around, frantically, for the French words to tell this man to go away. How did you say "closed" in French? All she could remember was the Spanish, *cerrado*. A lot of help that was.

"*Excusez moi*," she began, begging the man's pardon even though he was the one who had disturbed her, not the other way around. "*Il n'y a pas . . . nous sommes pas ouverts*," she stammered.

"We are not open," she thought she managed to say, though as it came out she realized she'd left out half of the negative in French, the *ne* that was supposed to go before the verb. Her sleep-addled mind was doing the best it could.

The man rattled something off in a scratchy voice, still smiling, still waving.

This is the problem with even attempting a foreign language. You managed to spit something out, and then they had the audacity to speak their language in return.

"*Je ne parle pas français*," she said, finally remembering how to say, "I don't speak French," the simple words bubbling up thickly, like crude oil, from her consciousness.

"This is okay, okay!" the man said, nodding eagerly. "I speak English very good, you see!"

"I'm sorry, *monsieur*, we're closed," Genevieve said, through the still-closed shop door.

"This is okay!" he repeated with enthusiasm. "I call myself Philippe. Philippe D'Artavel. I am a friend of your uncle's."

Oh lord, thought Genevieve. *Please don't make me deliver my uncle's death notice to an old friend, in French, no less.*

"*Je suis désolée,*" Genevieve said as she opened the front door so they could speak without the pane of glass between them. "I'm so sorry, but *mon oncle* . . . my uncle has passed away."

The old man looked at her, head tilted slightly, as though not understanding. Genevieve remembered the word for dead in French: *mort.* But surely there was a softer way of saying it, a euphemism like "passed away" . . . ?

"Dave is . . ."

"Dead," Philippe said with a nod. "I know this. He was very old. He was . . . what is the word? *Il était prêt.* Ready. He was ready to be dead. I am not ready now, but very soon. I am so old, can you imagine? Even older than Dave!"

Genevieve didn't know what to say to this.

They stood there for a long moment, staring at each other. Philippe D'Artavel stooped over his cane of polished wood, topped with a large brass lion's head. He was several inches shorter than Genevieve. His eyes were a light sherry brown that gave him a kindly expression, and the grin never dropped from his face.

"Would you like to come in?" Genevieve finally said, stepping back and waving him into the tiny shop.

"Okay, yes, thank you," he said. His *th* was

pronounced like a *z,* making the words sound like "zank you." Genevieve remembered, as a young teen, trying to coach her cousin Catharine, whose English was almost perfect except for her accent. At one point Genevieve actually reached into Catharine's mouth to pull her tongue out between her front teeth so she could approximate the very un-French *th* sound.

"I think you are . . . *Vous êtes l'Américaine, n'est-ce pas?*" said the man. "You are the American niece, I think?"

"Yes, I'm sorry." Genevieve held out her hand, blushing at having forgotten her manners. "I'm Genevieve Martin."

The man stepped toward her, and Genevieve remembered that the French preferred kissing to shaking hands. First one cheek, then the other. She leaned down toward Philippe, smelling a minty toothpaste, a subtle aftershave. She had never been a big fan of cologne on men, but this scent was understated, fresh. Expensive Parisian cologne, no doubt.

"I remember you as a girl," he said. "One time only. I was away most of that summer. But Dave, he tells me all about you. You are the little locksmith, *n'est-ce pas?*"

"Not so little anymore."

"But now you are a beautiful woman!" He shook one hand in the air, sucked a loud breath in through his crooked teeth. "*Ooh la la!*"

Genevieve couldn't help but return his smile. This, she had never forgotten. The ability of the average Frenchman to make a woman, no matter her age or appearance, feel beautiful. Their ability to flatter seemed ingrained, as much a part of the culture as wine and cheese. Where the Parisian women were cool, elegant, and distant, the men were flirtatious, teasing, and attentive. And bold: Here was an old man, stooped and wrinkled, shorter than she, with bad teeth. And he was flirting with her.

Even while she appreciated all this about Philippe, Genevieve felt bleary with sleep, and a headache was creeping up, the tension in her neck, the awareness of the back of her eyes, warning her of an incipient migraine. She needed coffee, and she needed it soon.

Genevieve thought longingly of the huge bottle of Excedrin in her carry-on. A sheepish Jason had brought it home the night before she left, saying it was a going-away present. *"Meager, I know, but you don't like gifts and I'm sure you're already over your baggage weight limit and I . . . I just thought it might come in handy."* The truth was, she had been touched. She wouldn't have guessed he had ever noticed what medication she used.

"May I help you with something?" she asked Philippe, hoping to hurry him on his way.

"Yes. Yes, if you please. Your uncle, he was working on my family's house. Now, he has all the information, all the original parts. Catharine tells me you come to Paris. You must finish this, I think."

"I'm not . . . I'm just visiting . . ."

"Dave has all the information. He has a *dossier* about my house, and the original . . . *Comment dit-on? Serrures?*"

"Locks?"

"*Oui, c'est ça.* Locks. He was cleaning them, fixing them."

"I really don't—"

"This is my family home. This is what I must do before I go."

"You're going on vacation?"

"*Non!*" He lifted his eyes to the ceiling and laughed again. "Before I join my good friend Dave. Up there, I hope!"

"I'm sorry, *monsieur*, but I just arrived and I'm really not set up to . . ."

Genevieve trailed off, distracted, as she watched another man rush across the street, making a beeline toward the shop. He was much younger than Philippe—about Genevieve's age—and was wearing a backpack, and a camera with a huge lens hung around his neck. Dark haired and well built. When he stood in the doorway, he loomed over the diminutive Philippe.

"We're not open," Genevieve said, trying to head him off. "*Nous ne sommes pas ouverts.*"

"What chance, a locksmith shop, right here!" he

said with a lilt that Genevieve assumed was from one of the British Isles. "And you speak English, no less. Brilliant. Listen, I'm a git—I locked myself out of my apartment. I'm after a lock-smith."

"She say she is not working here," said Philippe.

"I'm not really . . ." By now the headache was growing stronger, swelling, filling the space in back of her eyes, areas of which she was normally blissfully unaware. Taut tendrils of pressure reached out to her left temple. "I only just arrived, and I'm not actually a locksmith—"

"I really need this," the man said. "I'm in a real jam."

"Dave say you could open all the doors," said Philippe. "He say you have the touch."

"You see there? Dave says you can open all the doors, and I only need you to open just the one."

"True, I learned about locks from my uncle when I was a kid, but I'm actually a copy editor."

"A copy editor?"

She nodded.

"So . . . you couldn't help a fella out of a real jam? I'm close by."

Genevieve took a deep breath, blew it out slowly. "How close?"

"Right across the street." He pointed to a three-story building made of creamy stone, tiny black wrought-iron balconies at the windows. "The manager's not home, and I really need my wallet. Supposed to meet a friend for dinner at the Brasserie Bofinger."

"*Mais, c'est excellente, la* Brasserie Bofinger!" said Philippe. The two had a quick exchange in rapid French, apparently about the quality of the restaurant.

"He's really more a business associate," continued the younger man. "And it wouldn't do to stick him with the bill. You'd be doing me a real favor. My name's Killian, by the way. Killian O'Mara."

Genevieve swallowed hard and tried to fend off the headache through sheer force of will, as though it were a simple mind trick.

"Do you have any proof?"

"Proof of my name?" He gave her a quizzical look.

"Proof that it's your residence? A driver's license, a phone bill, something with your name and address on it?"

Both men looked confused. Genevieve tried again.

"I'm not . . . I have no idea what the laws are like in Paris, but where I'm from, locksmiths don't just go around opening locked doors upon request. How do I know you actually live there?"

Now they grinned at her.

"You're saying an intrepid thief might just hire a locksmith to let him into random apartments?" Killian asked.

"I . . ." Yes, she supposed that *was* what she was saying. This sort of thing was an issue in Oakland, and she was sure locksmiths were required to obtain proof of residency. Probably using a locksmith to gain access to a victim's lair was one of those things people would never think to do in France.

"All right," said Genevieve. "I tell you what: If you could go get me a large, very strong coffee, straight, no milk or sugar, plus a *pain au chocolat*, I will meet you at your house in fifteen minutes."

"Really? It's a deal. By the way, what's your name?"

"Genevieve Martin," said Philippe, helpfully. Pronouncing her name perfectly, of course. "She is the new locksmith of Village Saint-Paul."

"I'm really not a locksmith," Genevieve tried again.

"What happened to the Dave of the sign?" Killian asked.

"Dave died," said Philippe.

"I'm sorry to hear that," said Killian. "Was he a relative?"

Both men turned to look at Genevieve.

She burst into tears.

Chapter Eight

Angela, 1983

Pasquale (sweet, long-suffering Pasquale) has lost her patience with Angela.

"*Je suis désolée*," Pasquale says. "I am sorry, but you are in Paris! You must go out of the house while it is sunny. . . . It is not always so beautiful here. I insist—go out, walk around and see the sights!"

Angela knows there are sights: Paris is the City of Lights, after all, and when she came with Jim on their honeymoon she had been enamored by everything she saw. There were the obvious attractions like the Eiffel Tower and the Louvre and Notre-Dame, of course, but so much more than that. Like the ice cream at Berthillon on l'Île Saint-Louis. She had insisted they walk across each and every bridge over the Seine, looking down into the water. And then Jim dragged her to the Café des Philosophes in search of the radical discussion group.

That was back when Jim would speak of philosophy; he bought her a book from Shakespeare and Company: the collected letters of Jean-Paul Sartre and Simone de Beauvoir.

"Listen to this," Jim said, reading from the

book. "Jean-Paul wrote this to Simone: 'I love you while paying attention to external things. At Toulouse I simply loved you. Tonight I love you on a spring evening. I love you with the window open. You are mine, and things are mine, and my love alters the things around me and the things around me alter my love.'"

"What does that mean?" asked Angela.

"That he loves her, and that his love for her changes everything."

But Angela wasn't so sure. She thought maybe it meant that his love was ephemeral, hard to pin down. That the things around his love changed his love.

And as for Simone de Beauvoir, Angela knew there were feminist lessons in de Beauvoir's prose, but what most spoke to her was the sense of longing, the never-quite-fulfilled yearning of a couple destined to spend their lives together, while never actually marrying, never living together, never making the ultimate commitment.

Angela hadn't known how to put her feelings into words, and she wasn't ready to voice it to Jim, but there was something seductive about the challenge to love a man beyond all reason, to take everything her man could dish out. Not outright abuse, of course, nothing like that. Just like Lady Day singing, "Hush now, don't explain" and Janis Joplin, begging her guy to "take another little piece of my heart. . . . I'm going to show you . . .

that a woman can be tough." And Simone de Beauvoir, the woman who was described as the mother of the feminist movement, stating that her greatest achievement in life had been her relationship to Jean-Paul Sartre, the philandering philosopher who received so much more public acclaim than she in life, when she was arguably the more revolutionary thinker.

Angela had wanted, back then, to give herself to Jim in this way. Heart and soul. Rationality be damned.

But Jim was won over easily, expecting her only to be a partner and helpmate as they returned to the land, started a family, ate organic vegetables, savored the simple pleasures. Even in this he is not overly demanding; she escapes from time to time to sleep on a friend's couch on O'Farrell Street in San Francisco, just to get away. Jim is patient. He is steady. He is a good man.

She is very lucky. Everyone says so.

The weariness is heavy within her, dragging her down. She is exhausted. She went to bed before dinner last night and didn't get up until eleven today, but still she is fatigued. *Très fatiguée* is a French term that seems particularly apt not only to her body, but to her soul as well.

Perhaps it is oxygen deprivation. If a person stops breathing, eventually she must stop living, right? Or would pieces of her start to die off first, small bits not integral to life?

She turns this idea over in her mind as she walks.

The small toe would probably be first to go. Perhaps earlobes, hair, the fingernails, which had become virtually useless with the advance of civilization and the decline in the need for claws. Or perhaps it would be invisible parts inside one's body: the appendix, or tissue-thin linings, or tiny glistening organs one never even realized one possessed. Or maybe it would be parts of the brain or soul . . . her sense of humor, for example.

Angela crosses the bridge and finds herself on the Île-de-France, passing by the Cathedral of Notre-Dame. A swollen line of tourists waits to climb to the top to visit the gargoyles, while herds of visitors surge into the open entrance of the sanctuary itself. The tourists are red-faced and grumbling, cameras hanging around their necks, plastic bags bulging with tchotchkes purchased out of boredom or habit from the ubiquitous souvenir shops: mini gargoyles, music boxes that play "La Vie en Rose," tea towels and refrigerator magnets and T-shirts that proclaim a love for Paris, proof of one's international credentials upon returning to Spokane and Midland and Columbus.

Angela keeps her head down and pretends not to speak English, feeling embarrassed by the prosperous, well-fed Americans. The strong U.S. dollar brings them flocking to Europe, clogging medieval streets as they arrive in their air-conditioned tourist buses built for wide American dimensions. Middle-aged women in cardigans and sensible shoes, hair cut short more for convenience than with an eye toward fashion; middle-aged men in baseball caps and cargo shorts, displaying sturdy American legs. A few slouching teens forced to accompany their parents. They appear alternately enchanted and exhausted, limping through a city they have seen in movies and read about in books. It is part of the lore, the City of Lights.

But what that lore doesn't tell them is that Paris is a workaday place full of folks just trying to get to and from work. It is, like any other urban center, a vast, hurried, confusing mélange of streets and boulevards and museums and street people begging for change. There are more smokers here, true, and the streets are lined with cafés, and if you turn around you might see a plaque telling you that you are standing near the home of Victor Hugo, or you might find yourself, quite by accident, at the foot of the Eiffel Tower, looking up into its steel-and-lace guts—a building so lofty that, like tall buildings everywhere, it disappears when you draw near.

But in the end, Paris is still just a city.

So Angela skirts the tourists and keeps walking, past kiosks selling newspapers and cigarettes and gum and stamps, past outdoor café tables and tiny shops selling kitchen gadgets, back across the Pont Neuf, past the Louvre and the Palais-Royal, and down the avenue de l'Opéra. Now that she has started walking, it seems she cannot stop. Perhaps if she keeps walking, no particular destination in mind, she will eventually get some air into her lungs; she will feel herself breathing.

The day has turned cold and gray; the sunshine, as Pasquale had predicted, was fleeting. The Parisians are just as cold and gray, Angela thinks. They stand in stark contrast to the colorful, overeager Americans, like really well-dressed gargoyles come to life.

Except for him.

He is on his hands and knees, using chalk to draw a huge painting on the sidewalk in front of the place de l'Opéra. He scuttles around gracefully, adding dimension, bringing his picture to life. He has smudges of yellow and blue on his face; his big hands and forearms are covered in multicolored dust. His hair is so dark it is almost black, and when he looks up, his heavy-lidded eyes are a somber, and startling, light blue-gray.

"Bonjour, belle femme!" says a man sitting nearby in a folding chair, holding out a cup for people to give money. He is pudgy and sandy haired, with a pleasant face. Angela had been so absorbed watching the dark-haired chalk painter that she is startled by this voice. He repeats, in English: "Hello, beautiful woman!"

"I . . . hello," she says. She wishes she had thought to answer in French, but when she gets nervous, the words flee her mind. In any case, her accent is so bad she fears he would have known her origin anyway.

"I am Thibeaux. This is Xabi."

"Xabi?" She wants to hear the voice of the man covered in chalk, wants his remarkable eyes to lift again. So she asks, "How do you spell that?"

To her disappointment, the chalk painter remains silent, his head bent over his work.

So instead, Thibeaux spells the name for her: "*X-A-B-I.* It's short name for Xabier. Basque name."

Angela roots around in her bag for some francs but isn't sure how much the coins are worth in U.S. terms. She hasn't figured out the money here yet; she spends every day hidden in Dave and Pasquale's apartment, letting them handle the outside world.

The coins clank loudly as she drops them in the cup. Thibeaux hoots, rattles the coins, and gives her a huge smile. She blushes, not sure if the money is too much or if he is teasing her for putting in so little.

Angela walks around the chalk painting to see it from the proper perspective, and only then does she realize it is the Statue of Liberty, surrounded by scaffolding. Xabi is working from a black-and-white photo from the newspaper. She remembers reading that the statue was being cleaned for the first time in decades, a massive undertaking.

"Why the Statue of Liberty?" she asks, directing her question to the artist.

He sits back on his haunches, looks up at her, studies her for a long moment. Finally he says in accented English, "It seems a perfect metaphor, no?"

"How so?"

"America, held up by—how do you call this?" He points to the picture.

"Scaffolding."

"Yes. America, held up only by scaffolding."

"But scaffolding doesn't hold anything up. It's flimsy itself."

"Yes. Precisely. A metaphor. And of course the statue was a gift from France, so it is even more so."

An American couple walks by, laden with shopping bags, barely slowing as they look at the painting, ignoring Thibeaux's rattling of his cup. In a voice loud enough to be overheard, the woman says, "Don't these people have jobs? It's a Tuesday and they're playing with chalk!"

"Yup," the man responds. "Must be nice."

When they are gone, Xabi holds Angela's gaze, gives her a sardonic smile. Then he says, *"Ah, les Américains. Très gentils."*

Which meant, "Ah, the Americans. Very courteous."

In her halting French, Angela responds, "You can't refer to all Americans that way. It's a big country."

"Where are you from?" he asks.

Usually she tells people she is from Canada. It is so much easier that way. No one holds Canadians in the kind of disdain in which they hold Americans. But for some reason she tells this man the truth: "Mississippi, originally."

"There are many problems there, no? It is racist, I hear."

"It can be, yes. But there are good people there, too."

"Good people, like you?"

"Yes, just like me."

"Hey, you want to join us?" Thibeaux asks. Angela looks up, again startled to find him there, as absorbed as she is with Xabi.

Thibeaux has folded up his chair and gathered together the newspapers and is packing a small wooden box with chalk and rags, a spray bottle of water. He has been joined by several others: three men, one woman. They are dressed like bohemians: their clothes raggedy and covered in chalk and paint.

"This is Jean-Luc, Mario, Cyril, and Michelle. Artists, all. We are going to a restaurant right here, around the corner," he continues. "Xabi and I are painting murals there in exchange for food. Come with us."

"I . . ." Angela is about to beg off. She should beg off, shouldn't she? She isn't the kind of woman who joins itinerant bands of artists in restaurants.

On the other hand, this is Paris. And it is starting to rain, big fat drops staining the sidewalk a dark gray. No one seems to notice the chalk painting is already beginning to smudge and run.

Pasquale will be expecting her for dinner, but Angela could call from the restaurant and explain she'd met up with an old friend. It isn't that far-fetched. Everyone passed through Paris eventually, didn't they? And probably Pasquale would be relieved to have her home to her small family for an evening. Pasquale has been welcoming and warm, unfailingly hospitable, but now, as Angela puts herself in her sister-in-law's shoes for a moment, she realizes how disruptive it must be for her to have a woman sleeping in her daughter's room fourteen hours a day.

Angela falls into step beside Xabi as they walk to the restaurant.

"Won't the rain ruin your painting?"

He shrugs and says, "*C'est la vie.*" That's life.

"How long has it taken you to paint it?"

"Three days."

"What a shame, then."

"It is a . . . *Comment dit-on*? A process. The people, they give money because they appreciate that we are making art. No need to last forever."

The restaurant is charming, candlelit, and cramped. The walls are covered in sketchy, half-finished Chagall-like murals of people floating and dancing among puffy clouds over a Parisian skyline. The tables are full of tourists—American and Japanese, a few Germans—munching on pencil-thin breadsticks and drinking wine from straw-covered Chianti bottles.

The owner is a short, balding man named Pablo who wears a white apron over an impressive belly. He greets the artists with boisterous affection and ushers them into a back room with low ceilings made of arched brick groin vaults, like an old wine cellar. The walls are lined with wire shelves crammed with quotidian restaurant supplies: paper towels, napkins, tablecloths, unlabeled cardboard boxes. A massive, sturdy wooden table sits in the center of the room.

Thibeaux, Xabi, and Michelle grab plates and silverware and proceed to set the table. A basket of bread appears, a dish of creamy butter. Two platters dressed with pâté, sliced tomatoes, and tiny cornichons.

"No one has any money, of course," explains Thibeaux, "but this way Pablo gets art for his place, and we are fed. This isn't bad, is it?"

Pablo bustles in with steaming bowls of food that he sets on the table, family style. Stewed rabbit, potatoes, vegetables simmered in a buttery sauce. Some sort of meat dish. Pasta with tomato sauce. A hodgepodge unlike the carefully orchestrated dinners Angela is used to at Pasquale's table, or on the rare occasion when she has eaten at Parisian restaurants.

There are several bottles of wine without labels, and they use small jam jars as glasses instead of stemware.

After Pablo goes back to work and they are eating and drinking, conversation is intense. They have been joined by a few others, Chileans and French and Basque. They speak in a mix of French and Spanish and another odd language Angela doesn't recognize, with a very occasional translation provided by Michelle or Thibeaux.

Angela doesn't mind letting the vast majority of the foreign words flow over her. She is fascinated, watching them debate with passion and certainty and occasional flares of anger and bursts of laughter. It is as though she is watching a play.

Only she and Xabi remain mute. After dinner he removes himself from the crowded table, taking a seat on a barrel in the corner, crossing his arms over his broad chest. He looks like a painting, surrounded as he is by wine bottles and the low brick ceiling.

Finally there is a lull in the conversation.

"What is your opinion, from the land of Ronald Reagan?" Xabi asks, gesturing toward Angela with his chin.

"Don't blame me. I didn't vote for him," she holds up her hands, as though surrendering. "I try to stay out of politics."

"This is not possible."

She shrugs, smiles, and drinks a little more wine from her jam jar as the conversation swells with talk about the Reagan administration.

Angela forces herself, for several minutes, not to look at Xabi. When she finally does, she finds his brooding stare upon her. She meets his eyes; he does not look away. The intensity in his gaze makes her catch her breath.

Catch her breath!

She is breathing.

Breathing.

Chapter Nine

Later, Genevieve would wonder how to say "mortified" in French.

Both men reacted as men so often do to women's tears: They were immediately intent on quelling them. They escorted her into the rear apartment and sat her down at the dining table. Though Killian tried to go, Philippe insisted on running for the coffee and croissant, saying he knew a good place right around the corner and could ensure fast service.

Killian scooted out a chair, sat, and leaned

toward her. "Can't I help in some way? Isn't there something I can do?"

"I'm just . . . I just flew in from California last night, and I think it's the lack of sleep. I'm getting a headache—a migraine; I get them sometimes. I'm hoping to head it off with coffee and chocolate—the caffeine helps."

He smiled. "And chocolate's the best medicine anyway, eh?"

Genevieve tried to return his smile but failed.

"Do you have any medicine I could get you?" Killian offered.

"Um, yes, Excedrin—" Genevieve started to stand, but he placed a hand on her shoulder to urge her to stay.

"Where?"

"The red canvas bag, in the bedroom on the left."

He brought the bag to her, and she rooted through for the jumbo bottle while Killian got her a huge glass and a bottle of Perrier. She shook three white pellets into her hand, then tossed them to the back of her throat and chased them down with a full glass of mineral water.

He handed her a wet washcloth. It felt like heaven on her hot brow.

"Better?" Killian asked.

"Not quite yet, but I hope I caught it in time."

"I'd be happy to run to the pharmacy. You know how hypochondriacal the French are. I'm sure I could come up with an armful of herbal tinctures and various *digestifs*. In my experience the French are convinced just about anything can be cured with a good stiff drink."

She smiled, remembering her uncle giving her "medicine" for a stomachache that turned out to be an alcoholic fruit cordial of some kind, followed by an herbal chaser.

"No need, there's a whole cupboard full of such remedies right here. But I'll stick with caffeine. I'm . . . I'm very sorry I cried. I'm so embarrassed."

"Why would you be embarrassed? My mum always said a good cry was good for the soul. So, locksmith Dave, of the sign . . . he was your father?"

"My uncle," she said, tearing up again. She hadn't cried for Dave until right this moment. Now, in front of strangers, surrounded by the smell of his pipe, the rust of his old keys, she could feel the loss. Crying not just for his recent death but for all the years that had passed. All that time she hadn't come back, had hardly reached out. Long ago Genevieve had played tug-o'-war at a school picnic, and she still remembered the shocking sensation of the rough rope being violently wrenched through her hands, leaving her palms scraped raw. Dave's loss felt like that: an abrupt, stinging pain, followed by a long, lingering burn.

"I'm new in the neighborhood myself," said Killian. "Though I've been living in Paris for some time now, over in the ninth arrondissement."

"I didn't think anyone used those things anymore," said Genevieve, gesturing to the clunky camera hanging around his neck. She was hoping to get her mind off Dave, her discomfort, her desire to curl up in a ball in the corner, to wail like she had as a child.

He lifted the camera off his chest. "You mean this? I know—I'm old-school. Don't care much for phone cameras."

"What do you take pictures of?"

"I like to think of myself as an urban explorer, I'd say. Truth is, I go for the gritty, the manky."

"Manky?"

He gave her a lopsided grin. "Dirty, grimy. Abandoned, even better. D'ya ever see the photos of the ghost towns of Ireland?"

Philippe tottered back in, a white paper bag already stained with grease in one hand, a cardboard coffee cup in the other, and his cane looped over his arm.

"*Ça va?* You are feeling better?"

When Genevieve didn't answer immediately, Killian said something in French so rapid she couldn't understand. He ended with: "She'll be better soon."

"I'll be okay in a few minutes, I think," she said. "Thank you so much for the coffee."

"Okay, okay!" Philippe responded. "Then you will open this man's door, and come to my house?"

She took another deep breath and then released it slowly, starting to feel the effects of the medicine dulling the edges of the pain.

"Monsieur D'Artavel—," she began, but he waved a hand in the air.

"Philippe. Please! When a beautiful young woman calls me 'Philippe' it makes me feel like a man, *n'est-ce pas*?" He seemed to address this last to Killian, who smiled and nodded.

"Philippe, then," Genevieve said. "I will look through my uncle's things and see what I can find. But, just to be clear: I practice sometimes, just for fun, but I haven't really worked with locks since I used to follow my uncle around as a kid. Besides, I just arrived from California a few hours ago. Could you give me a few days to try to find your information and settle in?"

"Of course. You are a good girl, Genevieve. Dave always says this. I will wait, and you will come in a few days, okay?" He held out an old-fashioned calling card, the kind with his name and address and phone number.

"*Vicomte*?" she asked, reading the title before his name.

Philippe laughed and waved his hand in the air. "Just a little bit royal, perhaps not enough even to have my head off in the Revolution! I only include that so the people will treat me well at the *boulangerie*." He winked. "My house, she is not far, only two miles. Dave, always he walked."

"Today is Sunday, right?"

He nodded.

"All right, let me see what I can find out from my uncle's papers, and I will come on Wednesday if I find the file, the *dossier. Mercredi.*"

"Come on *mercredi* even if you don't find the *dossier*. We will have lunch."

"Lunch isn't necessary, thank you," Genevieve said, tucking her hair behind her ear, wondering if she looked as unkempt as she feared. She still felt headachy, and awkward in front of these two men. All she really wanted right now was to take a shower, to be left alone. "I'll just come and finish the locks, if I can."

"I have many doors at my house," said Philippe, waggling a finger. "You will see. We will need to eat lunch first."

"There's really no need," Genevieve continued. "I—"

A smiling Killian interrupted: "I think you're going to have to give up on this one, Genevieve. The French take invitations to lunch seriously."

Genevieve blew out a breath. She had dreamed of a new life as a locksmith in Paris, so why was she pulling back now? "All right, Philippe, thank you. I will see you for lunch on Wednesday."

"Okay?"

"Okay."

"Okay!" Another round of kisses, and he tottered off.

Killian raised one eyebrow. "You're willing to give my door a go?"

Genevieve nodded, grabbed her uncle's tool bag—an old black leather satchel—and followed Killian across the street.

Chapter Ten

1997

The morning after Uncle Dave picked up Genevieve from the airport at Roissy, she awoke bleary-eyed and out of sorts. Catharine was reading in bed, big ugly glasses perched on her nose.

When she saw Genevieve stir, she yelled out: "*Elle est prête!*"

Then, in a softer voice, she asked, "*As-tu bien dormi*? Did you sleep well?"

Tante Pasquale hustled in then, a tray in her hands, asking the same thing.

Genevieve nodded, mute. She had never been a morning person; even as a baby, her mother used to say, she woke up crying and combative, unhappy to release the bonds of sleep, to start her day. Making her mother miserable from day one, she supposed.

Pasquale set the tray on a little bedside table. There was a pot of hot chocolate; a cup and saucer; and a plate holding a baguette, a *pain au chocolat*, and a huge croissant. Beside these were two tiny pots of preserves: one orange marmalade, the other raspberry jam.

Genevieve had always associated hot chocolate with special events: the occasional camping trip or going to get a Christmas tree. Someone would pour hot water into powder, and if you were super-lucky they'd add a couple of marsh-mallows. Too impatient to let it cool, Genevieve always tried to drink it while scalding, burning her mouth. The anticipation of sweet liquid chocolate was now forever entangled with the memory of that searing sensation on her tongue.

"Eat, eat!" Tante Pasquale said. "And then you must go with your uncle, to make a little visit. And be sure to go by the *boulangerie* on your way home—you must remind your uncle, as he forgets and comes home without baguettes!"

"What a scandal," said Catharine in a sarcastic tone. "*Quelle horreur.*"

The hot chocolate was in a tiny white pitcher, and there was an oversized cup, as big as a bowl, sitting on the saucer. It was as if things had changed places, Genevieve thought. Like in a dollhouse where things were out of proportion, but you pretended everything was normal-sized anyway because you absolutely needed Barbie to have a cup of coffee or an apple, or whatever.

The entire room filled with the scent of rich cocoa. Genevieve sat on the side of her bed and tried to pour the chocolate into the cup. Instead of pouring like milk, it had a sludgy, slow quality as it drizzled into the cup. It was darker than she was used to as well, not the light brown of camping trips but a deep, rich brown closer to coffee. She began to wonder if Pasquale had merely melted down a candy bar.

She blew on it, sipped cautiously. It was the perfect temperature, not too hot at all. The thick liquid coated her mouth. Her entire soul was now wrapped in the divine substance: chocolate.

"Good, huh?" Catharine's loud voice interrupted her reverie.

"Um, yeah," Genevieve replied, suddenly embarrassed at her show of pleasure.

Catharine rolled her eyes slightly. "My *maman*, she is . . . how you say? Indulgent. Don't get used to it."

"Why?"

"Do you see a tray for me? She is doing this because it is your first morning here. It's not typical. I'm just saying." Catharine's English, though subtly accented, was excellent; Dave spoke to her in English, and she read a steady stream of American comics and novels.

Genevieve didn't reply, losing herself again in the chocolate.

"You dip the bread in the chocolate."

"All of them?"

"No, you choose. Whichever one you want."

Genevieve didn't want to be a pig, so she tore off a bit of the baguette and dunked it in the hot liquid, coating it with a thick brown glaze. She put the bit in her mouth. The crisp, chewy doughiness of the bread combined with the heavy sweetness of the chocolate to create an entirely new taste.

Genevieve started to feel overwhelmed. She hadn't even gotten out of bed yet on her first real day in Paris, and already things were so . . . *different.* The chocolate was fantastic, but foreign, nothing like the Hershey's chocolate bar she and Nick were very occasionally allowed to eat in s'mores when friends came for sleepovers. And she had never, not once in her life, been served breakfast in bed. Genevieve had a sudden visual of the morning light streaming into her room at home. She thought of the raucous call of their old rooster, Roscoe, whom they had to get rid of last year when the housing development encroached on their old working farm and the new neighbors started to complain. Knowing she had to check the chickens for eggs before school, even the mean old spotted one that always tried to peck at her. The familiar dread of having to face her classmates at school. And her mother, knocking on the door, yelling at her not to be late, carpool would be there in half an hour.

How Genevieve used to detest her mother in that moment, the bearer of such unwelcome news, standing in her doorway silhouetted in the morning light.

The memory of her mother brought the sting of unwelcome tears to her eyes. She bit her tongue, hard, loath to cry in front of Catharine. Homesickness sucked at her, a sick feeling in the pit of her stomach.

She pushed the rich chocolate away, wanting nothing more than to pull the covers back over her head and fall back to sleep. She felt a deep, dank yearning; a hollow, bleak, nauseating sense of disconnectedness, of being cast adrift. Abandoned.

"You have to get up," said Catharine with a snort. "They're going to drag you around to see tourist things. Notre-Dame, probably, and the *Tour Ee-FELL*."

"The what?" Genevieve asked.

"The *Tour Ee-FELL*!" Catharine repeated in a louder voice, as though increasing the volume would help.

At Genevieve's blank look, she finally rolled her eyes again and said in exaggerated English, "The *EYE-ful* Tower. Is that what you say?"

"Oh. I don't care about the Eiffel Tower."

"Well, he'll take you there anyway. You're an American in Paris; you have to do all those things. I remember your mother loved the gargoyles at

Notre-Dame. And there's the Louvre, and the Champs-Élysées. Get your camera ready. Click, click, go the Americans!" She shrugged and turned her attention back to her book. *"C'est la vie. Ça va."*

Chapter Eleven

Inside her uncle's bag of picks and sweeps Genevieve found a little foam pad to kneel upon; nonetheless, she was uncomfortable after a few minutes. She felt like a reluctant penitent, worshipping at the doorknob. But at least the lock was straightforward: a Garrison seven pin. She had cut her teeth on locks like these. It wouldn't take her long to open.

Killian was leaning against the wall, arms crossed casually over his chest. The hallway was narrow and disappointingly utilitarian: acoustic ceiling tiles, indoor/outdoor carpet. Though the building was historic, the corridor retained little charm.

"What brings you to Paris?" he asked.

"My uncle's death," Genevieve answered plainly, noting with mean satisfaction that the man retreated a bit, his easy smile faltering with her straightforward words.

"Sorry," he said. "A bit bold on my part."

"No, *I'm* sorry. I'm just . . ."

"Headache, still?"

She nodded, though the truth was that the pain had subsided. She had caught it in time. Either that, or the headache would hunker down at a low level for a while, hiding, fiendlike, ready to pounce when she went to sleep. She couldn't count the number of times she had drifted off with a muted thrum of faraway pain and awoken to the sickening sensation that her head was a melon under pressure, ready to crack open at any time.

A few moments of silence passed as she worked on the lock: probing blindly back and forth, forward and aft, taking note of the bumps and voids as she felt them, drawing a map of the mechanism in her mind, feeling the pins drop into position.

"So, you must be a good photographer," she said to Killian in an effort to make amends for her earlier rude comment.

"Sorry?"

"To afford downtown Paris. I hear it's pretty pricey."

"Ah, sure, 'tis. Truth to tell, the photography is just a hobby. I'm here working in computers."

"They're importing the Irish to work in computers?"

"Sure, yeah. English is essentially the technical language now, which makes it easier. And d'ya know that Ireland is a high-tech country these days?"

"Actually, I didn't know that."

"They call it the Celtic Tiger. At least, they used to. Unfortunately, the floor fell out of the industry a while back, so I'm a bit of a wanderer."

"Oh, that's too bad."

"You Yanks are still going strong, though, aren't you?"

"I guess so."

One of the prime reasons, Genevieve thought with sudden ferocity, for leaving the San Francisco Bay Area was so she no longer had to talk about computers. She knew—*lord,* did she know—that they were the future, that if only she'd majored in computers like her father had wanted her to, they'd all be sitting pretty today. *"With your math skills, you could have walked right into a program, made good money straight out of college,"* he'd said, the man who rarely spoke finding his voice when it came to trying to push his daughter into something she didn't want to do. Apparently forgetting that when his own parents wanted him to become a lawyer he'd refused, instead pursuing several hippie-inspired venues before deciding to "return to the land" and becoming a farmer, a vocation his own father saw as a repudiation of the upwardly mobile life he had worked so hard to achieve and pass down to his children.

Instead of majoring in computer science and engineering, Genevieve had studied English with a minor in the history of architecture—not even *actual* architecture, mind you, where she might have had a shot at a decent job. And then, to make matters worse, she told him she was thinking about becoming a locksmith, a job that just skirted along the definition of working-class, a job well on its way to becoming obsolete. A strange, old-fashioned profession.

"You might as well go into mapmaking," her father had said, teasing her over a dinner of whole-wheat pasta topped with organic vegetables. His softly spoken words carried a subtle but distinct edge hewn of anger.

"It could be worse," said Nick, matching his father's faint smile. *"She could become a watch-maker."*

"I thought I'd start making hourglasses in my spare time," Genevieve had replied, her words dripping with sarcasm. *"I hear it's the wave of the future. Just like small-scale family farming."*

In the end, she hadn't pleased her father or herself. Instead, she had become a freelance copy editor, mostly of technical manuals. Sure, it sounded boring . . . actually, it *was* boring. But it paid decently and gave her a lot of flexibility with her schedule. And she worked alone.

"I'm only here on a temporary contract." Killian's voice brought Genevieve back to the here and now. "My sister married a Frenchie, so I thought it'd be nice to spend some time with her, get to know my nieces and nephews. You okay?"

She nodded and resumed what she was doing; her thoughts had careened from her father's unwanted career advice to her dream about the door she couldn't unlock.

"Probably I'll end up in your neck of the woods next," he said. "Not that I particularly want to. No offense, but I don't much fancy working in Silicon Valley."

"I don't blame you," Genevieve said. "Sunnyvale isn't exactly Paris."

Finally she felt the mechanism give, that remarkable moment when the side pin slid, the cylinder released, the block was overcome.

She looked up at Killian, a triumphant smile lighting up her face.

His eyebrows rose in surprise. When he spoke his voice was quiet. "If breaking into my apartment makes you smile like that, I'll lock myself out every night."

Genevieve could feel her cheeks burn and looked back at the handle in front of her. She turned it and pushed the door in, then started to gather her tools.

"Seriously, Genevieve, that's a handy job, isn't it? You're good."

"This was an easy one."

Killian crouched opposite her and began to toss tools into the bag, where they clanked.

She stilled him, placing her hand over his. "I'll do it, thank you. They were my uncle's."

"Sorry."

"No worries, I'd just rather do it myself."

She felt his eyes on her while she stowed the picks and rakes, placing each piece carefully and precisely in her uncle's velvet-lined leather bag. Little soldiers, all in a row. Genevieve had always wondered at this: that her uncle surrounded himself with mess in all aspects of his life but this one. When he opened his locksmithing bag, it was a symphony of order.

She pressed the last one, an S pick, into its molded slat and snapped the bag shut.

"What do I owe you?" Killian asked.

"Oh, um . . . nothing."

She wasn't set up to conduct business; in fact, she had no idea when—if ever—she would receive the certification allowing her to work in France. The French were prickly about foreigners taking jobs from the native-born. Genevieve had been hoping she might qualify for some sort of exemption since she was Dave's niece and Catharine was happy for her to inherit the business, but she hadn't heard back yet on her request.

"Ah, c'mon, you did me a real favor. Let me pay you for your time and expertise."

"As I said, I'm not really conducting business. I'm just . . ." What *was* she doing here? "I'm just looking after things. I'm not set up to take money."

"You have to brave the famed French bureaucracy to get certified as a foreigner working in Paris, eh? Take it from me—it's not easy. My advice? With the civil servants here, *non* doesn't mean 'no.' Just keep politely insisting on what you need, don't let the paperwork get you down, and keep showing up at their offices. Eventually they'll give you what you want, just to be rid of you. It's a battle of patience. Remember what they say: '*Impossible' n'est pas français*."

" 'Impossible' isn't a French word?"

"Exactly. But 'bureaucracy' most certainly is."

"Thanks, I'll remember that," she said with a smile as she peeked through Killian's door to the apartment beyond. Funny, it had never dawned on Genevieve before that "voyeur" was also a French word. Like "entrepreneur," or . . .

Jet lag again. She was having a hard time concentrating. That, combined with the fuzzy hangover effect she felt after experiencing a migraine, even one she had managed to head off.

"At least come in, then, let me get you something," said Killian. "Probably it's hard to believe, me bein' Irish, but I'm not half-bad as a cook."

"I thought you were rushing to a dinner date."

He glanced down at his watch, making a sound of exasperated surprise. "You're right. Clear forgot. But I could make you another cup of coffee before I go, at least."

She would love one, but she didn't want to make small talk with this man. Or with anyone, for that matter. How was it everyone in Paris seemed to speak English? That hadn't been the case last time she was here, as a teenager. In fact, she had welcomed the linguistic divide. The less she understood, the less she would have to interact. She had been expecting to be able to pass a significant amount of time not having to speak to anyone beyond simply ordering a baguette.

Just her luck, to meet up with a native English speaker who lived right across the street.

Still . . . she looked through Killian's open door, curious. Peeking into other lives was her weakness.

"Would you like to take a quick look at the place, at least?" Killian asked, noticing her gaze. "The building's quite old. I'm subletting from a friend of a friend, or I'd never have found such a great place in this location."

"You don't mind?"

"Not at all," Killian said. "Feel free to look around. I'll just go grab my wallet."

The apartment was much more interesting than the hallway: Here the original architectural features remained. The ceilings were tall and decorated with classic French carvings. Cupids and garlands and egg-and-dart moldings were painted a creamy off-white; the walls were a French robin's-egg blue. A tiny kitchen looked out over rue Saint-Paul, and a doorway led to a bedroom; she caught a glimpse of an ornate metal bedstead. An old molded cast-iron fireplace, small by U.S. standards, was surrounded by shelves jammed with books and papers. A notebook computer sat on a small café table, a leather briefcase beside it.

But most fascinating were the photos. They were everywhere: hung on the wall, propped up on the mantelpiece and along the floor, and in messy stacks on a credenza by the bay window.

Some were black-and-white; others, sepia toned; still others showed muted, washed-out colors. Many faded off at the edges, producing blurred effects; some were slightly distorted, with strange, ghostly halos and wisps of light. There were plenty of gargoyles and ornate tombstones, but other, less expected, day-to-day scenes, as well: a pair of birds perched on a stone wall topped with jagged shards of broken glass; a big-eyed toddler who looked utterly alone, standing on a city street; rows of velvet theater seats in a building with a chunk of ceiling missing. Abandoned houses strewn with garbage and dust, their forlorn aspect intensified by the startling presence of a single child's shoe on the stair, or a ripped leather armchair in the middle of an otherwise empty room.

Genevieve was riveted and repelled at the same

time. The photos instilled in her a morbid fascination, a strange nostalgia for lives she had never known.

Finally her eyes alit on a framed color snapshot of a pretty woman, two little girls, and a dog. A wife and kids, probably. The decidedly pedestrian nature of the picture, after the sordid splendor of the others, affected her like a shock of cold water.

"I should go," she called out.

"Let me take you to dinner as a thank-you, at least. Won't you join my friend and me? It's really quite a good brasserie—Philippe was saying it's one of his favorites. Do you have plans for dinner?"

"Thanks, I . . ." She shook her head, trying to think of an excuse. But then realized she didn't need one. She was tired of subterfuge. "No, thanks. I don't want to."

"Sure, certainly, of course. Sorry to disturb. Thank you, again, for coming to my rescue. Let me know when you think of a way I could repay you for your housebreaking."

She left him there, knowing that she would not take him up on his offer. A quick peek into his life was all she wanted.

It was enough.

Chapter Twelve

Genevieve had barely walked in and closed the shop door behind her before the phone in the apartment started to ring.

Damn.

She glared at the old-fashioned telephone. All she wanted to do was lie down with a cold cloth on her forehead, eat her chocolate, and make sure the headache was really gone. Finally, after the fourth shrill ring, she picked up the heavy receiver.

Only then did she realize she had no idea what a person said upon picking up a phone in France. Which was beside the point, really, since, after all, once the person on the other end of the line began speaking French to her she was going to have to hang up anyway.

" 'ello?" she answered, dropping the *h,* as though that made the word French.

"Martin?" said a familiar voice.

"Mary!"

"I just had to make sure you made it to Paris. You haven't answered my e-mails."

"I'm sorry. I don't have Internet here at the apartment yet—it's on my to-do list."

"No Internet? That blows. Hey, I'm using my friend's phone and he's got unlimited international minutes, so feel free to tell me *everything*."

"It hasn't even been a full day since I arrived," Genevieve said with a laugh, but she was filled with warmth to hear from an old friend, and relief at the familiarity of the California accent. Because the phone was an old-fashioned landline attached to the wall with a short cord, she was forced to sit at her uncle's desk rather than walking around multitasking, as she would normally have done.

She closed her eyes and recounted her uneventful trip, the feeling of being back after so many years. Making an idiot of herself at immigration, the taxi ride, the smell of Uncle Dave's pipe, the outrageous feast of wine, cheese, and bread she'd treated herself to on the massive kitchen table. Her current plans for chocolate.

And then she told Mary about being awakened by Philippe and opening up Killian's door.

"No *way*. You're saying you've been in Paris less than twenty-four hours and you've already got two boyfriends?"

"I'd hardly say *boy*friends. One's about a hundred years old—"

"Don't be ageist."

"And he's about a foot shorter than I am."

"Now you're being heightist. Is that a thing? Besides, I thought Paris was famous for the whole May-September love-affair deal."

"I think that's supposed to be between an older

116

woman and a younger man. I'll keep my eyes open for a likely eighteen-year-old."

"But it sounds like this guy might have a great old house in Paris. Think of the possibilities! You could start an artists' colony when he passes away, name it in his honor. Personally, I think the first fellowship should go to yours truly."

"He's got bad teeth."

"Hmm." Mary pondered this as though they were being serious. "Okay, you're right, that might be a sticking point. What about the other one? Irish, huh? As in red-haired and florid, or dark and romantic?"

"I'd say somewhere in between. Good-looking, but I think he's married, or . . . something. There's something about him I don't quite trust."

"You might not be the best judge of male character right at the moment."

"Mmm," was Genevieve's noncommittal reply. She was eying the *pain au chocolat* Philippe had brought her. It taunted her from the big kitchen table, out of reach.

"Anyway," continued Mary, "here's what I think you should do: Take 'em both out for a spin."

"Out 'for a spin'? And what does *that* mean, exactly?"

"You know what they say: You have to get right back on the horse. Take those two out and, you know, get 'er done. Get it out of your system so you can move on."

"Get 'er *done?* Get *what* done? What . . . are you suggesting I *sleep* with these guys?"

"You're in Paris, aren't you? It's the city for lovers. What's keeping you?"

"Um, let me see: There's jet lag, and a migraine headache, and general distrust of all men. Not to mention the fear of pregnancy and STDs. . . ."

"Wait, wait, *wait.* Seriously, are you telling me you flew to Paris without any *condoms?*"

Genevieve laughed and realized she had put her legs up on the desk and was twisting the coiled cord around her finger while she talked, like a teenager in an old movie. Was she reverting? Or simply enjoying the moment, like she hadn't in so very long? Maybe Paris truly *was* magical.

"Mary, you are *so* number one on the things I knew I'd miss from home. I tell you what: If you promise to move here, I'll marry Philippe and found that artists' commune for you."

"You're on, sister."

Just as Genevieve had feared, a glance in the bathroom mirror confirmed that she looked a wreck. Her unbrushed hair was lank and mussed, her cheeks were pale, and smudges of mascara (applied long ago—before leaving Oakland) melded with dark circles of fatigue under her eyes.

Great. Just great. She was going to have to warn Mary that no marriage proposals were bound to be coming her way anytime soon. Not that she was seriously looking for such a thing—quite the opposite. But somehow looking slovenly upon her arrival in Paris seemed . . . cringeworthy.

So, first things first: She needed a shower. Just as Genevieve remembered, the device was jerry-rigged in a retrofitted closet decorated with jarringly 1970s harvest gold tiles. There was no curb, no curtain. Just a fully tiled floor and walls, with a showerhead sticking out of one corner of the room and a drain in the middle of the floor.

Bathrooms were the one thing in Europe that didn't live up to the American version. Who wanted medieval (or even Renaissance-era) charm in a lavatory?

Still, someone had left a stack of clean white towels, a bottle of herbal shampoo, and a big new bar of lavender-verbena soap. Had Catharine specified that her neighbor should leave these, too, along with the food?

Genevieve thought about the meager presents she'd brought Catharine from the States: a dozen *Star Trek* comic books, a T-shirt, and a coffee mug. Did Catharine still have a fondness for the science fiction series, or had Genevieve based this on an image of Catharine that was almost twenty years out-of-date? Also, two plastic bottles of barbecue sauce, because for some reason the French had yet to discover this American taste sensation and Uncle Dave always used to talk about missing "good Southern cooking." Along with this were two boxes of corn-bread mix and a can of okra. It wasn't much.

She cringed inwardly. Maybe she should just hide the stuff and go buy Catharine something nice here in Paris. . . . She was in the world's shopping mecca, after all. Surely she could find something worthy, something a person would value beyond barbecue sauce.

Genevieve turned the *chaud* tap on full strength and waited several minutes, but the water never heated up. Not even enough to take the edge off. Then she tried the *froid*, just in case the hot and cold lines had been crossed, but that was no better. Finally she forced herself in, trying to wash herself thoroughly without immersing her body in the freezing water.

She swore, caught her breath. Felt like crying, felt desperate.

First-world problems, she imagined Mary saying. The thought made her laugh as she emerged and dried off with a fluffy towel, teeth chattering.

No Internet. No hot water. Genevieve was prepared—eager, even—to embrace change in her life, but this was pushing it. She wrapped a blanket around herself and hurried into the main room.

Catharine had left her godmother's phone number on the bottom of her note. Genevieve placed the call, and after she'd stumbled through a few French words the receiver was passed to her cousin. After hellos and quickly catching up, Genevieve asked if there was normally hot water available.

"*Mais bien sûr*! The village may be behind the times in some ways, but yes, we have hot water. But you have to be sure the light is on fire."

"On fire?"

"The hot-water heater is in the closet in the kitchen, the one with holes in the door. You turn the knob for the gas and light the little fire, and—"

"Oh, you mean the pilot light?"

"Yes, that's it. We don't leave it on all the time, to save gas. I can give you the name of someone if you need help; there are many neighbors who could—"

"No, no, *merci*." Genevieve didn't want strangers trooping through what she was already coming to think of as her place. Not yet. "I'm sure I can figure it out, thanks."

"I am sorry my timing was poor. *Désolée* . . . sorry I am not there."

"It's okay, really. You had your plans, and I'm enjoying getting familiar with everything. It's good for me to discover things on my own."

"Oh, good, good. Genevieve, I wanted to ask you: Could you possibly visit my mother while you are there? I told her that I would not visit for a few days, but she forgets things. I left her address and the directions on my father's . . .

bureau. Comment dit-on? Desk. On his desk."

"Of course," Genevieve said as her gaze alit on the directions. "I was going to ask you about that—I would love to see Tante Pasquale."

"Good. I am back in Paris on Thursday. I would like to invite you to lunch. I am in the twentieth arrondissement, near Montmartre. There is Métro nearby. Close to my mother. It is not hard to find."

"Sure, of course," said Genevieve, wondering why Catharine seemed reluctant to come to the village, to what was still her home, her property.

"When you are on the Métro, make attention to the thieves. The . . . what do you call them? The ones who take from the pocket?"

"Pickpockets."

"Oh yes. How . . . obvious. So, everything else is going well? I asked one of the neighbors to leave some food."

"Thank you! I have been enjoying it. Thank you so much. But that reminds me—your mother always insisted we needed a fresh baguette every day. Is the Maréchalerie still the best *boulangerie* in the neighborhood?"

Catharine's chuckle was deep and smoky. If Genevieve didn't know Catharine and just heard her voice over the phone, she would have conjured an image of a woman with a wide, generous mouth, a voluptuous figure, and lush, long hair. Though Catharine had a few such physical attributes, they somehow added up to someone who seemed asexual. Always had. Even when Genevieve was in Paris as a young teenager, she remembered looking at the then twentysomething Catharine—the young woman still living in her parents' house, sleeping in a twin bed and reading comic books—and thinking she was the last person Genevieve could imagine talking to about sex. It would be like asking a female, geeky version of Mr. Rogers. Here she was in Paris, she remembered thinking, and her French roommate probably knew less than *she* did about the nuts and bolts of human anatomy.

"I'm glad to see you are still a little bit French," said Catharine. "This is the first question you ask me. Very good. Many Americans, they do not eat bread. I find this . . . confusing. How does a person simply decide not to eat bread? How does this even happen?"

This was another thing Genevieve remembered about Catharine: She always wanted Genevieve to explain America—and Americans—to her.

"I think it's mostly a diet thing. We just don't have the same relationship with bread. Not to mention that ours isn't as good as yours. So . . . about the *boulangerie*?"

"Yes, la Maréchalerie is still the rudest, and the best. So often these go together, don't you think?"

"Only in Paris."

"Oh, I think not, *ma cousine*," Catharine said with another chuckle. "I think not."

Chapter Thirteen

Angela, 1983

It is after midnight by the time they finish their meal in the back of the restaurant.

"Where are you staying?" Thibeaux asks.

"With my brother. In the Village Saint-Paul," says Angela.

"Of course you are," says Xabi in a sardonic tone. Angela wonders what it says about her that she is staying in the village, what he finds objectionable. But she hesitates to ask.

"Xabier, why don't you walk her home?" Pablo suggests.

"It's all right," Angela says with a quick shake of her head. "I'll be fine."

The wine has made her a little hazy, just enough to make her feel confident, yet simultaneously to doubt herself. She remembers a time when she walked everywhere, anytime, at three in the morning, no problem. Back then she hadn't given a thought to being out on the streets alone, unaccompanied, and a little tipsy from wine. Now, of course, she realizes it is foolish to take the risk. But there is a part of her that admires that old self, the audacious girl she'd once been, ready to take on the world. Unafraid, unabashed, undeterred.

Now she knows enough to be afraid. Now she is afraid of so many things.

"He is going your way," says Pablo, cajoling. "It is easy for him. And what is better for a man than to escort a beautiful woman? You will take her, Xabi?"

"*Bien sûr*," Xabi says with a frown. He pulls on a worn brown leather jacket. "Of course I will take you."

Angela thanks Pablo, Thibeaux, everyone, for the night, feeling awkward as she does so, as though she is thanking them for afternoon tea. But what is the proper etiquette after spending the evening drinking wine and eavesdropping on revolutionaries?

She nearly laughs aloud at this thought and thinks, *It is all right,* she will never see any of them again and will simply remember this night with fondness: a perfect souvenir from Paris, so much better than a commemorative key chain.

Xabi leads the way down the glistening cobblestone street. It is no longer raining, but the sidewalks are freshly washed from the downpour and the streetlamps and restaurant lights reflect brightly off the wet concrete. Angela wonders about Xabi's chalk painting: Has it been washed away, a multicolored kaleidoscope of pigments swirling in the puddles?

He lights a cigarillo. Offers her one. It is brown like a cigar, but much slenderer than the cigarettes back home. Delicate. Exotic. Angela takes it, though she doesn't smoke.

This. Walking together in silence. The air damp and cool, scented with rain and old stone and the Seine. A cigarillo in her hand because she is no longer Angela Martin, wife and mother. She is An-zhel Mart-ann, a woman who walks the wet streets of Paris with a handsome escort in the wee hours, a little bit tipsy on unfiltered red table wine, smoking.

Breathing. She is breathing. Finally breathing, with a smoke in her hand. Only in Paris.

Paris at midnight is not like any other city she has ever seen: certainly not San Francisco—which shuts down so early it's hard to find a meal past nine at night—or even New York. Here people are out in droves: huddled over coffees and beers in outdoor cafés, or lounging on benches, heads bent closely. There are couples walking arm in arm; others are leaning up against walls, lingering under bridges, pushing into one another, kissing.

Angela remembers watching an old movie set in Paris (what was the name?) in which one character tells the other: *It's midnight. One half of Paris is making love to the other half.*

"They have no large homes," Xabi says suddenly.

"Excuse me?"

"People who live in the city—it is very expensive here. The houses, the apartments, are very small. So they . . ."

"Make love on the street?"

He looks over at her, surprised.

She laughs. Oh yes, she may have had a little too much wine.

"Yes, sometimes. Or they meet at cafés, like their . . . what do you call the *salons*?"

"Living rooms?"

"Yes, like this, like the living room. There are many thousands of cafés in Paris."

"So, you're not from here, are you? Thibeaux said you are Basque?"

He nods.

"What is it like there?"

"It is . . . complicated. I have family in both France and Spain. But the legacy of Franco is still with us. It is still brutal in some ways."

"Franco died a while ago, didn't he?"

"Not soon enough."

"Is that why you came to Paris?"

"I came to Paris because here, the people support artists. Not the Americans so much, but others are very supportive. They throw coins, enough to live on."

"I'm sorry you don't like Americans." Is it the man, or the place, that makes Angela feel free to be someone she is not? To say the things she wouldn't say? "It's a shame we can't be friends."

Again he looks startled. Discomfited. She is glad.

"I never said . . . I never meant to say that."

"No, really. I understand. A lot of people don't like Americans."

"It is . . . the policies of the government. Not you."

She smiles. Smokes. They walk the rest of the way without talking, but somehow the silence between them feels companionable, not awkward. There is something about this man . . . the way he holds himself, the intense way he looks at her, as though there isn't anything else—anyone else—in the world.

They arrive at the Village Saint-Paul. Xabi steps back to read the sign on the front of the building.

"Your brother is a *serrurier*?"

She nods. "Yes, a locksmith."

"He opens doors? Is he good?"

"The best. Look." She pulls a pendant out from under her blouse. "He gave me this. It's a key from ancient Syria."

Xabi reaches out to lift the rusty metal, his light eyes studying it intently. The nearness of his hand to her chest makes Angela's heart pound, her senses sing.

"It doesn't look like a key," he says quietly.

"No, it doesn't, does it?"

"What does it open?"

"Only my heart," she says with a little laugh. Her joke falls flat, though, as Xabi gazes at her for a long moment without speaking.

Finally he drops the key, wishes her good night, and walks away.

Chapter Fourteen

That night Genevieve studied her French with renewed enthusiasm. Pawing through her phrase-book and dictionary, she pulled words together and jotted down several phrases in her notebook: *Il faut = I need, it must; J'ai mal à la tête = I have a headache; Est-ce que vous pouvez m'aider? = Could you help me?*

Though she wasn't able to fall asleep until well past one in the morning, her rest was blissfully free of locked doors, of any dreams at all, actually. She was awakened a little after nine by the sound of tapping at a window. Pulling on a black Oaktown sweatshirt over the T-shirt and shorts she used for pajamas, she went into the main room to investigate.

A middle-aged couple stood outside the kitchen window.

He was short and compact, with wide, slightly bulging eyes topped with wire-rimmed glasses. She was unsmiling and wore no makeup, her graying hair swept up in a severe chignon.

After a round of *bonjours*, they introduced themselves as Daniel and Marie-Claude Goselin. Marie-Claude spoke, while Daniel stood at her side, smiling and nodding. Much of Marie-Claude's meaning was lost in translation, but

Genevieve did glean that these were the neighbors responsible for leaving the food, the *nourriture sur la table*.

"*Oh, merci, merci beaucoup. J'aimais . . .*" Genevieve tried to say, "Thank you for the food. I loved it," but finally trailed off, foiled once again by gendered pronouns and the past tense. Still, the point was made. She hoped.

"We meet you when you are visiting when you are very small; I think you do not remember us. You are here now to tackle on your uncle's business?" the man asked in tortured English.

"Yes, I would like to, but . . . it is difficult to know how," Genevieve responded in equally tortured French. "I think I must get the papers of the government."

This engendered a long discussion between the man and woman, in which they appeared to be telling Genevieve the secrets for obtaining the necessary paperwork with which to conduct a business in the Village Saint-Paul. Because it was zoned as an arts and antiques district, some requirements were unique to the area.

"*Ne te rends jamais aux bureaucrates,*" Daniel concluded with a rueful shake of the head. "Never . . . *Comment dis-tu?*"

"Never surrender?" Genevieve translated.

"*C'est ça!* That's it!"

"I've been told that '*impossible*' *n'est pas français*."

"Exactly! This is what Napoléon says."

So they were taking advice from Napoléon now? As Genevieve thanked her neighbors for their advice, she started to yearn for a cup of coffee. She felt groggy and wondered what time it was in California (probably one in the morning?) but then chastised herself. *You're in Paris; there is no "home" time.*

Another man walked up to join their trio; he was large, American-sized, big-boned, and well-padded, with a florid, handsome face. He seemed shy, yet stood closely, as though already part of the conversation.

A conversation that had long ago outpaced Genevieve's linguistic abilities.

The man introduced himself as Jacques André. There was a lot of talking and pointing, and Genevieve realized they were trying to tell her where they lived—the couple on the other side of the courtyard's ivy-covered walls, the younger man through the arched walkway. The oft-repeated word *brocantes*—summoned up from her dusty memory, it meant "antiques"—made her suppose they were dealers, as were most residents of the area. Those lucky enough to have inherited homes here were able to live above or behind their shops, as Dave and Pasquale and Catharine used to do, while benefiting from frequent antiques fairs and arts events, as well as everyday foot traffic.

When there was a lull in the conversation, Genevieve volunteered, "Today I am going to visit my aunt."

It was a sentence from a beginning French class, and yet Genevieve felt inordinately pleased with herself. Already the language felt just a tiny bit easier, like a too-tight pair of leather shoes that, while painful, loosened ever so slightly each time she wore them. She just hoped she didn't develop the equivalent of linguistic bunions in the process.

Marie-Claude mentioned that in France most elderly parents lived with their families, and how sad that Pasquale couldn't live with Catharine, but the facility was very special, very modern. Alzheimer's was such a shame . . . *quel dommage.* Everyone shook their heads and the conversation stumbled to a gloomy end.

Finally, Jacques and Daniel brought out business cards.

Genevieve had to look for the number on the ancient phone to give to them, reading off the faded numbers from under a strip of yellowing tape, written by Pasquale, how many years ago?

But of course, the neighbors already had that number, as it was the same one Dave and Pasquale had had for decades. And besides, as Genevieve recalled, the custom in the village was less about phone calls and more this: to stop by and speak through windows. When they were flung open, it was taken as a sign that the inhabitants were awake and ready to chat. Or, in this case, even when they were closed, neighbors simply knocked and woke a person up.

After they'd bid one another *"bonne journée,"* Genevieve fixed herself a simple breakfast: a hunk of the (already stale) baguette with some cheese and pâté, and a cup of strong tea.

She started a shopping list: *coffee, baguette, vegetables, fruit, yogurt.*

Catharine had written out very careful instructions for visiting Pasquale, which she had fastened together in a thick sheaf like a handwritten instruction manual: where to find the Métro entrance, how much money was needed for the book of tickets (called the *carnet*), and even a description and diagram of how to use the machines. She included which exit to take out of the Métro station, and a little map of how to walk from there to the Alzheimer's facility.

Genevieve considered what Catharine had said about pickpockets. She doubted they could be any worse here than in San Francisco but supposed it was smart to leave her valuables in the apartment.

The Village Saint-Paul, as a nosy, close-knit neighborhood, felt secure, but just in case, Genevieve hid her passport and extra money in a little hidey-hole under the floorboards in the bedroom, which Catharine had shown her in confidence the last time she was there. She remembered Catharine saying, in a grave tone of voice: "I think they may have hidden Jews down here, during the war." The opening was only about as big as a breadbox, but the teenaged Genevieve had supposed perhaps it opened further, somehow, her imagination stoked by stories of Anne Frank and her family secreted behind the paneling. Only now did Genevieve realize that Catharine had probably been joking.

She packed forty dollars' worth of euros, a small water bottle, sunglasses, and a dog-eared old paper map of Paris she found on Dave's desk into a small leather satchel, then locked the doors and set out.

Genevieve felt almost like a native as she navigated the streets and found the Saint-Paul Métro stop barely three blocks from the village. Catharine's precise instructions were easy to follow. A gypsy family got on when she did, a little girl dancing, whirling, and clapping, while a man—her father?—played the drum, the loud bangs reverberating off the metal sides of the train. No one gave them money; Genevieve would have, but she didn't have any change with her and couldn't figure out what was appropriate, anyway. They exited at the next stop, without a word.

On the number 2 line Genevieve studied the big subway map and kept track of the stops: place de Clichy came right before her station, and Pigalle right after. She exited at Blanche and took a moment to get her bearings when she emerged from the underground. She was looking for 49, rue Blanche, not far from the famous Moulin Rouge.

On the map Catharine had written, *You can't miss it: It is a modern building, yellow with big crooked white strips in front of it, and stainless-steel details. It is an atrocity in the neighborhood, though some people love it.*

Her cousin was right: There was no way to miss the ultramodern façade. The steel-and-glass, yellow-and-white building stuck out like a colorful, modern, bumbling American among the elegant, staid Parisians.

Genevieve entered through the sliding front doors and signed in at the reception desk. She had practiced a couple of lines in French—*I am here to visit my aunt Pasquale Mackenzie. Could you please direct me to her room?*—but it wasn't necessary; apparently Catharine had called ahead and told them to expect Genevieve. A pretty, delicate-looking young woman emerged from a back office and greeted her in English.

"*Bonjour.* I am called Solange. Your aunt is on the second floor, room 211. Here behind you is the lift. I will put in the code for you."

"Thank you," said Genevieve, following her to the elevator.

"You are American?"

"Yes," Genevieve replied, trying not to be disappointed that people seemed to guess her nationality so readily. So much for fitting in with the locals.

"This code is for security, so the residents don't wander," Solange explained as she tapped numbers on a keypad. "We have many security features, because with the Alzheimer's this is a concern."

Genevieve nodded.

"Just like this, for example," said Solange, turning toward a stooped, white-haired woman who was shuffling toward them, leaning on an aluminum walker. "Madame Lyon, *pourquoi êtes-vous ici?*"

"*Êtes-vous américaine?*" The old woman asked Genevieve if she was American. She reached out and cupped one of Genevieve's hands in both of hers. Her hands were warm and dry, velvety soft. "*Merci, merci pour . . .*"

Genevieve lost track of what the woman was saying. She looked to Solange, who translated.

"She say thank you for coming, in the war."

"The war?"

"The Second World War. She remembers the Americans arriving, liberating her village when she was little girl."

"I . . ." Genevieve didn't know what to say. She'd had nothing to do with World War II, of course. But did Madame Lyon even realize what year this was? Should Genevieve simply accept the thanks gracefully, acknowledge her gratitude?

"She always does this whenever she hear anyone speaking English," said Solange, sounding annoyed. She was holding the elevator door open with her shoulder; every few seconds it tried to close, banging her softly. "Don't preoccupy yourself about it."

"*Merci*," said Madame Lyon one more time. She was still holding Genevieve's hand, her soft grip surprisingly strong.

"*Je vous en prie*," Genevieve said finally, practicing a line she had looked up last night: "You are welcome." There was a much less formal way to say this: "*De rien*," which meant, literally, "It is nothing." But World War II wasn't nothing. Genevieve remembered this from her last visit to Paris: The war was still alive, still acknowledged here in a way it wasn't in the States. France had been invaded, bombed, occupied. It would take more than a generation or two of distance from the events to forget.

Finally Solange led Madame Lyon away, and Genevieve rode the elevator to the second floor. She found her aunt's room at the end of the long hall.

Pasquale was sleeping. Her olive skin was dark against the white sheets; her eyes were closed but seemed to be moving, as though she was dreaming. Not wanting to disturb her, Genevieve took a seat in a molded plastic chair.

Tante Pasquale had always been petite; at

fourteen, Genevieve had already stood as tall as she. But now her aunt seemed truly tiny. Time (or was it the disease?) had only intensified her small build, shaving any extra plumpness from her until her bones poked cruelly at tissue-paper skin.

Like Catharine, Pasquale had a wide mouth, strong cheekbones, heavy-lidded eyes. But on Pasquale it lent an elfin appeal: a dark pixie with a sweet, secret smile. When she cast that smile in Dave's direction he would stop whatever he was doing—watching a game on TV, prepping vegetables, oiling his tools—and cross the room to embrace her. He would nuzzle her neck and whisper sweet nothings.

It was a breathlessly romantic gesture that always embarrassed Catharine, who would roll her eyes and snort.

But Genevieve had been enthralled with Dave and Pasquale's flagrant adoration, as well as their romantic story: the young American soldier who had loved a woman so much that he had forsaken his native land and stayed to help rebuild Paris from the devastation of war. Who had rarely returned to the United States, not even to visit. Genevieve's own parents had been devoted to each other, she supposed, but it always seemed more of a civilized partnership than a passionate love affair. Perhaps it was always like this for the offspring, Genevieve thought. Perhaps Catharine didn't recognize the adoration shining in her parents' eyes, or never interpreted it as romantic.

"*Qu'est-ce que vous faites là?*"

Genevieve jumped at the sound of a voice demanding to know what she was doing there. It was an attendant: dark hair pulled back in a tight bun, chubby, dressed in a baby-blue smock decorated with tumbling teddy bears.

"*Je suis ici visiter mon tante Pasquale. Je suis américain,*" Genevieve said, wincing because she got the gender wrong, referring to her aunt with the masculine pronoun, and to herself using a masculine adjective as well. "I am here to visit my aunt Pasquale," she had tried to say, adding, "I am American."

Mentioning she was American was probably wholly unnecessary, Genevieve thought, as the attendant gave her a frown.

"She no know you," the woman responded in English. She wasn't French either, Genevieve realized. From somewhere else; an island nation, maybe. Tahiti? Just as in the United States, the people working in the nursing home appeared to be mostly female, and many were immigrants. Her name badge read: *Pia.*

Pia held one finger up beside her ear and made circles in the air. "She crazy."

"I . . ." Genevieve trailed off, not knowing what to say. She wasn't going to argue the niceties of Alzheimer's with a health aide who probably knew her aunt much better than she did, at this point. Still. "I just want to sit with her until she wakes up. Is that okay?'

The attendant gestured with her chin toward the bed. Genevieve turned to see Pasquale's dark eyes were open. Her gaze was vacant, fixating on a spot beyond either of them.

"*Comment ça va, ma petite?*" Pia said, a big smile on her face. She continued in French, and Genevieve tried her best to keep up. Then she switched back to English. "You feeling better? Look who came from America to see you? From America, so far! Here is your nephew! And I bring you some lunch. Let's sit up and look pretty!"

Pia stacked two pillows behind Pasquale and helped her to sit higher in the bed.

Once Pasquale was arranged, Pia placed the lunch tray on a hospital cart that she positioned in front of her.

"She was dizzy earlier, so she stay in bed today," Pia said to Genevieve. "You help her, eh?"

"Of course."

"I be back. *Bon appétit, ma petite Pasquale!* Your nephew, she help you to eat, okay? *C'est le repas, le déjeuner.* Lunch! Mmmmm."

Chapter Fifteen

Pasquale

*L*unch. Pasquale didn't care for peas, and the milk was warm.

Did she even *like* milk?

During the war . . . she would have loved anything—anything—to quell the constant, gnawing, nauseating yearning deep in her empty belly. Her parents sent her away to the countryside, to her grandparents on the farm. Thinking it would be safer than Paris. But times were hard in the Franche-Comté too; the Germans had come through, set up shop in the nicest farmhouse in the valley, ate up the stores.

Paris . . . liberated. She returned too late to see the troops in their triumphant uniforms, marching down the Champs-Élysées.

She works in her parents' café near Montmartre. The American soldier comes in every day for coffee. Loud, smiling, everything a joke. Handsome, terrible accent. Younger than Pasquale by two years, she later discovers, but her father calls him "an old soul."

Thick wrists. Twinkling eyes. Dashing goatee. The scent of tobacco and something citrus. That Hershey's chocolate bar. She had nearly fainted from pleasure when it melted on her eager tongue. Not like the chocolate she had known from before the war; strangely sour, as though the milk had turned. But delicious.

"I think she's finished." A voice. A pretty woman, auburn hair, stands in the room. Her eyes as brown as that Hershey's bar, but sad. As though she carries a great burden.

Angela?

"Where'd you get that hair?" Pasquale asked.

The woman smiled. "From my mama, I guess. How are you, Tante Pasquale?"

Tante. Not Angela, then. But the hair . . . like Angela's.

Another moment passed, and Pasquale realized the woman was still watching her.

What had the question been? What was she supposed to answer? Had there been a question at all?

She hated this moment, when she realized the here and now had been taken from her, relentless, unyielding, slipping away like the proverbial wave upon the sand. She tried to reconstruct what had just happened—the words, the meanings— but it was as futile as trying to pin down that wave.

It was like when Catharine used to pester her, asking about her dreams. Pasquale would try to remember, but it seemed the more she concentrated, the faster the images skated away, fluttering just out of her mental grasp, before she could describe them. Sometimes she made things up to placate her frustrated daughter, to give her something to interpret. Oh, the stories Catharine would tell!

Her *nephew,* Pia had said. But Pia must have meant *niece.* The woman was still looking at her, expectantly.

What was she supposed to say?

She gave a polite smile, nodded. Pretended.

"*Ça va, Tante Pasquale?*" the young woman asked. "Done with lunch? *Finis*? I am Genevieve, Tante, do you remember me?"

Genevieve. Screaming in the night, awakened from a nightmare, sobbing as though her heart was breaking, calling for her mama. Was there anything more terrible, more wrenching than the sound of a child calling out from the anguished depths of night? Calling for a parent who would never come?

"Are you . . . you are Genevieve?" Pasquale asked.

"All the way from America," said another woman, taking the tray of food.

Pia, Pasquale remembered. The woman taking the tray was named Pia, and she worked here, in this place Pasquale lived now. Pasquale didn't live in the Village Saint-Paul anymore. Never again. No more friends dropping by and chatting through the window. No more relatives stopping by for couscous. No more Dave.

No more Dave.

Pain washed over her. Dave was gone. He had promised never to leave her, and yet he had. How could he have left her?

Then shame. For forgetting.

"Genevieve, *mon amour,*" she said, a huge smile breaking out on her thin face. "I don't believe it! What are you doing here?"

"She here for a little visit with her favorite auntie," said Pia.

When Genevieve came to them . . . The feel of her, sweaty and anguished, calling out in the night for her mother. Never had Pasquale known a child could cry like that, her small frame racked with sobs.

How many nights had they been awakened by her cries? Dave rushing to her, cradling her in his big arms, bringing her into the kitchen so Catharine could sleep. *Pasquale warming milk at the stove while Dave sits with Genevieve at the table, pushing the hair out of her hot face, her cheeks streaked with tears.*

"Why?" *Genevieve's question, simple and heart-breaking and impossible to answer.*

"*We cannot understand why.*" *Dave's voice is soft. "Only God knows the reasons for things. It will all be explained one day."*

Pasquale remains mute, her eyes fixed on the milk warming in the pan, making sure it doesn't scald. She wishes she could agree with Dave, that she could believe God has a plan, that someone is in charge, that such heartbreak would be explained. But Pasquale lost her religion somewhere around 1944. She knows that for some, the horrors of war increased their allegiance to God; but in her mind, no higher being would have orchestrated such atrocities or could have sat by and allowed them to happen.

"But écoute-moi, listen to me, Genevieve," Dave says to the girl in his arms, now hiccupping in the teary aftermath. "You will be happy again one day. You will live, and love. Sometimes love is all there is, but that is enough. Do you understand me?"

Is it enough? Pasquale watches his gentle, graying head bent low toward his niece.

Dave had always had more faith than she. The only time she'd seen it challenged was with everything that had happened with Angela. Pasquale had understood what Angela had done, and why, but Dave never could.

The woman spoke.

"You are beautiful as ever, Tante Pasquale."

Pasquale waved a thin hand in the air, and when she spied it, for a moment she couldn't believe it was hers. It was so skinny, the bones practically poking through, like in the war.

But this hand was old. Ancient, ropy blue veins standing out from grayish skin, gnarled knuckles. Her grandmother's hands, sloughing lavender off

145

the stalks they had dried in the sun. A circle of old women and children, working together to fill a huge basket, big enough for Pasquale to curl up in.

The rhythmic scratching noise of thin, calloused hands scraping away at the fragrant blooms. The mound of lavender blossoms. The murmur of old voices. Behind them, someone is grinding spices for the night's couscous. No meat, but there are carrots and onions, wild roots and haricots verts, *and of course the couscous one of the boys brought home—they didn't ask from where. Wild greens and twisted orange mushrooms, the chanterelles her uncle gathers from the forest.*

The woods are their salvation. They eat pigeons, the occasional cat. Rabbits. Dandelions. Roots. Anything.

The soldiers took the chocolate and coffee and butter first thing, but left them with some lard. The old women roast barley and mix it with chicory to replace the coffee, but chocolate remains a sweet, mouthwatering, long-ago memory.

When she complains, her grandmother gets her a scoop of cool well water from the bucket. Drink deeply. Think of good things, pleasant things. Not food, but the warmth of the sun on her skin. The strange, musky smell of the goat's pelt when she rubs her nose in it. The lowing of the cows, the ones the Germans haven't slaughtered, the ones that still provide precious milk and cream. *Her grandfather made some sort of deal with the head officer and they were able to keep two of their cows, but the soldiers confiscated the butter and cheese and most of the milk.*

Warm milk. Pasquale reached for the carton that was on the tray, but the tray was gone.

The young woman leaned over the table to hug Pasquale. She smelled like shampoo and fresh-cut grass and a little like the oil Dave had always used on his door locks. Reddish-brown hair fell in her face.

"Angela?"

"No, Tante Pasquale, it's Genevieve, remember?"

"Genevieve . . . Angela isn't with us anymore."

"No."

"It makes me so sad. . . ." Pasquale's eyes filled with tears. "Dave's gone, too."

"Yes, I'm so sorry."

"So many, gone. My brothers. But . . . there are babies, *n'est-ce pas*? There are always babies. Did you tell Jim?"

"Jim? You mean my father? Tell him what?"

"*Écoute-moi*, listen to me, Angela. You have to tell him. You have to. I know you don't like my advice, but you should listen to me on this."

"Tell him what, Pasquale?"

Pasquale glanced around the room: a vase of flowers, half a dozen glittery cards sitting on the windowsill. Acoustic tiles overhead, medical equipment discreetly pushed behind a screen. A bright yellow strip of metal visible through the window. Not at home. She was sick. She can't remember things. *Something on the stove is forgotten, catches fire. It is the last straw. Catharine insists she move.*

The woman in front of her, with Angela's hair. Her niece. *Genevieve.*

"It is so good to see you, Genevieve. All grown up! You are beautiful."

"*You* are the beautiful one, as always, Tante Pasquale," Genevieve said. "Catharine sends her love. She'll be back on Thursday."

"I wish I could cook for you."

Genevieve smiled. "Me too! I have dreamed of your couscous over the years. And do you remember when you used to make me *chocolat chaud*—hot chocolate?"

"Catharine won't let me cook anymore. Where is the milk?"

Chapter Sixteen

Outside the Alzheimer's facility, the streets were lined with traditional cream-colored stone and brick buildings. Fanciful black wrought-iron balconies, elaborate corbels under the eaves, carved shields over each doorway added grace to the blocky forms.

Genevieve walked down rue Blanche, past a long row of Vespas and motorcycles, noting a pizzeria and a couscous diner, a couple of dress shops, a cute bright red bar called Blabla (what a great name for a bar).

Though Genevieve had steeled herself against profound changes in her aunt, it was still a shock to see what the years, and Alzheimer's, had wrought. Why had she let Jason talk her into a honeymoon in Hawaii? She was one of those weird people who didn't particularly like sun *or* sand, much less resorts full of tourists. She should have insisted on coming to Paris, except that Jason said he had a friend with a condo where they could stay for free, and her aunt and uncle didn't have much room for them, and a hotel would have been expensive. And Parisians were snooty, weren't they? And Jason had a client in Hawaii; he could do a little schmoozing and then write off the whole trip; it would be a win-win.

But the truth was that Genevieve hadn't pushed the idea of Paris. Her time with Uncle Dave and Aunt Pasquale had saved her after the death of her mother. But . . . it was also an unwelcome reminder of such raw vulnerability, such a painful time, that to relive it was too grueling even to contemplate. Marrying Jason was the start to a new life, one without regrets, without dwelling on the losses of the past. Or so she had imagined at the time.

What had Pasquale been telling Angela to do, in

her reverie? What did she think Angela should tell Jim?

Probably it was some inconsequential confidence that the sisters-in-law had traded. Spending too much on a dress, drinking a little too much, losing a precious piece of jewelry. And what would it matter at this point, anyway? All the players were long gone, existing only in the memories of those who had known them. Still alive in Pasquale's mind more than in most, in that odd, Zen-like state of here and now (and very long ago) that afflicted so many with dementia.

Genevieve wondered how Catharine dealt with her mother looking through her, not recognizing her, answering questions that had not been asked. Since it had been so long, it was possible that even a healthy Pasquale would not have recognized her niece Genevieve after all these years . . . but what must it be like to have your mother's familiar eyes rest upon you with that unsettling emptiness, that lack of recognition? At the worst, even when Angela went into hospice, she had always recognized her children.

But . . . could Pasquale's admonition have been about something more? Could Angela have been troubled when she came to Paris? To Genevieve she had always referred to it as a carefree trip before having a second child; a visit to see her brother, Dave, in the City of Lights.

The brother she adored. Though . . . she had

never returned to Paris, and Dave had never come to visit them in California. Genevieve hadn't wondered much about it as a kid; it was simply the way it was. It was an expensive trip, and neither family had much discretionary income. But still . . .

Genevieve remembered one night, sitting on the floor with her uncle, hunched over a rusted lock they were putting back together. When she leaned forward, the strange old piece of metal she wore as a talisman fell out of the neckline of her shirt.

Dave's hands went still as he stared at it. Normally Genevieve didn't see much family resemblance between Uncle Dave and her much younger mother, but in that moment their eyes had the same cast: about a thousand years old.

"Um . . . I found this in my mom's drawer, after she died." Genevieve reached up to stroke the necklace. "It was in a package from Paris. Was it from you?"

He nodded.

"Do you think she would mind that I took it?" she asked, made nervous by his continued silence. "Or . . . do you want it back?"

"No, of course not," he said with a sad smile. "It's just as it should be. It looks good on you. It's a key. Originally from Syria."

"It's a key?" she held it up to look at it. It didn't look like a key.

He nodded. "Very ancient. Very special. Keep it safe."

She nodded. "You know, my mother always told me stories about you. She loved you so much. And Paris, too."

After a long pause he said, simply, "Did she, now?"

Genevieve tried to conjure memories of Angela—of the *woman* she had been, not just as a mother—but the truth was that her recollections were a vague jumble. Soft, capable hands. The sadness in her dark eyes. The quiet, stubborn insistence with which she stared down the neighbors at the city council meeting. Her sweet voice singing: *"I love you, a bushel and a peck . . ."*

Memory was a tricky thing. Not long after their mother had died, Genevieve had an argument with her brother over a huge pile of snapshots they were sorting through. Genevieve had a distinct memory of the family road trip to Yosemite, but Nick told her she hadn't been born yet; it was right after Angela came home from Paris. "The only way you were there was in utero," he'd said. Genevieve must have manufactured the memory from the familiar photos, kept on the mantel.

Toward the end, when Angela was in hospice, she had long talks with Nick and Jim. But not with Genevieve; Angela would just hug her daughter as hard as she could, and cry. Genevieve wished she could forget the odd stench of the room, the stinging tang of rubbing alcohol and the unpleasant stewed-food aroma that wafted down the hall from the cafeteria. At home, her mother had always smelled of baking spices: vanilla and cinnamon, yeast, sometimes citrus. That scent was gone, masked by the cloying, disturbing sourness of imminent death and, worse, the doomed efforts to keep it at bay. She had felt suffocated by those smells and by the tightness of her mother's grip.

As always, Genevieve's mind overflowed with questions she wished she could ask Angela, not as child to mother, but as woman to woman.

Genevieve looked up to see that she was in front of the Moulin Rouge. Outside, a swollen line of people waited for the doors to open. They had the harried, annoyed, yet determinedly cheerful demeanor of tourists. It felt surreal, slightly dreamlike, to walk out of a state-of-the-art medical facility and stroll past such a famous club, a place that looked like a movie set. But that's the way it was in Paris: everywhere she looked were sights so iconic as to seem like tourist clichés. The Eiffel Tower, Notre-Dame, the Arc de Triumph, the Louvre. Adorable florist shops and cheese shops and chocolate shops. Historic fountains and the bridges over the Seine and plazas chock-full of outdoor café tables under colorful umbrellas.

She considered trying to walk all the way home instead of taking the Métro, but the day had turned gray and rain looked imminent. Also, though the lunch at the Alzheimer's center hadn't looked very appetizing, it reminded Genevieve that she hadn't eaten much for breakfast.

There were plenty of restaurant dining options, but she wasn't up to lingering over a meal, alone, in a Parisian restaurant. Not yet.

So she zoomed back on the Métro, easily reversing her steps. It began to sprinkle as she made her way from the Métro stop to the Village Saint-Paul and was truly raining by the time she arrived back at the shop. She fitted the key in the front door and pushed it open to the sound of the ticking clocks. The dusty confines of the shop and apartment were warm and dry and felt like home.

She brought the cheese dome out of the fridge and laid it on the table beside a rather pathetic heel of stale baguette. Then she took out a small cutting board and sliced the remaining pear, which was already going soft.

Genevieve polished off the last of the cheese and ham just as she finished her novel. She would have to go grocery shopping tomorrow. Not to mention *book* shopping. Like most readers, she felt nervous without a stack of novels at her disposal. In fact, she sometimes wondered: What did people *do* if they couldn't read? On the other hand, maybe without those hours lost to novels she would have become a championship knitter, or a rock climber.

Luckily, Paris was, hearteningly, still a city of books. Across the street and a few doors down was a bookstore called the Red Wheelbarrow—surely, given their name, they would carry books in English?—and of course there was the famous Shakespeare and Company, not far from Notre-Dame.

Then it dawned on her that Uncle Dave used to keep a small bookshelf full of novels in English. He lent them out only to his closest friends and even had a personalized stamp, a hefty metal object with his name in a bold, blocky script that reminded Genevieve of something from the Cold War era, like pictures from a history book about the Soviet Union:

DAVE MACKENZIE
Under Lock and Key, Serrurier,
Rue Saint-Paul, Village Saint-Paul

Dave had handed her the stamp and a big ink pad. *"Could you go through the books and make sure they're all stamped? That way they're sure to make their way back to me."*

Genevieve had been avoiding the master bedroom since she'd arrived, hesitant to face those ghosts. But now she opened the heavy wooden door at the end of the hall to reveal a simple chamber, virtually unchanged. The small double bed was neatly made, covered (as always) in a wedding-ring quilt made by Pasquale's mother and aunts and given to the young couple as a present upon their marriage. Tante Pasquale's dressing table was topped (as ever) with a lace-edged linen runner and several dainty bottles of expensive perfume, a rare luxury. There were a series of baby and school pictures of Catharine on one wall, a few other family members. And two framed photos of Genevieve: one, standing with Dave and Pasquale and Catharine in front of Notre-Dame; the other a high school graduation photo she didn't remember sending. Perhaps her father had done so.

Uncle Dave's highboy still held a little pewter dish full of coins—they used to be francs; now they were euros. Every night he emptied the coins from his jingling pockets; in the morning he would hand a few to Genevieve and send her to buy baguettes.

"The government pays a subsidy to bakers, to keep baguettes affordable. There were too many hungry people during the war; now at least one can always buy baguettes!"

Along one sidewall was a low bookcase jammed with English-language novels and collected essays: Ernest Hemingway. Mark Twain. Henry Miller. F. Scott Fitzgerald. Henry James. Gertrude Stein. Harriet Beecher Stowe. Americans, all, who had found their way to Paris and left behind a bit of their hearts.

Genevieve pulled out *The Autobiography of Alice B. Toklas*, by Gertrude Stein.

It dawned on her that she shared her hometown of Oakland, California, with the American expat, who had set up a celebrated salon in Paris not far from the Luxembourg Gardens, where she entertained the likes of Pablo Picasso and Ernest Hemingway. Stein had, in fact, given Oakland one of its few claims to fame, famously remarking: "There is no *there,* there."

Genevieve took the book into her bedroom and set it on the nightstand, but she didn't feel like reading at the moment; in fact, she was alert to the point of fidgety. It must be jet lag: tired at the wrong time, wide-awake at odd moments.

Should she go out for another walk? It was raining in earnest now, a steady beat of droplets drumming loudly against the casement windows. There was probably an umbrella here somewhere, shoved behind holiday ornaments in one of the few overstuffed closets. Catharine had encouraged her not to be shy, to help herself to whatever she wanted. Still . . . while Paris in the rain sounded romantic, it also sounded cold and dreary.

She had noticed rags and a mop and bucket in the closet where she found the pilot light for the water heater. But if she was going to clean, first she needed music.

Genevieve flipped through the albums by the old phonograph, hoping to find Edith Piaf or

Jacques Brel or something else typically French. The sort of music that would be on the soundtrack of a Hollywood movie set in Paris. But to a record they were American, probably music for a homesick Dave: Hank Williams, Frank Sinatra, Tony Bennett. Finally she chose an album and put it on the turntable, clumsily setting the needle in the groove as Dave had taught her so long ago.

The apartment filled with Patsy Cline's voice singing "Crazy for feeling so lonely . . ." as Genevieve dusted and swept and washed the floors, every stroke of her arms making the apartment feel more like hers, like home. For real.

It would be an exaggeration for Genevieve to suggest she *liked* housework. But she was enough of a farm girl, she supposed, to feel uncomfortable having people doing the work for her. Jason had tried to hire a housecleaner many times. Most of her friends would have loved the idea of their husbands suggesting such a thing. But Genevieve felt it beyond awkward: What was she supposed to do while they cleaned, when she felt compelled to pick up a mop and work beside them? Should she kick back and read a book, lifting her feet while they swept under her? Or should she hand over the keys and take a walk, allowing virtual strangers access to her things?

Jason insisted she was being paranoid. But Genevieve had walked through people's private spaces when she was young. She had peeked through drawers, shattered the invisible barriers that protected their privacy. She hadn't hurt or stolen anything, but she had *seen*. And even though she didn't really have any secrets worth protecting, the thought made her feel too . . . exposed.

Genevieve was dusting the front room when she remembered her promise to Philippe D'Artavel. His *dossier* must be hidden somewhere on Dave's crowded desk. After looking through a couple of messy stacks of bills (some with notations in Catharine's upright French-style hand, evidence that she had gone through his papers), she finally found the current job files, piled on a side table in one dim corner of the apartment.

They were labeled in Dave's spidery, all-caps script:

MLLE CORRINE GERARD,
35 RUE DE VENISE

M JEAN-PAUL ANGELINI,
1134 RUE SAINT-SAËNS

M PHILIPPE D'ARTAVEL,
283 1/2 RUE DE TRACY

MME MICHELLE VELAIN,
6P RUE EGINHARD

The files were full of receipts and photos and notes:

> Husband passed away, charge half price
> Yale or Corbin Ironclad locks, take photos for book
> Install modern security at points of entry but maintain antique locks throughout—replace master bedroom lock with salvaged pancake lock or push-key lever lock

Genevieve brought Philippe's file over to the dining room table, then filled the electric kettle and put the water on for tea.

Wind and rain batted at the windows. A man ran by holding a newspaper over his head, then ducked into the shelter of one of the arches. A cat yowled piteously until a little red door opened and it dashed inside.

Genevieve returned to the table, spread open the dossier, and thumbed through the notes and pictures. Whenever Dave encountered antique locks and keys, he documented them by photographing them and drawing a schema of each, along with historical notes. He had planned to include all of these in his book: *Love Laughs at Locksmiths*. There were captioned photos of the different items. But the quality was terrible; they were grainy, amateurish. Probably taken by Dave himself with an impossibly old camera he had salvaged.

Genevieve picked up Philippe's dossier and out fell a hand-drawn map. She studied it from several angles before she realized it was of the *souterrain*, the catacombs.

What was *that* doing in the file?

The kettle whistled. She took a bag of Earl Grey out of an old tin and placed it in the coffee mug she had brought with her, the only souvenir (besides clothes and toiletries) she had brought from America, from her past life. A life that already felt eons ago, although it had been only a couple of days. If she were to return to the U.S. tomorrow, almost no one would have noticed she'd gone, and yet she already felt as though she'd lived a lifetime in Paris.

There was nothing quite so useful as travel, she decided, to illustrate Einstein's theory that time could shrink or lengthen relative to one's situation.

Though Dave was messy, he had his own method of organization. He had kept a page or two for each room in a house, documenting its lock or sets of locks, and on each was a letter and a number: *E-7, W-4*. These corresponded to bins under his workbench in the shop, with some overflowing onto shelves in the living room.

Genevieve found the bins corresponding to Philippe D'Artavel's house and brought them back to the kitchen table. She spread out several pages of *Le Monde* newspaper she'd found in a tall stack in the living room, then set out the old locks.

She took her time, cleaning and putting them back together with Patsy Cline crooning in the background, getting her hands dirty with oil and grunge, loving the smell and the motor memory.

"Your mind is concentrating and yet not, which is a neat trick. When you give yourself over to a lock, you don't need meditation," Dave would say, laughing. *"One day some Zen master is going to figure this out and create a whole new craze, learning to meditate while working as a locksmith!"*

But as Genevieve focused on the antique lock in her hands (beautiful, shaped like a lion's head), taking it apart, cleaning and oiling the parts, then putting it back together, her mind wandered back to her encounter with Tante Pasquale.

What had Pasquale been advising Angela to tell her husband?

Chapter Seventeen

Angela, 1983

"What happened to the other painting?" Angela asks two days later, when she returns to the place de l'Opéra, in front of the *palais*. The picture of the scaffolded Statue of Liberty is gone, replaced now by a half-finished rendition of Chagall's *Birthday*. "Did the rain wash it away?"

Xabier is crouched over the painting, his big hands covered in multicolored chalk dust. He is wearing his blue sweater, also dusty. His cheeks are shaded with several days' growth of dark beard.

He does not seem surprised to see her. As though he knew she would be back. His astonishing gray-blue eyes meet hers and do not turn away. His glance lingers too long; it is too intense. The question dies on her lips long before there is a response, and when it comes, it is from Xabi's friend Thibeaux, who laughs.

"It was not popular with the crowd. *N'est-ce pas*, *Xabi*? It required more work and skill than any painting he has done, and yet . . . it gathered the least money."

"I guess the American tourists did not understand my point," says Xabi.

"Or perhaps they did, and that was the problem," she quips. Angela feels exhilarated, pleased by her own audacity.

She had been surprised at herself ever since she dressed this morning, taking extra care with her hair, brushing it and letting it hang in soft, shining sheets around her face. She also applied a little makeup, but not too much. She'd been taking note of why Frenchwomen seemed so chic, and one reason was this: their makeup was subdued, subtle, in stark contrast to the American-style big hair and multicolored eyelids.

She had allowed Pasquale to take her shopping on rue du Commerce, a quiet street not far from the Eiffel Tower crowded with boutiques, to buy some new clothes. The things she wore on the farm were loose and natural; they might as well have been burlap sacks. Pasquale had been far too polite to say anything, but it is clear that Angela's Berkeley-inspired hippie style is not prized in Paris. The French do not wear baggy clothes; they are neat, tidy, tucked in, well pressed.

So this morning she put on a new summer dress of white cotton. Strappy red sandals with a small heel. A matching leather purse. A striped straw hat.

"You are looking *très parisienne*," said Pasquale when Angela emerged from the bedroom. "*Très chic!*"

Angela had refused the baguette, butter, and jam

Pasquale offered. She was too nervous to eat. She was going to go by and check on the progress of the painting.

That, in itself, makes her pause, ask herself what she is doing.

Her wedding ring encircles her finger, a plain gold band of reproach. She wasn't going to do anything, but still. How would she feel if Jim had dressed nicely, in his single Brooks Brothers shirt he kept for weddings and other special occasions, dabbing a bit of cologne (or all-natural vanilla extract) behind his ears, and then walked oh so casually by a beautiful street artist that he couldn't stop thinking about?

Part of the reason she wants to go, Angela tells herself, is for the much-needed dose of reality. Xabi has come to her in her dreams for the past two nights; those light, flashing eyes promising a treasure trove of secrets. The way he communicates so much through his stillness. The scent of him: tobacco and some sort of unfamiliar spice. The sound of his voice, which he uses so rarely: deep and resonant, making her think of curling up under a tree and listening to him read aloud poetry by Pablo Neruda, or perhaps Shakespearean sonnets.

That last reminds her of being in Paris with Jim on their honeymoon. They sat in the little park behind Notre-Dame as he read passages from Jean-Paul Sartre's *Being and Nothingness* to her.

Angela had wanted to climb to the top of the cathedral to see the gargoyles, but Jim had declared it too touristy, as though reading Sartre in the park wasn't par for the tourist course.

Angela didn't really understand philosophy, and mostly didn't care. But she pretended she did, for his sake. Jim had been so excited to stumble upon the Café de Philosophes, but when they got a table there were no intense philosophical debates, no students or masters discussing the finer points of existentialism. Only tourists like them, and a few French locals having lunch. They wound up ordering the plat du jour as always, while Jim tried to laugh off his disappointment.

At the time Angela had been embarrassed for him and wished he'd drop the whole thing. But now she wants some of that back: Jim as the boy who yearned to unlock the truth of existence, the meaning of life. The one who sought understanding, some sort of significance beyond growing food. The farm was more than just a way to make a living, of course; it was a lifestyle, a way of bringing his politics back to the very core: to the plates on the table. To sustenance. What could be more essential?

But when had their ideals turned so inward, so small? Food was politics—Angela knew that. And she was very lucky; everyone said so. And yet.

And yet . . . she had put on her new dress,

brushed her hair, dabbed some of Pasquale's perfume behind her ears.

And she had come to see what Xabi was painting.

"Do you like Chagall?" he asks her, finally looking up from the shading on the woman's black dress as she flew through the air, kissing her man. A physical manifestation of love and freedom, romance and magic.

"Very much," Angela says.

"He painted the ceiling in the opera house, you know. And . . . I think perhaps he is more pleasing to Americans. His paintings are very . . . romantic."

She smiles. Nods. Breathes. Does not look away.

"Yes. Yes, they are."

Chapter Eighteen

When Genevieve was a young teenager, being in France had been about strangeness: the odd tones and impossible consonants of the language that swirled about her, the unfamiliar shows on TV, the unusual foods covered in delicate sauces, the peculiar expectation that children could (and should) take care of themselves, running through the streets in search of baguettes.

Now it was a never-ending river of nostalgia,

overlaid with a torrent of anxiety-producing logistical details: whether to leave the pilot light on, should she get a cell phone (and how?), where to buy groceries, does she need a special certification to be a locksmith in France over and above the license to work as a foreign national, and if so, how should she proceed?

There were basic things to fret over, as well: With a rude jolt that morning, she was reminded she had left the U.S. without tampons. Would she have to ask for them by name, and if so, how did you say *tampon* (or was there a polite way of referring to such things, like "feminine sanitary supplies"?) in French? Did they sell such things in grocery stores like in the U.S., or in the ubiquitous pharmacies marked by the neon green crosses? Parisian pharmacies were places not only to fill prescriptions but also to find a wide array of homeopathic remedies, tonics, and alternative cures. The workers wore white lab coats and offered copious health advice on everything from hangnails to digestive problems to hormone replacement.

But Genevieve did recall this, at least: to bring her shopping bag with her. There were several hanging from a hook near the refrigerator: sturdy leather straps on tightly woven flexible baskets. There were a few smaller canvas options, but she chose one of the baskets because they were prettier, and it made her feel very French to walk down the street with a basket over one arm, as though she were playing a role in a movie. But here they carried their bags without self-consciousness, and always had: Few stores provided bags, whether paper or plastic, and those that did charged for them. What had become an environmental issue in California was here simply a matter of tradition.

First things first: the *boulangerie*.

In France, when the bread is sold out, the store shuts down. At the really good bakeries, this often occurred shortly after the lunch hour. Pity the Parisian hostess or host who didn't manage to get to his or her favorite *boulangerie* on time.

Genevieve walked two—or was it three?—blocks down rue de Rivoli, then took a right on rue de Sévigné. But it didn't look right. The streets seemed tantalizingly familiar, yet also foreign. When she arrived at a distinctive triangular corner for the second time, she realized she had been walking in circles and had to laugh at herself.

She was like a child at Disneyland, easily distracted, looking up so much that she risked losing her footing.

Genevieve had always had a good sense of direction, and she had gotten cocky after making it to Pasquale's nursing home and back without any problem yesterday. For fear of looking like a tourist, she had been resisting consulting the paper map she had found in the apartment and shoved into her basket at the last minute. Finally she took it out, pinpointed her location, and realized she had missed the *boulangerie* by only one block.

La Maréchalerie means "blacksmith shop" in French, and the building was decorated with horseshoes and the head of a horse emerging from a shield. Genevieve had been confused by these as a teenager: What did horses have to do with bread? She remembered rushing back to the house and looking up the name in her travel dictionary but was still just as confused until Catharine told her it was merely an old building made into a *boulangerie*.

"They don't take things down here, or change things," said Catharine, clearly disdainful of her cousin's interest. *"They just leave the name, and the horse decorations, and make their bread."*

There was a line out the door, mostly women and children, all with baskets hanging off their arms. Genevieve took her place behind a chubby middle-aged woman, and they traded quiet *bonjours*. The delectable smell of freshly baked bread wafted over them.

The old front-door lock, Genevieve noticed as she waited, was in the shape of a horseshoe.

There is a danger in not knowing exactly what you want at a Parisian *boulangerie*. Behind the counter was a glorious selection of bread in various shapes and sizes, from golden to dark brown; slender baguettes and fat, round, mushroom-shaped loaves and assorted muffins and croissants. Genevieve practiced what she would say as she progressed up the slow-moving line.

The young woman behind the counter was small and pale, with the fine bones so typical of the French—high nose, prominent cheekbones, elegant and refined. She had soft-looking brown hair that was long and swept up in a ponytail, and striking gray eyes. She moved with a natural grace, frequently rising on her tiptoes to reach bread for customers. *She could have been a dancer,* Genevieve thought, imagining her pirouetting around the back of the bakery, rolling out dough for croissants, twirling over to the ovens. . . .

Genevieve had reached the front of the line. The shopkeeper's *bonjour* was grudging, nonspecific. Said with a sigh.

At the last moment, out of cowardice, Genevieve asked for two baguettes instead of one because "two"—*deux*—was easier to say than "one"—*un* or *une*, depending on the gender of the word. And Genevieve couldn't remember whether baguettes were male or female. Because of their shape, one might assume male, but the word ended in *ette*, which sounded female. What *was* it with gendered nouns, anyway?

So in the end she asked for two baguettes, two croissants.

The shopkeeper grabbed the baguettes and flung them down onto a large square of paper, on the diagonal, rolling them up with the speed and surety of one who had worked in a *boulangerie* for many years.

She passed them to Genevieve and used tongs to put the croissants in a small paper bag. Genevieve handed over a bill and the woman made change without looking at her, turning to say *bonjour* to the next in line without so much as a *Je vous souhaite une bonne journée*, I wish you a good day.

Despite the less-than-warm interaction, Genevieve smiled as she left the shop.

She had survived her first shopping expedition and now had delicious bread in her basket, the baguettes sticking out as in any travel advertisement for France. Next she should find the cheese shop and the greengrocer and the butcher. . . .

She got to the corner and paused. Genevieve didn't remember these places like she did the *boulangerie*—her *tante* Pasquale deemed *that* shopping too important to be entrusted to children. Genevieve should have thought to ask Catharine, or the neighbors, for their recommendations of the best local vendors.

On the large boulevard, she spied a big neon sign that read: CASINO.

This was not a place to gamble; it was a chain of grocery stores. Supermarkets, Genevieve knew, were very *American* (not in a good way) and she really should support the small, traditional, family-owned shops. No doubt the quality was much higher. Still . . .

In a supermarket she wouldn't have to interact with the shopkeeper and ask for what she wanted. She wouldn't have to practice her French, using up her precious mental energy. It was a cop-out, probably (surely), but she was newly arrived in Paris, after all. She could cut herself some slack.

Genevieve slipped into the Casino through the automatic doors.

The store was much smaller than a typical American grocery, but set up on the same principle: aisles stocked with canned goods, a refrigerated section with eggs, cheese, packaged meats. But instead of Oscar Mayer cold cuts like bologna and pastrami, there were several types of prosciutto and *jamón serrano*, salamis made of rabbit and wild boar. Hanging beside these were various pâtés, including foie gras.

Foie gras had been deemed illegal in California because of cruelty to animals; Genevieve was vague about the details, but since foie gras wasn't a subject that came up frequently in her life, she had been happy to support her more socially conscious friends in their moral outrage. But her brother, Nick, found it infuriating; he used to import the delicacy and made a fortune selling it to local foodie restaurants.

Genevieve chose a packet in honor of her brother.

Nothing fancy, just your everyday foie gras.

She perused diminutive, prettily labeled jars of cornichons and capers and olives, then lost all track of time in the spice aisle, studying whole vanilla beans in skinny plastic vials and herbes de Provence in jumbo plastic gallon containers. There were cute little boxes with interesting spice concoctions she had never heard of and had no idea how to use. She added a few to her basket, just because she liked the packages and pictured setting them on the too-empty counter in the apartment. If nothing else they would make great presents for people back home.

Back home.

Was California home? Was she going back? Would she be bringing spices and scarves as souvenirs for friends, talking about her time in France in the past tense, referring to it as a small chapter in her life? As her mother used to do.

Genevieve had read somewhere that most Americans died within five miles of where they were born. Which only went to prove that even if a place really sucked, it retained a certain gravitational pull, like a planet forcing moons and satellites to remain within its orbit. But even Genevieve, who had wanted so much to escape, had to admit that the familiarity of home held some comfort; knowing what to expect, how to proceed. How not to look foolish. It had been only a few days, just a tiny drop in the proverbial bucket of life, but . . . how long would it take an expat in Paris, for example, to truly feel at home? Would she ever? How long had it taken for Ernest Hemingway or Gertrude Stein? It had taken a world war to drive Stein from her Parisian apartment.

As Genevieve approached the checkout counter, she realized she had been adding items to her basket with no thought as to how to pay for them. Was she carrying enough cash to cover the groceries?

"Bonjour," she said to the bored-looking woman sitting on a high stool behind the register. Genevieve knew this, at the very least: *Bonjour* was the opening gambit to all discussion, and its omission was considered rude to the point of disdain.

"Bonjour, madame," replied the cashier in a bored tone as she whisked the items, one by one, across the scanner. When she was done she announced the total.

In halting French, Genevieve asked whether she could use a credit card.

"Bien sûr." Of course. The woman held out a metal-and-plastic contraption about the size of a thick paperback novel, with a cord that fed into the register.

Genevieve swiped her card. The woman read something on the register, frowned. Looked at Genevieve and shook her head.

There were now two people in line behind Genevieve, a man and a woman. Dressed in business garb, they had only a few items apiece, probably on their lunch breaks, trying to grab something quickly. Genevieve smiled at them apologetically; they appeared as world-weary as the cashier, and not at all interested in her contrition.

Try not to be so American, Genevieve told herself. Americans were considered goofy and overbearing, she knew. They smiled too much, were too eager to please even while mucking everything up. Puppylike, but without the cuteness.

She ran her card through the electronic thingy a second time, but it still didn't work. The woman at the register did not crack a smile. She asked Genevieve something in rapid French. Genevieve froze like a deer in the headlights.

The well-dressed woman behind her in line stepped forward and said, in English, "Your card, she needs a chip."

"A chip?"

"Yes. The American cards, sometimes they don't have the chip."

Genevieve fished around for her cash but the cashier pulled out a second machine, an old-fashioned one that took a physical imprint of the credit card, and then had her sign the slip.

The cashier handed her the paper receipt and said, "*Bonne journée, madame.*"

Genevieve was dismissed.

Clearly she needed to get a card with a chip, she thought as she loaded her groceries into her basket. Which would mean a French bank account.

Genevieve had been allowing herself not to think too hard about the actual logistics of moving. She had come to France on the standard tourist visa, but it would allow her to remain for only three months. If she actually wanted to take over her uncle's shop, she knew it would require a long process of wrangling with the infamous French bureaucracy, as her neighbors had already tried to point out to her. Maybe Catharine could help. And if Genevieve really wanted to make a go of it, it might be worth hiring a lawyer to help navigate the system.

Not to mention, she might need a local lawyer to help her look over divorce papers, whenever *those* happened.

She didn't want to think about that. For a little while, at least. Genevieve could grant herself a few days of respite from worry, of simply enjoying being in Paris.

On the way back to the village, Genevieve remembered she wanted to buy flowers to replace the dead ones in the sadly neglected window boxes. Though she passed several florists, their buckets of flowers casting splashes of lurid color on the rain-washed sidewalks, there were no live plants.

She couldn't think how to ask for them. When she got home she would have to look up the word for "nursery," as opposed to "florist," and ask her neighbors for suggestions.

Genevieve turned a corner and found herself under the covered, vaulted gallery of the place des Vosges.

Memories flooded through her. She and Dave and Pasquale—and Catharine when she would deign to join them—had eaten many a picnic here in the small park in the center of the square. It was one of the few places in Paris where people were allowed to sit on the grass, something that was usually a no-no in France.

She remembered once when their plans were foiled by a sign placed at the edge of the grass: PELOUSE AU REPOS.

"It means: The lawn is resting," said Tante Pasquale.

"What? Why?" asked Genevieve, disappointed.

"Grass is a living thing," said Dave. *"And like every living thing, it needs a rest now and then. We have to stay off for a little while."*

"Does this mean we can eat at a table like civilized people?" asked Catharine, making them all laugh.

Now, as Dave had taught her to do, Genevieve looked up in search of plaques on the sides of the buildings. One gave a brief history of the place de Vosges: In the seventeenth century, Henri IV demanded an opulent residence within the city, an assembly of thirty-six redbrick and stone pavilions surrounding the majestic, tree-shaded square. It used to be called the place Royale.

Today the *place* was full of pricey art galleries and a few restaurants. On one corner a young woman dressed in formal attire played the cello, its deep tone reverberating off the groin-vaulted ceiling. Genevieve crossed the square via the park, which was full of families picnicking, children chasing bubbles, young couples lounging on the grass.

On the other side, another plaque: Victor Hugo had lived there, at number 6 in the place des Vosges. Of course he did. Victor Hugo. As in *The Hunchback of Notre-Dame* and *Les Misérables*.

Genevieve had flown in from Oakland a few days ago and now was standing in front of Victor Hugo's house. She was suddenly gripped by a tourist's notion: that the world was magic.

But then part of the wonder of a city like Paris was all the famous writers and artists it had embraced over the years. If she walked far enough, would she stumble upon plaques honoring Baudelaire and Hemingway and Fitzgerald? In fact . . . maybe she really should set up an artists' commune, as Mary had suggested. She could host her own salon, follow in Gertrude Stein's footsteps, start a tradition for the new millennium, foment a link between Paris and Oakland, of all places.

As Genevieve headed back to the village to drop off her groceries, she realized she was smiling broadly. Just like an American.

Chapter Nineteen

1997

"Love laughs at locksmiths," said Uncle Dave.

"What?" asked Genevieve, not looking up from her task. An old lock was held tight in the table vise on the side of the workbench. Dave had shown her how to pop off the back with a screwdriver and then do the same with the second panel.

"I'm thinking of using that for the title of my book on the history of locks and keys. Have you ever heard the phrase?"

Genevieve shook her head, biting her lip in concentration. She took the keyhole out of the lock, set it aside, and then, just as Dave had shown her, made three incisions, one on top and one on either side of the cylinder. The metal casing fell away, displaying the key pattern.

"That's it," said Dave. "Now remove the thinner casing, see? And this one here, and then you see the pins, *voilà*!"

Like an anatomy student at an autopsy, Genevieve studied the insides splayed out in front of her. She was enthralled. All those years of turning doorknobs and using keys, and she hadn't realized the metal cover plates hid a whole world of pins and plugs and casings. Hadn't thought about it at all, really; never pondered the magic inherent in a door being locked one moment and unlocked the next, simply by inserting a specially cut piece of metal called a key.

"You see the pins on the keyhole?"

She nodded and reached out a finger to touch them.

"Careful—they're loose now. Don't drop them—you won't know how to put them back in the right order."

"What do they do?"

"Locks are basically just a series of pins of varying length. The pins must align to release the mechanism." He held a key over the line of pins to demonstrate. "The serrated edges on the key push the pins so they line up. When they line up correctly, the plug is released, and that allows the lock to turn."

"It's that simple?"

He laughed. "That's the basic idea, but there are many variations on the theme, and lots of improvements on the original design. Some are downright diabolical! But believe it or not, we still use essentially the same lock that was

181

invented by Linus Yale Jr. in 1861. His father had invented the first tumbler lock, the type that could be operated with the famous skeleton keys, like this." He held up one of his old keys that he loved so much. The metal bar was round, as opposed to modern flat keys. "A lot of the old places around here still have these types of antique locks on the doors."

"They still work?"

"Oh, of course. They'll work forever unless they're improperly dismantled, destroyed by carelessness. Sometimes the old brass wears down over the years, but it takes a lot to hurt one of these babies."

He patted one of his antique locks lying on the workbench. The metal was decorated with scrollwork so elaborate it looked like a work of art. Several of the old locks and keys were tagged with explanations for the book Dave was writing. He had drawers of old keys, bins full of them, and sometimes rather than pick a lock he would simply try one key after another because, as he said, "there is something delightful about helping a key find its way back to a lock, so it can do the work it was meant for."

Genevieve continued to peer into the mechanism, delicately pushing at the loose pins with her index finger, imagining how they moved in the secret darkness, hidden behind the lock plate.

"Now that you've got that open," Dave said, "make a key for it."

"*Make* one?"

"Sure."

"Me?"

"Who else? You're the one who took it apart."

Dave showed her how to remove the top set of pins, leaving the bottom pins in place. She studied the guts of the device for another moment and then started to fit the casing back over it, careful not to drop any of the pins.

"You put the blank into the keyhole to see where you need the grooves. Use a metal file to shape the blank into a key so that when you use it, the remaining pins lay flat. You see?"

As she started to file the blank—a laborious process—she asked her uncle, "So what does it mean? Locksmiths laugh at love?"

"It's the other way around: Love laughs at locksmiths. Important distinction!"

Uncle Dave's laugh easily filled his tiny shop; Genevieve imagined it could fill nearby Saint Paul's Cathedral, or even Notre-Dame, the way it boomed, lush and generous and green like the fennel bushes back home. One of her chores on the farm was to dig up the fennel, all the way down to the taproot that reached deep into the earth, keeping the plants verdant despite northern California's cyclical summertime drought. Genevieve hated weeding but she chose it over cleaning out the animal pens; at least the fennel smelled good, like licorice, and the bushes had no thorns. Only sheer tenacity.

Uncle Dave was like that, Genevieve thought. Whether a lock was threatening to overwhelm him with frustration or Pasquale was chastising him or he was recalling some terrible memory from a war-torn Paris . . . still his eyes twinkled; he laughed his booming laugh. It was as though Dave had a taproot reaching down through the dark underground to glean every possible drop of moisture from this life.

"It's a quote from a Shakespeare poem, one of the long ones," said Dave. "In French they say, *l'amour force toutes les serrures*, which means 'love forces all locks.' For once the English is more poetic than the French, *n'est-ce pas?*"

Genevieve nodded, though she still wasn't sure what he was talking about. But speaking of love— she took her eyes off the mechanism for a moment to glance up at Dave's grizzled jaw, feeling a sense of . . . what was it? Joy, and connection, and life. A bright spark lighting up the dreary, bleak days she had felt ever since her mother's illness overwhelmed her, mired her whole family in the tar pit of sorrow and regret. Last night, as she crawled into bed in the room she shared with her cousin, Genevieve realized she was . . . sort of . . . in love. Not in a creepy way; it wasn't romantic love or anything. But everything Dave did held her enthralled, enraptured. She loved the way he left a trail of rusty nuts and bolts and hardware throughout the house, the way he ate as though each and every meal was a revelation, the way he waggled his crazy eyebrows when he told a joke.

At home her silent, dutiful father seemed to sleepwalk through life, rarely laughing or speaking, even before her mom got sick. And Angela, when she was alive, had plodded along as though keeping her eyes on the muffin pan in front of her was the only thing keeping her going, as though if she looked up from her task, she would float off. And indeed, Genevieve had often come upon her mother gazing out the little kitchen window that overlooked the carrot patch, and she seemed to be a thousand miles away. But whenever Genevieve asked her what she was thinking about, Angela would stroke her daughter's hair, cup her chin in her hand, smile into her eyes, and say, "*You,* of course."

Genevieve would smile in return, but she knew her mother was lying. She knew it with the unshakeable sense of a child tuned in to every nuance of her parents' actions.

Sometimes her mother seemed caught in an endless circle, an inescapable vortex made up of three points: stove and counter and freezer. She would spend long hours preparing whatever was in season. Peaches or figs or cherries. Canning tomato sauce and pickles and apple-plum sauce. Filling the commercial freezer with carefully wrapped hunks of organic meat that came back from the butcher in lieu of the chickens or pigs or turkeys that her father had taken to slaughter. Angela's only breaks were to drive carpool and to drop off cupcakes at school events—whole-wheat carrot cake with no processed sugar, the healthy option that remained (embarrassingly) on the table long after the chocolate chip cookies and brownies and lemon bars had been devoured.

Or she would stay in bed for days at a time with a "sick headache," a washcloth on her brow, staring at the wall.

Had her mother ever been truly happy? Joyous and passionate and full of life, like Uncle Dave?

Once Genevieve finally finished filing the key, she painstakingly reassembled the lock, then tested the key. It stuck a little, but it worked. The new key opened the lock.

Uncle Dave hooted in triumph.

"Would you look at *that?* On your first try! Perhaps you will go on to best your old uncle, eh?" he said, ruffling her hair and sending chills of proud delight down her spine. "Since you did so well, I will show you something very special."

He opened a skinny drawer and extracted a black iron ring, full of different kinds of skeleton keys.

"What is it?" she asked, her tone reverential.

"It's a Victorian burglar set. Can you believe that? One of these will open just about any old padlock from the era. Just imagine."

"You mean some burglar had these made to break in to places?"

"Exactly. What do you think of that? I use them every once in a while to open old padlocks, that sort of thing. But mostly I just think they're sweet as molasses."

"So they won't open all the doors anymore?"

"Not all, of course not. But back in the day . . . they probably opened most of them. Just like love—this is what the saying means. Love laughs at locksmiths: love cannot be locked in or out. Remember that, Genevieve. Love has its own set of burglar keys!"

When she returned home from Paris, Genevieve's father picked her up at the San Francisco airport and they rode the hour home without exchanging a single word—Jim not recognizing his daughter's sullenness as anything more than what it had been before she had gone to France.

But this was much worse, for now Genevieve had been betrayed. Not only was her mother gone, but she had been sent back to Petaluma, to the farm, where her father and brother worked in the muck, apparently content. Exchanging occasional cheerful complaints about the harvest, remarking upon the heirloom tomatoes and the special spotted chickens. Asking for nothing else. Nothing more.

But she had tasted something *more* and now realized what she had been missing. Genevieve had tasted Paris.

Genevieve could walk for hours, and she did, making up stories in her mind. Before going to Paris she used to imagine she was a secret CIA operative, living an undercover life on a farm in Petaluma but actually keeping an eye on a suspiciously James Bond–like billionaire intent on ruling the world from his secret lair underneath one of the big new houses that were relentlessly encroaching upon their farm.

But she had returned from France with a secret talent. She was a superhero, and her special power was not flying or becoming invisible, but unlocking doors. Letting herself in.

She emerged from a small copse of trees to see the Landons' house. It was huge, with a swimming pool and a three-car garage.

She knew the family was away, enjoying the last week of summer vacation before school began. Probably in Hawaii or Jamaica, someplace exotic and expensive where they could work on their tans. The three Landon girls were blond and pretty and always wore the right clothes. Mr. Landon sported a deep tan and unnaturally white teeth and golfed a lot; Mrs. Landon was thin and energetic to the point of frenetic. The Landons had gone up against Genevieve's parents at the city hall meeting about the keeping of livestock—specifically, the aromatic pigs—in what they kept referring to as a "residential area."

Not long after Angela's death, Mrs. Landon and her girls had come by the house with a casserole and a sympathy card, at which point Mrs. Landon had earned Genevieve's undying enmity by making her cry in front of her trio of perfect daughters, who all made sympathetic clucking noises although they'd never once spoken to her in their entire pampered, hypocritical lives.

Genevieve stared at the Landon place for a long time as an idea formed. She looked around: The house was shielded from the road by trees on all sides. Unseen, unnoticed.

She wouldn't *hurt* anything. She just wanted to see if she could do it.

She went to the front door and rang the bell. If someone answered she'd pretend she was raising money for a band trip. She wasn't in the band, but how would they know? Kids were forever raising money for band trips, knocking on endless doors and begging for spare change to be allowed to play their instruments—one of those things that grown-ups were always claiming they wanted kids to do, but which they weren't willing to pay for.

No one answered.

"Choose your point of entry," Uncle Dave had

taught her. The front door was usually equipped with the most difficult lock. She circled the house and knelt before a set of French doors on the back patio, by the pool.

She rubbed the key she wore around her neck.

"Defeat the lock. Gain entry. Will you let yourself be defeated by a silly old lock?"

Genevieve studied the lock before her. It looked like a Schlage single side pin. She hesitated.

"A locksmith never abuses the power to open locks."

But he had sent her back.

A wave of anger surged inside of her. Uncle Dave had sent her back here, to the middle of nowhere, where she took long rambles and no one thought to ask where she had gone. To silent dinners with her father and brother. To collecting eggs and weeding the vegetables before school, and then sitting through endless classes with hateful students who wore the right clothes and giggled about boys and who made her feel ugly and awkward. A freak.

Now it would be even worse, as hard as that was to imagine. Now she would go back to school as the kid whose mother had died.

Her mother was *dead.*

When her mom first got sick, no one would tell Genevieve what was going on. She was fourteen, but they treated her like a baby, like she couldn't handle the truth. Her father, her brother, the doctors. So she looked up cancer on the Internet, and that's when she learned why no one would talk to her about it. She read about how, a lot of times, cancer took root and grew inside of people because they were unhappy. She read that sick people could *choose* to live or to die, that overcoming cancer had to do with the power of your spirit, your desire to heal yourself.

Genevieve had begged her mother to choose to live. She had lain in Angela's skeletal arms, ignoring the stifling heat and strange smells of the sick room, and cried and pleaded with her. Genevieve promised to make her mother happy, to do everything right and not complain anymore, ever. She would learn to bake and knit and whatever else Angela had always tried to teach her that she'd railed against.

Adults—the very few to whom Genevieve disclosed any inkling of this sort of thinking—told Genevieve she was wrong, that Angela was dying of a disease, that it was nobody's fault.

Genevieve nodded. But she didn't believe them.

Genevieve had begged. And then her mother died anyway.

She had known, deep down, that Angela was unhappy. Sometimes (many times) Angela would get that faraway look in her eyes and stare out the kitchen window at the carrot patch. Or she would focus on Genevieve, her gaze so intent that Genevieve would look up from her puzzle or her book, having felt its weight from across the room. Nothing was as sad as that look on her mother's face; it was the expression of someone who wouldn't protest overmuch should some hooded figure with a scythe show up to escort her away from this life.

"Do you think you can die of being sad?" Genevieve once asked Uncle Dave.

Her uncle's hand had stopped toying with the lock in front of him. He set down his pick and turned to Genevieve, crouching before her and speaking in a voice as soft and gentle as a cat's paw: "You will be happy again one day, *ma chérie*. You must believe your old uncle Dave. You must not give up, *ever*—you hear me? You will go on to live your life; you will not die of this sadness."

Genevieve had opened her mouth to correct him but then didn't say anything, awash in embarrassment that she had been thinking not of her own sadness, but of her mother's.

The mother who had chosen to abandon her.

Genevieve took her favorite S pick out of her jeans pocket. She had been carrying it around with her ever since she had become a Paris-trained superhero.

It took her almost an hour, but she was patient. She did not give up. She defeated the lock.

Stealthily, she wandered around the Landons' house, imagining life in their shoes. They had a fully stocked bar and a massive television with about a zillion videos (no surprise there). She flipped through a few pages of Brittney's diary (boring, mostly about boys and clothes) and then snooped through Mrs. Landon's powder blue, perfumey bathroom with gold fixtures (his-and-hers master baths) and found a jumbo-sized vial of Valium in the medicine cabinet.

Genevieve felt awash in a combination of guilt and disappointment. The Landons' lives were as pretty yet empty as she would have imagined; one of those ornately decorated Easter shells with the egg blown out.

She left, carefully relocking the door and promising herself she wouldn't do it again. She lied.

Chapter Twenty

Genevieve had made plans to meet Philippe at Le Petit Feu, "a wonderful café where they treat me like the royalty I am," he said with a laugh over the phone when he called to make arrangements. She had, once again, attempted to decline lunch in favor of getting straight to work on his house, but he insisted.

So Genevieve packed the dossier and all the old locks that pertained to Philippe D'Artavel's address into a large canvas bag she found in Dave's shop.

She hesitated when deciding what to wear: normally she would dress in jeans and a T-shirt; though locksmithing wasn't always dirty work, it involved plenty of kneeling. But if she was meeting Philippe for lunch in a restaurant . . . she finally decided on a black pullover, jeans, and boots, covered with her overcoat. And her key necklace, of course.

At the last moment she borrowed one of Pasquale's silk scarves—Hermès, in shades of red and gold—that had been draped over a lampshade, and tied it around her neck. It took her three tries to get a knot even approximating something stylish, but the scarf was so pretty she decided it was good enough.

She picked up her uncle's bag of picks and sweeps and oil, then took a moment to study the dog-eared map of Paris, figuring out her route to the café. It was a little over a mile away, but the bag wasn't heavy and the day was sunny.

The Petit Feu was as adorable as every other brasserie on every other corner of Paris: the name on the big front window was in gold gilt and lettered in the elongated Art Nouveau script; wrought-iron tables topped with fresh flowers spilled out onto the sidewalk; unsmiling apron-clad waiters hustled by with trays or loitered nearby.

Philippe was seated at a small table outside, hands perched on his cane.

"Genevieve Martin! *C'est la serruriere américaine!*" he said as he rose to greet her. They kissed each other on one cheek, then the other. "The American locksmith, thank you for meeting me here."

"How could I refuse? A date with a handsome Parisian royal?"

His laughter was rusty but loud, more a cackle than a chuckle.

She took a seat and when the waiter appeared, she used some of the restaurant French she had studied last night and asked for the menu, please: "*Le menu, s'il vous plaît.*"

"Okay! Good choice!" said Philippe, before carrying on a long and animated discussion with the waiter. Genevieve didn't even try to understand what they were saying, instead enjoying the sunshine. It was a cool day, but not overcast, and outdoor heaters kept the tables comfortable. Parisians loved outdoor dining so much that only a downpour kept them from enjoying the fresh air.

It was only after the waiter returned with an appetizer that Genevieve realized she had made a classic American mistake: in France, *la carte* refers to the list of offerings, while *le menu* refers to that day's special two- or three-course meal. By asking for the *menu* she had already ordered her lunch.

Good thing she was an omnivore, she thought as a terrine was laid in front of her. Alongside this was a small pitcher of chilled rosé and a wineglass.

"The wine, it comes with the *menu*," said Philippe as he poured wine from his own tiny pitcher into his glass and raised it in a salute: "*À la vôtre!*"

Philippe asked her how she was settling in, whether she had enough to eat and had found the best *boulangerie*. He laughed when she confessed that after her trip to the *boulangerie* she had chickened out and gone to the Casino. He gave her a few recommendations for butchers and greengrocers, though he suggested she ask her immediate neighbors for their favorites in the neighborhood.

"Otherwise, you walk too far every day, I think."

Genevieve smiled. "I don't mind. I like to walk. So, tell me, how did you and my uncle Dave know each other? Was it during the war?"

"No, no. Dave, he comes here after the war is over. But . . . you know, it takes time. Even after Hitler was gone, it takes some time for things to get back to the normal."

"The rebuilding effort?"

He nodded. "Yes, and even to get all the Germans to leave. Back then, communication was difficult; not even everyone knows the war is over at the same time. *Écoute*, did you know I had been captured, was going to be killed before the soldiers left?" He mimed a rifle, taking aim, squeezing one eye shut, pulling the trigger. "*Comment dit-on?*"

"You were going to be shot?"

"*Oui*, yes, exactly. Because I work against the soldiers. But when the city is freed, I am released. I am lucky. Others were shot while the soldiers go—they kill many prisoners before they go back to Germany."

"That's terrible to imagine. So you worked against the Germans? In the resistance?"

He nodded, sipped his wine.

"I've always wondered," Genevieve continued, "how many people took part in the resistance?"

"*La résistance?*" He pronounced it *ray-zis-TAHNCE*. He shrugged, tilted his head, pushed out his chin. "There were . . . I have heard people say twenty thousand. A lot, but not enough for a country this size, *n'est-ce pas?* We cannot do much, but we do what we can. We take down the road signs, put the holes in tires, cut the lines for power and communication. We bomb gas depots. Oooh, you must try this pâté."

He pushed his plate toward her and she tried a bit: creamy and salty and rich. Then she offered him her plate in return; he slathered a chunk of terrine onto a piece of crusty bread, popped it in his mouth, gave a thumbs-up sign, and washed it down with rosé.

"The bells of the churches, it sound like all the

churches of Paris—they start to ring on the twenty-fifth August, 1944. That is how we know we are liberated! Because of the bells, you see? I was a prisoner, but I wake to the sound of the church bells. The soldiers hear it, too, and they run away!" He laughed so hard he started to cough, then took another sip of wine. "The Second French Armored Division march down the Champs-Élysées toward the Arc de Triomphe. There has . . . there has never been a more beautiful sight than those French soldiers coming along the Champs-Élysées—other than a beautiful woman, of course." He ended with a wink and a smile.

"You were a war hero," Genevieve said.

He shook his head, wagged a finger. "No, I was no hero. There were many heroes during the war, but I was not this. I fight for my city, *la fraternité*. My . . . *Comment dit-on*? *Ma patrie*. I did what I have to do; you would do no less if the Nazis march down your street, kill your neighbors, your family. Believe me, I know this."

His rheumy eyes were bright, and for a moment Genevieve caught a glimpse of the dashing fellow he must have been. The young man who had defaced road signs and cut power lines, who laughed at his Nazi captors running away on the morning he was set to be put to death. Images from a hundred movies and books flickered through her mind: children hiding in secret rooms, the infiltrators and collaborators and double-crossers, the families being packed into cattle cars and transported to death camps.

"I would hope I would fight," Genevieve found herself saying. "I don't know how brave I am, but I hope I would have fought beside you."

"You would have," he said with a firm nod. "I see courage in you. You should see how you would fight. You Americans, you don't have people come on your land to take you over. You go other places to fight instead—isn't that true?" He chuckled. "Believe me, it is easier to fail that way, in some foreign land when you don't know why you are fighting. It is different to fight for your homeland. Do you know this man, Jean-Paul Sartre?"

"The philosopher? A little bit . . . I mean, I read a little Sartre in college."

"He said the Nazis gave us a gift. And this was it: Their cause was wrong."

"Their cause was wrong? That was the gift?"

"Yes, exactly. All decent people agree on this, that the Nazi cause was wrong. It was, how do you say? Black-and-white. That is not typical; usually there is more than one side to every conflict. War is complicated. Like love."

The waiter came and whisked away their appetizer dishes with quiet efficiency, replacing them with the main course, or the *plat principal*. He uttered a quick, "*Bon appétit*," and rushed off without asking if they needed anything else.

Philippe yanked his head in the direction of their server and smiled. "The waiters here, they are . . . *Comment dit-on? Pas gentils?*"

"Rude?"

"*C'est ça!* They are rude here, *n'est-ce pas?* This is what Dave tells me, that in America every waiter is your best friend! He says in America, your waiter tells you his name! Okay!"

Genevieve smiled and gave a little nod/shrug of acquiescence. She did find Parisian waiters intimidating. "They're different here—that's for sure."

"We don't leave him extra money."

"Oh, let's leave him something." Genevieve had waited tables one long, hot summer while in college. She knew exactly how much tips meant to servers, so even if the service was iffy, she never stiffed them. "He's doing his job, even if he isn't friendly."

"No, I mean that here in Paris, no one leaves money—except the American tourists, who don't know the custom! This is why they are not friendly. It is *service compris*. They are paid by the restaurant already. Sometimes we leave a few coins, but that is all."

"Really?" She craned her neck to look at the middle-aged man who had been attending to them. He was leaning against the wall in the back of the restaurant, arms crossed over his chest, chatting with another waiter.

"Also, they used to be happier when they could smoke. Now there is no smoking inside the restaurant, *quel dommage*, eh?"

Genevieve was just as glad she didn't have to secondhand smoke a pack of cigarettes along with every meal, so she didn't agree that it was a shame, but she just smiled and nodded as she tasted her duck breast, *magret de canard*. It was moist and succulent. The rosé was crisp and dry, the perfect temperature. She didn't usually drink wine during the day, but when in Rome . . .

"Anyway, Sartre was a great thinker," continued Philippe. "He was a friend of mine."

Her head popped up. "Really? You knew Jean-Paul *Sartre*?"

"Maybe I exaggerate . . . We were not the best of friends, but we were *copains*. Friends. We would get together at the Café des Phares, talk of what was happening. You know, much of his thought, his philosophy, came from the terrible things from the war. It was a hard time."

Now that she thought about it, Genevieve realized that of course, Jean-Paul Sartre had been writing in the fifties and sixties. Somehow in her mind she had always grouped him with other philosophers, old dead men all, timeless. It was hard to imagine them as living, breathing humans, hanging out in cafés with rude waiters serving them the *menu*.

After the main course came the dessert, a choice

of crème brûlée or chocolate mousse. Genevieve was stuffed, but Philippe ordered one of each without asking her. "Or would you prefer cheese?"

"No, dessert sounds great."

"We will share, okay!" he said with a wink. "You want coffee, too, okay? Espresso?"

Chapter Twenty-one

Angela, 1983

Angela asks Pasquale and Dave, "What do you know about the Basque region?"

"Oh, it is beautiful, this area," says Pasquale. "I like it very much. The people are a little different; they have their own language, their own cuisine."

"Would you like to visit?" asks Dave. "It's a long trip from here, but there's always the train. . . ."

"No, I was just wondering. I met someone from there and realized how little I knew about the Basques and their history."

"Under Franco, the Spanish Basques were not allowed to speak their language. It was very hard, and not so long ago," says Dave. "Franco died only a few years ago. Nineteen seventy-five, I think. Things are still working themselves out."

"Even after his death, though, there are still many

forces at work. It was not only Generalissimo Franco who tried to repress the Basques. Last year there were Spanish death squads sent across the border, into France."

"Death squads?" Angela asks.

Dave gives Pasquale a significant look. "It is a fight happening far from here. Yes, it is a tragedy, but it is not our tragedy."

"Until someone brings it home, to Paris," says Pasquale. "This sort of thing has a way of making itself known."

But now Angela is back with the group she likes to call (in her mind) the Revolutionaries, sitting outside Pablo's café, at tables that spill into the street since there is no traffic at this hour. Thibeaux and Michelle and Cyril and Mario and Pablo. And Xabi, of course. He is sitting across the table from her, smoking, avoiding her eyes. And for some reason—probably because he will not look at her—she wants more than anything else to make him talk, make him engage in conversation with her.

"Where did you live before you came to Paris?" Angela asks him.

Thibeaux answers: "Biarritz. We were both there, weren't we, Xabi?"

Xabi nods, stubs out his cigarette.

"You don't like tourists, but you lived in Biarritz?" Angela asks. "Isn't that a tourist mecca?"

"That's where the jobs were," Thibeaux says.

"That's one thing you can say for tourists: They bring the money, eh?"

"But you're originally from Spain?"

Finally, Xabi nods, leans back, meets her eyes. "I have family on both sides of the border. Ours is not France or Spain, but the Basque country, Euskadi. But yes, I was born in Franco's Spain."

"So you speak French as well as Spanish?"

"I grew up speaking Euskara—what you call the Basque language—as well as French, and *castellano*."

He practically spits out the last word.

"*Castellano*? That's Spanish, right?"

"You call it Spanish. We call it the language of the government. We Basques don't consider ourselves Spanish. We never really did, but after Franco things became much worse. He outlawed our language, our culture."

"How do you outlaw a culture?"

Xabi looks at her a long time. His beautiful light blue eyes. "Exactly."

The café is virtually empty; no food is being served at this hour. The only other customers are the patrons lingering over their coffees and drinks: two young couples apparently in love, a pair of elderly men debating loudly, a middle-aged couple dining in silence.

"You must miss the Basque country. You speak of it with such love."

A long pause. She notices that Thibeaux casts Xabi a significant glance.

"It is . . . different there," Xabi finally responds.

"Enough of this talk," Thibeaux says, getting up to pour more wine. "The Basque country is the past. Let us rejoice in the now; isn't that what you say in California?"

Angela finally looks away, down the dark street, toward the spires of a church that reminds her of a mini Notre-Dame, visible over the rooftops. To change the subject, she says, "Do you know, I've been to Paris twice, and I have never seen the gargoyles atop Notre-Dame?"

"That is a shame," says Thibeaux. "Did you know Victor Hugo wrote his books about the gargoyles and the hunchback in part to save the building? He was a genius. He wrote, 'All the forces in the world are not as powerful as an idea whose time has come.'"

"That's beautiful," she says. "I love Hugo's writing."

Thibeaux takes the empty wine bottle into the restaurant and starts arguing with Pablo, probably trying to get him to donate yet another bottle. Michelle and Cyril are talking, heads bent, deep in conversation.

Angela looks up to find Xabi's eyes on her.

"I think you must go," he says. "A lover of Victor Hugo cannot come two times to Paris and not visit the gargoyles, high and low."

"High and low?"

"There are gargoyles below the ground, as well."

"How do you mean?"

"You do not know the catacombs?"

She shakes her head.

Again, Xabi looks at her for a long time. What is he thinking? Never before has she wished so fervently to be able to read someone's mind. Does he despise her and her American ways? Or . . . is it something more? Does he find her as fascinating as she does him? Is he interested in her . . . and if so, does she want him to be?

She dressed for him this morning, she reminds herself. Angela is nothing if not honest with herself; never play coy—tell the truth. She had wanted him to notice her, to cast his intense eyes over her body, slowly, taking her in. The intensity that burns in those eyes promises secrets in the dark; it hints at a kind of connection she hasn't known for too long.

It promises breath.

The jarring, terrible truth is that when she spends time with Xabi her lungs are full of air, oxygen soaring through her, making her feel alive and aware and awake.

She and Jim used to make fun of a song on the radio, singing it to each other in falsettos reminiscent of having sucked on helium: "Love is like oxygen: you get too much, you get too high, not enough and you're gonna die."

Angela has been dying, and now she is high. Perhaps too high.

This is ridiculous. She has to get ahold of herself. She is a wife and mother. Her thumb plays with her wedding ring in a nervous habit, spinning it around on her finger. Is it her imagination, or is it looser than it used to be? Has she somehow been losing weight, even while indulging in thick hot chocolate and creamy cheeses and Pasquale's irresistibly rich sauces? Probably she has; she is so distracted that for the first time in her life she keeps forgetting to eat.

She is like an adolescent girl with her first crush.

What she needs to do, right this second, is to pack her bags and book a flight back home. Back to the farm, to her husband who needs her—at least needs her help with the animals and the harvest—and back to the warm, sticky hands of her son.

Tricky Nicky, who told her on the phone just last night that she should have fun because he and Daddy had everything under control.

Nick is such a mini-Jim. She loves him for that. She loves him for that, and yet it drives the spike further into her heart. Because just as when she talked to Jim, when she spoke to her son (flesh of her flesh, as she gripped the phone and cried with longing and yearning and a mother's love), she absolutely could not breathe a single deep breath.

What is wrong with her? She is a terrible person.

"Could you take me to the catacombs?" she hears herself ask Xabier.

He stills. He sits there across the table, absolutely still. And yet his brain is moving a mile a minute; she can tell by that penetrating look in his eye. How can he possibly be so still and yet so riveting? Rather than blending into the background—the way Jim did—he demands all her attention, like a teacher she'd had in eighth grade who used to lower his voice, rather than raising it, thereby quelling the students, who quieted to hear what he was saying. Xabi had the same gift: He somehow demanded attention, even while remaining silent and unspeaking. Especially while silent and unspeaking.

"On one condition," he finally says. "I will not take you to *l'empire de la mort*, the tourist catacombs. You can take a tour for that. I will take you to the real catacombs."

Thibeaux—emerging from the restaurant with another bottle of wine held triumphantly over his head—hoots and says something in rapid French.

"All right," Angela says. Another hoot from Thibeaux, another unintelligible sentence, and shakes of the head from Michelle and Cyril. "Let's go."

"They say people risk leaving their souls down there, in the *souterrain*," warns Michelle, shaking her head. "There are ghosts."

"But the American is not afraid. Are you?" Xabier asks with a tiny half smile.

"No," says Angela, breathless, yet high on oxygen. "I am not afraid."

Chapter Twenty-two

Despite the espresso, Genevieve was ready for a nap by the time she and Philippe walked the three blocks to his house. His cane tap-tap-tapped on the sidewalk as they made their way slowly but surely down the street, he stopping to greet neighbors and joke with children as they passed.

But her drowsiness fled when they stopped in front of a three-story stone building on the corner.

"This is your *house?*"

The building took up the entire corner, and she would have guessed it held several apartments, not a single home. It was historic and lovely, but upon second look she saw signs of neglect: window frames were sagging; the paint had chipped off of the trim. A corbel had detached from the eaves. The filigreed balconies decorating the windows showed rust and corrosion.

"Yes, it is quite beautiful. It *was* quite beautiful. . . . I am very sorry to say that I have not had the money or the . . . how would you say, the heart?" he patted his chest. "I have not had the *courage* to make the repairs it needs."

He used an old-fashioned skeleton key to open the main lock, inserting it into an antique lock plate. It was decorated with scrollwork and a lion's head, reminiscent of the brass cap on his cane.

"I was so happy when Dave restored this lock for me. It is so lovely, I think. But he says it is not secure enough—I suppose I must stay safe from rascals like him and you! So then he gave me this one, the modern, electronic one."

The electronic keyless entry looked almost ludicrous next to such a historic door and key. But there was no denying that they were much more secure against people with picking skills than the antique models.

Philippe said the code out loud while he put it in: "One-nine-four-four—the year Paris is liberated," he said with a wink. "Now you can enter anytime you want—if you are like your uncle, you can open this old lock easy, even without a key, and then enter the code and *voilà*!"

They stepped inside the foyer.

It had a strange, dry-yet-dank smell. What was it about vacant houses? Even when full of furniture, they gave off a stale, unused feeling. Unbidden, Genevieve's mind flashed on the photos she had seen in Killian's apartment: it was the scent of abandonment.

"You don't live here?"

Philippe shook his head. "No. I live with my

daughter, in the Levallois-Perret. It is near her work and the children's school. My grandson is *autistique*. Special needs. This place . . . we have many problems with plumbing and electricity. Very expensive. Too much, to open all the walls and . . ." He trailed off, gesturing at exposed wires running down one wall, water stains on the ceiling, a chunk of plaster that had fallen from a decorative medallion over the door. "It is beautiful but maybe it is too much for the modern world, eh? *Comme moi*, like me, it is a relic from another time."

"But it's such a beautiful home." And in Paris? Genevieve didn't know the details, but she was pretty sure Paris was like New York or San Francisco in this regard: A historic home right downtown would be worth a fortune, no matter its state of repair.

"Right now, we get the locks done and maybe after, my children figure out the rest. It will take much time and energy. I will be gone soon anyway."

Their voices seemed to echo off the bare wooden floors. The house appeared scavenged: There were discolored squares on the wall where paintings had once hung; grooves in a carpet where a chair used to sit; an upholstered chair by a table, without its mate on the other side. There were crystal chandeliers strewn with cobwebs; a broom rested against what looked like a Louis

XIV credenza. Her eyes immediately searched out the interior doorknobs—cut crystal—and those exposed to sunlight were turning various shades of lavender. Uncle Dave had taught her the color was the result of manganese in the glass, which dated the crystal to before 1920.

"When the sunlight hits these knobs over time, it brings out the color of flowers. There's a metaphor in there somewhere, don't you think, Genevieve?"

There were also plentiful signs of incomplete packing: cardboard boxes and stacks of newspapers, as though someone had begun the process but had gotten distracted before making much progress.

Philippe made his way to a huge dining room table, larger and finer than the one in Dave and Pasquale's house. That one was sturdy and blocky, made for a farm family; this one was elegant, with claw feet holding balls, and was topped with a once-shiny lacquer. There were no matching chairs.

Philippe started digging through one of three cardboard boxes atop the table.

"I want to show you. . . . Yes, yes, it is here, *voilà!*" He pulled out a large photo album, laid it on the table, and splayed it open. "Here, it is a photo of your mother, Angela. You see? You look very much like her."

"My mother?" Genevieve put down an old book

on the history of Paris (leather bound, marbleized endpapers) she was inspecting and joined him at the table. "I didn't realize you knew her."

"Of course! Back then, when she came, she was helping my wife to organize these photos. Even then we did not live here, can you imagine? Even then we had started to move out, and still we have not finished!" Philippe laughed. He had a way of announcing things as though he himself were astonished by what he was saying. As though pleasantly surprised by life as a whole. It was not hard to imagine him and Dave as fast friends.

"Look how young we were! And here, this is my beautiful wife, Delphine."

It was a group of six, seated at a long table in what looked like an old brick wine cellar.

"We are here to a cabaret. Aux Trois Mailletz, in the Latin Quarter. Oh, such a time we had." He laughed. "You know, here in Paris, they play music and sing all the night. There is no closing time like in your city. That night we go there, the music is playing, the people are singing . . . we order wine and do not come home until the sun comes up!"

Uncle Dave must have been in his fifties, still dapper, his goatee salt-and-pepper. Beside him sat a smiling Pasquale, her hair up in a stylish coif, a silk scarf at her neck; she had always had the easy elegance so many Frenchwomen seemed to inherit at birth. Philippe sat with them, a bit older, already gray, with a lovely woman beaming at his side. Then there was Genevieve's mother, Angela, in a blue-and-yellow scarf Genevieve thought she recognized from Pasquale's bedroom. Sitting beside Angela was a striking, dark-haired, light-eyed man. All but the young man were smiling.

"Who's that?" Genevieve asked.

"Who?"

"The handsome man, here."

"Xabier."

At her questioning look, he added with a laugh, "With an *X*."

"Who was Xabier?"

There was a slight pause, then a small shrug. "A friend. To make the couples even. Boy, girl, boy, girl."

An awfully good-looking friend, Genevieve thought. But then, as Mary had pointed out, she'd only just suffered her first migraine and she had two eligible bachelors—two men, at least—knocking on her door. She supposed this was one of those things France is famous for, like *pain au chocolat* and museums and cafés.

"Okay! Now I leave you to your work," Philippe said. "I am going now to play chess, in the Jardin des Tuileries. I am too old for *petanque*, but my head, I can still use it. My friend comes with his car, so I wait for him outside."

"Good for you. So, I'll just replace all the locks Dave took out? Do you know if he had gotten to everything, or do you want me to double-check . . . ?"

She brought out Dave's notes and his schema for the house and laid them on the table. Clearly she didn't have enough locks in her bag to fit all the doors in a house this enormous.

Philippe laughed and waved his wrinkled hand in the air between them. "You look around, work on whatever you find. Do not be shy—enjoy! To Dave, this was like a child's fantasy, all these locks. Although there are a few doors that might not be worth opening."

He looped a scarf around his neck—a black-and-white herringbone pattern in soft-looking wool—grabbed his cane, and turned toward the front entry.

On the way out, he turned back and said, "Genevieve? Perhaps not all the doors need to be opened. But . . . I will leave that to you."

Chapter Twenty-three

Alone in Philippe's house, Genevieve felt as she had when she was a kid: like a trespasser. But Philippe had given her leave, so she snooped around, fascinated at this peek into another time.

Up the broad sweep of stairs, she found five large bedrooms on the second floor—in France, they called it the *first* floor, she reminded herself—and on the third, a row of small, cell-like chambers, which could have been storage closets, or perhaps servants' quarters. Only two small beds remained, old iron frames with shallow mattresses, which were still, oddly, made up: linens in faded shades of green and yellow. There were cardboard moving boxes here and there, assorted lamps and side tables, small area rugs, and a few scattered papers, but by and large the sense was of a fine house right after the war, abandoned and looted.

Three of the doors (paneled, made of heavy oak) were bereft of their plates and knobs, displaying bare circles cut into the wood. Genevieve checked Dave's schema and found three brass door fittings (locks, knobs, plates) that had been labeled and tagged as belonging to this floor. Each was packaged in a separate plastic bag, with little notes written in Dave's all-caps handwriting. It was typical in fine old homes for the nicer parts of the house to be decorated with expensive crystal, ornate metal, or carved wood knobs, while in the servants' quarters and work areas the fittings were made of less expensive brass.

She took the first apparatus out of the bag, placed the kneepad before the door, and started to fit it into the hole, screwing in the baseplate.

Her hands shook.

She was no locksmith. Yes, she had shown great promise when she'd learned the basics of locks at her uncle's knee. And yes, she had continued to practice, spreading out newspapers on a card table and taking apart old mechanisms or picking padlocks, driving Jason crazy with her "incessant need to fiddle with locks" in the evenings when he just wanted to relax and watch TV. And yes, she installed and fixed locks for people as a volunteer with an Oakland-based group that worked on old homes for the elderly.

But none of that made her a qualified locksmith. What if she screwed something up? What if she ruined one of the D'Artavel family heirloom locks?

"Treat the lock with respect, Genevieve, but do not let it defeat you."

She let out a long breath, hushed the voice of doubt in her mind, concentrated on her work, and persevered. Upon finishing with the first doorknob, she tested it thoroughly: did the device latch properly? Did the lock engage? And, most important, did the keys work easily?

Yes. She felt a sense of pride; she had done it.

She hung the old key off the knob by a loop of scratchy twine, as her uncle always had, and moved on to the next lock.

Genevieve imagined the clanking of the key ring at the housekeeper's waist as she moved about the house, busily attending to the business of her employers, the other servants under her thumb. In grand old homes such as this one, the housekeeper and the head of the household (usually the patriarch) would each have had a copy of the skeleton key, allowing them access to each room. Back in the day, maids and grooms were not granted the right of privacy from their employers. That was a modern invention.

She wondered why Philippe would want the locks cleaned and repaired and replaced, even while ignoring the plumbing and electricity. Was it a whim of an elderly, ever-so-slightly addled mind? Or was he simply determined to have the house whole again, to be sure all the original parts were brought back and to see her uncle's job through to completion? Maybe he had the notion of restoring it to what he remembered from growing up here as a boy.

Plumbing and electricity were relatively recent inventions, after all; these locks might have preceded such modern conveniences by centuries.

Genevieve was methodical, almost meditative, as she proceeded room by room. *A locksmith can't rush the work.* There was no point to it—if you lost your patience and hurried, you had to go back and start from the beginning. She didn't know how much time had passed (she needed to get a watch!), but she must have been working upstairs for almost two hours by the time she finished, polished the knobs and plates to a dull brass sheen, and checked the dossier for what was next.

There were several doors that needed work on the second floor: each bedroom, and closets within each bedroom. But she didn't have enough time to finish them all today. She descended to the main floor so she would be sure to hear Philippe when he came back in.

Typically there were fewer lockable spaces on the main floor, as there were fewer private areas. She checked her uncle's notes again: the library, the front guest room, the pantry. She found the cleaned and repaired antique locks for those three rooms in her bag.

Leaving everything on the dining room table, Genevieve looked around and got her bearings.

The library was small but still packed with a quantity of beautiful little volumes that made her wish she could read French easily. Oak shelves reached up to the ten-foot ceilings, and two tall windows provided a mellow light. A cracked leather chair and ottoman sat beside a desk covered with papers and dust. The floor was studded with stacks of very old, very yellow newspapers and crumbling magazines.

As she stepped out of the library, Genevieve noticed an intriguing little door off the hallway, tucked under a steep stair. It was small and very old. The wood was full of tiny wormholes and was slightly warped, the knob and lock plate very old brass, unlike the finer crystal knobs on the rest of the doors on this level.

She checked her uncle's schema, but this door was not included in the dossier.

The lock was a simple double-acting tumbler lock. The metal had corroded over the years, making the mechanisms stiff. *"Sometimes the soft brass wears down on antique locks; warm it with a hair dryer."* Even easier: Her uncle's bag included a small can of WD-40. A good application of the lubricant, and she was able to work the pick and the guide.

She could feel the pins falling into place. It wasn't that hard. There was no way her uncle would not have been able to open this door if he'd tried. But then . . . Philippe had said that some of the doors weren't worth opening. Perhaps "some doors aren't worth opening" was a polite way of telling her to mind her own business and stick to the original plan regarding which locks were to be serviced.

Still. If there's one thing a locksmith hates, it's a locked door.

Not that Genevieve was a locksmith, but (reflecting on her work upstairs with a little thrill of satisfaction) she was getting pretty darned close.

And Philippe had invited her to look around, to make herself at home. Most likely this was just some forgotten little closet: full of dusty old linens or outdated vacuum cleaner parts or expired canned goods.

Just as the lock was opening (that magic moment of release) Genevieve remembered her dreams. She hesitated, overcome with a quick, heady rush of fear. Wordless, primordial. *"Some things behind the doors are not meant to be seen."*

"Will you let yourself be defeated by a silly lock?"

Chapter Twenty-four

Genevieve reached up, wrapped her hand around the knob. Pulled.

The door creaked loudly, protesting.

Beyond the opening was a long, dark, dank staircase.

Leading to a basement, most likely. It was probably nothing more sinister than Philippe's *cave*—pronounced *khawv*. She had learned during her teenage sojourn in Paris: Anyone with enough space, even the humblest Parisian, kept his or her own wine cellar. Dave used to have a small one in a cool interior closet; someone (probably Catharine) had already cleared it out, replacing the old bottles with new cleaning supplies.

But whatever this was, it had been long abandoned. Genevieve would bet that the door hadn't been opened in many years.

In her uncle's bag was a heavy-duty head-mounted flashlight. She pulled her hair back into a ponytail and pulled the device over her skull, adjusting it to a smaller size. Genevieve felt silly, like a kid dressing up as a miner for Halloween, but this way she could carry the locksmith bag in one hand and keep the other free to hold on to handrails or grapple with the stone walls . . . or fight off ghosts or vampires.

Whatever she might face in the sooty dark that lay below. It felt reassuring to have at least one hand free.

To the left was a switch—not a flipper but a little round disc. She twisted it. A light came on, illuminating the upper staircase. Dim and thready, as though having a hard time making it through the dank air. She was amazed (and grateful) it worked at all. It was an unadorned, old-fashioned bulb, with a visible filament. She prayed that it didn't pop.

The stairway was narrow, enclosed by walls made of gray stones and fat, tan-colored bricks. Thick cobwebs were strewn along the walls and hung from the stone ceiling.

Genevieve descended. She took her time, making sure of her footholds. She kept her free hand on the stone wall for balance, but there was no rail, and the steps were steep. The air was stale: must and moisture in equal measure.

How long had it been since anyone had been down here? Years? Decades, maybe?

These stones felt different than the rest of the house. Ancient. Just how old *was* this building?

The overhead light barely reached to the base of the stairs. She twisted her head around to shine the flashlight this way and that. It revealed a dark hallway, nothing more. She paused, hoping her eyes would adjust to the shadows.

Finally, carefully, and with a sigh of relief, she set foot on level ground.

Something slapped her in the face.

She squeaked and flailed, imagining spiders. But it was only a chain. Heart pounding, she pulled it. Another feeble bulb came on, this one lending its glow to the distant stretches of the hallway, which continued about twenty feet, then took a sharp right. The stones in the low ceiling formed an upside-down U.

From an American's vantage point it was hard to believe homes this old even remained standing. In California buildings were lucky to survive fifty years, much less centuries, before being torn down to make way for something new, or being tumbled due to earthquakes or shoddy building materials. But this . . . to what had these walls borne witness over the years?

Several openings and doorways led off the hallway. Pipes and wires ran exposed along the walls.

Slowly she made her way forward, torn between fear and reverence. All of her senses felt heightened with the dread of the unknown: of spiders and rats and ghosts and wildly reclusive French serial killers.

But also reverence for the history before her eyes. The cellar must have served as storage and perhaps as workshops for generations of D'Artavels. Could it have been used during the war? It wasn't much of a stretch to imagine hiding whole families down here, or young men and women with heads bent low over a barrel used as a table, plotting sabotage against the Germans.

The first doorway was open: The perimeter held racks and a few wooden cages and appeared to have been the storage room for wine. Here again, the ceiling formed an arch, this time a low, broad one. Wine *caves* made a positive out of dank underground places. *"The mold is good for the bottles,"* she remembered Dave telling her, as he pulled from the rack a dusty bottle covered in a thin layer of gunk. He had wiped it off with his big, roughened hands, apparently uncaring of the grime, to show the label: a pen-and-ink drawing of an old castle. *"We humans may not like it, but it's good for the bottles to look like this."*

Philippe's wine racks were virtually empty; only half a dozen bottles remained. She felt a little thrill as she pulled one out, blew off the dust and cobwebs. *Aloxe-Corton*; *Domaine Gaston & Pierre Ravaut*, from Bourgogne, 1959. She should bring one up to show him. Perhaps Philippe had valuable wine down here that he'd forgotten about for the past fifty years. But then . . . more likely it was very interesting, very historic vinegar.

The next chamber was full of rotting wooden boxes and old metal chairs, a couple of cots, picture frames, plus a window frame with two broken panes. A box of Christmas ornaments: She picked one up, wondering how much this would fetch in a vintage store in San Francisco—a pretty penny, no doubt. Glittery glass balls and little candles made of ceramic, with tiny lightbulbs for flames.

There were a rusted child's bicycle, iron rods, chairs, a brass bedstead. Even a surfboard in one corner—so surely someone had used this storage space relatively recently. Everything was covered in a thick layer of dust and grunge.

Where did it come from, this grime? Did the old stone walls settle, sending a gentle mist of mortar sifting down over the years? Did the footfalls of those overhead dislodge minuscule bits of brick and stone, lathe and plaster? Did rats scamper over boxes, leaving behind trails of dirt? The spiderwebs were so thick they were fluffy veils, furred with dust.

She peeked into another room: a utility sink, a long stone counter. A few old mismatched dishes, buckets, an ancient mop. In the corner, a strange contraption of tubes and glass receptacles that looked suspiciously like a still. Perhaps Philippe's grandfather spent time down here, cooking up the kind of botanical extract so common in France: this *apéritif* made from a special herb that grows only in the Italian Alps; this *digestif* from a mixture of flowers that grow only in Provence; this tincture made with holy water from Lourdes. Probably with a little more poking around she would find the cupboard of homemade concoctions, all in dusty bottles labeled by hand in that scrolly, loopy kind of writing they taught in the French schools.

In the floor of the utility room, half-hidden by a wooden box, was a large, ornate grate. Probably this room was built on the same principal as the shower in Dave and Pasquale's house: simply mop and send the water down the central drain.

Still, the metal on the grate was so ornamental Genevieve crouched down and bent her head to focus the flashlight on the metal, trying to discern the design: Art Nouveau–inspired swoops, elongated lilies, and stylized reeds. This was so typical of a long-ago time, when even the simplest bit of utilitarian metal was carved and molded, meant to be beautiful even though it would remain underfoot, providing humble service in a basement utility room.

She was pushing herself up when she noticed something odd.

Beyond the grate was not the opening she expected; instead, it dropped down about a foot, and there it stopped, blocked by a piece of wood. Genevieve took the gear off her head and pointed the beam of the flashlight beyond the grate, trying to make it out.

It was a piece of wood with hinges on one side. Like a trapdoor. A trapdoor equipped with an elaborate antique lock.

Genevieve couldn't be sure . . . but it looked like one of her uncle's special locks. She looked closer . . .

"*Genevieve, es-tu la?*"

Chapter Twenty-five

"Genevieve?"

Genevieve emerged from the room and hurried down the little hall to see Philippe standing in the square of light at the top of the basement stairs.

"Yes, yes, I'm here," she called as she climbed the stairs.

"What are you doing down there?"

"I'm sorry, I didn't mean to—"

"No, no, is okay. But this door has been locked many years. I am surprised . . . for a long time no one has gone there. I think there is nothing but trash there."

Genevieve closed the door behind her. "There are a few bottles of wine—would you like me to bring them up, see if they're worth anything?"

For a moment Philippe remained silent, his gaze fixed on the old wood of the door. He had a faraway, unfocused look in his eyes that reminded Genevieve too much of her *tante* Pasquale. Philippe's mind seemed so sharp most of the time, but if he'd been old enough to fight when the city was liberated seventy years ago . . .

"That door hasn't been opened for a very long time. We used it during the war, but . . ." He shrugged. "We lost the key."

Used it for what? she wondered. Clearly the cellar had been used after that—the wine was dated 1959. But Philippe didn't volunteer any more information, and something in his eyes stopped her from asking.

"Do you want me to make sure you have a key that works?"

He stared at the door for another moment, then shrugged and smiled, back to his old self. "We decide later. Right now, you must stop working; it is time for *apero*."

"*Apero? Qu'est-ce que c'est?*" What is *apero*? she asked.

"It is . . . snack before dinner."

Genevieve was still full from lunch. And she had indulged in a flaky, buttery croissant for breakfast this morning, feeling almost virtuous for not having a *pain au chocolat*. And now she was supposed to eat a snack before dinner? So much for her nebulous plan to lose weight while in Paris.

She followed Philippe into the kitchen. He started opening plastic bags he'd carried in with him, placing things in small bowls and plates. Cheese puffs, crackers, blanched almonds glistening with olive oil and studded with rosemary. He cut thin slices from a hard salami that had a tag stamped with the silhouette of a tusked boar.

"This is very good, *saucisson de sanglier*," said Philippe. "Wild pig sausage. You see, they put the picture on so you know of what you are eating: rabbit, deer, duck."

"I should tell my brother. He makes sausages like this—he could start the tradition in California."

Philippe held out a shallow bowl of cheese puffs, his eyes lighting up. "You try these. So good! *C'est à mourir.*"

Americans were enthralled by the cheese and wine when they came to Paris; perhaps the French were swayed by fried cheese puffs.

He shook the bowl as though to entice her further. Genevieve took a cheese puff and crunched on it. Philippe watched her closely, thin white eyebrows arched in anticipation.

She made a yummy face and nodded. "Mmm."

"What do I tell you? Delicious, are they not?" He brought three glasses to the counter, then poured a deep red wine into two of them. "The doctor, she tells me Bordeaux is good for the health. This is why I am so old, I think!"

"But still handsome."

He laughed heartily, slapping the counter. Then he gathered up the wineglasses and headed to the dining room.

"Please, Genevieve, to bring the plates to the dining table, and two chairs from the kitchen so we sit down."

"Of course," she said as she gathered the plates, balancing two on her forearm as she'd done in her old waitressing days. "So, speaking of wine, would you like me to bring the old bottles up from the *cave*?"

"Later, maybe. Next time you go down. Probably they are no good, but it would be an interesting experiment to see."

"Yes, I wondered about that," Genevieve said, returning to the kitchen for the chairs, old metal with plastic-covered cushions. "So, you haven't been down there since the war?"

"Oh, of course." He waved a hand in the air. "But not for a long time. I leave it to the rats. And, how do you say, to the *fantômes*?"

"A . . . ghost?"

"*Oui.* And the ghosts."

"You think there are ghosts down there?"

"*Mais oui.* Always there are ghosts. Perhaps you are not old enough to know this. We carry the ghosts around with us." He tapped his chest, over his heart. "We are the ones who cause the ghosts, you see? The memories of the past. That *cave*—

we used it during the war. War causes many ghosts."

"What did you use it for?"

He crunched on a cheese puff. Pondered. Took his time. "To hide the people."

Genevieve's heart fluttered slightly even thinking of someone hiding down there. "I thought you said you weren't a hero. Hiding people in your basement sounds heroic to me."

He shrugged, sipped his wine. Remained mute.

"There is a little trapdoor under a grate in the utility room," Genevieve said. "It looks like it has one of my uncle's locks on it."

"Yes, it had an old lock before that was too easy to open. Dave changed it for me. But you don't need to worry about that. There is nothing to open in the *cave*. But tell me, Genevieve, do you know about *les souterrains*?"

"The catacombs? I've heard of them. There are thousands of bones, right? My uncle refused to take me to see them when I was here before. I guess he thought it would be too scary."

"Not thousands of bones—*millions*. Paris is a very old city, with a lot of bones! The graveyards were emptied in the eighteenth century, and the bones moved to the *souterrains*. *L'empire de la mort*, the empire of the dead, they call it. But there are many kilometers of tunnels down below our feet, many more than just the rooms of bones. But most tunnels are closed to the public. *Interdits*, forbidden."

"What were they used for?"

"First they were made by accident, by bringing out the stone. The limestone which you see now in all the old buildings of Paris—like this one! After, some were used to bring the water around the city, or to take the bad water away. . . ."

"Like sewers?"

"Exactly. Sewers and other things—who knows? But there are hundreds of kilometers of tunnels. We were lucky for this because we use them in the *résistance*, to get around the city secretly. But also the Nazis found parts of the tunnels and used them as bomb shelters, and to move around also. You can see there are still things written in German on the walls, even some old Nazi toilets down there!"

"I had no idea."

"But people get lost, you know; if you don't know your way around you can get lost or hurt yourself." He held up a shaky finger and wagged it slightly, as though in warning. "People have disappeared, never to be seen again. Many in the *résistance*, they knew the tunnels well. But still . . . sometimes they are in a tunnel right next to the soldiers but they don't know! One day, I was not there, *merci à Dieu*, but their paths crossed! *Imagine!* Just imagine what surprise they feel!"

"What happened?"

His laughter faded. He shrugged, ate another cheese puff. "Two of our friends were killed; we were lucky it was not more. But the soldiers turned and ran away. It was because of the surprise the Nazis feel, *ils avaient peur*. They have . . . they are afraid. Afraid of the ghosts."

"Ghosts again?"

"Not one. Many, many ghosts in the tunnels, I think. The tourists, they are scared to think the catacombs are full of the bones, millions of bones. Maybe there are ghosts there, too, but the ghosts I am thinking of are more recent."

A shadow passed over his eyes. On such a smiley countenance it was startling to see sudden sadness descend. It reminded her of Dave whenever she spoke about her mother.

The melancholy mood didn't last long. The doorbell sounded, a series of graceful chimes.

Philippe pushed himself up with his cane with surprising speed.

"Would you like me to get it?" Genevieve asked.

"No, no, don't be ridiculous. I am still the man of the house. You sit; you have been working hard all day."

Genevieve opened her mouth to protest—her day hadn't been particularly grueling, after all—but then realized there was no point in going up against one so determined as Philippe D'Artavel. So she did as she was told, sipping her wine and studying her surroundings.

One edge of the little basement door was visible from her seat at the table. She gazed at it and wondered. Could there be actual ghosts down there in the catacombs, forever roaming the tunnels beneath the streets of Paris? If the bones of millions were stored in the ossuary, surely the law of averages would suggest that there would be at least one or two confused spirits, wouldn't there?

Not that Genevieve believed in that sort of thing.

But . . . there were ghosts, and then there were ghosts. Philippe was probably right: It was the living who kept the ghosts alive, carrying them around, whether as protective talismans, or as prisms through which to view their lives, or as a stone around their necks set to drag them into the depths.

Genevieve feared she kept her mother's ghost alive, kept it strapped to her back like a proverbial monkey.

"Look who is here!" Philippe said as he tottered back to the kitchen. "Look who drops on to us!"

Down the hall behind him came the Irishman, Killian O'Mara.

"Hi," said Genevieve as she stood to greet him. She didn't buy for a second Philippe's "surprise" that Killian had stopped by uninvited; witness the third wineglass on the table.

"Good to see you again, Genevieve." Killian's

voice was deep and warm. He gave her the Parisian double kiss, one on each cheek. She felt the slight abrasiveness of his whiskers on her cheeks, caught the scent of him: soap and an ever-so-slight musk. A manly scent that didn't come from a bottle. "Oooh, cheese puffs!"

"*Très délicieux*," said Philippe as he shoved the bowl toward Killian and poured a glass of wine.

"This house is incredible, Philippe," Killian said, looking overhead to the beams and intricate moldings. "When was it built, do you know?"

"It was my grandparents' house, and then my father's. And it was old even before that! The main part of it is eighteenth century, but old houses are like castles: many start small and then get bigger with the years; each generation builds more. So there is no one year they are built. The *cave*, for example, it is very old, as *l'Américaine* discovers today."

Killian turned to Genevieve, eyebrows raised. "The *cave*?"

"It's more than just a wine cellar. There are several rooms down there."

He was clearly intrigued, and Genevieve remembered the kind of photographs he took. They chatted for a while: about what kind of work Killian was doing in Paris, and how Genevieve should approach the authorities about getting a business license (the theme of French bureaucracy being a favorite trigger for unsolicited advice, apparently), and then Philippe told them about his daughters and grandchildren.

He teared up when he spoke about his wife, Delphine, who had passed away more than twenty years ago.

"But it is like yesterday," he said. "She was . . . a wonderful woman. She made me laugh! I miss her every day. Soon I will go to be with her."

Killian met Genevieve's gaze across the table. It was hard to know how to respond to something like that: People here seemed to have a matter-of-fact, straightforward attitude toward death, but it was difficult to conceive of Philippe no longer existing on this earthly plane. He seemed so very alive, so vibrant, and Genevieve was sure the world would be a sadder place without him. Just as it was without Dave.

"Philippe," Killian said finally, changing the subject. "You might be the man to ask: Any idea how I can get into the secret underground tunnels, *les souterrains*?"

"There are tours," said Philippe with a nod. "Tours of the bones every day, but I think maybe you have to make the reservation."

"No, I've seen that, actually. It was fascinating. But I was more interested in the other tunnels, the ones that aren't open to the public. Folks seem quite secretive about them."

Philippe pushed his chin out, shrugged. "They are *interdits*."

"We were just talking about the tunnels," said Genevieve. "I hadn't realized they were used by the resistance when they were fighting against the Germans—and also by the Nazis themselves. Philippe says there are underground bunkers."

"But they are dangerous," Philippe said, picking up the plate of crackers and shuffling into the kitchen. "I think it is best you not attempt to go in there."

"Did I say something wrong?" Killian asked Genevieve in a low voice after Philippe left the room.

"He was just telling me about losing some of his fellow resistance fighters down in those tunnels," she answered. "Maybe he's feeling sad."

Killian and Genevieve grabbed the rest of the bowls and glasses and brought everything into the kitchen.

"Philippe, would it be all right with you if I came back sometime to photograph the house?" Killian asked. "I have a small camera with me, but I'd really love to bring my good equipment and take some decent shots."

"This house? *Bien sûr*! Okay! You come back with Genevieve, she show you around. She knows how to get in now; she does not need me. She can—*comment dit-on?*—get in like the thieves."

"Just as she did with me. Quite the housebreaker."

"Actually, Philippe, I'll need another day, at least, to finish all the locks here," said Genevieve. "I told my cousin I would have lunch with her tomorrow, but I can come in the afternoon, if that works for you."

"*Non, non*. Don't come back tomorrow, because they say it is going to be a beautiful day. Go to see the sights! This is a beautiful city, *la belle France*! And Catharine lives in the twentieth arrondissement," Philippe said. "Too far."

"She says it's not far from where I went to visit my aunt. Métro stop Blanche."

He nods. "Near Montmartre, the famous hill for artists. You should visit this while you are there. Also, it is right near Pigalle."

"What's Pigalle?" Genevieve asked.

Philippe laughed and bright red flags of a blush appeared on his cheeks.

"It's the naughty district," Killian explained. "Strip shows, sex shops, and the like."

"That doesn't sound much like my cousin Catharine."

"It's been cleaned up in recent years—it's also the home of Moulin Rouge and a few other famous clubs. You lads seem to love it."

"Us lads?"

"Americans."

"Ah." *But I'm not the typical American tourist,* Genevieve thought as she gathered up her uncle's tool bag and put the dossier back together. With

Philippe's permission, she stashed the canvas bag full of locks in a hall closet.

"But then," Killian added, "I suppose you aren't much like a typical American tourist, are you?"

Genevieve looked up from her task, startled that Killian seemed to have read her mind.

Their eyes met and held for a moment. There was something about Killian's easy, smiling, helpful manner that seemed familiar. . . . She couldn't quite put her finger on it the other day, but now she realized what it was: He reminded her of her uncle Dave. No wonder he and Philippe were already getting along like long-lost pals.

Still . . . warning bells went off in her head whenever she was near him. Probably Mary was right—it was the result of her twisted view of male-female relationships lately. But still.

"Okay, I am busy man so you two must leave now," said Philippe. "Killian will walk you home, Genevieve," he said as he escorted them both to the front door. It had started to rain, so he shoved a large black umbrella in Killian's hand. "You make her to stay dry, okay? Okay! *Je vous souhaite une bonne soirée!*"

Chapter Twenty-six

Killian put his arm around Genevieve, lightly, to be sure the umbrella covered her as well as him. She could feel his warmth and once again caught the scent of him: not of cologne like Philippe, just a really good manly smell, mingling with the scent of damp wool, and rain on city streets.

She felt two strong emotions, simultaneously: First, she wanted to be back in the quiet apartment among her aunt and uncle's things, the rusty keys and antique locks and incessantly ticking clocks; and second, it felt exciting, thrilling even, to be walking through Paris on a rainy day, quite literally in the arms of a charming, interesting man.

Genevieve didn't expect—or even want—anything to happen with Killian, but she couldn't deny the cinematic perfection of the scene: the big umbrella, the Hermès scarf, the way their legs moved in step along the cobblestones, dodging puddles and downspouts.

"Let's take the long way back," Killian said. "There's something you absolutely should see."

"Thanks, but I really should get home."

"You sure? This is France, Genevieve. Even though Paris is a big city . . . the pace is different here. What are you rushing home to, exactly? D'ya have a cat to feed?"

Genevieve opened her mouth to say it was none of his business, that she could plan her day as she saw fit. It would be easy enough to claim she wanted to get out of the rain, that she was tired from working (all three hours of it!) and wanted to relax. But the words didn't come.

Killian was right. Why was she in a rush to get back to the Village Saint-Paul? To go through Dave's files, read more about Philippe's house, see if she could find any other tidbits of information about it and that one Schlage side pin that was driving her nuts . . .

But there was plenty of time for that. And she *was* in Paris.

"Like I told Philippe, I've set aside tomorrow for sightseeing."

"This isn't a typical tourist spot, to be honest. But it's something that a locksmith absolutely has to see, and, if at all possible, it's best seen in the rain. You willin' to chance it?"

She smiled, gave in. "Sure, okay."

Ten minutes later they arrived at the Seine and strolled along it toward the Palais-Royal.

"All the *bouquinistes* are closed because of the rain," Killian said, shaking his head. "What a scaldin'. It's not as though it's bucketin', is it?"

"Sorry, you lost me. What language are we speaking?"

He laughed. "I was saying it was a shame these big green boxes aren't open, since it's not raining that hard. The *bouquinistes* sell—"

"Oh, I remember these!" said Genevieve. The green wooden stands were set out in a long line bordering the Seine. They were locked up tight at the moment, but when their tops were flipped open they displayed used books, old maps and drawings, calendars, and a few tourist tchotchkes. "I used to love looking through the old papers. My uncle bought me a map of the Île de la Cité and an old engraving of a gargoyle."

"Here's an interesting factoid about Paris: Did you know in order to have one of these stands, you have to be a librarian or have another relevant degree, else there's a seven-year wait to receive a license?"

"Really? That's . . . impressive." Though it did give her a funny feeling in the pit of her stomach: If it took seven years (or advanced degrees) to operate a box of used books on the shores of the Seine, how long would it take to receive her locksmith credentials?

"The French take their books seriously," said Killian. "It's one of the things I love about Paris."

"I've been meaning to go by Shakespeare and Company."

"Love that place. Did you know they have beds among the stacks?"

"Beds?"

"Apparently it was so overrun with sleep-deprived students, the owner wanted them to be able to nap."

Genevieve smiled at the image. "Sleeping among the stacks of books. What could be better?"

"Spoken like a true book lover. But my very favorite bookstore in all of Paris is Le Pont Traversé, near the Luxembourg Gardens. Not so many tourists."

"Have you been to the Red Wheelbarrow, on our street? I've tried twice, but it's been closed."

"They're off on vacation, I think, but they'll be back."

"I finished both my novels, so I'll have to find some new books soon. And I'm sorry to say my French isn't good enough yet, so I need English books."

"You don't travel with an e-reader?"

"I'm old-school. I like paper."

He nodded. "I do as well, come to that. I like the feel of them in my hands."

"In fact . . . I don't know, I guess I'm becoming an anachronism. I find some of the old technologies so elegant: like watches, and paper maps. Maybe that's why I'm so attracted to locks. They're old-fashioned. My uncle told me the kind of lock and key we still use today was invented in 1871. There have been some improvements, but it's the same basic device."

"Really? I don't suppose I've ever thought much about the history of locks. Fascinating, though, isn't it?"

"It is, at least for some of us. There are locks dating back to ancient Mesopotamia—wooden ones, back then. These days things are changing, of course—everything's moving toward electronic systems, sadly."

As Genevieve said this last bit she remembered: *Killian is a computer guy.* She waited for him to look at her with that mixture of disappointment, curiosity, and pity that Jason always did when she decried the effects of electronics on contemporary society.

But instead, he smiled and said, "That's yet one more reason to like Paris. There's an appreciation here for that sort of thing. Good food, cooked slowly; artisans who make things by hand; books; and probably locks, too."

"Old-fashioned photography."

"That, too. In fact . . ." He shrugged, looked out over the Seine. A small barge floated slowly past; ducks waddled on the banks; couples held hands as they walked. "I think the French are traditionalists."

"As in, conservative?"

"I wouldn't say *conservative,* certainly not politically, but careful about change. The fresh and novel is treated with suspicion. You American lads are quite the opposite, normally: Anything new is considered exciting, good. You're a very optimistic people."

"I've never been quite in step with 'my lads,' I guess. Either with technology or . . . optimism."

She could feel as well as hear the rumble of his laugh. "And on that note: Here we are."

They stood at the base of the Pont des Arts, one of the many bridges over the Seine, connecting the Left Bank to the Right. As compared to many of the bridges in Paris, such as the famous Pont Neuf, this one was plain and uninteresting.

But the rails were covered in padlocks.

Hundreds—thousands?—of locks. So many that the sides of the bridge looked like great banks of solid metal squares and rectangles, hearts and circles.

"What is this?" Genevieve asked in wonder.

"They call it the Love Locks Bridge. Sweethearts attach padlocks marked with their initials or names to the sides of the bridge, then toss the keys into the water below to seal their love. *Ce sont cadenas de l'amour.*"

"Wow."

"It's become such a popular tradition that city workers have had to cut out and replace entire panels of fences too heavily laden with locks; occasionally one will fall into the Seine. Which isn't the end of the world, I suppose—I imagine the Seine's seen much worse—unless, of course, it happens to hit a passing barge."

They stood in the middle of the bridge, studying them.

"Amazing, isn't it?" Killian said. "A tribute to love, in the city for lovers."

"Looks like a lot of work to me."

He burst out laughing.

"I'm serious," Genevieve said, though she smiled. "This is the sort of nightmare I'd have when my uncle Dave used to sit me down with locks and make me open them, one after another. He'd get old locks from his antiques-dealer friends, and I wasn't allowed to get up until they were all open."

"That sounds a little harsh."

"It wasn't, not really. He was trying to get my mind off my mother, I realize now. She had just passed away when I came to stay with them. Dave was a sweetheart. He'd make a big show of how I had to open every lock in the pile, but then he'd sit down on the floor with me, cross-legged, and tell me stories and jokes as he helped me work my way through the pile. He was . . ." She sighed. "He was a very good man."

Killian looked down at her. "You were lucky, then. To have him in your life."

She nodded, feeling a lump in her throat, and gazed at the Seine. Couples were walking along the banks, arm in arm. A child threw bread toward a small group of ducks. A tourist boat chugged slowly down the river, descriptions of the sights blaring out over the loudspeaker, first in Japanese, then in English.

Genevieve felt the soft weight of a hand on the back of her head. She glanced over her shoulder to see Killian looking at her intently.

He pushed a hank of hair out of her eyes, blown by the wind off the river. She was afraid he would do more, but after looking into her eyes for a moment, he smiled and edged back a minuscule amount.

"May I take your picture?"

"I don't take good pictures."

"I'll be the one taking the pictures."

"I meant—"

"I know what you meant," he said with a grin. "But I don't believe you. May I?"

"I thought you told Philippe you didn't have your cameras with you."

"I always carry a small one." He handed Genevieve the umbrella and pulled a small black case out of his backpack. "Just a cheap one, for snapshots. I like to muck with the exposure, so I leave the door open a tiny bit, see?"

She peered at the oddly homemade-looking device.

"So, may I?" He asked again. "Genevieve Martin, standing amongst the locks."

"I . . ." She blew out a breath, shrugged. "Okay, if you insist. But I'm keeping the umbrella."

Feeling awkward, she stood by the bank of

locks and allowed him to snap away. Apparently heedless of the rain, he didn't take one photo, but dozens, so many that she started to laugh and shake her head. The wind whipped her hair across her face, and she pushed it back, eventually forgetting to care that he was still snapping away.

"Why d'ya suppose they call them 'locks' of hair?" Killian asked finally, as he put away his camera. "Is there a connection, d'you think?"

"Good question," said Genevieve. "I know lovers used to give each other bits of their hair as a gesture of trust and loyalty; maybe they 'locked' people together?"

He nodded. "Good story, true or not."

"Is it the same word in French?"

"I don't think so. . . ." He thought for a moment. "*Serrure* means a lock on a door, and locks of hair would be . . . *chevelures*, I think. I don't know if there's another. We'll have to look it up."

"Where did you learn your French?"

He shrugged. "Old girlfriend. Shall we keep walking?"

They walked past place de l'Hôtel de Ville, and Killian pointed out a café named Caféothèque de Paris.

"I've been told by my coffee-drinking friends that this place sells the only decent coffee in Paris."

"Really?" Genevieve took note of the locale. "You know, I've noticed . . . I always assumed the

French would have great coffee, but it was so much better in California."

"Yeah, I've heard that. They've got decent espresso and the like, but coffee per se? Not so much. But you should check out the Caféothèque. They roast their own beans, and it's a nice little café."

"Do they have Internet access, do you know?"

"I'm not sure, but there are plenty of cafés that do. Don't you have Internet at your place?"

She shook her head.

"I could help you set it up, if you like. I recommend going with the company called Orange. You can place an order by phone, get a box. There are bound to be some problems, as there always are, but I'm happy to help you install it."

"Really? That would be great."

"I could pay you back for your housebreaking the other day."

"You really should stop calling it that."

"I enjoy it," he said with a smile. His voice was gentle as he looked down at her. "Makes me feel like I'm hanging out with a mysterious someone from the Parisian underworld."

Chapter Twenty-seven

Angela, 1983

The entrance to the catacombs is through an abandoned train tunnel. They have to hop a fence, negotiate a steep slope, and walk down weed-strewn old railroad tracks.

Xabi moves aside a metal plate, like a manhole cover, in the side of the tunnel wall.

The opening doesn't look much bigger than a cat door.

"That's . . . the entrance?" Angela asks.

"You are not afraid, remember?" he says.

Xabi has brought a pack and he shows her the contents: a compass and a hand-drawn map of the catacombs. Flashlights (the kind you put on your head, as well as carry in your hand). Extra batteries. Water and snacks. It seems strangely nurturing of him to have come so prepared, almost Boy Scouty. Perhaps there is an equivalent group in the Basque country, Angela thinks, trying to imagine a juvenile version of the man in front of her, a scarf around his neck. Wondering how to say "always prepared" in Euskara.

The only scarf she can imagine him wearing is red, with a white outfit and a beret, ready to run with the bulls of Pamplona. That is a Basque city, she knows, having seen a documentary on the famous annual escapade. It seems fitting, now that she looks at him with that in mind. She imagines him turning and fixing a bull with an icy stare if it dared try to run him down or skewer him with its horns.

"People have been lost down there," said Pasquale when Angela asked her about *les souterrains*, the underground. "Lost, and perhaps someone later finds their bones. Or they are simply gone, never to be seen again."

They built on the natural caves. The Romans were here two thousand years ago, and they mined the limestone to build their buildings. But to these have been added, over the centuries, waterways and sewers and basements and storage units and even underground factories.

"You see how it is separated naturally? This little place here?" Xabi points out a tiny crevice in the stone, his hands for once not covered in chalk dust. Now she sees they are deeply tanned, with long, tapered, calloused fingers.

"Here, they put the piece of wood, *comme ça*. The air is moist—you feel it? As the wood gets more moisture, it gets bigger, and over time the split, she gets much bigger. Then the workers can get in and cut, and pull out the big piece of stone. You see? The mining created so many caves, hundreds of kilometers of unmapped caves. And then people used the caves for many things. When there were too many people in Paris and they realized the dead people caused a problem, they moved the bodies here."

"Here?"

"*Ne bouge pas*," he says. "Don't move." He seems to be listening, standing near the small hole in the wall about four feet off the ground. All Angela can see within is darkness.

"*Allons-y*," he says, looking back over his shoulder with a grin. She has never before seen him smile, and the sight makes her forget for a moment. Forget that she is underground, in a tunnel clearly marked *interdit*, forbidden to enter, and apparently is about to allow herself to be swallowed up by a black hole.

"In . . . in there?" she asks once the magic of that smile falls off. "That's the only way?"

"I thought you were not afraid. *As-tu peur?*"

"No," she says, raising her chin.

She thinks about the woods where she grew up, how as a girl she would try to poke her head into the small animal burrows she would find. She had always wondered what it was like to be inside such a thing: walls, floor, and ceiling dirt, only one direction to go.

"I go first," he says. "You follow. You are smaller—if I can go, you can go."

She nods and watches as he steps on a chunk of concrete to hoist himself up, shining his light first, then pulling himself through with a few muffled grunts.

It strikes her, then, as she watches the bottoms of his shoes disappearing into the black nothingness: She, Angela Martin, is standing in a dank tunnel under the streets of Paris. No one in this world, other than Xabi, has the slightest idea where she is. Her brother and sister-in-law, her husband and child, her friends back home . . . she could disappear now into nothingness, float away, or melt right into this ground, leaving behind no trace, no sign. Her bones would blend with the thousands already housed here, out of time, out of place.

It is the closest she has ever come to vanishing, and it is at once seductive and disorienting, alluring and terrifying.

"Angela?" comes Xabi's muffled voice.

Angela tries to remember: Is this the first time he has ever actually used her name? He pronounces it with the soft *g*, making it sound exotic and beautiful.

"Angel, are you coming?"

Some of the tunnels are large; others are narrow and make her feel like they are entering the crypt of an Egyptian pyramid; still others have the broadly arched stone ceilings common to wine cellars and church basements. One tunnel has water running along a trough in the center, forcing them to straddle it, one foot perched awkwardly on each of the side curbs.

There are occasional medieval carvings and admonitions in Latin; some passages are marked with street signs, indicating what lies so many feet overhead.

What surprises Angela is the graffiti: it is everywhere, from the banal *(Marco was here!)* to the artistic.

Xabi leads the way through one more tiny, animal-sized hole, and they are suddenly standing in an assemblage of open rooms, as spacious as a restaurant.

"There used to be a factory down here," he says. "For making beer."

"They made beer in the catacombs?"

"Yes. And many other things. They grew mushrooms, too, called the *champignons de Paris*. Maybe they still do; I don't know."

"So this used to be a brewery? And now . . . an art gallery?"

Clearly they are not the first visitors to this locale. In fact, its walls are covered in paintings: cartoons and abstract drawings but also intricate murals: the Mayan calendar, a delicately rendered version of Caravaggio's famous Bacchus.

Makeshift tables have been set up, many holding remnants of candles, some with evidence of picnics: crumpled white butcher paper and empty wine bottles lying on their sides.

"But who paints down here?"

"Whoever wants to, I suppose."

"You mean people haul all their art supplies in here, and then stay down here for hours, painting?" asks Angela. "Why? Who will ever see them?"

"We are seeing them."

"But . . . why not paint them up above?"

"I think because this is a very special place. You can feel it, I think, how special it is down here, almost like a kind of cathedral."

She nods. He is right. She feels it.

"A friend tells me in English there is the expression: art, for the sake of art," says Xabi. "You know this?"

"Yes: art for art's sake."

"Art does not always hang in the Louvre. Sometimes it is made for other reasons. Just for itself."

"Like your chalk paintings?"

"Exactly." He smiles. "Although—those chalk paintings also pay my rent."

Xabi takes her deeper into the tunnels. He shows her a beautiful, deep stone well, with a circular stair leading down to the water.

"This was what they used to mix the concrete, when they were building columns to support the tunnels."

They passed many such columns as they

progressed through the underground. They seem hodgepodge, made of random stones and hunks of concrete, crooked and organically formed, like something that might grow under the ocean or appear on the pages of a Dr. Seuss book.

"They were built because some of Paris started to fall into the tunnels, because of too much weight."

"You're saying all of Paris is held up by these columns?"

"Only part of Paris," he says. "But, yes."

As they continue, they walk down tunnels that become tighter and smaller. Or does it just feel that way? Occasionally Xabi stops and refers to his map, checks markings on the wall—some official, some graffiti—then continues on.

Angela is fascinated yet terrified. Does he really know where they are going? Pasquale's warnings ring in her ears: tales of people who went exploring and were never heard from again. What had possessed her to entrust herself so completely to this man?

Finally they turn a corner, and Xabi invites her to sit on a little stone ledge.

"You are tired, I think," he says. "We will rest a while, have a snack. But first we will take a moment with the ghosts of the *souterrains*."

He sits beside her, takes the flashlight from her hands, and clicks it off. Then he extinguishes his own light.

They are plunged into absolute darkness. The only sound is the rasp of their breathing, echoing off stone walls. Angela fancies she can hear their hearts, the blood rushing through their veins.

"Do not be afraid," Xabi whispers. "The ghosts, they will not harm you. They only want to be seen."

But Angela has to fight the panic that claws at the base of her throat. She has never been claustrophobic, but this is different. This is all encompassing. She reminds herself that far above them, sixty feet overhead, Parisians stride down boulevards, cars idle at lights, tourists gawk. There is daylight, and breezes, and everyday pleasures and annoyances. All the hustle and bustle still exists.

But here, in the belly of the city, they sit in the dark. Unknown, unseen.

"Where are you from?" Angela asks him. She can't think of where she is, who she is. It is all here and now, all in the moment.

"I told you. From Euskadi, the Basque country. In the mountains."

"But . . . who are you? Why are you in Paris? Why are you here with me now?"

"Why are *you* here? Where is your husband?"

Silence. Total and utter silence, along with the dark, enveloping them.

Angela has to struggle to keep herself grounded. Closes her eyes, tries to remember, to fight against the nothingness. This was what she wanted, yearned for, as she avoided her husband, her child, wanting only to sleep, to be absent. This nothingness. This terrible, all-encompassing nothingness.

"Be careful what you wish for," her mother used to tell her.

"I am sorry, Angel," Xabi says finally. "That was wrong of me to ask. And it is not important. The only thing is this. Here, now, you, and me."

She feels the warmth of his hand cupping hers. The feeling is so welcome it is a blessing, a grace.

Another human being. She is not alone. Tears sting the back of her eyes.

And then his arm is around her, and his mouth is on hers.

The kiss is elemental, essential. The spirits of the tunnels wrap around her; the ghosts of the empire of the dead.

Beware *l'empire de la mort.*

His lips, his hands, are life. They are heat and light and connection. They are everything.

Chapter Twenty-eight

"And this is the BHV," said Killian as he and Genevieve passed by a busy corner on quai François Mitterrand. It had stopped raining, and waiters were already wiping off outdoor tables and chairs, turning on the outdoor heaters, and beckoning to passersby.

"And the BHV is . . . ?"

"A kind of general store, a department store. But not terribly fancy. Furniture, clothes, fragrances . . . and downstairs is sort of like a DIY store, with hardware and garden supplies. The sorts of things that can be hard to find in all the small little boutiques. There's also the Monoprix—that's a handy place."

"Do they sell flowers there, to grow in window boxes?"

"Actually, if you walk the other way, on the other side of the Pont Neuf, there are a bunch of garden shops. Pet stores, too. Also, there's an open-air market near Notre-Dame on weekends, with a lot of garden stuff."

"You're like a walking guidebook."

"I try," he said with a smile. "I think sometimes it takes an outsider to help navigate the city. Natives will show you the things they love, and of course you need to make time to see all the famous sites and wander through the Louvre. But sometimes a person just needs a wrench or a pencil or, I dunno, a towel. Not to mention a good cup of coffee."

"Well, I appreciate it. I'm . . . I feel like I'm still getting my sea legs under me. It's been a little overwhelming."

"There's always a bit of an adjustment. You've

only been here, what, a few days? And besides, you're still mourning your uncle. So, you're going sightseeing tomorrow?"

"Yes, I think I should. I'm looking forward to it."

"Too bad I have to work, or I'd volunteer to shepherd you around."

I'd rather go by myself, Genevieve thought. Killian looked dapper, his wet hair slicked back from his face, using the big black umbrella as a cane now that it had stopped raining. He was interesting and funny (and smelled like heaven), but the last thing she needed right now was a man clouding her thoughts and muddying her emotions even more than they already were. Besides, she had to deal with Jason (and the dissolution of their marriage) before even entertaining such notions, and she *really* didn't want to think about that yet.

She needed . . . time, she supposed. Just time.

"You're not dead, Martin," Mary had told her. But she had felt that way for months, maybe years: untouched by joy, by life in general. Going through the motions, phoning it in. She could already feel the magic of Paris working on her, but it took time to bring a person back from the dead.

As they strolled past a typical little Parisian corner bistro, Genevieve recognized a woman seated by herself at an outdoor table. Genevieve knew her from somewhere, but other than her neighbors, whom did she know in Paris?

The woman looked up, and her gray eyes met Genevieve's gaze.

Then it dawned on her: This was the shopkeeper from the *boulangerie*. The petite, pretty woman who made change without looking and moved like a dancer. A decidedly grumpy dancer.

Genevieve didn't think the woman would remember her, but as she and Killian walked by, the baker raised her chin a fraction of an inch in greeting.

"*Bonjour*," said Genevieve.

"*Bonjour*," the woman responded with a curt nod. She then said something too rapid for Genevieve to understand. Killian responded, and they had a brief exchange in French.

"I am Killian O'Mara," Killian said. "And this is Genevieve Martin."

"I am Sylviane Michel. *Enchantée*." She lifted her chin in Genevieve's direction. "Where you from?"

"The United States."

She rolled her eyes and made a *c'mon* rolling gesture with her hand. "Yes, I know this much. Where in the United States?"

"Calif—"

"*California?*" Sylviane cut her off, smiling and sitting up straighter. "Really? I love California!"

"You know it?"

"Please, sit down." She gestured to the seat opposite. "You have time for a *pastis*?"

"Um . . . sure," said Genevieve.

"Alas, I'm sorry to say I have to run," said Killian. "I have dinner plans, and I have to change into something dry. Genevieve, as always, a pleasure. Here's my number. Please let me know when you plan on going back to Philippe's so I can tag along and photograph the place. Unless you prefer to work alone?"

"No, that's fine. I'll let you know."

He gave Genevieve a double kiss good-bye, then spoke to Sylviane in French, excusing himself. Both women watched as he ambled down the boulevard.

Genevieve felt Sylviane's curious eyes on her.

"A *pastis*?" Genevieve took the seat across from her. The iron chairs were painted robin's-egg blue, spindly yet sturdy. In French, she ventured to ask: "*Qu'est-ce que c'est?*"

"You don't know *pastis*?"

Genevieve shook her head.

"No? But you must know this. You like absinthe?"

"I thought absinthe was illegal."

Sylviane made an impatient, dismissive gesture. "It was. But that was a long time ago, when it made people go crazy and . . . what is the word when you cannot see? When the eyes do not work?"

"Blind?"

"Yes, blind," she gestured with her pointer finger: *Exactly*. "Absinthe, before, it used to make people be this sometimes."

"But it doesn't anymore?"

"No, I don't think so." She shook her head, a little wrinkle of a frown between her eyebrows; then she stuck out her chin and shook her head again, with finality. "No, I'm sure it is no problem; that is why it is no illegal now. Is a shame, though, probably the ingredients were what helped all that creativity, what do you call? For the artists and musicians. But now it is safe."

She let out a deep sigh, as though lamenting the passage to safety.

"So . . . *pastis* is like absinthe?" Genevieve asked.

"Oh! Similar, but I like it better. You like . . . what do you call? Licorice? Smell." She lifted her glass to Genevieve.

It was a slim, tall glass, with one ice cube and a milky amber liquid. It smelled strongly of anise.

"I . . ."

Sylviane signaled to the waiter standing by the door. She gestured with her chin, holding up her glass in one hand and her pointer finger with the other.

"So, Genevieve, tell me: You are here for little visit? A vacation?"

"Not really. Actually, I'm hoping to take over my uncle's locksmith shop. The *serrurier* on rue Saint-Paul."

"Dave? Locksmith Dave is your uncle?"

She nodded. "*Was* my uncle—he passed away."

"Yes, yes, I know. I was so sorry; he was a wonderful man. He make us laugh!"

"He was always joking," Genevieve said with a nod and a smile. "I remember him taking me to your shop a long time ago, when I visited as a teenager."

"The Maréchalerie is the best *boulangerie*. Everyone, they know this."

"Do you like working there?"

"Like? What do you mean, *like* working there?"

"I just . . . you seem a little grumpy when I go into the shop in the mornings."

"What means 'grumpy'?"

"Um . . . unhappy. *Triste*."

She shrugged. "My *grandparents* work at the bakery; my *parents* work at the bakery; *I* work at the bakery. My whole life, I smell like bread." She held out one slim arm. "Smell! Smell me. Fresh bread, isn't it so?"

Genevieve stifled a smile and made a show of smelling her arm.

"Most people think that's a good thing," Genevieve said. "People love the smell of fresh bread."

Sylviane made a rude-sounding snort, sipped her *pastis*, and stretched back in her chair.

"You know, there aren't many women bakers in Paris," said Sylviane. "The men, they think the women can't do it, but my father, he has five sons: Jean-Luc, Jean-Baptiste, Jean-Marc, Jean-

Paul, Jean-Claude. But not one wants to be a baker. Not one!"

"You have five brothers named Jean?"

"*Comment*? *Non*, they are Jean-Luc, Jean-Baptiste, Jean-Marc . . . oh, I see what you are saying. Huh, never have I thought of this! Anyway, not one want to learn to be baker, so now it's me. Like you, I think. Or there are many women locksmiths in America?"

"I wasn't actually a locksmith in America. I was a copy editor."

"What is that?"

"I checked publications before they were printed."

"Like books?"

"Technical manuals, mostly."

"Sounds boring."

Genevieve just nodded.

"Anyway, this is why I am—what is the word you called me?" Sylviane asked.

"Grumpy."

"Grumpy, as you say. But you know what? I don't want to talk about bread—I want to talk about California! I love cinema. You like cinema? 'Movies,' you say in America?"

"Sure, I like movies."

"Rom-com, you know this?"

"Um . . ."

"I *love* American movies! Especially rom-com." She squinted, lifted her delicate chin and growled, "Go ahead, make my day."

"I'm not sure *Dirty Harry* qualifies as a romantic comedy," Genevieve said with a laugh.

"I like all American cinema, but mostly rom-com. *Harry Met Sally*—she had a—what do you call? When you have sex and you finish? She had it right there in the restaurant! *Quelle coquine!*" She leaned over the table and pounded it, letting out a great hearty laugh that seemed incongruous with her petite stature.

The waiter chose that moment to arrive at the table with a little brown tray holding a tall, slender glass, a bowl of ice, and a small pitcher. He set the glass on the table: It was one-third full of a clear, pale amber liquid. The waiter dropped a single square ice cube into the glass, then added a little water from the diminutive pitcher. As soon as the water hit the alcohol, the liquid started to cloud up, like a chemistry experiment.

"*Merci,*" Genevieve said, captivated by the theatrical presentation of the drink.

The waiter did not respond. Sylviane fixed him with a look of mild disdain, remaining silent until he left. As soon as he did, she leaned forward again.

" 'You complete me.' What does this mean?"

"It's supposed to mean that he didn't feel like a complete person until he met her—it's romantic, I guess."

"That's what I thought." She waved her hand, dismissing the idea. "But . . . I don't like that. Men and women don't need each other like that. You know Simone de Beauvoir? She does not wait for Jean-Paul Sartre. When he is an ass, she does her own thing; she takes many lovers. I like *Runaway Bride*; did you see this?"

Genevieve nodded, her mind reeling in the attempt to keep up with Sylviane's thought processes, careening from de Beauvoir to *Runaway Bride* in one breath. Thank heavens they were speaking in English.

"I like Julia Roberts. You remember the movie where she says Chagall paints pictures that look like the way love is supposed to feel? Like, floating. I think that is true, because Chagall was French, you see?" said Sylviane. "I like also when Julia Roberts is a—*comment dit-on?*—a *putain*?"

"A prostitute? You mean *Pretty Woman*."

"Yes! I think I might like to be prostitute in LA—what you think?"

Genevieve opened her mouth to reply but didn't know what to say. She wasn't sure whether Sylviane was joking.

"I would not be smelling like bread, you see?"

Genevieve smiled and sipped her *pastis*. It was strong and a bit cloying—almost overwhelmingly so. It filled her nostrils with the aroma of anise, coated her tongue. The smell reminded her of the fennel bushes on the farm; she had spent half her childhood yanking out those stubborn plants.

Mostly she liked the setup, so very *not*

American: the slender glass, the single square ice cube, the clear liquid gone cloudy, the tiny pitcher of water sitting at the side.

"Too strong?" Sylviane asked. "Put more water in if you want. That's why he leaves the pitcher."

"No, it's good."

She smiled and raised her chin. "We make a Parisienne of you, you see! So, tell me, Genevieve, you are living here now, truly? You are to be a *serruriere*, a locksmith like your uncle? Here in Paris? *Vraiment*?"

"Maybe. I'm not sure. I think I would like that. I don't yet have the right visa, though, or the certification."

"You know the . . . *Comment dit-on*? The secret to bureaucracy here in France? Never give up. Do not listen when they say *non*; just keep appearing until they get tired and give you your papers."

Genevieve laughed.

"I am not making joke," said Sylviane. "So you really want to stay here in Paris? Forever?"

"Maybe."

Sylviane studied her for a long moment; then her eyes flickered down to her ring finger.

"You are not married?"

Genevieve opened her mouth to say, *No, I'm not married,* but couldn't quite get the words out. She managed an awkward little squeak, an uttering between an "eh" and an "mmm," but that was about it.

"*Désolée.* Sorry." Sylviane waved a delicate hand in the air. Her nails were cut short, manicured, buffed. "Maybe you and me trade places, eh? You stay here—I go California. Tell me, you see the movie stars?"

"Not really. I saw Tom Hanks in passing once, but that's about it. I live in the northern part of the state, nowhere near LA."

She looked disappointed. Explaining to Europeans that Hollywood was only a small section of LA—and a much smaller portion of the whole state—was invariably a letdown to them.

"It's a really big state," Genevieve said. "I think almost as big as all of France."

Now skepticism filled Sylviane's gray eyes. "I don't think this is so. You exaggerate."

"Maybe. I'm not very good at geography. But I do know it takes about six hours to drive from my house to LA, and that's only about half the state."

Sylviane's eyes widened slightly; she ducked her head and stuck her lower lip out in a way that conceded Genevieve might have been telling the truth. "That *is* a far way, then."

Genevieve nodded and sipped her *pastis.* Now that the shock of the taste on her tongue had ceded to a luscious licorice glow, it was growing on her. She was starting to feel mellow, filled with a warm sense of well-being.

Sylviane was watching her carefully, smiling. "You like it, the *pastis*?"

"Yes, I do."

"Okay, good! But be careful—it is very strong. More than it seems. Make you dance all night, on the boats on the Seine. So, did you see this movie called *Addicted to Love*? It has a Frenchman in it—oh, he makes me laugh! He says Frenchman in America is like Superman; he can do no wrong. Is this true?"

"Um . . . I don't know about Superman, but it's true that a lot of people like the French accent."

"Like me? You think I would do well with my accent in America?"

Genevieve smiled. "I'm sure you would. They'd love you."

"Or *French Kiss*—you see that one? They film it right here in Paris! Jacques Brel on the . . . what do you call this? The music."

"The soundtrack. I love that movie."

"*Moi aussi*! Me, too! Hey! We have a night to look at movies sometime?"

"I would like that very much."

They exchanged numbers, and then Sylviane insisted on paying the bill.

"I have to go." She rolled her eyes. "Dinner with my family. You stay here, finish. No hurry. You keep the table all night if you want; this is how we do in Paris. No hurry. But we will be together soon, Genevieve Martin, *serruriere extraordinaire*!"

They did the double-kiss good-bye, and Genevieve breathed in Sylviane's fresh-bread perfume.

Genevieve remained at the table, people watching, finally feeling at home and relaxed in a Parisian restaurant. So much so, in fact, that she decided to take Sylviane's advice and linger, and even ordered a dinner of *moules frites*, mussels with fries.

And wine to go with it.

Chapter Twenty-nine

Once again, Genevieve was awakened by the sound of the shop buzzer. She really needed to make up a sign, hang it on the door. She was *not* open for business.

In fact, yesterday's mail had included an official notice: It was bright pink and consisted of many pages. She had worked on decoding it for almost an hour with her dictionary at hand but still wasn't certain what it meant. All she knew for sure was that it didn't say, *Welcome to Paris! We need all the locksmiths we can get!*

But license or no, Philippe was right: She couldn't leave her uncle's clients' projects half finished; no matter what happened, at the very least she needed to finish up with them. Uncle Dave would have wanted that.

Genevieve glanced at the calendar: This was the day Catharine was coming back to Paris. Could she be the one at the door? Wouldn't she come to the apartment door on the courtyard side? Or surely she kept a key to the place?

The buzzer rang again: loud and insistent. Genevieve finally surrendered, threw on yesterday's clothes, ran a comb through her hair, and went out to the shop. It was a woman named Anna, with a baby in a stroller. She spoke English well and explained that she was a neighbor, pointing to an apartment building down the street. She had known Dave; apparently he had spoken to everyone who would listen about his American niece.

"It's nice to meet you," said Genevieve after the long introduction. "But I'm not actually a locksmith, and the shop's not open for business. . . ."

"Please, I must get new keys made. You won't believe my list of things to do today—if you could do this I would appreciate it! I must find a dress; tonight my husband and I have a babysitter. This is rare."

The cutting machine sat on the counter, and there were plenty of blanks hanging on the twirling display. The machine was straightforward; Genevieve was pretty sure she remembered how to use it. The keys in the woman's hand looked like standard models, so if her uncle had the appropriate blanks, it would take her all of five minutes.

Anna took her whimpering baby out of the stroller and jostled him, bouncing foot to foot, side to side.

"*Bien sûr,*" Genevieve said finally, holding her hand out, palm up, for the keys. "*Pourquoi pas?*"

Of course, why not? She was already beginning to sound like Dave, Genevieve thought. He had always believed he was a popular installation in the neighborhood because Americans were well liked after the war, but Genevieve knew it was much more than that. After all, Americans had fallen out of favor many times over in the intervening decades. He was popular because he was a smiling, happy soul, glad (eager, even) to do favors for friends and neighbors and passersby. He had the kind of relationship with his neighbors (and his neighborhood) that Genevieve had never known; even when she was a child, on the farm, there was a palpable distance between the Martin family and their neighbors, most of whom were urban financiers who liked to think of the semirural locale as bucolic but who disliked the reality of animal smells and sounds and had urged the city council, more than once, to rezone the area to a livestock-free zone.

Genevieve offered the still-fretting child a set of keys to jangle. The young mother cast her a grateful smile. Anna's harried state made Genevieve wonder what it would be like to raise a baby in a city like Paris.

"You said you have a babysitter coming?" Genevieve said, making conversation as she picked out the appropriate blanks. These were new keys, with a common thickness and size.

"*Oui*, but it costs a fortune. My mother and father live in the countryside, near Bergerac. So I have no family here. This is why I must buy a dress, you see? I want the evening to be perfect. What do you call it, a date?"

"Yes. You're looking forward to an evening away from the baby, it sounds like."

"Mostly I am looking forward to a good dinner. And you know the Parisians: If you want to bring a dog to a nice restaurant, it is no problem, but a child? This is impossible."

"Is that true?"

"The *French*," Anna, the Frenchwoman, said with a roll of her eyes. "Impossible."

"I thought '*impossible*' *n'est pas français*," Genevieve said with a smile as she moved toward the cutting machine. "You might want to cover your ears; this will be loud."

But the baby seemed entranced by the loud whine of the saw. A few minutes later, Genevieve handed the new keys to Anna and explained that she couldn't take money for the job. The young mother offered some now-familiar advice as to how to deal with French bureaucracy.

The phone started ringing just as Genevieve was holding the door open for Anna and her baby, who was strapped back into the stroller. Genevieve locked the door of Under Lock and

Key behind her, waved, then hurried into the rear apartment to catch the call on the sixth ring.

"'ello?" She *still* didn't know how to answer the phone in France. *Put that on the list.*

"Genie."

Jason. Genevieve glanced up at the cuckoo clock, but of course its ornate hands were not showing the right time. Still, she knew there was a nine-hour time difference; he must be calling in the middle of the night.

"Hi," she managed.

"So, how's Paris?" His voice had a chatty, genial quality, with that barely there looseness she knew came after a few drinks. Jason was one of those guys who never appeared particularly drunk, just jovial. She had learned early to take the car keys before he started in on a third drink, even if he seemed perfectly sober.

"It's . . . good. Great. Beautiful, of course."

"Rainy?"

Like strangers on a train. Worse, actually. With a stranger, at least, a person wouldn't feel awkward exchanging small talk about the weather. With a stranger Genevieve wouldn't feel ice crusting over her heart. With a stranger she wouldn't feel this nausea in the pit of her stomach at the very sound of his voice.

"Yes," she answered. "But I found an umbrella in the closet."

There was a long pause.

Yes, but I found an umbrella in the closet. Genevieve cringed at the inanity of her own words. On the other side of the telephone line, probably stretched out in their bedroom, was the man she had held (how many nights?) in that big brass bed with the goose-down comforter. The man with whom she had exchanged vows at an informal ceremony at the farm: the barn strewn with garlands of flowers and a huge banquet table set up on the lawn; Nick had dressed up the goats with flower-and-laurel leis that they immediately ate off of one another, to everyone's amusement. On the other end of the telephone line was the man who had mourned with her when her father died . . . *but,* she reminded herself, feeling the ice hardening her heart, he was already with Quiana by then.

One of the cruelest cuts of infidelity was the shadow of doubt it cast backward, onto everything that came before. Was it all a lie? The time she and Jason had stubbornly packed a picnic and gone to the beach despite the chilly forecast, then huddled over a fire because neither would admit how cold they were, then wound up laughing and making love on the deserted stretch of sand? When they were painting the bedroom a butter yellow and Jason dabbed Genevieve's nose with paint and said he hoped it brought a sunny glow into each and every one of her days? When she leaned on his shoulder and cried for her father, told Jason about the silent, stoic man Jim was, how his lack of demonstrativeness sometimes drove her crazy and yet that he was a good father, one who never left her in doubt of his love . . . when she was telling Jason all of that, spilling her heart, opening her soul . . . was he thinking of another woman's lips? Of her smell, the sounds she made when he was inside her, the feeling of her moving beneath him?

"So, the flight was all right?" Jason continued.

"Yes, it was fine, thanks. Everything's fine. What's up?"

"I was just checking in. You said you would e-mail me when you got settled."

"I don't have Internet set up yet. And no cell phone, either, so I'm a little cut off."

Another pause. Genevieve knew he was thinking, *"She* wants *to be cut off."* And he was right, she realized with something akin to surprise. She certainly hadn't been rushing to get connected. Obviously this couldn't go on forever; she had bills to pay online and people to contact. This was the modern world; as tempting as it was, she couldn't hide in her medieval-era Parisian village forever.

She cleared her throat. "As a matter of fact, one of the neighbors has offered to help me get Internet set up, so I should be online soon."

"Oh good. That's great. I've tried calling this number before, but it just rang and rang; there was no voice mail."

"Things are a little different here—it's kind of like the 1950s. Only better dressed and beset by ennui."

He chuckled. Genevieve always could make him laugh.

"In the meantime," she continued, "this is the best way to reach me. And you have the street address, right?"

"Are you suggesting I write you a letter on paper?"

"I know, shocking, right? But you know me, I'm an old-fashioned sort."

"All right, I . . . I just wanted to make sure you were okay."

Genevieve took a moment, trying to force down the lump in her throat. She didn't want him to hear it in her voice. *Remember the humiliation,* she thought, blowing a breath out of taut lips, trying to maintain her resolve. She wasn't herself with Jason; didn't know who she was, really, but she knew they hadn't been good together, even before Quiana sauntered onto the scene. Skinny, blond Quiana.

"I'm fine, Jason, thanks. How are you doing?"

"I'm . . . well, it's been rough. I don't want you to think this is easy for me. I know I screwed up, big-time." She could just see him, ducking his head in an adorably vulnerable, *aw shucks, ma'am, didn't mean to trample your rosebush* kind of way. She heard the tinkle of ice in a glass:

probably a scotch kind of night, single malt of course, aged eighteen years, "old enough to vote."

"Okay, well, I really have to go. Thanks for calling. Sleep well," Genevieve said in a rush, needing to get off the phone.

"G'night, Genie."

Genevieve needed a watch.

The last one she remembered owning had Tinker Bell on it, from a family trip to Disneyland when she was eight. Despite the fact that Genevieve enjoyed the *idea* of old-fashioned watches, the reality was that she had become accustomed to checking her cell phone for the time. But though she had brought the phone with her in case of emergency, the international rates were exorbitant, so she had simply left it turned off.

Part of her—out of touch, on vacation, no schedule—appreciated the novel sensation of rarely knowing exactly what the hour was, and it was good for her to practice her French by asking strangers for the time. But still.

Catharine kept telling her to take whatever she wanted, to use whatever she needed. So Genevieve went into Dave and Pasquale's bedroom and pulled open the top drawer of her uncle's highboy. In the jumble of loose change, miscellaneous receipts, yellowing letters, old combs, military medals, jewelry-sized boxes: There it was, the watch she remembered him wearing: big face and hands, aged brown leather strap.

An old man's watch. Far too large for her arm. Nonetheless she strapped it on. Even after she'd pulled the strap as tight as she could, it still spun around on her wrist. She loved it. It reminded her of Uncle Dave.

Genevieve was about to shut the drawer when she noticed the handwriting and return address on one of the letters: *Angela Mackenzie Martin, 2510 Apple Tree Lane, Petaluma, CA. USA.*

It was written on the crinkly, tissue-thin blue paper that people used to use for airmail. Genevieve took it out, turned it over in her hands. The postal stamp was smudged, making the date illegible.

Now she *really* felt like she was snooping. Reading someone's mail was a step too far, wasn't it? On the other hand, both parties were deceased. It wasn't as if either of them would care.

Slowly, carefully—as though it might bite—she opened it.

Inside the envelope was a single piece of stationery. It made a crackling sound as she unfolded it. Three olive leaves fell onto the top of the bureau; probably from the small orchard of trees they had out behind the turkey shed. Angela always liked to send dried flowers or leaves in her letters.

Blue ink, her mother's handwriting. Only two words:

I'm sorry.

As Genevieve was making herself a cup of bad coffee (she would have to try the place Killian had showed her yesterday), she flung open the window. The air was cold but fresh. The rain-washed stones of the courtyard glimmered in the morning sun; geraniums bloomed pink and red, trailing from tiny balconies and window boxes. There were a few small tables and chairs where neighbors liked to take their morning coffee, and an old white bike—complete with flower-filled basket—leaned against a stone wall. Big painted Italian pots held fragrant herbs and small topiary manicured in the shapes of spirals and balls.

What had gone on between Angela and Dave? Was this why they hadn't visited, all those years? What could have been so serious to have caused such a break?

Her heart hurt for them both.

What could—

A tapping at the window. She looked up to see her neighbors Daniel and Marie-Claude.

After a round of *bonjours*, they invited her to join them for espresso.

"Oh, thank you, but I have to run—I am going to visit Notre-Dame this morning, and then I'm going to have lunch with my *cousine* Catharine."

"Please give them our love," said Daniel. "To Catharine and Pasquale."

"I will."

"Catharine never comes back here," said Marie-Claude with a sad shake of her head.

"Never?" Genevieve asked.

"Too many memories, I think."

They all fell silent for a moment.

"Maybe, when a little time has passed, it will get easier." Even as she said the words, Genevieve felt as though they were trite, a platitude. Still, trite was often true. *"Time heals all wounds,"* her mother used to say. *Healed, perhaps,* Genevieve remembered thinking, looking at her mother's arm, *yet not without leaving scars.*

"Perhaps I could join you tomorrow morning," Genevieve suggested. "Or I'd love to at least come by and look through your store. I remember my uncle used to get old locks from some of his neighbors. . . ."

"*Oui, bien sûr,*" said Daniel. "I put them aside, always for him. Always he is working on his book. You are looking to complete his book, I think?"

"I . . . I didn't . . ."

Marie-Claude clucked and said to Daniel in a chastising tone: "It is not because she asks about locks that she is going to finish his book."

"Ah. Sorry," said Daniel. "*Quel dommage*—it is only that it is a shame he did not finish."

"Maybe . . . perhaps I will."

Chapter Thirty

1997

Of all the tourist meccas in Paris, the only one Genevieve specifically asked to go see was the top of Notre-Dame. Home to the famous gargoyles.

Her aunt and uncle were not up for climbing the steps, and Catharine (already put out that her parents insisted she accompany them on their "family outing") just laughed and said she would visit the gargoyles in her dreams.

They waited with Genevieve in the long line, though: Catharine perched on a balustrade on one side of the cathedral, reading her book the whole time, sighing when she had to get up and move as the tourists shuffled forward, one group of twenty at a time.

Uncle Dave made the most of the long wait by browsing the tourist traps that lined the street. He kept insisting Pasquale and Genevieve check out the treasures he found, bringing one after another over to the line for them to look at, sometimes with a shopkeeper yelling at him to *either buy it or bring it back*: tiny hand-crank music boxes that played tinny renditions of "Frère Jacques"; aprons covered with the famous *chat noir*—black cat—of Paris; silly snow globes featuring the Eiffel Tower.

When finally they reached the head of the line, Uncle Dave looked apprehensive about letting Genevieve go by herself. At the last minute he offered to go with her, but Pasquale pooh-poohed the idea, saying he would collapse before he was halfway up.

"I'll be okay," Genevieve had said. "I'm not a baby."

"I know *you* aren't," he said with a wink. "But *I* am. I'll wave at you!"

"You won't be able to see me, all the way up there."

"I'll wave anyway, just in case. Look for me!"

The circular stone stairs wound up, up, up the tower, narrow and steep. Genevieve climbed, keeping a steady tempo, following on the heels of the man in cargo shorts in front of her. There were so many people right behind that she prayed she wouldn't stumble, for if she did, she would knock over everyone below her like dominoes, all of them falling and thumping their way down the steep stone steps and spilling back out the side doors of the church.

She could see the headlines: GENEVIEVE MARTIN CAUSES TOURIST CATASTROPHE!

There were grooves worn in the center of the stones, the rock worn away fraction of an inch by infinitesimal fraction of an inch over the centuries. She imagined brown-robed monks and black-robed priests, and perhaps a hunchback or two in rags, climbing the never-ending stairs to the tower to ring the bell.

When she finally emerged at a platform, Genevieve was disappointed to find they were not at the level of the gargoyles yet, but instead at a visitors' center. Yet another place to buy souvenirs, as well as the ticket for the rooftop visit. Some of the sightseers, incredibly, decided not to ascend any farther, already defeated by the rigors of the steps.

But Genevieve figured she had come this far, why stop now?

Up farther, so many steps, round and round and round. Until emerging, finally, at a platform partway up the church façade. The gargoyles' lair.

The view of Paris below was stunning, of course: the Eiffel Tower; the star of streets radiating from the Arc de Triomphe; the Seine flowing around narrow islands as it snaked its way through the city; the faraway dove-white dome of the Sacré-Coeur perched atop the butte of Montmartre.

But it was the gargoyles that held everyone's attention and elicited oohs and aahs. And Victor Hugo's ghosts were alive and well up here in the tower: the hunchback condemned to forever toll his bell, the beautiful gypsy to whom he lost his heart.

Genevieve knew the real story. She and her

mother had seen Disney's cleaned-up version (they called it Quasimodo-lite) last year, even though Genevieve was too old for cartoon movies, because Angela really wanted to go and talked her daughter into it. They had shared a bucket of buttery popcorn and hooted at Frollo, then applauded when he met his well-deserved end.

But in Hugo's original tale, Esmeralda sure didn't live happily ever after. In fact, when the beautiful, free-spirited Esmeralda was forced to choose between the noose and the man (the real monster, Frollo), she had chosen death. And then the ever-loyal hunchback had lain down beside her body and died of starvation. Later, when someone tried to separate their skeletons, his bones turned to dust.

Love was destined to destroy you, was Victor Hugo's basic message, as far as Genevieve could tell. A couple of years ago Genevieve had wanted to believe in love. But now . . . now that her mother's abandonment had nearly killed her, she understood. Hugo got it right. Love was out to get you. To destroy you.

"Are you going to let that little lock defeat you? Love defeats every lock, Genevieve; trust your old uncle."

She knew Dave believed it when he said things like that, and she wanted him to be right. But she wasn't sure.

Genevieve looked down to the courtyard in front of the cathedral. It was a dizzying height, and the plaza was full of groups of tourists, but finally she spotted Dave and Pasquale. Dave was looking up, waving both hands. She couldn't see the expression on his face, but she imagined he was smiling, calling out to her.

He probably couldn't see her but simply hoped she could see him. The off chance that she could, she imagined, was enough for him to make a fool of himself. Gladly. He was like that.

The gargoyles were worth the climb: Some seemed so real they could easily have been demons turned to stone. One appeared to be biting the head off of some much smaller creature—a tiny man?—clutched in his claws. Another was contemplative, his monkeylike face resting in the palms of his oversized hands, as he observed his domain. Others stuck out their tongues, bared their teeth, made faces. Their expressions were so elastic and whimsical it was hard to believe they were carved of stone.

Yet another, apparently made from stone of a different quarry, had not withstood the weather: the face was half gone, the carving sloughing off over centuries' worth of pelting rain and hail. These melted sculptures seemed more sinister, somehow, than the well-preserved ones, as if they were spirits emerging from their stone cocoons.

Genevieve suddenly remembered the scars on

her mother's arm, the injury she had never explained to Genevieve. The slick, melted-looking surface. After her mother's death, Genevieve asked her father about it.

He'd said, *"Paris,"* and that was all.

Chapter Thirty-one

Genevieve started up the steps of Notre-Dame, hitching her backpack higher on her shoulder and remembering the last time she'd been here, as a teenager, how she had prayed she wouldn't trip.

The backpack was heavy with the presents for Catharine: *Star Trek* paraphernalia and a little taste of the South. After long consideration, Genevieve had decided to bring what she had to her cousin and perhaps buy her something else while she was in Paris.

She wished she didn't feel so awkward around her cousin. Catharine wasn't a bad person; she was just off-putting. Or so Genevieve had always felt. And Catharine's insistence on Genevieve's divulging her dreams wore on her. It seemed to her that certain things should remain private. How was it that Catharine was so annoying when her parents were so lovely, so warm and welcoming?

But then, Genevieve wasn't much like either of her parents, was she? She had aspects of each, she imagined, but she certainly wasn't her father. As for her mother . . . that was harder to know.

Had her mother climbed these steps? She must have. There was that photo of her and Dave here with the iconic gargoyle, the monkey-faced one with wings looking out to the city below. The tour was so orchestrated that every visitor stepped the same way, so their feet would be falling on the same spots.

Did each person leave a minuscule trace? Was there some sort of historical butterfly effect? Did the footfall of one's mother (or one's fourteen-year-old self) leave something behind: the tiniest imprint, the tiniest groove in the stone?

Her mother had come to Paris and had her picture taken in a cabaret, sitting beside a handsome man. Why had Genevieve never known this? Why were there pictures in the farmhouse of Dave in Paris, photos of Angela and Jim on their honeymoon, but only the single one of Angela's later trip?

Or perhaps there were dozens more tucked away in photo albums or shoe boxes. Nicholas had dealt with their parents' things after their dad passed away. He had asked Genevieve if she wanted anything and she begged him not to throw anything away until she had a chance to go through it; but of course she had never made the time, or the mental space, to do so. Had he kept the items in boxes that he tripped over, swearing at her each time? Or tucked in the closet of the spare room, or out in the barn where the insects and vermin would eventually eat through the cardboard and ruin everything so he could feel justified in throwing out the leftover effluvia of not one but two lives?

Like everyone else huddled out on the parapet, Genevieve wished she were alone. But the other tourists jostled and pushed around her. A trio of children spotted ice cream for sale in the courtyard so far below and started to whine about the heat (though the day was chilly and overcast) in a play for a cone upon descent. Two teenage boys spotted friends waiting for them sitting on benches in the courtyard and yelled down, repeatedly, apparently convinced that if they only bellowed loud enough the girls would hear and (Genevieve presumed) be impressed.

But most took photos. So many photos and videos that Genevieve wondered if they were actually seeing anything in the here and now, or whether they would return to their homes in the suburbs of Columbus and Nagasaki and Berlin and look at the photographic evidence of their visit, and say: "Hey! Would you look at that! There was a gargoyle eating the head off a little man. Honey, do you remember a gargoyle eating the head off a little man?"

The walkways were covered in a heavy wire mesh. It made her feel like a bird caged high above the city, crowded into this jail with a flock of foreign fowl. She hadn't remembered that from the last time she was here. Clearly someone—or many someones—over the years had attempted to climb over the stone balustrades in order to obliterate themselves, or to grab an *awesome* photo opportunity, or to prove he or she wasn't afraid.

Or perhaps the mesh was put up to keep tourists from petting the gargoyles, some of whom appeared to invite such ignominious treatment.

To the rear was the steeply pitched roofline of the cathedral below. This roof was unseen from any other vantage point, but nonetheless it was decorated with a line of statues along the eaves. All men: popes or bishops or saints, Genevieve supposed. Realistic (idealized) men, each of which was probably the work of a master crafts-man. Still, it was no surprise that everyone came to see the horrifying gargoyles, rather than the martyred saints.

Why would the church higher-ups commission such fearsome sculptures from artisans through the years? And for that matter, why were there a host of them guarding the roof of the greatest cathedral in Paris? This had never occurred to her, but now Genevieve was burning with curiosity. Why would they build a magnificent Christian sanctuary, then top it with demons?

A docent urged the pack of visitors to move

along ("others are waiting in line for their turn") and showed them the access to the bell tower. Only a few climbed these stairs. They were wooden and clearly redone recently, and featured a jarringly modern sign with no words, but a picture of a stick figure falling on its head: *faites attention*, be careful.

And then they were invited to climb farther up, to the very top of the spire. There were no gargoyles here, but an amazing view of the city of Paris, laid out before them like a 3-D map.

Winds buffeted Genevieve, whipping her hair around her, Medusa-like. She enjoyed the feeling of it, even while realizing she would need to find a restroom to put it right. No self-respecting Parisian would ever walk around town with wild snakes for hair. But for the moment she reveled in the sensation: it made her feel base, primordial. Part of the elements.

A visual struck her: What if she were to turn to stone right here and now, hair forever wild, a stricken, slack look upon her face, hands made into claws that clutched the balustrade?

What would Catharine make of that? she wondered with a laugh.

One of the ice-cream whiners eyed Genevieve with concern, and she realized she must have looked like a crazy lady with her hair whipping about her, standing alone, laughing aloud. The thought made her laugh some more.

Next time Catharine asked about her dreams, Genevieve would tell her this: She stood at the very top of Notre-Dame, winds pummeling her, and she was turned to stone, condemned to use her demonic powers forever to guard the church.

Or could she be guarding the tower from the line of saints and martyrs below?

Chapter Thirty-two

Angela, 1983

Angela introduces Xabi as a friend, nothing more. Dave does not believe her; the suspicion and worry are clear in his blue eyes. But Angela wants them to meet him, to know who he is.

Part of her expects them to fall in love with him, just as she has.

She enlists Pasquale's help. Pasquale does not approve, either, but she is French; she has seen a great deal. She has a more complicated perspective on love and loyalty than does Dave.

"Let's have one night together," Angela begs. "Just one night. We'll go out and hear music, dance, enjoy. I've always wanted to do that with you. Please, just this one night."

When Angela had come to Paris with Jim for their honeymoon, Dave had suggested just this: that they all go out and enjoy the Parisian

293

nightlife. But Jim was not one for dancing and music; clubs were too loud, too expensive, too frivolous. He loved strolling the museums and gardens during the day, but he would have been happy to be in bed by ten every night.

Pasquale intervenes. So Dave says yes.

They all meet at Philippe and Delphine's house for *apero*. Philippe and Xabi get on well, and Philippe takes him down to the cellar to pick out a bottle of wine. They are down there so long Angela goes down after them.

She finds them in a storage room, looking through an ornate grate in the floor.

"What is that?" she asks.

Philippe laughs. "A route to *les souterrains*; we used it during the war. Can you believe it?"

Xabi stands back, watching her, saying nothing as she gets on her hands and knees to look at the little trapdoor beyond the grate.

"This is a route to the underground?" she asks.

"*Mais, bien sûr.* Of course. During the war, this saved many lives. Because of this, you see, I could hide the people and if the soldiers search the house, they can escape."

"But . . . you keep it locked, right? So someone won't find it from the tunnels, and come into your house this way?"

"Who would do such a thing?" asks Philippe. "I can't imagine who, or why. It is not like in the war, when we needed such secret routes."

Angela glances up at Xabi. His eyes, intense as always, are on her. Studying, assessing.

"I think you should lock it," Angela says. "Just in case."

"Okay, no problem," says Philippe as he replaces the grate, stands, and rubs his hands together to wipe off the dust. "But enough of this! Now is the time for *apero* and music and good friends! Take it from an old man, both of you," he says, looping his arms through theirs and escorting them out of the room: "Evenings like this—with good wine, good music, good friends—they are what life is all about."

Chapter Thirty-three

The Métro was easy and fast. But Genevieve decided next time she would ask Catharine how to travel by bus, so she could see the sights. It was befuddling to pop up from the underground, almost like a groundhog emerging from its dark lair.

Paris was huge and, with the exception of Montmartre, mostly flat. If you couldn't see the Seine or the Eiffel Tower, it was difficult to orient yourself. In Oakland, Genevieve always knew her basic compass points: the hills to the east, the ocean to the west. But in Paris? Which way was which?

Here at the base of Montmartre, the neighborhood was more working-class, less full of tourist attractions than the Marais, which surrounded the Village Saint-Paul. Farther up, topped by the glistening white basilica of the Sacré-Coeur, was the famous hill of artists; Montmartre was where Picasso, van Gogh, Renoir, and so many others had lived (cheap, back in the day) and painted and fomented the artistic revolution of Impressionism, which would challenge the entrenched dominance of the European art elite. Genevieve remembered tiny winding cobblestone streets full of shops and cafés and, mostly, artists with their portable easels: selling portraits and landscapes and cityscapes of all kinds.

Her cousin Catharine's place was nowhere so interesting: she lived on a nondescript street in a nondescript 1950s building, a few blocks from the base of the butte. The shops were not fancy—corner grocers and tobacco shops—and several signs were written in Arabic as well as French.

Genevieve translated the little plaque beside Catharine's doorbell: JUNGIAN-INSPIRED DREAM INTERPRETATION AND COUNSELING.

Catharine answered the bell within seconds, buzzing Genevieve in. Genevieve stepped into the apartment house foyer and spotted her cousin standing in an open doorway down the hall.

Catharine was plumper than the average Frenchwoman, and today she wore a cream cardigan with a pastel spray of embroidered flowers on one shoulder, over a boxy blue T-shirt, along with a dark skirt and sensible walking shoes. Genevieve wasn't exactly a fashion plate herself, but such lack of panache was striking in a woman born and raised in Paris. Here, even working-class house-wives had a certain je ne sais quoi. Catharine, on the contrary, seemed almost American in her lack of élan.

But in one way she was a true Parisienne: She smoked like a chimney.

After hellos and a tobacco-scented double-kiss greeting, Catharine invited Genevieve to step inside. "You see, this is where I do my work."

The front room was set up with a large sand table in the middle. Built-in shelves at the back held hundreds of little figurines: people and animals and mythical creatures of all sorts. And objects: tiny bags of money and little houses and diminu-tive bathtubs.

"I think you didn't believe I would make a living from my vocation. No one did. But here I am—the sand table is very illustrative. It reveals many things. I have many clients."

"I'm glad for you, Catharine. This is great."

"Please, have a seat." Two comfortable arm-chairs sat on an angle around a small round coffee table. "And if you are moved to play with the sand table, well, that is what it is there for. I will interpret for you."

"Thanks," Genevieve said as she took a seat. "Maybe later."

"How are things in the *village?* How do you get on?"

"Things are great. The neighbors send their regards. They miss you."

Catharine didn't respond. She took a long draw on her cigarette, then got up and opened the window. Genevieve took a deep breath, thankful for the fresh air.

"Oh! I brought you something from America. Not much—you probably don't even care about *Star Trek* anymore . . ."

Her cousin sat up, intrigued, as Genevieve pulled the bundles out of her backpack. Catharine opened the plain brown packages to reveal a stack of comic books and laughed her husky laugh.

"*Mais, c'est magnifique!* I love them, thank you! It is, what do you call . . . a 'guilty pleasure,' right?"

"Exactly," said Genevieve with a smile.

"I know people think it is silly, but to me the *Star Trek* always promoted peace and harmony, mutual understanding. There is nothing wrong with this, is there?"

"Not at all."

"My father always told me that these were the beliefs of the United States. Of his home. Perhaps less so when the later problems happened, with Vietnam and all of that. Still, he never stopped

298

missing it, you know. So the gifts of barbecue sauce and corn bread, perfect! Always he talked about moving back to his country, but this was impossible."

"But . . . I thought he stayed because he loved Paris so much."

"Oh, he did love Paris," she said with a nod. "He did, but you know my father; I think he would love anyplace. He loved life, so he loved wherever he was. You should have heard his dreams! So optimistic. But he never stopped missing America, and Miss-iss-ipp-i."

The word Mississippi tripped clumsily on her tongue. Even among French speakers fluent in English, the Native American names were difficult: Oklahoma and Minnesota and Mississippi.

"Then why didn't they move back?"

"My father was afraid everyone would see my mother as a . . . how do you say? A . . . well, my father always said 'the n-word.' He said you weren't allowed to say it."

"The . . . 'n-word'?"

"You Americans," Catharine said, a cloud of smoke muting her words. "How do you react so strongly to a mere word? It is a word, not a bomb."

"It harkens back to a traumatic, disgraceful time."

"We've known our fair share of those here in France, too. You don't see us banning the word 'Nazi.'"

"Nazis were the perpetrators, not the victims."

" 'Dirty Jew,' then."

That one made Genevieve wildly uncomfortable as well. Like so many students, Genevieve had read *The Diary of Anne Frank* in middle school. Genevieve remembered, at the time, studying her classmate, Marvin Zimmerman. He was the only Jewish person she knew well, and she had wondered: If the Nazis marched into the classroom right then and there, and they all kept their big traps shut—even Richie Aguilar, who didn't like Marvin because he beat him in the long jump—how would anyone be able to see it in him? And if he managed to blend in, who would have been the first to break, to betray him? Probably Richie. He was a real weasel.

On Genevieve's long walks through Paris she had seen numerous brass plaques. They weren't all street signs or homes of literary figures. Some of them were remembrances from the war: FORTY SOULS TAKEN FROM THIS CORNER, 9 MAY 1943, WITH THE COOPERATION OF THE VICHY GOVERNMENT. A sign over an elementary school entrance read: 11000 ENFANTS FURENT DÉPORTÉS DE FRANCE DE 1942 À 1944 ET ASSASSINÉS À AUSCHWITZ PARCE QU'ILS ÉTAIENT NÉS JUIFS. NE LES OUBLIONS JAMAIS. Which meant: *11000 children were deported from France from 1942 to 1944 and killed at Auschwitz because they were born Jews. We will never forget them.*

Genevieve found it stunning that the French were willing to make this history public, to keep it alive. She tried to imagine similar plaques in the United States: *Here the U.S. Cavalry massacred forty-seven souls, children among them, because they inhabited ancestral land rich with mineral deposits.* Or, *Here, sixty-two humans were sold as slaves in a disgraceful combination of commerce and inhumanity, their only crime having been born African.* Would a person be able to walk a single mile without seeing every tree, every block, studded with such declarations?

"I am thinking the fear of this word is related to your guarantee of happiness, but I am not certain how," Catharine said, bringing Genevieve back to the conversation at hand.

"Sorry?"

"You have a constitutional guarantee to happiness, right? That's . . . what is the word? Incredible. This is it. *C'est incroyable.* I've never heard of such a thing; one cannot guarantee happiness."

"Incredible or not, how is that related to the use of such a hurtful word?"

She shrugged, smoked. "As I said, I have not quite figured this. It is just a hunch."

"And just FYI, it's a guarantee of the *pursuit* of happiness, not happiness per se."

301

"Ah. This is interesting."

"You French are pretty funny, too. A chain-smoking psychic?"

"I am not a psychic. I'm a dream interpreter. More a therapist than a psychic."

"That makes the chain-smoking even worse."

Catharine just laughed and waved off her cousin's concerns with an angular hand.

"Okay . . . so back to what you were saying," Genevieve said. "Why did your father fear your mother would be called a . . ."

"Go on. You should practice."

"No, thank you. I think we're going to leave this one filed under cultural differences."

"*Un 'nègre,' en français.* Is that better? You'd rather speak in French?"

"No, my French is still lacking, I'm sorry to say. I'm afraid I might miss something. But why was he afraid of that?"

"Truly, you are asking me this? Because she is. As am I."

"You are . . . ?"

"Black. *Noir. Nègre.* Whatever you want to call it most delicately. My grandmother is Algerian; didn't you know this?"

"I thought . . . I only heard about her father, the artist."

"My mother's father was French, but her mother was Algerian. She was raised here with her family, but she is from Algérie."

Genevieve studied her cousin, the deep olive-tone complexion, the ample mouth. In her mother Pasquale's features it was even more pronounced, now that she was looking for it.

"Here it is not the same thing, I think," Catharine continued. "We have a different relationship to this race issue. My father always tells me, 'In America, if you are a little bit of something others consider 'other,' you are that thing. This is why Josephine Baker comes here to France, so she can be something other than just . . . *une nègre* all the time. She wants to be known as a person and an entertainer, not just by the color of her skin."

"I always thought Dave fell in love with a Parisienne—your mother—and wanted to stay and help with the restoration efforts after the war."

She nodded. "I believe this was the story he shared with his American family. And it is not untrue. But, Genevieve, why do you look so down? It was not to hurt anyone, this story. Don't you know we all tell stories, and those stories are never finished until we leave this earth. Now that he has passed, my father's story ends like this: an American in Paris to the end of his days. Tell me your dreams, Genevieve, *ma petite cousine*, and we will help tell your story."

"I think for now I'll settle for lunch. I'm starved."

Chapter Thirty-four

"Would you like to take the funicular or walk?" asked Catharine as she and Genevieve approached the hill. "There are many steps up the butte of Montmartre, but sometimes the line for the funicular gets long."

"Let's walk. It'll be good for us; we can work off our lunch. A preemptive strike."

It was slow going. There were hundreds of steps, and Catharine paused frequently to cough and catch her breath, and once to light up a cigarette. Genevieve bit her tongue to keep from remarking upon the connection between cigarettes and lung capacity; she had to fight against the self-righteousness of the native Californian non-smoker.

Along the way the steps were lined with souvenir shops and, surprisingly, fabric stores. When Genevieve asked about them, Catharine explained, "This has always been this way. The zone had the textile factories, and so there have always been fabric stores here."

They were increasingly jostled by tourists the higher up the hill they went. Street performers dotted the sidewalks, with circles of spectators around them. The neighborhood was even more crowded than the Marais or near Notre-Dame, but then the streets were smaller here, akin to those in the Village Saint-Paul.

"The artists must have the license to put their stands here," Catharine said. "And there are many rules: They cannot force anyone to pay for a portrait—if they make your portrait but you don't like it, you don't have to buy it. Also, the artists must always keep an original piece of art on their easel." She lowers her voice. "I think sometimes they get line drawings from China, and then just fill in the colors. But then, I am a cynic."

"Seriously? Paint by number?"

She laughed and shrugged. "They are hooligans, *n'est-ce pas*? They are artists. They cannot be expected to follow the rules. In the summer many of them go on vacation, and the *restos* put out more tables and chairs. It is a pity because that is when most of the tourists are here, too. Ironic."

"*Resto*?"

"Short for 'restaurant.' Speaking of which, we will eat here, down this alley, as the food is much better off the tourist track."

A mere two blocks over, the crooked cobble-stoned street was empty. Here there were homes and small businesses and several more fabric stores.

Catharine stopped and stubbed out her cigarette before gesturing toward a place that looked like a deli, with a counter in front for ordering sandwiches *à emporter*, to go. But then she led the way through a brick arch that opened onto a charming back room. Windowless, it had low brick groin vaults and yellow stone walls. The limited menu was written in chalk on huge magnum wine bottles set on each table.

Three couples were seated at a table in one corner, raising their wineglasses in a toast. It put Genevieve in mind, again, of the photo she had seen at Philippe's house. Angela looked young (so very young) and vibrant in that picture. Happy. With a man other than Jim by her side. Not for the first time, Genevieve reminded herself that a man sitting next to her mother in the picture didn't, in itself, mean a thing. Especially in Paris, where the men were flirts and it was de rigueur to mingle and seduce. It was second nature to Parisians. Perhaps not to Catharine, she thought, looking across the table at her cousin, but to most Parisians.

"Do you know anything in particular your mother would tell my mother to be truthful about?" Genevieve asked after they placed their lunch orders.

"How do you mean?"

"When I saw your mother the other day, she thought I was my mother, Angela. And she was urging me to tell my father something."

"I wouldn't worry about it. My mother persists in a dream state now. Ironic, really, since she never wanted to tell me her dreams, and now that is virtually all she does."

306

"Yes, I understand. But . . . I don't know. I wish I knew my mother better. Can you tell me anything about her, about when she came to visit?"

"I was just a girl. I don't remember that much about her. I know there was a falling-out, but that was all."

"A falling-out? With your parents?"

"With my father."

"What kind of falling-out?"

She shrugged. "It was . . . I don't know. It had to do with her injury."

"Her arm."

Catharine nodded.

"What happened?"

"I was not permitted to know what happened. A lot of whispers. There are secrets, and then there are not." She left off with yet another shrug, digging into her *salade composée*.

"So you don't have any idea what the falling-out was over, or what happened to her arm?"

Catharine shrugged, ate, and remained silent.

Leave it to Catharine to start talking in circles just when things start getting interesting. Genevieve felt a surge of unreasonable irritation, and on its heels envy, that Catharine had known her mother back then, had shared a room with Angela and yet refused to tell Genevieve in detail about every nuance, every shared story or confidence or bobby pin. What Genevieve wouldn't give to go back in time, to have been a fly on that wall.

She turned back to her own delectable meal of *entrecôte aux cèpes*—steak with mushrooms—and tamped down the ridiculous impulse to throttle her cousin.

They traded a few remarks about Catharine's extended family in Paris and her godmother's place in Provence, and then Genevieve told Catharine about Nick and his wife. Finally, Catharine brought up her eternal question:

"So, are you going to tell me your dreams?"

Genevieve considered making something up, perhaps the fanciful scene still in her head from earlier atop Notre-Dame. But instead, she told her cousin the truth.

"The only one I remember that's interesting is me trying to open a locked door and being unsuccessful. But then . . . when I finally get close to opening it, I feel afraid, like maybe I shouldn't open it."

"You are afraid to see what is behind the door?" Catharine's intense gaze drilled into Genevieve, making her feel uncomfortable, embarrassed.

"I should have gone with the gargoyle thing."

"Excuse me?"

"Nothing. Sorry."

"So you are afraid of your own curiosity."

"Well, you know what they say . . . curiosity killed the cat."

"But 'satisfaction brought it back.'"

"Is that really the next line?"

Catharine merely raised one eyebrow at her, as though to say *You see? I do have some knowledge.* The waiter came to whisk away their plates. They both ordered espresso.

"What I find interesting is that you should have such a . . . *prosaic* dream."

"Probably I'm worried about failing in my new endeavor here in Paris. Not very exciting."

"But this was also my father's profession, do not forget. And he came into your life at a very important time. So perhaps you think he is hiding something from you?"

"In the dream he's urging me on, encouraging me to open the door."

"Ah! This is interesting. But you do know that in your dreams, you play every role, do you not?" Catharine was getting fidgety, playing with the leftover silverware. She looked around the restaurant, as though searching for something. "I can't *believe* there is no more smoking in Parisian cafés. We are in Paris, are we not? This is hardly civilized."

"Do you want to step outside?"

"No, no, I will survive. So, when I was thinking about you, I always think of Jean-Paul Sartre."

"We look alike?"

"No, of course not . . . oh, you are making a joke. But you do know what Sartre's most famous play was about, don't you?"

Genevieve thought for a moment . . . she wasn't that familiar with French literature, much less philosophy. She had a vague notion that Sartre wrote about choice and existence, all of which led to a lot of ennui and world-weariness. After Philippe had mentioned him the other day, Genevieve had intended to look him up. But without an Internet connection at home, such activities were difficult. She should find the library and dedicate a day to studying. But then again . . . if she couldn't understand philosophy in English, trying to plow through it in French seemed like a rather wasted effort.

"*Huis Clos*," Catharine said helpfully. "In English it's usually called *No Exit*."

"Oh, right." Genevieve realized she was playing with a little bit of spilled salt on the tabletop, moving the grains around. She feared Catharine's hawk eyes might decide the shapes meant something, and abandoned them. "That's the one where Sartre says that hell is other people? That sounds about right."

"You are joking again. What I meant to point out is that *No Exit* is about people locked in a room. They can't open the door, can't get out."

"You're saying they are in need of a locksmith?"

"In a spiritual sense, yes. They need to learn the truth in order to set themselves free."

Genevieve gave Catharine a look out of the corner of her eye. "I'm not sure that's what the play's about. I thought they were in hell, always wanting something they can never have, and that there's no way out no matter what."

"'*L'enfer, c'est les autres.*'"

"That's what I said: 'Hell is other people.'"

"Yes, but it does not mean exactly that. It means that we can only know ourselves through others' perceptions of us."

"Really? Huh." Genevieve had no idea how this related to her dream but was afraid to ask. Was Catharine saying that she was afraid of what other people thought of her?

"When you were a teenager, you idolized my father. And then you found out that he and your mother had not spoken in some years. That he was angry with her. And you felt very upset about that."

"I did?"

"You don't remember? That is why you were angry when you left us."

"I don't . . . ." Genevieve tried to think back. That time was so odd in her mind: She remembered certain scenes with startling clarity, while others were murky or gone altogether, as though she had been on drugs. Not long after returning to Petaluma from Paris, when her grades took a nosedive and she was caught red-handed breaking into a neighbor's house, Genevieve was ordered to go see a therapist. The woman—who wore a lot of loose natural fibers and smelled of patchouli oil—told Genevieve that "memory confusion" was normal for "young people" who had gone through "traumatic events." Apparently it was common to forget things entirely, especially if those things challenged important parts of the psyche that needed to be protected.

"I thought I was angry because I didn't want to leave Paris," Genevieve said.

"That, too, maybe."

"And you really don't know what happened between them?"

"I don't," she said with a firm shake of her head. "But he never forgave himself. When he found out that Angela was sick, and then died before he could even arrange to go visit her . . . well, for the first time his dreams were full of hastiness, and grapes that were sour."

At Genevieve's questioning look, Catharine explained, "These are symbols of rejection, loss, and regret. Mostly regret."

Genevieve sipped her wine, wondering what could have happened between the siblings.

"So, you see," Catharine continued, "there are things worse than locked doors. It is the secrets they keep that threaten to destroy us."

Chapter Thirty-five

After lunch Catharine and Genevieve went by the Alzheimer's center to visit Pasquale. She was vague but pleasant, not at all like the other day, when she seemed to be in a different world entirely. Together they strolled through a courtyard garden attached to the building. Genevieve had been hoping Pasquale would say something further about Angela and Jim, but while Pasquale didn't recognize Genevieve, she chatted about things in the here and now: the color of the leaves, a spider on the wall.

"This is one thing that is so difficult with the Alzheimer's," said Catharine as they left the building. "There are good days and bad. You never know who you will meet. Come, I will walk you back to the Métro. Unless you want to come play with the sand table?"

"Actually, I was thinking I'd walk back."

"*Walk* back?" Catharine's jaw dropped. "That's . . . I don't know, four or five kilometers, at least. Maybe more."

"I like to walk, and it doesn't look like rain. Is there a route you would recommend?"

Catharine's look of horror finally ceded to resignation. She gave a slight shrug before lighting a cigarette. "I suppose . . . in a car the most direct route would be the rue des Martyrs, this way. I will walk you there. You will not get lost?"

"If I do I'll just ask someone to point me toward the Seine. I can find my way from there."

As they walked, Catharine promised to try to find someone who could help with the paperwork for the locksmith shop—of course, Genevieve had forgotten to bring the bright pink papers to share with her.

"You bring them next time. It is probably too bad you alerted the authorities that you were coming—probably you could have worked for many years with no one noticing."

"Maybe, but it's too late now. And besides, it would be pretty embarrassing to be deported from France."

She shrugged. "The secret to dealing with the bureaucrats is to keep insisting—they try to defeat you with requests for more papers, more documentations, but if you persist, eventually they will cooperate."

"So I hear."

"Well, we are arrived. So, you head down that way until you hit rue de Faubourg Montmartre, continue to rue de Montmartre, and turn right at rue du Louvre. Then straight on toward the Seine, as you say."

"Thank you for lunch, Catharine. It was wonderful. And thank you for everything you've done—letting me use the apartment, the food, everything."

"It is no problem," she said, waving away the gratitude. "I have no use for the place. It is good it is occupied by someone happy to be there."

"I . . . I adored your parents, you know. They saved my life, I think."

Catharine shrugged noncommittally, looked away.

"All I mean is . . . you were lucky to have them as parents."

"Do you know something? No one believes me when I say this, but it is the truth: It is a terrible thing to be the only child of a couple in love."

Genevieve stuck to the path Catharine had suggested, proceeding down rue des Martyrs toward rue Montmartre, because she wasn't up for getting lost in Paris. Not yet, anyway.

Normally she loved walking without a plan, crossing streets when she had the light or turning the corner when something caught her fancy. Oakland was crisscrossed with little pedestrian alleys and staircases leading through backyards and behind residential lots, quaint relics of the WPA era, when the government used to employ people to construct neighborhood improvement projects. Sometimes Genevieve walked so far she would look up, almost as if coming out of a trance, to find herself in a "bad" part of town.

But she had never experienced anything worse

than strange looks from men lingering on corners, or dogs rushing their chain-link enclosures, barking and snarling. In fact, in recent months she had been walking so much that she quickly wore out the soles of her shoes, buying new ones every couple of months. It had become her one big wardrobe expense.

Walking was one way to keep her mind off the desire to let herself into whichever place she wanted: an empty house for sale, a crypt, a warehouse. Genevieve wasn't motivated by greed, not for objects, anyway. She was fascinated by the intimate details of other people's lives. What made them tick, how they organized themselves . . . especially what made them happy. She hadn't given in to the compulsion since she was a kid, but it bothered her that she still felt the pull.

It was a pull that increased the unhappier she became.

She'd tried talking to a counselor about it once, but the young therapist hadn't been trained in how to maintain a poker face, and his quick look of surprise and worry was enough to keep Genevieve from returning for a second session.

So she walked. Jason would have preferred her to work out in the gym at the club, using a treadmill "like a normal person." But Genevieve liked the view: Life unfolded before her slowly, like a surreal foreign movie taking its time to set the scene before getting to the meat of the story.

All leading up to some really depressing point, of course, as foreign movies usually did. That life was pain, or the banality of evil. Something like that.

And as she walked down the rue des Martyrs, Genevieve definitely felt as though she were strolling through a movie set. Even given the relatively humble neighborhood—the tourists rarely ventured far from the butte of Montmartre—everything was impossibly charming.

Could the deep yellow façade of the *coiffeur* shop (with *Dames* and *Messieurs* written on either side of the door in Art Nouveau script) be any cuter? Or how about the pharmacy, with its arched Gothic windows painted a chalky blue, a pretty white-coated woman standing in the doorway, chatting with a handsome deliveryman?

How long would it take for the wonder to wear off? For buying aspirin in such a place to begin to feel normal, even ho-hum? Did a person ever stop seeing (feeling) the beauty, the history of Paris? Did stone walls begin to feel cold and depressing, to the point where she would ever yearn for the plastic, standardized façades of an Applebee's or an Olive Garden?

There must be some similar franchises in France, she felt sure. Out in the suburbs, in newer areas, there must be big-box stores and chain restaurants. Probably they were as uninspired and soulless as in the U.S., no better or worse.

But one thing was sure: Spending the day "walking in Paris" sounded a lot more glamorous than spending the day doing the same thing in Oakland.

Chapter Thirty-six

Angela, 1983

Xabi is consulting his map, flashlight beam fixed on the paper. Angela peers over his shoulder. They are back in the catacombs, exploring.

"Look, it looks like . . . we are almost directly under Philippe and Delphine's neighborhood," she says.

"Yes, I think you are right." He glances at the map, then casts his light above, where the arched ceiling of the tunnel cedes to a vertical shaft, one of many, that lead up to the surface: perhaps to a manhole in the middle of the street, or yet another tunnel . . . or to someone's basement. A rusted ladder is attached to one side.

When he looks back, Angela is staring at him.

"Angel, why do you look at me like that?"

"Did you know that—before? That we were under Philippe's house?"

"Why would it matter?"

She doesn't know. But it seems significant.

"Why were you so curious about the *cave* the other evening at *apero*?"

He stills. Extinguishes his flashlight, then takes hers from her hand and turns it out as well.

Next he wraps his arms around her, enveloping her with his scent. He whispers, "Always you are looking for something suspicious, I think. But it is your own guilt speaking to you, Angel, making you afraid."

"Xabi . . ."

"I know you and I should not be together. But when I hold you like this . . . how can this feeling be wrong? How can it be denied?"

Inky darkness flows around her. Again she feels the strange nothingness, the disorienting sensation of being in pitch black, unknown by all in the world but him.

He takes her hand. "Come, I want to show you something."

They walk in the dark, just a few steps. Then he turns his light back on to illuminate a wooden door. When he opens it, she sees there is a small cot made up with sheets and blankets, a tiny table. A candle and a bottle of wine. There is a sketchy mural on the wall over the bed: a man and woman floating in space, surrounded by stars, kissing.

"What is this place?" Angela asks.

Xabi smiles. "It is a place for us. Not exactly a castle fit for a queen . . . but a little room that's just for us."

He steps close to her, takes her in his arms. The world comes down to this: to him and her, no names, no faces, just two souls mingling, connecting. Breathing.

When they meet the others at the café that evening, the mood is not as jovial as she has come to expect. Even Pablo seems formal, makes himself scarce. Xabi's friend, the always-laughing Thibeaux, isn't laughing. He draws Xabi aside, speaks to him in hushed tones. Xabier shakes him off.

Thibeaux storms out. There are many significant glances cast about the room, but no one speaks.

"Maybe . . . I think I should go," Angela says, standing. She's not sure what's happening, but she does not feel welcome. She is an interloper.

"Don't go, Angel," Xabi says. "Wait for me a moment; I be right back. I walk you home, if you don't want to stay. Wait for me, okay?"

He slips out after Thibeaux.

Michelle comes to stand beside Angela. Michelle had always been friendly enough, but now she seems nervous. "Be careful of him, Angela. I say this as a friend."

"Who?" Angela asks. "Xabi or Thibeaux?"

Michelle raises her eyebrows, then shrugs. "Both, I suppose. But I was speaking of Xabi. He is already a ghost. Seriously, *Américaine*. You should go back to your home. There is only trouble for you here."

Angela waits another fifteen minutes, sipping her wine. Eyes are on her, there are a few whispers, a few inconsequential comments traded, but by and large silence reigns.

Finally, she realizes: Xabi has not come back for her like he'd promised.

Chapter Thirty-seven

As time passed, Genevieve fell into something of a routine: visiting with Sylviane at the *boulangerie* in the mornings when she bought her baguette and a morning croissant; making copies of keys for people who refused to believe she wasn't open for business; and going through Pasquale and Dave's papers and tchotchkes and hardware and memories, sorting out the precious from the disposable. She bought her coffee at the Caféothèque, walked endless boulevards and tiny cobblestone alleys, and took time to sit in the place des Vosges—or one of a thousand other charming parks—with her journal, jotting down useful French phrases and describing the city around her: the sights and smells, her memories and regrets.

She wrote a postcard to Jason saying simply: "Doing fine. Hope you're well." And several to Mary, fitting as many tiny letters as she could in the available space and trying to capture in words the floating sense of *rightness* she was starting to feel in Paris, as though she had finally found a place where she fit in.

Every day Genevieve met more of her neighbors in the village, and she made a Herculean effort to remember all of their names; Anna brought a homemade chocolate mousse as a thank-you for Genevieve's help, and an upstairs neighbor brought by a welcoming bouquet of flowers.

Twice Genevieve had offered to finish the job at Philippe's house, and twice he had demurred, preferring instead to "have the company of a beautiful woman" for day trips: first to the Musée d'Orsay to "make visit" with the Impressionists, which then required a long lunch afterward to recover; and then a day trip, when he hired a car to take them out to the Palace of Versailles.

Philippe walked so slowly that each trip was limited in scope, but as Genevieve relaxed into the slower pace she realized how much more she saw by not trying to take in the entire palace, but instead focusing on a few rooms: Marie Antoinette's elaborately draped bed, and the nearly hidden door out of which she was said to have escaped—temporarily—the Revolutionary mobs; the amazing gold-gilt rococo hall of mirrors, out of which the gardens of Versailles were visible in all their formal, manicured glory.

One day Genevieve screwed up her courage (and, on the advice of her neighbors, packed snacks and water for the long line) and went down to what she thought was the proper governmental office to discuss getting an official work permit, but since locksmithing was a special case, she was sent to another office, and then another. All of which required different forms to be filled out, which she did laboriously, dictionary close at hand. Finally she managed to land an appointment with a horrid little man named Monsieur Lambert, complete with slicked-back hair, quivering bowtie, and the special sort of obstinate self-righteousness common to petty tyrants everywhere.

The good news was that he spoke excellent English. The bad news was that he read her the riot act regarding the arrogance of Americans taking good jobs away from the French, and the need to schedule a shop inspection; he also informed her that if she wanted to become certified as a locksmith, she would have to serve an apprenticeship. She would not be able to proceed until she had a vital signature on one set of paperwork and a stamp on the other. He handed her a ream of new forms to fill out, and Genevieve finally did what everyone had been advising her not to do: She gave up.

Not permanently, of course; she just needed a little time to regroup, before she broke down and cried in front of a little weasel like Lambert. Or worse, came down with another migraine.

Just keeping food in the house seemed to be a full-time job. Genevieve thought back to how gracefully Pasquale had provided meals for her family every day. To do it right, the neighbors had informed Genevieve, one must go to the best butcher, the best cheese shop, the best fish store. These were not necessarily the most *expensive,* but the best, and one knew about them only by asking the locals. There were occasional disagreements—engendering long and dramatic discussions—but by and large most agreed on which were the finest shops. Then there were the farmers' markets: there was one near the Hôtel de Ville on Wednesday and Saturday, and others throughout the city on a daily basis. Paris was not like California, where one could buy grapes or avocados out of season. Perhaps such items could be had if one scoured the city, but in general the food available was whatever was in season: squashes in winter, peaches in summer. Many were *bio*, short for *biologique*, which meant "organic." And some came from people's yards rather than big farms: many came to sell their apples or plums or whatever they happened to be inundated with that week.

But besides acquiring food, sightseeing with Philippe, taking long walks, and fighting bureaucracy, most of Genevieve's days were spent listening to old records while she cleaned out and organized the apartment, piece by piece.

Catharine had assured Genevieve, repeatedly, that she was not violating anyone's privacy and that she should help herself to anything she wanted. Catharine also told her it was a comfort to know her *petite cousine* was caring for the apartment and going through her parents' things.

Genevieve began to make a pile of personal items she thought Catharine might want one day, even if it was too soon now: photo albums, Dave's military ribbons, Pasquale's (and Catharine's?) christening gown, packed away in a special box.

She riffled through the other letters in the top drawer of Dave's bureau, but she found nothing from Angela besides that one note: *I'm sorry.* She thought back to the missive she had found so many years ago with the antique key she wore around her neck. It had been in her uncle's upright, all-caps handwriting and had simply read: *You hold the key.*

What was with such cryptic notes between a brother and sister?

Could there be a treasure trove of letters from Dave to Angela, hidden in one of those boxes Nick had taken out of the closet but then stored because none of them could bear to go through them? Were they, even now, moldering somewhere in the back of the barn?

She considered calling her brother and asking him. But then she imagined his bewildered, exasperated, yet patient response: "I'm up to my ears with turkey hatchlings right now, Gen; you want me to go through all the old boxes to find what? Letters from a dead man to a dead woman? Any particular reason it's so urgent?"

And what could she say in return? Why did it matter? *Did* it matter?

Not really. Not at the moment, anyway. It could wait. In the meantime, she would follow up with her uncle's other pending projects: she went through the dossiers, found the locks by their numbered tubs, cleaned and oiled the ones that weren't already shiny and easily opened.

Next up, Genevieve was going to tackle cleaning out the shop.

Marie-Claude became friendlier over time, her stiffness fading away bit by bit, on a daily basis. She got to the point where she almost smiled when she saw Genevieve. They communicated with a smattering of English, a little French, and a lot of hand gestures.

"It is cold to sit outside today," said Marie-Claude one morning, wrapping her arms around herself and shivering exaggeratedly. "Please, I invite you to join me inside my shop, La Terre Perdue, for an espresso."

"I would love that, thank you." Genevieve had taken to carrying her small phrasebook and dictionary, along with her journal and pen, wherever she went. She wrote down "outside" and "inside," having made out the words from their context. She asked Marie-Claude how they were spelled; to her American ear, French words sounded so profoundly different from the way they were written, it was daunting.

She wrote: *Outdoors = dehors, sounds like dore (with a soft "r"—almost doh). Indoors = dedans.*

They took seats at a tiny café table behind the register. The shop was crammed full of so many fascinating items that Genevieve could barely take it all in: beautiful antique furniture of course, but also a taxidermied squirrel dressed in a tiny waistcoat, framed paintings of severe-looking matriarchs, a Nazi helmet. There were fanciful Murano glass chandeliers and vintage store signs, rolling pins and a wooden ice-cream maker, dolls and lamps and an old typesetting drawer.

Daniel appeared and said his effusive hellos, then brought over a shoe box full of old locks.

"We keep these for Dave, always. But now . . . you want them?"

There was a rusted iron padlock, and a couple of relatively new locks, which weren't much good for anything but practice. Genevieve remembered many an evening spent at the kitchen table with Uncle Dave, newspapers spread out, trying for hours to open a lock.

"Feel it, Genevieve. See *it in your mind, draw a mental map of what you are feeling, the voids and the pins. Never give in to frustration!"*

Then a young man—tall, pale, and thin—came into the shop. Marie-Claude introduced him as their son, Luc. He carried an aroma of tobacco so strong Genevieve could smell him across the room. Luc didn't say much and remained standing by a shelf of antique baby items. Neither did he join in the conversation; indeed, his sole purpose appeared to be to translate when his parents were stuck for a word.

Marie-Claude inquired after Pasquale and Catharine. They chatted for a few minutes about the state of the village, and Marie-Claude mentioned that while it would be nice to have an American around to translate for the tourists, perhaps it wouldn't do for *too* many Americans to move in. Daniel and she began a spirited discussion about how the Americans had taken over one or two sections of Paris and while they both enjoyed Americans, this was simply not right.

Genevieve sipped her espresso and smiled gamely, attempting not to be too American.

"Tell us, Genevieve, what do you do while you are in Paris?" Daniel asked.

"Yesterday I went to Notre-Dame and climbed to the top to see the gargoyles. *Comment dit-on* 'gargoyle' *en français?*" She asked how to say "gargoyle" in French.

"*Gargouille*," said Luc.

"Ah, easy, then." They laughed. "It is almost the same."

"How about the paperwork?" Daniel asked. They had helped her to decipher the bright pink notice she had received, and sent her to the office from which she had scurried away in defeat last week. "How does it go?"

She told them of her efforts and her ignoble end.

They shook their heads, said a few rapid words in French about *bureaucrates*, sucking air loudly between their teeth.

"You shouldn't have told them you were here," said Luc. "It would have taken a long time for them to figure it out."

"Yes, that's what my cousin said. And it's true that even without the license I *have* done a little locksmith work—*j'ai travaillé comme serruriere.* My uncle left a few projects incomplete, so I have been finishing things at one house. Philippe D'Artavel. Do you know him?"

Marie-Claude's lips pressed together in a disapproving line, and she glanced over at Daniel.

"Did I say something wrong?"

Marie-Claude mumbled something that sounded like *tret*. Daniel made a tsking sound and gave her a sharp look.

"What does that mean?" Genevieve asked.

"She doesn't mean this, exactly," said Daniel. "It is very complicated."

"*Traître*," Luc repeated. "Means 'traitor.' "

Marie-Claude looked it up in Genevieve's

dictionary and showed her. It was spelled virtually the same but when spoken it sounded like *tret*.

"*My* Philippe?"

"Philippe D'Artavel, *oui*."

"But, I thought . . . I thought he worked with the *résistance* during the war. He was a hero."

"Yes, this is true, in the *guerre mondiale*," said Marie-Claude. "But then, you know, with the *guerre d'Algérie*. Then things changed."

"The Algerian War? I don't . . ." Genevieve trailed off, feeling, once again, as inadequate with history as she had when her uncle had picked her up at the airport, at the age of fourteen. "I'm sorry to say I don't know much about the Algerian War."

Try *nothing*. She knew nothing about the Algerian War.

"When was it, exactly?" Genevieve asked.

"In the fifties, mostly."

"The Algerian War was like our Vietnam," said Luc.

"I thought the French were in Vietnam, also," said Genevieve.

"Yes, we were. But then we got out in time," said Luc. "You were there long time, I think. When we are in *Algérie*, it lasts a long time. Eight years."

"My husband and I," said Marie-Claude. "We are Black Feet. The Pieds-Noirs. This is the name for French people born in Algérie. We were forced from our homes; we had to leave everything and come back to France. My family had a winery there. We lost our land; that is why the shop is called La Terre Perdue."

"I'm so sorry."

"It's complicated," said Luc.

A rapid-fire discussion ensued among the family members; tempers flared. Finally Luc excused himself, claiming he needed a cigarette, and left.

Luc's departure left Genevieve flipping through her dictionary with renewed fervor.

"The young people, they don't understand how it was," Daniel said. "Luc never lived in Algérie; he does not know what it is to be forced out of home."

Genevieve nodded, thinking that if the Algerian War had anything in common with the U.S. involvement in Vietnam, she wasn't surprised there would be a generation gap. And even with Vietnam . . . Americans had been fighting on foreign soil. What would it be like to be forced from one's home?

"I'm afraid I still don't understand. Why do you say that Philippe was a traitor?"

"He did not support his country during this time. He was part of a group of intellectuals—they wrote articles, voiced opposition to the war, even sent money for the other side," said Marie-Claude. "You have heard of Jean-Paul Sartre?"

Sartre *again*. Genevieve was going to have to

catch up on her philosophical reading just to keep up with conversation.

"He writes a lot about this," Marie-Claude continued. "He did not support his country."

"It is not because he writes about this that he does not support his country," said Daniel, smiling, clearly trying to smooth things over. The peacekeeper. "But . . . he sees things differently."

"My family lost their winery; we had to leave our home," said Marie-Claude. "I find this hard to forgive."

"There are two sides to every story," said Daniel.

"I meant to ask," said Genevieve after an awkward pause in the conversation. "Did you happen to know my mother, Angela, when she was visiting my uncle, a long time ago?"

"We were away when she arrived," said Daniel. "No one stays in Paris in August!"

"But we met her briefly, after she was hurt," said Marie-Claude.

"What happened, do you know? How was she hurt?"

The couple looked at her with curiosity; only then did Genevieve realize how strange it must sound, that Angela's own daughter did not know how her mother had been injured.

"She only told me that something had happened here, in Paris," Genevieve continued. "I never learned the details."

Now Marie-Claude and Daniel exchanged a significant look. When Marie-Claude spoke, it was in French. Genevieve thought she said:

"There was an accident, and soon after, she went back home. But it is so long ago. It does not matter now."

Chapter Thirty-eight

The day was gray but the rain held off; a dozen people milled about rue Saint-Paul, carrying shopping bags, peeking into storefronts. Genevieve glanced up to the second story of the building across the street: The lights were on in Killian's apartment.

She hesitated for a moment, but then again . . . the Irishman had repeatedly offered his help. And, as Mary had pointed out, what were the chances some good-looking guy would show up, quite literally on her doorstep, the day she arrived in Paris? It seemed almost like fate.

Not that she was interested in anything of a romantic nature. Not at all.

Genevieve thought back on her awkward phone call with Jason. She had been consciously trying to avoid thinking about it, but the truth was . . . the small, scary truth was that maybe what had happened between the two of them wasn't Jason's fault. He was a decent, hardworking man, and in the big scheme of things, they were a very fortunate couple. And he wanted to please her— how many times had he demanded, "Just tell me what I can do to make you happy, Genie. Just *tell* me, and I'll do it."

True, he had said it in an exasperated tone, but still.

Maybe there was some deep part of her that was lacking. Jason had certainly insinuated as much: that she was locked down, closed up— more affectionate toward her ancient locksets than toward him.

Perhaps . . . perhaps having her mother die so early had damaged her irreparably. Or maybe she was more like her silent, brooding father than she had ever wanted to admit.

Probably what she really needed to do was get some therapy—not Catharine's dream interpretations, but something solid. She would do that, Genevieve decided, just as soon as things settled down a little more. Already she was settling into a routine in her new home, so within a month or two she would figure out how to get certified to work, and find a professional to talk to. (Surely there were Parisian counselors who spoke English!) In the meantime, her therapeutic plan was to walk the streets, linger in parks, write in her journal, and meander through the Louvre "slow looking," as Philippe had taught her.

In any case, Genevieve thought as she

approached Killian's apartment building, since she didn't trust (or even like) men at the moment, this Irishman would remain a harmless friend. An innocent flirtation at most.

Stroking the key that hung at her neck, Genevieve screwed up her courage and rang the bell at the front door. Killian buzzed her in without a word. She climbed the steps to the second floor to find his door left wide-open. She approached it cautiously, finally sticking her head in.

"Hello?" she ventured.

"*J'arrive*," he said from the direction of the bedroom.

As before, she was struck by his photographs. Old mansions ravaged by time, abandoned, debris-strewn hallways. The most poignant and unnerving images depicted rooms that looked as if their inhabitants had just left, with pillows thrown carelessly on the bed and bath towels still hanging from a railing over a tub. One image showed a table with six place settings, dusty but intact, with vegetation peeking through open windows.

They looked . . . haunted. Like Philippe's basement.

Some buildings seemed to carry a certain *something* in the air. Could it be the spirit of their former owners? She and Jason once went to a formal dinner party at a historic Bernard Maybeck–designed house that had miraculously escaped the Oakland fire. Genevieve kept losing track of the conversation, as wrapped up as she was in the sensations of other lives having been lived in that same space, their wants and dreams and desires leaving a residue just as real as dust in the grain of the wood, the cracks and crevices. She wouldn't have been surprised had some apparition floated by in a flapper dress.

Jason made fun of her afterward, when Genevieve asked him if he'd felt the same; she hadn't confided in him again about such thoughts.

"Genevieve?" said Killian from the doorway of his bedroom.

She jumped, dropping several photos on the table.

"Sorry if I scared you," he said.

"Guilty conscience," she said with a rueful smile.

"I thought you were someone else, but it's lovely to see you. How is everything?"

"Good, thank you. Keeping busy. I was wondering, since you offered, whether I might impose upon you for a couple of things."

"Of course. What can I help you with?"

"Ordering Internet service. And also, since my French is so bad, do you think you could call two clients who had unfinished business with Dave and schedule appointments with them for me next week? I'm sure I can make myself understood when I see them in person, but I get intimidated over the phone. I think I need body language."

He laughed. Then he got on the phone and placed an order with a company to begin Internet service at Dave and Pasquale's apartment. They were supposed to send a box and instructions, but since it was a new service, he also set a date for the installation.

Then Killian placed phone calls to Madame Corrine Gerard and Monsieur Jean-Paul Angelini, Dave's two other outstanding clients, chatting and laughing with them on the phone. He set up two appointments for the following week.

"Thank you so much for your help," Genevieve said.

"No problem at all. Although . . . I was half hoping you were here to invite me to look through Philippe's house."

"I will, I promise, next time I go. He said he would be back next week, and we'll set a day then. I'll let you know."

"All right, then. He's quite a guy, isn't he? How *old* do you suppose he is?"

"I was trying to figure that out. If liberation was in 1944 . . . that was seventy years ago."

"Right. And he was already fighting, so even if he was very young at the time . . ."

"In his nineties, I'm guessing."

"Amazing. He seems to have his head, though— I'll give him that."

"Yes. He really is quite a character."

She considered asking Killian about what the neighbors had said about Philippe, but then Killian knew Philippe even less than she did. And the last thing she wanted to do was to become a gossip, spreading stories about a little old man who had been extremely kind to her. The village was like a small town, after all. She remembered her mother telling her about the wildly efficient gossip network in the small Mississippi town where she was raised: *"The tyranny of the tongue,"* she'd called it.

"This is really nice of you," she said. "I'm sorry to bother you on your day off."

"Not at all. Happy to help."

"*Everyone* seems happy to help. In fact, besides the rude waiters, everyone has been so nice here, I'm a little shocked. I thought Parisians were supposed to be cold and standoffish."

"That hasn't been my experience. Not at all, in fact. It's sort of like a small town, especially neighborhoods like this one. France is still old-fashioned that way, a bit like Ireland. Maybe that's why I like it so much. The countryside is even more so—the people are cautious at first, but once they realize you're trying to speak their language and you're not a jerk, they welcome you with open arms."

"I've never been outside of Paris."

"What, never?"

"It's only my second time to France; my first, I

338

was fourteen. I came to stay with my aunt and uncle after my mother died, but Dave and Pasquale were working and even though they offered to send me to the country with relatives, I wanted to stay with them."

"We should take a trip. I know you lads are used to long car trips—gas is more expensive here, but it's still worth it. Or there's the train, of course, but with a car you can get off on the rural roads, little narrow highways threading through tiny villages. Within a couple of hours outside of Paris you can be in Bourgogne, or go the other way toward the Loire Valley. I like the Dordogne, myself. The Southwest is really lovely, truly *craic*."

"Crack?"

"It's great, fabulous."

"Ah. Where I'm from that's the name of a street drug."

"Of course, I should have known that from the movies." He smiled, his eyes crinkling as he did so. Their gaze met and held for a long moment.

"*Bonjour?*" came a voice from the door. It was a woman, pretty and chic in that oh-so-Parisian way. Ice-blue linen sheath dress, heels in which Genevieve would have pitched face-first into the cobblestones before managing her first ten steps. Tiny little leather purse in metallic silver.

"*Bonjour, Liliane, ça va?*" said Killian, hurrying

over to her. Genevieve watched as they did the usual double-kiss greeting. "Liliane, this is a new neighbor of mine, Genevieve Martin. Genevieve, this is Liliane Monnier."

The women exchanged *bonjours* and kissed cheeks. When Genevieve leaned in she was surrounded by a very subtle cloud of perfume and powder.

"You are American?" Liliane asked.

"*Oui.* Sorry."

"Why do you apologize?" the woman demanded. She hadn't yet cracked a smile.

"I . . . uh, it was a joke. Sorry. I mean, sorry for being sorry earlier. I was just . . ." Liliane continued to stare at her as though confused and displeased. Genevieve could feel her cheeks flaming. What was *wrong* with her? It wasn't as though she was in competition for Killian, for heaven's sake. Of course he had a girlfriend. He was charming, kind, good-looking, gainfully employed. He was what Mary would have called a Unicorn, that mythical creature so many women—and in the San Francisco Bay Area a good percentage of the men—were looking for.

And Liliane was a perfect Parisian girlfriend.

"Genevieve's just moved here. Quite a change from California, as you can imagine," Killian said, coming to Genevieve's rescue. "Genevieve, we were just stepping out to get a bite to eat. Won't you join us?"

Liliane's perfect eyebrows raised, just a smidgeon.

"No, no thank you," said Genevieve. "I'm headed out to meet a friend myself. Thanks again for all your help, Killian. *Bon appétit, et à bientôt.*"

Genevieve did her best at waving a breezy wave, and left.

Chapter Thirty-nine

Angela, 1983

The shop buzzer rings. Dave goes to see who it is; it is evening, far too late for shop hours, but sometimes there are emergencies. Dave hates to see anyone locked out.

He returns to the apartment a moment later.

"It is for you," he says to Angela.

She enters the shop. Xabi is standing outside the closed door. Waiting patiently, despite the rain. He is still; unspeaking, unmoving. Wet, soaked through, without an umbrella. Their eyes meet through the pane, raindrops streaming down the glass like tears.

"You should tell him to go," says Dave from behind her.

Angela is startled at the sound of his voice. She looks over her shoulder to face her brother.

There has been a palpable distance between the siblings ever since the night in the cabaret. It was a glorious night full of wine and song, and yet Dave kept studying Xabi, turning his eyes back to Angela. It was obvious to them all that Xabi was much more than just a friend. Dave is happy to see his sister happy, but at what cost?

Angela told Dave—and herself—that she would stop seeing Xabi, that she wanted just the one perfect night. And she tried. The next few days she made a point to spend time with Dave in his shop, asking him questions about his work.

He showed her a recent acquisition: a Victorian-era ring of skeleton keys.

"These will open all old locks?" Angela asked.

"Not all of them, but a lot. I am so pleased you are interested. . . . I thought you didn't care about my old keys," he said with a wink.

"I guess you've worn me down. It's fascinating, isn't it? Thinking you can open all the doors."

"It belonged to a thief, I believe. Either that, or an old locksmith like me, eh? And yes, the keys on this ring will open most doors in old Parisian houses. That's why something like this is still dangerous, even though it's an antique."

And now Angela feels the tug: Dave on one side, Xabi on the other. She should do as Dave suggests, tell Xabi to go. She should book a ticket back to California; she should return to her family.

And yet.

"I need to talk with him," Angela says.

"Are you sure you know what you're doing, Angela?" Dave asks.

She does, and yet she doesn't. For the first time in years she knows absolutely, positively, what she wants. What she yearns for and dreams of. She is breathing so deeply, every molecule of her soul feels vibrant, alive, humming. Because of him. Because of the man standing out in the rain. And yet . . . he had left her at the café. Hadn't returned for her.

And Michelle had warned her against him. Why?

"I just need to talk with him. I'll be back soon. May I borrow your coat?"

Dave hands her his big khaki raincoat, the one with the plaid flannel lining. She rolls up the sleeves, kisses his cheek, puts the hood up, and goes outside.

"You abandoned me," she says without preamble.

His eyes, beautiful and intense.

"I didn't. I'm so sorry, Angel. I didn't mean to. I came back, but I know it was too long. It was . . . impossible to come sooner."

His voice, low and seductive.

"Why?" Angela asks.

"Just please believe me; it was an impossibility. I am sorry. Can you forgive me?"

"I just want . . ." Already she feels lost to him

again. Simply standing near him, seeing his eyes, hearing his voice, imagining the feel and the scent of him . . . Reason flees her mind. "I feel like something's going on. I don't understand. Someone said . . . someone said you were trouble, and that I should stay away from you. That you were a ghost. What did she mean?"

"It was Michelle, no?"

"What did she mean that you were a ghost?"

"Will you walk with me? I will try to explain."

They head toward the Seine, then descend stone steps to walk along the banks. The rain is soft; he is soaked already, but neither cares if they get wet.

"You know that for many years, for generations, the Basque people have been ruled by others. Dominated. And you probably know, also—I'm sure your brother has told you, since he does not approve—there were people who reacted to the oppression through violence."

Angela thinks of the first night when she saw him and his friends huddled around a table in the back room of the Chilean restaurant. She had thought they looked like conspirators, like revolutionaries. Like the French underground, fighting the Nazis. It had seemed romantic . . . but this seems base and ugly.

"Are you telling me you're a member of the ETA, the Basque terrorists?"

"No! What a thing, to assume this conclusion. No, in fact, my whole life I worked to avoid this.

But . . . my older brother Rémy, he was involved. Nothing specific, he helped to raise money, he lived in France and managed to find some supporters here. But then he stopped with everything, decided he wanted no part; he walked away from it. He asked me to come work with him, good job at a hotel in a French Basque village in the Pyrénées. Rémy and I. He was . . . he was like a hero to me, my brother."

"What happened?" she urges when he trails off.

He lets out a long breath. Stops walking. "One night, four men come in—Spaniards. We think they are tourists, like everyone else. They asked for a special Calvados, an apple brandy. I went into the back room to find it, and . . ." He blows out a long breath, gazes at the buildings lining the other side of the Seine. "That is when I heard it: bam bam bam!"

"Gunshots?"

He nods. "The sound of death. The sound of violence finding my brother, hunting him down like a dog. When I came out, Rémy was on the floor. Still awake, but bleeding. I held him, I cried out for help, but everyone had run to hide. I tried to stop the bleeding . . . there was so much blood. I never knew there was so much blood in a person. It was everywhere."

Xabi looks down at his hands, as though he can still see the blood on his hands. His face is wet, raindrops mingling with tears.

"Finally one of the waitresses called an ambulance, but it was too late. I held my brother, I begged him to stay alive, but I watched as the light left his eyes, felt the spirit lift from him as his blood soaked into my clothes, my skin. I had to call my mother, to tell her she had lost a son that day."

"I'm so sorry," Angela says, facing him, wishing she could think of something more apt to say, something more meaningful. She strokes his wet head; he bows it, touching his forehead to hers. Cries.

After a long moment he lifts his head, sniffs loudly.

"So, you see, I should be dead, too. Where I am from, if you cheat death, you are in between life and death. A ghost."

"But . . . they wouldn't have killed you, too, would they? They targeted your brother because he had worked against them, right?"

He throws up a hand, angry. "Who knows what goes on in the heads of murderers? For years I told my brother, I convinced him: Violence was not the way. But then . . . what is the result? He is defenseless when they come after him. We were living and working in another country, and still I held his bleeding body in my arms . . . and as I did, that was when I understand. That moment, I came to understand what he had been trying to tell me: There is no such thing as a bloodless revolution.

Sometimes violence is the thing left to us. It is self-defense."

"That isn't true, Xabi. Violence is never the way. Surely there's—"

"That is the American in you speaking," he says, cutting her off. "You have no idea what it is to live this way. Try to imagine you may not speak your language, you must adhere to another's beliefs. To have the state kidnap and kill its citizens, to do whatever it wants with your lives. No way to react, no power at all to respond. Can you understand what it is to live like that? Like animals."

"But . . . hasn't the ETA kidnapped and killed, too?"

"That is their only defense, to use the methods of the rulers against them. I used to agree with you. I wanted only to be permitted to live my life in peace. That ended on the day they crossed the border, they came to France to kill my family. It ended on that day."

Angela tries to wrap her mind around all of this. How would she have felt if it had been Dave, mortally wounded and bleeding in her arms? Something like that must change a person.

"And Thibeaux?" Angela asks. "Was he angry over something to do with all of this?"

"Thibeaux's story is even worse than mine. He smiles a lot, but he is just . . . He gets nervous around foreigners."

"I thought you were the one who didn't like Americans."

"Lately I find myself changing my mind." He gives her a gentle, sad smile.

She looks up at him. Caresses his face, wipes the tears from his cheeks.

"So now what? You remain exiled in Paris and make your paintings and . . . hate the Spanish government? And then what?"

He shrugs. "For now, that is all there is."

Chapter Forty

Once again, Genevieve was awakened by the shop buzzer.

Dammit. She was making a sign and putting it up. *Today.*

On the other hand . . . she supposed she could just ignore it. For now, Genevieve took a moment to splash water on her face, but the buzzer rang again. Repeatedly. She gave up and stumbled to the door.

It was Sylviane, wearing form-fitting jeans, little brown boots, and a tiny jacket, with a floral scarf tied at her neck. She carried a huge bouquet of flowers in fall colors: orange and yellow and green.

"Today is my free day! I go to the cemetery, bring flowers to my grandfather's grave. Would you like to come? Americans like cemeteries, I think?"

"Um . . . What time is it?"

"Early. I know. Is because I am a baker, I get up very early. Is too early? Are you okay? Not sick?"

Her gray eyes swept over Genevieve, widening ever so slightly in alarm.

Probably Parisian women roll out of bed looking ready for a photo shoot.

"I, um . . . I'd love to go. Come on in and just give me a few minutes to get dressed. Could we get coffee on the way?"

"Of course. We go to Montparnasse Cemetery. You will love it, I know. This is marvelous! 'Girls' day out' you say in English, right? Girls' day out in the cemetery!"

The graves were raised slabs sitting above the earth, as Genevieve had once seen at a cemetery in New Orleans. Mounted on many of the marble and granite headstones were oval pictures of the deceased, along with their names and dates of birth and death, and quotes from the Bible. Most were strewn with flowers, from the fresh to old, dried stalks, along with other remembrances: framed family photos and small bottles of eau-de-vie and handmade cards covered in childish scrawl.

Two old black-clad women hunched over interments, tending to rosemary and lavender bushes; one young man sat beside a slab, absolutely still, his hand resting on the shiny pink granite.

"Why there are no rom-coms filmed in cemeteries?" Sylviane asked as Genevieve inspected the ornate scrollwork on an ancient crypt lock.

"Rom-com in a cemetery?" Genevieve laughed. "I'm not sure the average American audience has such a relaxed view of death and dying."

"Really? Why not?"

"We don't associate cemeteries with romance. Not normally, anyway."

Genevieve thought of one rare occasion when she had convinced Jason to walk with her in Oakland's Mountain View Cemetery. Designed by the same man who developed New York's Central Park, Mountain View was located on a lovely rolling hillside with some of the best views of the Bay Area, and as Jason pointed out, it seemed particularly Oakland of the locals to use a cemetery in lieu of a public park. Catching their breath after climbing a hill, they stumbled upon a couple hidden behind a monument engaged in a particularly intimate act. Both were well dressed, attractive, and grown-ups, in their thirties, at least, apparently overcome by the moment. Jason had been appalled, but there was something about the scene that appealed to Genevieve: It seemed somehow fitting that death be balanced out by life, by love. What could be more fitting? Eros and Thanatos.

Jason had laughed and responded: "More like John and Ho."

Genevieve loved walking through that cemetery and noting the old-fashioned names and a few famous ones, like architect Julia Morgan, the Ghirardelli family of chocolate fame, or the famous Black Dahlia. But Mountain View didn't hold a candle to Montparnasse, which boasted headstones that read "Baudelaire," "Julio Cortázar," "Porfirio Díaz," "Samuel Beckett."

Sylviane said a prayer over her grandfather's grave and placed the flowers in a little vase attached to the headstone, filling it with water from a nearby spigot. Afterward, she and Genevieve strolled the grounds, taking in the somber beauty of the graves, the poignant evidence of lost loves and lamented parents, of mourned children and missed opportunities. Ever since her mother died, Genevieve had yearned for something like this: a place to come, a physical location to go to ponder her mother's existence. When she was young Genevieve would kneel under the sycamore tree, but somehow it wasn't the same; it was just another corner of the farm, the air stinking slightly of manure, Genevieve's melancholy interrupted by the ridiculous gobbling of the nearby turkeys or one exigency or another of the vegetable patch.

Angela's last wishes, to have no memorial but

to be scattered under that sycamore tree, had to be honored, of course. But like everything else associated with death, Genevieve realized, gravesites were so much more about the living than the dead. What had Philippe said? *"We carry the ghosts around with us."*

Their boots crunched as they walked on the gravel paths between the stones. Most of the monuments were fairly plain, but a few family crypts were decorated with stained glass and Corinthian columns and graceful statuary. Sylviane showed Genevieve one of her favorite sculptures: a distraught woman sitting upon a low wall, holding her head in one hand, her hair falling down to obscure her face.

"That looks like what grief feels like," said Genevieve.

"I agree," Sylviane said, tilting her head and studying the sculpture for a long, silent moment. "But come, I show you one that looks like love."

It was a nude woman, sculpted of pure white marble, draped on her back over a mound.

"Julio Ruelas was a Mexican artist who died here in Paris, too young. Only in his thirties. He loved the music of the gypsies who camped right outside the cemetery walls, and he asked that he be buried here so he could always hear the music."

"Do they still play?"

"Oh, not nearby, not anymore. They get chased away."

352

"And what's the story of the sculpture?"

"That?" she pushed out her chin and gave a Gallic shrug. "I think it's a young man's fantasy, probably. A beautiful naked woman adorning his grave? Oh! I know another one I want to show you—maybe this is the *woman's* fantasy, I think."

Gold gilt mosaic tiles spelled out FAMILLE CHARLES PIGEON on a memorial stone; in front of this was a larger-than-life sculpture of a woman lying in bed, a man sitting at her side with an open book in his hand.

"You see?" Sylviane said with a laugh. "A woman's fantasy: a man reading to her while she is happy in bed! Okay, come, we have some more famous people to visit."

A short while later they came upon a simple cream-colored slab littered with little slips of paper and a few bright red lipstick kiss marks on the stone. Two names were inscribed on the headstone: Jean-Paul Sartre and Simone de Beauvoir.

"Very famous romance," said Sylviane. "I think you must know these two?"

"Yes, I've heard of them. You mentioned de Beauvoir the other day. They never married, right? But were together their whole lives?"

"Exactly. Very *romantique*, and I say that word in French on purpose. I think maybe it means something else in your language. They had a long relationship in writing."

"Through their letters? An epistolary romance, I think they call it in English."

"Not just letters, also through their philosophy, I think, and their scholarly writings. I don't really know; I have never been this, a philosopher."

"Me neither. I mean, everyone read a little Sartre in college, but I wouldn't know enough to speak about him. Do you know Philippe D'Artavel from the neighborhood? He mentioned he actually knew him."

"Really? That is not too surprising—I think Philippe must have been involved in the intellectual circles of his time."

"What are these little papers?"

"Train tickets. It is tradition. Sartre supported the workers, you know, during those times. The government, she raises the rates on the Métro. This is very hard for the workers who use the train to get to work; they don't have cars. So Sartre opposes this; he says it is unfair to the working peoples. He and a group of people, they print up . . . how do you say, *faux*?"

"Faux . . . you mean fake? False?"

"Yes, fake tickets to give out to the poor people."

"They printed counterfeit train tickets?"

"Counterfeit! Yes, this is the word. So now people leave the tickets, like a tribute. We French like to strike, to shut things down. We are very dramatic."

"My cousin was just talking about the play called *Huis Clos*, by Sartre. Do you know it?"

"A little, but I am no expert. Mostly what I know of Sartre, he says that people are condemned to be free. This is their tragedy. They are free to choose."

"Do you believe that? You don't think people are forced sometimes, pushed by circumstances beyond their control?"

"I think it came in part from his experiences in the war," Sylviane said with a shrug. "After all, if everyone, together, had refused to cooperate, the atrocities wouldn't have happened. We were free to be *collaborateurs* with the Nazis. And some were. Many, actually."

Genevieve didn't know what to say. Wondering, as she had when she was with Philippe, how brave she would have been in the same situation. She steered the conversation back to safer terrain. "So you're a fan of Simone de Beauvoir?"

"*Mais oui*, of course. She was very amazing for her time, I think. Very early, smart feminist. She said that women define themselves through their men, because it is easier than to embrace their freedom and enter the world. They are born a person, but *become* a woman, in relation to a man."

"Do you think that's true?"

"For her time, maybe it was revolutionary thought. I think things have changed. I *hope* they have changed," Sylviane said, running her hand along a little filigreed iron fence encircling a slab decorated with a weeping angel. "Still, it was a great love affair she had with Jean-Paul. Very famous . . . She said their love was *essential,* not contingent. But I think maybe what that means was they could have other lovers. What do you think of this? I like it better in the movies. I could never let a man I love be with someone else, could you?"

Genevieve reflected on the moment she found out about Jason and Quiana. It was completely unintentional; she had known things weren't perfect in their marriage, but frankly she had been too wrapped up in her own mind to think about it. She had been working a lot, logging plenty of hours; as a freelancer she had to take the work when it came. She'd also been putting in time with her volunteer organization, culminating in a big work weekend. And Jason had been busy with a new account down in San Jose. So if they hadn't been particularly close, she put it down to being busy, to the day-in, day-out running around that constituted modern life.

One night Genevieve sat down to Jason's computer, since it was powered up and sitting on the kitchen table, meaning to log in to her e-mail account. But his was already open.

There were messages—*dozens* of messages—from the same woman. A woman she vaguely remembered meeting at one of the interminable, several-course dinners they'd hosted with a circle of "friends" who were so much more Jason's than hers. As she noted the unusual name she remembered: thin, blond, stylish; that lean-and-hungry look. While pouring before-dinner cocktails she remembered thinking: *They look good together, Jason and Quiana.*

She'd actually thought that.

Genevieve didn't read the text of the messages. At least she had spared herself that indignity. But the subjects were clear enough: *re re re last night. Your hands. The heat of your lips on mine.*

Shock washed over her: cold, then hot.

Really? Was this it? Were she and Jason just one more statistic now? One of nearly half the marriages that don't work out? Was it that simple?

They had first met while working as volunteers at the food bank—trying to fill mesh bags with carrots was no mean feat, and they had laughed while they attempted different techniques. He was in graduate school at the time, and she found him grounded and passionate, upbeat and fun, even while talking about things like bringing social justice to the computer world. But over the years the spark in his eyes faded (it seemed to Genevieve) in direct proportion to the money he made. Weekends spent volunteering at the food bank ceded to dining in the hot new foodie restaurants, collecting expensive California wines, being seen in the newest locales.

In contrast to Jason's, Genevieve's income was steady but didn't grow much. She had fallen into copyediting while wondering whether to go to graduate school to "learn a useful skill" or try to come up with something else. As a self-employed person, she received no bonuses or even paid vacation days; it wasn't as if there was a corporate ladder to climb. The advantage to working for herself, of course, was the freedom to set her own schedule: she volunteered a little, but mostly she used her time to wander through Oakland's Chinatown or walk around Lake Merritt or hike through the redwoods. Nosing through thrift stores and salvage yards for old locks and keys. Passing time.

Jason started to harass her—in that teasing, husbandly way that made it hard to pin down—saying that all those hours she spent on volunteering and walking could have been put to better use. But when she wasn't working or walking or fixing locks, her life took on a dreamy, watercolor nature.

Among so many other things, she didn't want to think about why she refused to talk with Jason (or even herself) about having children. The thing was, Genevieve realized as she took in the significance of the e-mails, she *did* want children. She always had, in a nebulous, *maybe later* kind of way. But the moment the knowledge of Jason's infidelity washed over her, Genevieve made an even deeper realization: She didn't want *Jason's* children. *She didn't want Jason at all.*

She felt shocked, a sick sensation deep in her stomach; she had sucked in great gulps of air and blew out several hard breaths to slow her pounding heart, her fluttering belly. But ultimately, she had to admit the truth: The knowledge of Jason's infidelity didn't make her want to fight for him; instead, it made her think of flight. Of freedom. Suddenly she wanted to escape from the trap of their marriage with the fervor of an animal willing to chew off her own limbs.

She had wanted *out.*

Chapter Forty-one

Sylviane handed Genevieve her phone to take her picture and mounted the steps of an ornate crypt to pose. Then she beckoned for Genevieve to come up and join her.

"Come, we take a selfie, you call it, is that right? Of both of us! Beautiful women in cemetery!"

They laughed and took a few more shots before ambling back toward the entry gates of the cemetery.

"Thank you for bringing me here, Sylviane."

"You are welcome. This is a good cemetery. The

other really good one is Père-Lachaise. That one has Jim Morrison and Oscar Wilde. And the one in Montmartre has Degas."

"Your cemeteries are like a list of who's who."

They walked past a large memorial to the airmen of World War II.

"Could I ask you something?" Genevieve asked. "Have you ever heard anything about Philippe D'Artavel's involvement in the Algerian War?"

"I think he did not support the war. It was very controversial. Many of the people of his genera-tion, they see this sort of thing as a treason. But me, my age, it is different."

"Different how?"

"The great war, you know, with the Nazis, it is still very real to the ones who lived through it. Of course, this is natural. They were here, some of them starved, they were abused, their neighbors were taken away. Have you seen the signs, about the deported people?"

"Yes. They're . . . so sad."

"This helps keep it alive. And so there was a great nationalism after the Germans are defeated, this is only natural, I think. But the younger generation, we look back and see it more complex. The Algerian people—they were a colony; it was wrong what we were doing there. The Pieds-Noirs, the French people who lived there, I understand it was hard to leave their country, and they saw it this way. But the

Algerians saw it as *their* country; this is only natural, too."

Genevieve nodded, thinking of Vietnam, Iraq, and all those other places she knew about only vaguely. Politics had never been her strong suit. But she knew how involvement in such wars could divide a nation.

"So Philippe, and even Sartre and a lot of other people, asked the question, why are we there, in Algérie? But you can imagine, a lot of people don't like that idea."

"That makes sense, I guess," said Genevieve.

"Is very complicated. This is why I don't like politics. I like romance more. So tell me about the Irishman. *Comment s'appelle-t-il?*"

"Killian?"

"*Oui.*"

"There's not much to tell. He works in computers."

"*Vraiment*? Really?" She stuck her chin out in a very French move. "He seemed more interesting than that."

Genevieve laughed at how Sylviane's thoughts mirrored her own. But then she felt compelled to be fair.

"There are a lot of interesting people working in computers," she said.

"Oh, I know, I know." Sylviane made a rolling hand gesture. Genevieve always thought of Italians being the ones who used their hands to talk, but lately she realized the French did as well. "But what else is his story?"

"He's a photographer. He likes to take pictures of abandoned buildings."

"Ah! You see, I knew there was something more. Why abandoned buildings?"

"I don't know. I guess the same reason some of us like cemeteries."

"Huh," she said, as though conceding the point. "Has he been to the Frigo?"

"The *frigo* . . . ? Doesn't *frigo* mean 'refrigerator'?"

"It does, yes. The Frigo used to be a place where they made ice. A factory. But it was abandoned, so the artists moved in and made it into their atelier."

"Really? That's great."

"I don't know . . ." She shrugged. "The neighbors complain, of course, because the artists are young and loud. They take over buildings a lot. The city tries to get them out but they refuse to leave. So the city buys the buildings and lets the artists have their atelier and gallery."

"They gave the building to the artists?"

"What else could they do?"

Genevieve smiled. "I don't know . . . I think in California there might have been tear gas involved."

"What is 'tear gas'?"

"I just mean to say the police probably would

have moved in and arrested the artists, if they wouldn't leave."

"And then what would happen to the building?"

"It would probably be left to rot. Either that, or turned into expensive lofts for people who work in the computer industry. Anyway, I think Killian's more interested in the catacombs. *Les souterrains.* Do you happen to know how to get in—not to the tourist part, but the other section?"

"*Les souterrains* . . . they scare me." Sylviane shook her head and shivered, pulling her shoulders up to her ears. Genevieve could hear her mother's voice: *"A goose walked over your grave."*

Upon reaching the gates, they both turned back and took one last look back at Cimetière Montparnasse. It was a peaceful place, with merely a handful of people—mourners and tourists—strolling among the headstones, birds tittering in the trees. Genevieve was only sorry they couldn't hear gypsy music in the background; it would have made it perfect.

"Okay, enough of death," Sylviane declared. "How about we do something fun?"

"Like what?"

"We need to go clothes shopping."

"Clothes shopping?"

"I saying, just look at you."

Genevieve glanced down at her jeans and sweater. "What?"

"I think you must dress better if you wish to secure the love of this Irishman."

Genevieve laughed. "I have no intention of securing the love of any man, Irish or not."

Sylviane hit her lightly on the arm and made a hand gesture of exasperation. "What are you talking? He is a beautiful man."

"The problem isn't him; it's me. I've separated from my husband, but I'm not in any way ready to be in a relationship."

Sylviane spoke with exaggerated patience, as though she were explaining something to a stubbornly dimwitted student. "I am not saying a *relationship*. You do not need to *be* with him, just attract him. It is always good to attract the man; this does not mean *relationship*."

"And besides, I think he has a girlfriend."

"Of course he has a girlfriend! He is a beautiful man. This is no reason not to make him fall in love with you. At least a little."

Genevieve laughed. "I see I have a lot to learn about romance."

"*Mais oui, bien sûr.* Of course, romance was invented in Paris, did you not know this? This is why the Frenchwomen, we know how to attract the man."

"So, speaking of that: What about you? How is your love life?" Genevieve asked as they started down the boulevard Edgar-Quinet.

Sylviane let out a long sigh. "I don't so much

know about the men here. Hey! Maybe I need American man, eh? Maybe a rom-com type? You know any I might like?"

"I don't think I'm the best matchmaker at the moment. And I'm sorry to say, I don't think most American men are like the heroes of the movies. No one is, to be fair. Have you noticed how rom-coms always come to an abrupt end after the marriage proposal? It's all downhill from there."

Sylviane shrugged. "Anyway, I am going to take you to Galeries Lafayette. You need new dress. It is a fantastic mall, good boutiques, and from the roof café there is the best view in all of Paris."

"That seems like quite a claim. What about the views from the tour Eiffel or Notre-Dame . . . ?"

Sylviane said something quick and dismissive in French. "Anyway, you will see. Galeries Lafayette. We will get lunch, and new dresses, and then we will have *apero*!"

Chapter Forty-two

Angela, 1983

"What is this?" Angela asks, her hands shaking.

They are in Xabi's apartment, the one he shares with Thibeaux and whatever itinerant artist or drunken revolutionary might need a couch on which to sleep. It reminds Angela of a student's hovel: the mattress on the floor, the stained towels, the threadbare curtains hanging crooked in the window. They have no money and don't seem to care; the refrigerator is empty but for a single beer and an old Chinese takeout container full of crusty rice.

When Angela suggests that she could bring in some groceries, make dinner, or perhaps even rehang the curtains, Xabi nuzzles her neck and calls her his "little American bourgeois." She learns it is not revolutionary to be concerned about such things as a nice home, a nice meal.

But then, she is not a revolutionary.

She is, quite simply, a woman in love. A married woman, in love with a man other than her husband. What is she doing here, still?

She holds out the paper for Xabi to see.

He takes it. "That, my love, is none of your business."

"The writing is in Euskara."

"Yes."

"And it appears to be a map of the Spanish embassy."

"I need to go there to renew my passport."

"Why all the Euskara, then, with arrows?"

"Why all the questions about nothing?" He balls up the paper and tosses it in the kitchen trashcan, where it lands atop a banana peel and coffee grounds. "It is nothing. What is wrong, Angela? Are you angry?"

Last night, late, she lay in Xabi's bed, drifting between sleep and wakefulness, her body still flushed and subtly vibrating in the aftermath of their lovemaking. In the other room Thibeaux and Xabi and a few others were talking in low voices, in a combination of French, Spanish, and Euskara. Angela knew high school French and spoke a little Spanish but not a word of Euskara. Still, she made out a few phrases:

Spanish embassy. Day after tomorrow. Five o'clock.

She looks into Xabi's beautiful eyes. They are so deep she wants to drown herself in their depths, like diving into a gorgeous pool of blue. They make her forget, lose herself, what she knows.

"Tell me, Angel," Xabi says, his big hands holding her arms gently, telegraphing their warmth to her blood. "What is wrong?"

She starts to cry. "I am a married woman, Xabi. I have a son. I shouldn't be here."

"Shh," he says, pulling her to him. Kissing her hair. Speaking soft and low. "I know. I do . . . I know it is impossible. But for here, and now, let us love. That is all. Just for now. We don't have long, I know. I know."

Later, when she is lying in his arms, she will wonder whether he meant their time was limited because she will be going back to America, to her husband and son . . . or because Xabi will be gone, the day after tomorrow, after doing something terrible at the Spanish embassy, something spoken of in whispers in back rooms.

She gets up, pretends she needs to use the toilet. The trashcan in the kitchen still holds the banana peel and coffee grounds, but the wadded-up piece of paper is no longer there.

Chapter Forty-three

"You look wonderful today," said the fourth neighbor Genevieve passed the next day as she headed out to find the bookstore Killian had told her about: Le Pont Traversé.

She was wearing a new blue dress, simple but elegant, with a fitted jacket, tights, and boots. After a halfhearted struggle at the department store, Genevieve had given herself over to the eager Sylviane, who treated store clerks as she did waiters: with imperiousness, as though they were her own personal staff. They, in response, hustled to do her bidding. Genevieve wound up buying several pieces: three dresses, the jacket, slacks, two tops. A nice pair of medium heels. Sylviane urged her to buy a couple of silk scarves and was mollified only when Genevieve said Pasquale had several Hermès at home she could use.

Genevieve's heart had skipped a beat when she signed the final sales slip. She used the credit card she shared with Jason, so he would receive the bill; she would have to call and warn him and transfer some money from her savings to cover it. But then, she thought with a rueful smile, *this* was the kind of crisis Jason would be able to understand—would, in fact, probably approve of.

Sylviane had helped Genevieve back to the Village Saint-Paul with all her bags, and after sharing some wine, she insisted on experimenting with Genevieve's hair, showing her how to sweep it up in a neat chignon, and giving her a few makeup tips.

When Genevieve looked at herself in the mirror this morning she realized the only part of her that looked the same as when she arrived was the antique key hanging from the chain around her neck. Girls' day out had never been quite so instructive, in Genevieve's experience.

"Genevieve!"

She turned to see Killian trotting up to her. His jeans were dirty, there were streaks of light brown on his shirt, and his boots were caked in mud. He had his pack slung over his shoulder the way he had the first morning they met.

"I take it you've been out exploring?"

"Ah, yeah. A bit manky. Do I look a wreck?"

Genevieve smiled and, in her new outfit, tried channeling Sylviane. "A little smudge on your cheek; hold still."

She reached up and slowly wiped a little dirt off his whiskery cheek.

"There," she said in a quiet voice. "All better."

His gaze held hers for a long moment.

"You seem . . . very Parisian today," he finally said.

She smiled and looked down at her clothes. "I had a makeover by a native Parisian. What do you think?"

"It's not just the clothes," he said with a slow shake of his head. "It's an attitude."

She smiled again. "So, shall I deduce from your dirty face that you found your way into the tunnels?"

"Not quite. I found a few short ones, but not the jackpot."

"They aren't all connected, though, are they? I mean, I heard they were left over from the old quarries; some were used for sewers, others for basements and such."

"Sure, yeah. Some are, some aren't, apparently. In fact, some of these really old places might have access points—did you happen to see any-thing when you were down in Philippe's basement?"

Only a strange little trapdoor under a grate, she thought. Most likely it was some sort of clean-out that led nowhere more interesting than a sewer pipe. Still, why would it have been outfitted with such an elaborate old lock, in that case?

"Anyway," Killian continued, "I have a couple of other irons in the fire; something's bound to shake out sooner or later. I've got feelers out to a few cataphiles."

"Cataphiles?"

"That's what they call the fellows who know their way around down there. It's not exactly legal, so it's not straightforward to get in touch. But I am undeterred."

An optimist. An optimist willing to color outside the lines, to crawl through tunnels that were *interdits*, forbidden.

"So, where are you headed?" Killian asked.

"I'm on my way to the bookstore you mentioned, the Pont Traversé?"

"Yes, that's the one. Have you eaten?"

"Not really, but . . ." Genevieve trailed off with a shrug.

"What? Tired of me asking, or tired of French food?"

"No, no, believe me, it's not that. I just . . ." Should she confess that she didn't have the heart to eat in a café alone? And since she spent the whole day yesterday with Sylviane, she hadn't managed to shop for groceries.

Eating was such a long, drawn-out affair here. Genevieve respected the custom in theory, but it did make it difficult if you just wanted to grab a quick bite. Sure, there were plenty of people eating by themselves in restaurants, and certainly a grand tradition of people lingering over tables while writing in their journals or reading a book.

No one would look askance as they might in a restaurant in the U.S., where they hoped to turn the tables quickly. Here, no one rushed you. If you claimed the table for three hours, dawdling over the cheese plate or your café au lait, so be it. In fact, getting the bill in a Parisian eatery usually entailed waving the waiter down, sometimes repeatedly.

Nevertheless, Genevieve felt awkward, wondering where to put her hands, whether anyone was watching her. Of course, the other night she had enjoyed her meal at the brasserie after Sylviane left her at the table. . . . Perhaps *that* was the secret. She smiled to herself, thinking of writing *Genevieve's Guide to Paris*: Get hazy on *pastis*!

"Sorry," she continued, realizing Killian was still waiting for her to finish her thought. "I just didn't want to take the time for a sit-down meal. Is that awful? Not very French of me, I know."

He grinned. "I know the feeling. It takes a while to relax into the lifestyle, I think, especially for Americans. Your lot rushes about, don't they? Eating in cars, all that."

"I suppose so."

"I have the perfect solution for your problem: a relatively quick lunch eaten while standing in the street. But it's delicious. And besides, in my muddy state, I shouldn't be imposing myself on a restaurant."

"Really? Where?"

"Have you been to the Jewish quarter? The Pletzl?" At her head shake, he went on: "It's not far from here, in rue des Rosiers. . . . You'll love it."

She checked her watch. It was nearly two, and just in case . . . "How late is the bookstore open, do you happen to know?"

"Until midnight."

"Really? Midnight?" She smiled. "I love this city."

"Come on, then. Best falafel you've ever tasted."

They crossed the busy boulevard called rue de Rivoli, then ducked back into a web of narrow side streets lined with boutiques selling everything from upscale kitchen items to fine children's clothes.

"I remember my uncle telling me that 'the Left Bank of the Seine is to think, the Right Bank to spend,'" said Genevieve as they passed by an art gallery.

"I've never heard it put that way, but I suppose it makes sense," Killian said. "The universities and all are on the other side of the Seine, while most of the big stores are over here. Though these days, I'm afraid you spend a lot just about anywhere in Paris."

"And think just about anywhere as well?"

"One can only hope."

Rue des Rosiers was a tiny cobblestone street crowded with pedestrians. Whenever a car came by everyone shuffled begrudgingly out of the way—it was slow going. Down near the end of the block the crowd was particularly thick outside a restaurant called L'As du Fallafel. A line ran down the block, and young men with notepads approached to take the order from anyone who lingered long enough to read the big sign with the posted menu, which was, in itself, very simple: a choice of falafel or schwarma, which was a grilled blend of lamb, chicken, and beef.

Killian ordered one of each, saying that they could share or she could have either one; he liked them both equally.

A young man took their money and gave them a receipt. But when Killian guided Genevieve toward the end of the long line, disappointment clutched her. She hadn't realized the line was for *this* restaurant, but now they had already paid, it was too late to go elsewhere. Her stomach growled at the thought of food, and the aromas of spices and roasting meat wafting out of the restaurant were enticing.

She was overcome by a grumpy, American sentiment: *Couldn't we just get something easy, maybe a drive-through?* Why did everything have to be such a *big deal* in Paris? But she kept quiet and allowed herself to be escorted to the back of the line, cattlelike, with the others. She kept their place while Killian availed himself of the rest-room to wash up.

"Now, it's a good thing the line's long, because there are a couple of things I need to know from you," said Killian upon his return.

"Um . . . okay . . . ," Genevieve hedged, her stomach sinking. This was the last thing she wanted, to have to get up close and personal with some guy. Why couldn't she have kept her big mouth shut? Why did she allow Sylviane to sway her? Why had she wiped a *smudge* off Killian's cheek?

"First, do you want your sandwich with all the add-ons, and second—and, most important—do you want *harissa*?"

She smiled in relief. Questions about food, she could handle. "Yes, the works, but no onions; and second, I might, if I knew what *harissa* was."

"*C'est piquante*. . . . Hot sauce."

"Oh yes. Definitely hot sauce."

The man in front of them turned around. "Haven't had these before?"

Genevieve shook her head.

"You're in for a treat," he said in a jolly accent that she assumed was Scottish. It didn't sound like Killian's Irish lilt, and it was more charming than the standard British inflection.

They chatted for a few minutes; then he turned back to his wife and started speaking what sounded like fluent Vietnamese. Genevieve realized that the young men behind them were speaking something that sounded like Hebrew, and she caught snippets of American English and Spanish.

Genevieve looked at Killian and raised one eyebrow: "You brought me to a *tourist* attraction? I thought this was some secret gem only the locals knew about."

"Well, now, it's hard to keep a place like this a secret once Lenny Kravitz starts tweeting about it. Paris is the most visited city in the world—did you know that?"

"And you're saying just about everybody who visits winds up at L'As du Fallafel?"

"Sooner or later. This, and the ice cream at Berthillon."

Genevieve smiled, remembering the kids whining for ice cream while atop Notre-Dame. Perhaps it was hunger, but it was dizzying to consider how long ago it felt she had been mingling with the gargoyles, even though it had been only a couple of weeks. And Oakland was another lifetime entirely. She had a moment of feeling out of time and place: How could Genevieve Martin be standing here in this place, in this time? Her eyes landed on yet another plaque, which declared that forty-eight people had been deported from the corner during the war. Little children, old women, it didn't matter. No mercy.

And now Genevieve and Killian stood in an

absurdly long line awaiting falafel and *schwarma* stuffed into pita bread, and the toughest decision they were facing was whether they wanted *harissa*. Surreal.

Even though Genevieve had plenty of time to formulate her French sentence asking for what she wanted, when they finally got to the head of the line and handed their ticket to the men at the window, she was struck by stage fright. Killian stepped in and ordered for her, joking around with the servers in fluent French.

Within seconds, Genevieve and Killian were walking away holding fat, heavy, foil-wrapped sandwiches so stuffed with fillings it was hard to know how to approach them. In what seemed like a highly un-Parisian scene, dozens of people stood around, leaning against buildings, and eating right there in the alley. Killian and Genevieve found a section of wall to lean against and joined in.

Killian watched as Genevieve took her first bite of falafel. Raised his eyebrows. "Worth the wait?"

"Mmmm," she replied, nodding, her mouth full.

Halfway through they switched, so they each could sample the falafel and the *schwarma*. Both were delectable, enhanced by salted cucumber and shredded cabbage and roasted eggplant and *harissa* and tahini.

"It's great to see this neighborhood coming back like this," said Killian as they ate. "It was emptied out, of course, during World War II. The Jewish deli there on the corner? It used to be a jewelry store; it was bombed in 1942."

"Bombed? I thought . . . people were rounded up and taken away. I didn't realize there were bombings."

"The anti-Semitism had been building for some time. Nasty stuff." He shook his head. "Bombings . . . so impersonal. Horrific."

His eyes took a far-off cast, and there was something about the way he spoke that made her wonder.

"Is there still a problem in Ireland, with the violence?"

"Not nearly as bad as it once was, but yes, there are still tensions. I wasn't involved in any of that, but I spent a lot of time and energy making sure I kept out of it. There's . . . there was right and wrong on both sides, plenty of violence. It's not an easy situation, nor is it an easy truce."

After they finished their sandwiches, they strolled through the ancient neighborhood of the Marais. The streets were full of cafés and shops, tourists and locals alike.

On one largely residential corner they passed by a building with a sign: MUSÉE CARNAVALET.

"Have you been in here yet?" Killian asked. "It's a great museum, focuses on the history of

Paris. Look, they're doing an exhibit about one of you lads, Josephine Baker."

"That's right, my cousin mentioned Baker lived here."

"Shall we go in? It's free."

"Free and dealing with 'one of my lads'? How could I refuse?"

The exhibit included early film footage, reels of Baker dancing virtually naked, covered only in endless strands of pearls and feathers, or in a skirt made of bananas. Her dances were raunchy even now; Genevieve thought she must have been a phenomenon back in the day.

"She was really something," Killian said as they checked out a mannequin sporting one of her skimpy costumes, made primarily of ostrich feathers. "Did you know she owned a castle in the Dordogne?"

"A *castle?* Josephine Baker bought herself a French castle?"

He nodded. "She did very well here. Hugely popular. Her theme song was: 'J'ai Deux Amours: Mon Pays et Paris.' "

" 'I Have Two Loves . . .'?"

He nodded. " 'I Have Two Loves: My Country and Paris.' She stuck with France through the war, too, and was even suspected of espionage on behalf of the Allies. As you can imagine, this only increased her popularity. She not only bought a castle, but then she adopted a whole slew of children from all over the world, a 'rainbow tribe' long before Angelina Jolie thought of it. She was a true original."

Genevieve referred to the pamphlet (in English) she had nabbed from the kiosk upon entering. She read aloud: "The castle is called Château des Milandes; she lived there from 1937 to 1969. But listen to this: It says she ran out of money and eventually lost the place. Apparently she 'wound up on the kitchen stoop, confused, asking to be let back in.' " Genevieve looked up from her reading. "That's the saddest thing I've ever heard. I wish I didn't know that part."

Killian turned to Genevieve, stopping her.

"Just because something has a sad ending doesn't mean the entire interlude was sad, Genevieve. Josephine Baker was a groundbreaker; she lived an extraordinary life."

She shrugged. "I suppose."

"And then Grace Kelly stepped in and offered assistance, so ultimately she was taken care of. Oh, look at this." He stopped in front of photos of exotic animals. "She was a collector of animals as well as of children. She had quite the menagerie."

"William Randolph Hearst did the same thing in California, but he had to build his own castle to show them off. No genuine articles in the real estate listings in that part of the world."

"Do you miss it?"

"What?"

"California? That's your home, right?"

Was it her home? She shrugged. "It's beautiful. Everyone loves it. You should go."

"That's not what I asked you. Paris is a beautiful place, too. But some people prefer not to be surrounded by too much beauty. The contrast to their inner feelings can be depressing."

"You have a very strange way of looking at the world, you know that?"

He granted her a crooked grin and shrugged. "Well, you know the Irish, we're a morose lot. I do believe we enjoy the gray weather, at least most of the time. It suits our moods and makes it a reasonable choice to go down the pub all day, imbibing and grumbling."

Perhaps that was why Killian had left Ireland, she thought: He seemed of an ever-sunny disposition. She smiled, and their gazes met and held for a beat.

And then Genevieve remembered she was married. Not for long, and certainly not happily . . . but the knowledge was there nonetheless, the gold band still in her jewelry box.

She turned away, looked at a picture of a pen that had been built to hold a jaguar. The big cat's eyes seemed huge and sorrowful as it gazed out at the photographer. "The cage seems small, doesn't it?"

"Aye," Killian said very softly behind her. "Very small. Depressing."

Genevieve looked over her shoulder. "Does that mean we should go drown our sorrows 'down the pub'?"

"I think that's precisely what it means."

Chapter Forty-four

"And here I thought 'down the pub' was just an expression. I had no idea there were *actual* pubs in Paris."

Killian and Genevieve were seated at the Bombadier, in the Latin Quarter.

"It's a very cosmopolitan city. The tourists want typical Parisian things, of course; that's understandable. But the locals want the occasional Mexican food, Ethiopian food . . ."

"British food?" She lifted an eyebrow in question.

He laughed. "I wouldn't go *that* far. They may be cosmopolitan, but they're true epicureans. You won't find anyone rushing to sample British fare, I fear. It's the scotch they're after in a place like this."

"So really it should be called a Scottish pub."

"You're a real stickler for details, aren't you?"

She smiled and took a tiny sip of her whiskey, making her eyes water. It was mellow, aged, excellent. Still, she wasn't a huge fan of hard liquor, and the smell reminded her of Jason. She remembered how she used to love smelling it on his breath, tasting it on his lips. *Whiskey kisses.* The memory made her sad and left her yearning for something she wasn't ready to admit.

"So," Killian said, "you mentioned you were a copy editor, right? D'ya work on novels, then?"

"No, training manuals, technical booklets, that sort of thing."

"Ah," he said, taking a sip of his scotch.

He was too polite to say what Sylviane had: *Sounds boring.* And it *was* boring. It took skill and a detail-oriented nature, and Genevieve liked to think she was the best damned freelance copy editor in the business. But really . . . what had she offered to society, to the greater good? Had her efforts kept the world of training manuals free from the scourge of misused ellipses, from the menace of the misplaced comma? And who really cared?

On the other hand, grammatical errors put her teeth on edge, and she did find a certain satisfaction in maintaining standards. And again, she had been able to make a living in the Bay Area, a feat easier said than done, all while maintaining her own schedule.

But she wanted more.

"One great thing about it is that once I have Internet, it's something I could do from here if I need cash."

"That is a plus, for sure. And here I thought you

weren't wild about computers," he said with a smile.

"They aren't my happy place, but I am as dependent on them as everyone else, I suppose."

"And . . . what does your husband do?" said Killian.

"My—how—I mean—is it that obvious that I'm married?"

He lifted one eyebrow.

Genevieve sat back in her chair. "He's in computers, of course. But . . . we're not married, or not for long, anyway. We're all over but the paperwork, at this point."

"I'm sorry."

"Thank you. It's for the best." *I don't want to talk about it.*

"So, tell me about Philippe's basement," Killian said after a moment. "Anything good?"

"I'm sure you'll enjoy it—it's a bit manky, as you would say. The only thing really odd was a little trapdoor under a grate."

"A trapdoor? Did you open it?"

"Not yet. It's locked. It's probably nothing exciting. Most likely it's a disposal pipe, maybe a sewer entrance they keep closed to keep the rats out."

"Still, worth a look, don't you think?"

"Maybe," she said with a shrug. Why did she even mention this to Killian? He probably wouldn't have noticed it on his own. And what was it about the door that bothered her? *Her uncle had put a special lock on it. Why?*

Her turn to change the subject. "So, tell me, how did you get into photographing abandoned places? I mean, that's what you do?"

"Essentially, yeah. Some of the gang call themselves Urban Explorers—the whole movement is known as Urbex. But that seems a bit pretentious to me. In fact, I had no idea I was part of a 'movement' until my mate pointed it out to me. For me it started out as more of a . . . compulsion, for lack of a better word."

Genevieve nodded. If there was one thing she understood, it was the unruly desire to enter places that are supposed to be off-limits.

"The first place I went into was this creepy old abandoned house on the outskirts of Dublin. I had passed it a thousand times, and finally I couldn't fight it anymore. I had to have a peek inside." He shook his head, looked out into space. "I was so excited, enthralled by the space. Every room, every artifact from a bygone era, from a past life . . . Sometimes I think I'm more a ghost hunter than an 'adventurer.' "

"Philippe says there are ghosts in the catacombs."

"I wouldn't be too surprised."

"Do you really believe in spirits?"

He paused for a long moment, took a sip of his scotch. Shrugged.

"I like to think that by taking photos of bits of history, the spirits and memories that come through the dust and decay . . . that I can capture part of the essence of the people who once lived there. That's why I never stage anything—it's like an Urbex code: You just take photos of things exactly as they are. I think human life leaves traces of energy behind, in the walls and the furniture, just as we leave behind our old curtains or letters or shoes. Does that sound crazy?"

"No, it sounds just about right."

"Which is not to say I'm looking forward to encountering any real, Hollywood-style ghosts, though, I have to say. I once went into an old hotel. . . . Doors kept slamming, my equipment wouldn't work. . . ." He played with his scotch, then flashed her a crooked grin. "I'm not saying there were *ghosts,* but I was pretty happy to get out of there."

After another sip of scotch, Genevieve ventured, "Liliane is lovely."

He laughed and nodded. "Yes, she is."

"Are you and she . . . ?"

He shook his head. "She's lovely, as you say. But she's not the right one for me, or maybe I should say I'm not right for her. She just hasn't figured that out yet. I've still got her fooled."

"And how do you know who's right?"

"That's the million-dollar question, isn't it? I'm

no expert in love. In fact, I've been engaged twice but married nary a once."

"What happened?"

"Well, the first time hardly counts. We were both pissed."

"Drunk?"

"Terrible, isn't it? Youth. We were kids, really. Anyway, that didn't work out; we were clearly too young. And then more recently . . . my ex, Claire, is a wonderful woman. I just . . ." He trailed off with a shake of his head. "It sounds silly to my own ears when I say it aloud, but she couldn't handle my explorations, to be honest. Just couldn't deal at all."

"She didn't like you getting manky?"

"Exactly. And it's not that my wandering around in empty buildings is more important than the woman I'm with, but . . . if she can't understand why I'm so interested, I think that signals a problem, don't you? Case in point: My da, he's into horses. Just adores them. And my ma loves to go to high tea, see a play. They don't agree on anything, and that in itself would be okay except that they use their time together to tear down each other's interests. Ended up despising each other."

"Are they still together?"

"Oh, yeah, sure. The Irish stick together, makin' each other miserable till the day they die." He gave Genevieve a crooked smile, took a drink, then gazed at her. "They'd both like you, though, I'll bet."

Genevieve looked around the pub, avoiding Killian's eyes. It was late afternoon, but the pub started to fill, mostly with men, stopping by after work. In addition to French she heard a smattering of English in a variety of accents from all over the world. Paris truly was a world capital.

"So, you really want to take over your uncle's locksmith shop?" Killian asked.

"I think so, yes. I'm thinking about it, anyway."

"And yet you're working for free?" he teased. "Fine way to run a business."

"As you said yourself, the French bureaucracy is legendary."

"Sure. But you have to be tenacious."

Genevieve shrugged and sipped her scotch. "I'll get around to it. I've done some of the paperwork, even spent a day down at the offices, but I think maybe living in Paris is sapping me of my American can-do attitude."

He laughed.

"If you want to know the truth, I think, at least partly . . . I think I'm here trying to capture another time, another moment."

"Your famous summer in Paris when you were young?"

"In part." But truthfully there was more to it than that. Her mother had also come here. What had Angela been doing in Paris, all those years ago? There was something about it that had always seemed odd, some doubt niggling in the back of Genevieve's mind. The way Angela spoke about Paris with such sad reverence, the fact that she never went back again. The photo of her, eyes shining with happiness, in that cabaret beside the handsome young stranger. Her *tante* Pasquale urging Angela to tell Jim something.

Killian waited for her to elaborate.

"My mother came to Paris the year before I was born. She always told me she was 'on vacation,' just a little trip away from her husband and son."

"Your father and brother?"

"Right. Now I think maybe there was more to it."

"More, like what?"

"Like . . . maybe she wanted to leave my father, move to Paris." Genevieve hadn't put her finger on it until right this moment. Hadn't allowed the concept to formulate in her mind, as though voicing it would be the catalyst that would unify and harden the vague inklings into suspicion.

"What makes you think that?"

Genevieve searched Killian's eyes for signs of doubt or skepticism or an edge of lewd curiosity. But all she found was frank interest, sincerity.

"I don't have any real reason," she said, still holding back. "Just a few things: My aunt said something, and there was a photo in Philippe's house."

"Philippe knew your mother?"

She nodded. "Better than I did, in some ways. I wish I could have known my mother as an adult."

"A lot of people have troubles in their marriages, Genevieve. It doesn't make them bad people."

"I know. It's not that. I just wish I could have known *who* she was."

"You mean as a woman, besides being a mother?"

"Exactly. It seems to me that we start to see our parents as real people—fallible, with needs and desires of their own—only as we become adults ourselves. I had that with my father but not my mother. I lost her when I was still a child."

"So in your mind she's more symbol than flesh and blood: an icon of maternal love."

"*Yes.* I have vague memories of her: the way she smelled, the feeling of her arms wrapped around me. But . . . they're all about *me,* really. Who was she, as a person? What was she like when she was here in Paris, for example, far from her husband and child? Was she . . . *happy* here? And if so, why did she go back?"

After a long moment, Killian raised his glass in a toast.

"I guess that makes us both ghost hunters, then. Here's to the two of us, Genevieve. Mad as hatters."

Chapter Forty-five

Angela, 1983

Angela awakes in the hospital. Her brain is fuzzy. Her head throbs, her skin stings, and she can't feel her arm, which is strapped close to her body.

The last thing she remembers is going to meet Xabi in front of the opera house, but he never arrived. Then she realized what day it was.

It couldn't be, could it? He had sworn to her there was nothing to worry about.

Still.

She had wondered. Lay awake at night, worrying. Looked up the address for the Spanish embassy, wondering if she should say something, do something.

So when Xabi didn't show up at la place de l'Opéra, Angela hopped the Métro to Alma-Marceau, running the rest of the way to the embassy. Yelling at the guards outside the front door, trying to warn them.

An old blue Renault was parked out in front . . . wasn't that Thibeaux's car?

And then . . . she can't remember anything else.

"What happened?" Angela asks the nurse.

The nurse is kind and apologizes for not

speaking English well. But she speaks very slowly in French, so Angela can understand.

"There was a bombing. A man ran all the way here, to the hospital, with you in his arms. A very handsome man."

"Who . . . who was he?"

"Are you feeling well enough to read? *Voilà*, the newspaper."

There is an article. No photo of the man who carried the American woman to the hospital, but a description. Dark hair, light eyes. Apparently injured. He is now being sought in connection to the bombing.

The bombing of the Spanish embassy. Three people had been killed, ten wounded.

"Also," the nurse says, "I am sorry to say this, but the police will need to speak to you. Do not worry; it is just in case you saw something, perhaps, or someone. Because the terrorist bombings are a big problem in Paris, of course. How could they not be?"

"Tell me . . . could you please tell me about the man who brought me here? Was he hurt?"

"He would not stay for medical care, but he wanted to be sure you would be all right. And you will be fine—you have a minor concussion, and your arm was burned, but you should regain the use of it. Also, you have some scrapes and bruises, but nothing serious. I'll get the doctor."

The doctor—a large, florid man who smells of

tobacco—assures her of the same. She will have significant scarring, he notes, and if she wants plastic surgery she can pursue that at a later date. Right now the main thing is to heal from the wound, keep it wrapped and safe from infection.

"*Et ne vous inquiétez pas pour le bébé.* No worries at all, madame. Your baby will be just fine."

"Baby? What *baby?*"

Chapter Forty-six

Sylviane was enthralled with Genevieve's cousin's sand table. From the moment she and Genevieve walked into Catharine's office, she had been recounting dream after dream and setting up figures at the sand table: She favored pink-and-purple princess motifs, and flowers, with a bottle of booze and a rusty old gear shaft thrown in for good measure.

"Catharine! Tell me, what does this say about me?"

Genevieve had gone to meet Sylviane at La Maréchalerie very early this morning. It was Sylviane's day off, but Genevieve had asked to see how baguettes were made. The key, according to Sylviane, was using the very best ingredients—not all flour is the same!—and giving the loaves a special twist just prior to baking. While they watched a very handsome young Italian man (biceps glistening in the heat) twisting the dough, then putting raw loaves in the oven and extracting the freshly baked ones, Genevieve told Sylviane:

"I think we need to fix up my cousin Catharine."

"Fix? She is sick?"

"No, sorry, it's an expression. I would like to take her out shopping and have you dress her like you did me."

"She is Parisian, is she not?"

"She is; it's just . . . she's a little different. I think she could use your help. Lunch is on me."

"Good, I love that! You are looking good, you see? Because of me!"

Genevieve smiled. "Exactly."

So now they stood at the sand table and Catharine interpreted for the overeager Sylviane. Her dreams revolved primarily around love affairs, and many sounded suspiciously like the basic storylines of romantic comedies.

"And you, *ma petite cousine*?" Catharine turned to Genevieve. "Have you had more dreams about not opening the doors?"

"A few." *Yes*. She had been plagued by them, in fact. Which bewildered her, since during waking hours Genevieve was feeling so much happier: worried about her visa, of course, and wondering how to set up an apprenticeship and how she was going to manage to get the shop certified. But she had faith in the advice of her well-meaning neighbors; she had been gathering papers and documentation according to Monsieur Lambert's list and planned to schedule an inspection of the shop as soon as she got it cleaned up and organized.

The truth was, Genevieve was falling in love with Paris and with Parisians. She felt more alive than she had in months (years?), and she intended to follow everyone's advice and be so stubborn and compliant with the bureaucrats that they would eventually surrender and give her what she wanted. After all, *"impossible" n'est pas français.*

"Do you know the story of *l'oiseau de Fitcher*? 'Fitcher's Bird'?" Catharine asked.

Genevieve shook her head. "I don't think so."

"Oh, I do!" said Sylviane.

"I will tell you," said Catharine, with a quelling glance at Sylviane (*"I* will tell the story"). " 'Fitcher's Bird' is about an evil trickster who captures innocent young women, marries them, and carries them back to his home, which is full of riches. He gives them a set of keys to the whole house but says, 'This one key, you must not use.' "

"Sounds like the legend of Bluebeard."

"It is similar. But I like this version better."

Genevieve smiled. "How come you get to pick and choose the fairy tales that best describe the human condition?"

Catharine shrugged and blew out a cloud of smoke. "Because this is my office."

"She is right," said Sylviane in a grave tone.

"Okay, sorry I interrupted. Please go on," said Genevieve. "I take it the young woman opens the door against his advice and sees something she shouldn't?"

"Precisely," said Catharine. "His previous wives, all dead. Very gruesome."

"*Tu as oublié l'oeuf*," inserted Sylviane, then translated for Genevieve: "She forget the egg."

"Oh, you are right. Yes," said Catharine. "I forgot to mention the husband also gave her an egg to hold."

"And what does the egg do?" Genevieve asked.

"When the girl goes in the forbidden room, there is blood everywhere and some gets on the egg," volunteered Sylviane. She took a cigarette from Catharine's open pack on the desk. "But of course blood cannot be washed off an eggshell."

"I thought you quit smoking," commented Genevieve, not relishing sitting in the small office with two smokers.

"I did!" Sylviane shrugged and got up to open the window. "I don't buy them anymore. Is different when they are from someone else."

"Okay, so the blood doesn't wash off the egg," said Genevieve, coming back to the story. "Now it sounds like Macbeth."

"I know you are making fun, but there is a reason so many stories include similar elements," said Catharine. "Just as our dreams do. We share the culture of humanity."

One aspect of this idea made Genevieve uncomfortable; she wasn't sure she wanted to share her most private thoughts and dreams—and symbols—with the rest of the world. On the other hand, it also made her feel connected, and curious as to what the disparate members of humanity held in common.

"When the egg is dropped in the blood, it is stained," continued Catharine. "This is symbolic of knowledge: once you know something, you cannot go back, cannot unlearn it."

"Then how come I can never remember my online passwords?"

"You like to joke. I know this. You Americans like to joke; you are always laughing. Smiling. But not everything is funny."

"I like the funny Americans," said Sylviane with a shrug.

"Sorry," said Genevieve, chastened. "Please keep going, Catharine. Blood gets on the egg and she can't wash it off."

"Exactly. So then the trickster returns, sees the blood, and she meets her bloody fate in the secret chamber."

"I'm telling you, these damsels really should have taken a decent self-defense course."

"Except that they aren't young women at all, of course," says Catharine, an edge to her voice betraying her impatience. "They are vulnerable parts of our psyche; this is what I'm trying to tell you. That is why they are always young and most often female. Every character is simply some aspect of us."

"*Vraiment*? Really?" Sylviane perked up at this last piece. "This is very interesting."

"Why do you think fables are so powerful?" said Catharine. "They are not fantastical tales about girls and wolves, or such a thing. They are about our own inner workings."

Sylviane smiled broadly and nudged Genevieve. "Your cousin, she is very interesting."

"You're right; she is," said Genevieve, nodding in agreement.

"Then her sister comes," continued Catharine. "But the sister is clever. She puts the egg in a safe hiding place first, and only then does she open the secret room. And what do you think she finds?"

"I'm guessing it's not good," said Genevieve.

"Not at all. There she finds her sisters' bodies all . . . how do you say, all divided? Arms here, legs there, head cut off?"

"Chopped up? Dismembered?"

"*Exactement*. Exactly. They are dismembered, but the last sister is able to put the pieces back together and her sisters come alive."

"So they are parts of the psyche that she is repairing!" Sylviane declared, apparently a convert to Catharine's interpretation. "So, Genevieve, this means the locked room in your dream is a part of your *psyche* that's all locked up! What do you think about *that?*"

Sylviane and Catharine had a lively exchange in French.

"Couldn't the dreams simply be a result of me thinking about becoming a locksmith?" asked Genevieve. "And dealing with the inherent frustrations of the profession? Not to mention the ordeal of trying to get my certification from the French bureaucracy?"

Catharine stubbed out her cigarette, agitated, and waved one hand in the air. "If you insist on the most obvious of interpretations, this is fine. But I can assure you, *ma petite cousine*, there is much more to this than you think. Our dreams are the route through which our inner selves speak to us."

"But maybe some rooms are *meant* to remain locked," Genevieve heard herself saying. "Why can't *that* be the lesson of the egg in the story? If you follow orders and don't open the door, you won't get chopped up."

"Just because you don't see the bodies doesn't mean they aren't there," said Sylviane in a sage tone. "You never see *Silence of the Lambs*?"

"She is right," said Catharine. "And, Genevieve, my father used to say that if there's one thing a locksmith can't stand, it's a locked door. And I think you are already more of a locksmith than you know."

Chapter Forty-seven

"Genevieve Martin, I am come back, you see? Okay!"

Philippe stood outside the shop window, smiling and waving with his cane.

"Philippe! So nice to see you," Genevieve said as she opened the door. "We've missed you."

"*Ooh la*," he said, sucking air in between his teeth and shaking one hand as though burned. "Look at you, you look *très parisienne*! You have gone shopping, I think."

Even while Genevieve smiled and thanked him for his compliment, part of her wondered: How unkempt did she look before, that everyone reacted so strongly to her new look? She had never been a fashion plate, but she had always considered herself at least presentable. But, then, this was Paris, she reminded herself. The standards were high.

"You come to my house?" Philippe said. "Finish with the locks maybe?"

"Yes, I'd be glad to. I finished with Monsieur Angelini, so once I complete your job only Madame Gerard is left."

"But you have many more customers, I think. Always the people need the locksmith."

"I'm not sure. I'm having some trouble getting

my paperwork signed and stamped. Apparently the stamp is very important. And even then . . . I would have to apprentice before becoming certified as a locksmith. It's complicated."

"I know another locksmith, on the other side of Paris—he was a friend of Dave's. I am sure he could help. I am happy to introduce you."

"Thank you. Let me get a little further with the paperwork, and then I might take you up on that."

Genevieve had spent yet another day down at the visa offices, armed with all the paperwork she could think of: passport and visa (of course), a recent utility bill in her name (to show she was actually living in the village and paying bills); a notarized letter from Catharine (notaries were much more formal and expensive here than in the U.S., Genevieve had discovered to her chagrin), testimonials from her neighbors (Marie-Claude and Daniel had gathered the notes and presented them to her as a gift in a bundle, along with a jar of homemade cherry preserves), and the sheaf of forms that had been thrust into her hands by Monsieur Lambert (which Genevieve carefully filled out and asked Sylviane to proofread).

Still, Genevieve had yet to obtain the necessary signatures, much less the treasured stamp. She had been given more forms to fill out and had scheduled a shop inspection.

But despite all of this, Genevieve felt content to remain in her strange limbo. Occasionally she would wake at three in the morning and start to worry, her mind tripping over a thousand hurdles yet to clear and conjuring disastrous what-if scenarios. But in general she was stubbornly *not* thinking about what would happen if she failed to arrange the paperwork with the proper authorities and never received a work permit. Or, even if she managed that, how would she get through the locksmith apprenticeship? Also, she didn't want to think about Jason and the next steps in the divorce.

In fact, all she wanted to do was play with her uncle's old locks and keys, open a door or two, and hang out with Sylviane and Killian and the neighbors and even Catharine. Killian had come by and (with the vociferous assistance of Daniel and Jacques) set up Genevieve's Internet connection so she had been able to pay some bills, but even so, other than sending Mary a chatty note, she had barely checked her e-mail.

She was existing in a charming, lavender-scented bubble of good food, art, and wine; it was an oddly sensual, seductive half-life.

"Never give up with the authorities, Genevieve," said Philippe. "And eventually you will succeed!"

"Thanks," she said with a smile. "So, would you like to come in for *apero*? I don't have cheese puffs, but I just came back from the store."

"How can I turn down such an invitation from a beautiful woman?"

She held the door for him as he used his cane, tapping his way into the apartment.

"It has been a long time since I am here," said Philippe. "Pasquale, she has the magnificent dinners here—do you remember?"

"I do," she said. "I have dreamed of those dinners over the years."

"Her couscous . . . never have I found a restaurant that comes near her quality."

"I've had the same thought myself. Here, sit, and let me get you a glass of wine. White, red, or rosé?"

She served them both glasses of chilled Muscadet, a dry white wine from the Loire Valley, then arranged a few snacks: seasoned walnuts, sliced green apples, thinly cut rabbit sausage, and an artichoke dip she had indulged in, on a whim, from a Greek delicatessen she had strolled by near the Champs-Élysées.

Genevieve asked Philippe about his time at his daughter's house, and he told her stories of his grandchildren and their pet hedgehog—a word for which Genevieve had to retrieve the dictionary after he unsuccessfully tried to describe the little animal.

"Philippe," Genevieve finally ventured, "could you tell me about my mother, what she was like when she was here?"

"Ah, your mother, she was lovely! *Très belle femme*, very beautiful woman on the inside, too, in her heart. Very sensitive, very . . . passionate."

"Did she seem happy to you?"

He tilted his head, considering. "I think . . . when first she comes, no. She sleeps a lot when first she comes. But then she becomes happier. She offered to help my Delphine with packing, *très gentile*, very nice."

"Do you know what happened to her arm?"

He looked at Genevieve for a long time, his rheumy eyes focused and intense. "You do not know the story? *Vraiment*?"

Truly? he asked. Genevieve shook her head.

He opened his mouth as if to speak, but then hesitated. After another moment, he said, "Always Delphine tells me: When one does not know the whole story, one should not speak."

"But my *tante* Pasquale, she was confused when I visited and she thought she was telling my mother that she had to tell Jim—my father— something. Do you know what it was? Did it have to do with the accident?"

"I am sorry, Genevieve. I do not know. What happened with Angela was an accident . . . she was an innocent tourist, too close to—" He cut himself off, his gaze shifting toward the court-yard. "Aha, look, your neighbors! *Bonjour, ça va?*"

Daniel and Marie-Claude had approached the open window, but upon seeing Philippe they nodded stiffly, wished Genevieve and Philippe a good day, and kept walking.

"They are the Black Feet," Philippe said,

yanking his thumb toward the window. "With very long memories, I am sad to say. Do you know about the Black Feet? From Algérie."

"Why are they called Black Feet?"

"Ha! Funny name, I think. Some say it is because they stomp the grapes, stain their feet. Or maybe it is because of the dark soil, the land. I do not know."

"What were you about to say, about my mother? She was too close to what, or to whom?"

"You know, these things are very complicated, Genevieve. What happened with your mother . . . it reminds me of what happened, *précisément*, with the Black Feet. Everything has so many sides. When Jean-Paul Sartre goes to Algérie, he sees what is happening: that now we *French* are the colonialists. You see, it is because of what happened with the Germans that I follow Jean-Paul in this. We fight not only with our bodies, but with our minds—we fight the colonialism, the invasion of the Germans, you see? But are we not doing the same thing in Algérie? Eh, Genevieve, this artichoke, is very good!"

He ate some dip, took another sip of wine, sat back.

"This is why some of us fight against the war, because this is not why our grandfathers fight the revolution against the king, against tyranny. We have a constitution; people forget the ideals of the *fraternité*."

"That does sound a lot like what happens in the U.S. when we go to war: Some people say it is only patriotic to support the war, and others say it is more patriotic to oppose it. The only thing everyone can agree on is to support the troops."

" 'Troops'?"

"The soldiers. The people who are sent to fight."

"Ah, *oui*, I agree with this. The soldiers go where they are told, *n'est-ce pas*? And even sometimes I think this about many Germans; maybe they did not want to be here. The soldiers who arrested me during the world war, they were boys, my age at the time. War is terrible for everyone, on all the sides."

"So you spoke out against the Algerian War. And you suffered for it?"

He shrugged, stuck out his chin. "I was not alone, you know. Many people were against this war. One famous group supporting Algérie is made of one anarchist, one Trotskyist, and one Roman Catholic priest! *Imagine!*"

Philippe laughed so hard he started coughing.

As he took a moment to regroup, something else occurred to Genevieve.

"My *tante* Pasquale, her mother was Algerian."

He nodded. "Yes. Yes she was."

"Was Pasquale involved in this?"

"We all were, in one way or another."

"Philippe, please, can you tell me what happened with my mother?"

He looked at her with such sadness in his old eyes. "I cannot, Genevieve. I am sorry, but I cannot."

Chapter Forty-eight

Angela, 1983

Several long days pass before Angela is released from the hospital. The gendarmes have questioned her repeatedly; she tells them nothing. Not a thing about Xabier or Thibeaux or Pablo or the others. She is silent, tearful, the innocent American tourist.

What they did was wrong, horrific. And yet she cannot bring herself to turn them in.

Dave comes to sit with her; he is frightened for her welfare—she is young and healthy; she will heal. But, unlike the police, Dave is not fooled by the "innocent bystander" mien she has adopted. He peppers her with questions about Xabi. *"Last name? Do you know where he lives? He is Basque, isn't that so? Has he been involved in the troubles? Who are his friends? Angela, you must tell me before someone else gets hurt."*

She is nauseated, cannot think. Her mind is muddled—by the drugs or the concussion?

What baby?

When she is allowed to go home she is tucked into the little bed in Catharine's room, and Catharine is relegated to the couch so Angela can have privacy. Pasquale flutters about, trying to make her comfortable, but the only thing that eases the headache and the horrifying burning sensation is drugs. She sleeps.

Her dreams are hypercolored, psychedelic. In them she is calling out for Xabi. Yelling at the young guards in front of the Spanish embassy. They can't hear her. Pointing at the blue Renault. Running but not getting anywhere; her legs won't carry her.

She awakens, screaming. *"Xabi, no!"*

Philippe and Delphine bring flowers and a few items Angela left at their house—her notebook, a sweater. They are so sorry for her troubles. They thank her for all her help packing, but Delphine has lost her interest in the project and wishes to join her sister in the countryside. She is disturbed by the incidents—bombings are too much, too reminiscent of another time. They are leaving Paris for a few weeks, going to the South of France.

Before Philippe leaves, he asks Angela: Does she know anything more about Xabi? Where might he be hiding?

When she shakes her head, begins to cry, they tell her to rest. The most important thing right now is to get well.

The D'Artavels, too, have been questioned by the police about Xabi. Because Philippe was known to support the Algerian cause, he is looked at with particular suspicion. This is another reason they are leaving Paris, Dave tells Angela, accusation in his eyes.

A few more days, and the pain subsides to a muted, incessant throbbing.

Angela keeps thinking about the little room they found in the catacombs under Philippe and Delphine's house. She would never be able to find her way back through the tunnels without Xabi to guide her, except . . . what about that grate in their *cave*, with the trapdoor beneath?

At her suggestion, Philippe had Dave put a lock on it. Does Dave have an extra key? Even without one, Dave would know how to pop it open, probably in a few seconds. She had witnessed this how many times? He could open just about any lock, would buy old padlocks and door sets at thrift stores and the swap meet, practice constantly, just for fun.

But if she asks for Dave's help, he will tell the authorities. Of course he would. She would have done the same in his place.

She would do so now, if it weren't for the fact that she loves Xabi so desperately. How could someone on the outside understand? The gentleness in his voice, the warmth in his hands, the secrets in his eyes. His haunted heart.

"I am already a ghost."

When Pasquale goes out to the market, Angela takes a flashlight and rifles through Dave's shop until she finds his Victorian ring of skeleton keys, the ones that he told her opened most locks in old Parisian homes.

She slips out, woozy but revived by the fresh air. She takes a cab to Philippe and Delphine's house. Tries the skeleton keys on the front door—it opens with the third try.

She lets herself in and moves without hesitation to the door that leads to the basement. Descends slowly and carefully down the steep stone stairs, stopping twice to rest. She breathes deeply, fighting vertigo and nausea.

Down the hall, into the utility room. She removes the grate and once again uses one of Dave's skeleton keys to unlock the little trap-door.

Lets herself down the rusty ladder. It is awkward, painful with only one arm, with her head aching and spinning. But she makes it. The catacombs are freezing, dank, and dark; the flashlight does not illuminate nearly enough. She shivers.

At the door to the secret room, she hesitates. Listens, ear to the damp wood.

"Xabi?" Angela says finally, knocking softly. "Xabi, are you there? It's . . . Angel."

As though this is a courtesy call, as if she is

welcoming him to the neighborhood. She feels like laughing—the idea is so absurd. Her thoughts are a jumble; she has to focus to keep her mind on the task in front of her.

No answer. She is wrong, then.

Has he fled Paris? Is he already abroad, on the run? Hiding out with relatives in the Basque country? Or . . . had he been seriously injured? Could he have already . . . ?

Angela tries two more skeleton keys before she finds the one that opens the lock. She pushes the door in slowly.

The beam of her flashlight sweeps the little chamber: There are more blankets on the old cot. Bottles of wine, packages of food, gauze, rubbing alcohol, and ointment. Newspapers.

She feels an arm snake around her neck, cutting off her breath.

Chapter Forty-nine

"This is amazing," said Killian. He had been photographing Philippe's house, taking dozens of shots while Genevieve finished up with the locks on the main floor, but now they both stood in the basement, at the bottom of the stairs.

"How long's it been since Philippe was down here?"

"Decades, I think," Genevieve answered. "He's

been living over at his daughter's house, and even before . . . I get the sense that he and his wife only used part of the house."

"A place like this, in this section of Paris . . . ? It would bring in a bloody fortune. Is that why he's havin' you fix it up, then, to sell it?"

"I'm not sure what he wants to do with it, to tell you the truth. He seems undecided. He said something about his daughter getting a new job, and that maybe they'd have the money to fix it up. As you noticed, the plaster is falling and the plumbing's ancient. Who knows what shape the structure's in, underneath it all."

"Are we perfectly safe down here, d'ya think?"

Genevieve smiled. "Let's put it this way: If this house were in California, I don't think I'd spend much time down here, waiting for an earthquake. But the earth doesn't shake much around here, does it?"

"Don't think so," he said, but his words were muffled as he held a series of cameras up to his face, focused on various corners of the old cellar, and snapped away.

Out from the old leather bag came half a dozen different cameras: a Polaroid, a disposable, something that looked like an antique box camera. Several sported tape or pieces of cardboard attached to them.

At her obvious interest, he said, "A camera is really just a dark chamber with light-sensitive paper. I've been thinking of building my own. Have you heard of Mendel Grossman, who snuck a homemade contraption into the Jewish ghettoes and took photos of them, right before they were emptied out by the Nazis? A camera can be a revolutionary device."

"Nothing very revolutionary down here."

"Oh, I don't know. . . . What about the door you told me about, the one you're afraid to open?"

"I'm not *afraid* to open it. Philippe said not to bother."

"I would think you'd be annoyed by such a thing. Locksmith creed and all that."

"How do you know about the locksmith's creed?"

He chuckled, pointed the camera straight at her, and took a shot before she had a chance to turn away.

"So, really?" he continued. "You're not even going to try to open the trapdoor? Where is it?"

She brought him into the utility room and showed him the ornate grate. He passed the beam of his light past the grill and illuminated the little door beyond.

Killian looked up at her, eyebrows raised. "Now, that's interesting, isn't it? Shall I lift the grate so we can take a closer look?"

Genevieve hesitated. There was something about that door and that lock . . . far too much like something she would stumble across in one of her dreams.

"Have you ever heard the tale of 'Fitcher's Bird'?" Genevieve asked.

"Sounds familiar, but I don't really remember."

"It's related to Bluebeard—all about damsels who marry a rich man who gives them everything they ask for, with one catch."

"There's always a catch."

"Right? When he goes away, they mustn't open one particular door. All the others are okay, but this one is off-limits. So of course they're overcome by curiosity, open the door, and find all his former wives chopped to bits."

"You think you're going to find a bunch of Philippe's former wives chopped up behind the door?"

"No, of course not. It's probably a waste pipe, or maybe an empty closet."

"That would be a disappointment."

"That's what usually happens, I remember my uncle telling me. You work for hours at opening some mysterious little door . . . and then you have the triumphant moment when you defeat the lock, and then it turns out to be an empty nook, or worse."

"Worse?"

"He told me once he found the remains of an animal. It wasn't pretty."

"But you don't think that, this time. I can tell. You're dying to open it."

"When I asked Philippe about it, he started talking

about the catacombs. He worked with the resistance, and they used the catacombs to get around. I can't seem to get the whole story from him; it usually devolves into warnings about ghosts."

Killian looked at her, a gleam in his eye. "Seriously? Well then, of course we have to open it."

" 'We'?"

He smiled. "I'm your moral support. I'm here to document the discovery, run for *pain au chocolat*, hand you your tools—whatever you want. I'm at your command. Shall I?"

After another moment's hesitation, she nodded.

He lifted the metal grate and leaned it against the wall.

Genevieve crouched and gazed at the door.

"It's an antique lock. I think my uncle put it on—it looks like one of his favorite lockplates. I recognize the maker and the scrollwork."

"And . . . ?"

"That means I don't want to hurt it, since it's antique; and it might be hard to defeat, since my uncle put it on. He was the best."

"And now you're set to be the best, carry on in his footsteps."

"That's a little optimistic, isn't it? I don't even have my work permit yet."

"If you really want it, you'll get it. I have faith in you. I recognize a stubborn nature when I see one."

Killian lay down on his stomach so he could inspect the door. Finally he sat up and brushed the cobwebs off his hands. "We could try removing the hinges."

Genevieve gaped at him, aghast.

He gave her a lopsided smile. "Let me guess: A locksmith wouldn't do such a thing."

"I should say not. That could damage the door, and the lock. And besides, it would be admitting defeat."

"Seems to me like not even trying is admitting defeat from the start."

Who was she kidding? She couldn't say no to opening a door like this; she would dream about it the rest of her life. Better by far to be disappointed by some prosaic assemblage of ancient plumbing hidden behind the door.

She opened her uncle's bag and took out a leather sack full of keys. Then she stretched out on the floor, belly down, and tried the first one in the lock.

"This might take a while," she said.

"How many keys d'ya have there?"

"More than a hundred."

He let out a silent whistle. "And you think one of them might work?"

"It's worth a try. My uncle loved old locks and old keys. This"—she held up the old iron key ring full of skeleton keys—"purportedly belonged to a thief back in the Victorian era."

"Really? That's *craic*." He came over, checked them out. When he leaned over her, she could smell him, feel his warmth in the cool damp of the basement.

"Crack, again?" Genevieve said, trying to ignore his closeness.

"Fun, interesting. Out of the ordinary." He smiled down at her, holding her gaze a beat too long. When he spoke again, his voice was very low. "Like you."

Genevieve could feel she was blushing as she focused on the lock. "Unfortunately, the thief's key ring doesn't seem to be doing the trick this time. Like I said, this may take a while. You should probably go take your pictures."

She didn't look up while she tried key after unsuccessful key. She could hear the soft clicks and purrs of Killian's cameras, and she wondered what those dark eyes were finding: interesting cracks in the stone walls, a corner full of cottony spiderwebs, a discarded children's rocking chair?

Finally she looked up to see that he was taking pictures of her while she worked.

"I don't take good pictures."

"No worries, *I'll* be taking them."

"I mean I'm not very photogenic. I don't like having my picture taken."

"Well now, those are two different things. Sometimes they go together, most times not. People think they don't look good in pictures because it's not the way they see themselves. But if the photographer is gifted, he or she sees beyond the surface."

"And you fancy yourself that good, do you?"

He grinned. "Ah, sure, yeah," he said in an exaggerated Irish accent. His cheekiness made her smile despite herself. "Have you ever seen yourself when you're focusing on a lock?"

"No, I . . . never really thought about it, I guess."

"You just wait 'til you see the photos. The ones from the Love Locks Bridge turned out brilliant— I'll show you next time you come by."

"Hey, that reminds me: My uncle was writing a book about antique locks and keys before he died. I was thinking of trying to finish it for him. Would you be willing to take photos of some of the pieces?"

"I'm not sure I'd be the best photographer for a project like that, but I'll take a look at it, at least. I'd be honored."

"Great, thanks." Genevieve hadn't decided upon finishing the book until right that moment. But now, as she lay on a cold stone basement floor, trying key after key in the lock, sensing her uncle doing just this as he installed the lock . . . perhaps Philippe was right: She had carried Dave's ghost with her down into this basement. He was with her in the keys, the lock, the process. Her new friends were right to call her the American locksmith. She would fight the bureaucracy, use her stubbornness, and then take up her uncle's mantle.

"What happens if you can't find a key to fit the lock?"

"I'll pick it. But I figured this was worth a try since I'll bet my uncle put this lock on. And if I can find a key that fits, I can give it to Philippe so he can open it again—which would be much easier than me making a new one."

"Ah."

"The only thing is . . ." She leaned over as far as she could, using the flashlight to try to peer inside the keyhole of the lock. "This is a very strange lock. It looks like a standard antique Yale on the outside, but inside . . ."

"What is it?"

Genevieve made out edges and grooves that made no sense. And then she realized: The exterior lock plate was a decoy.

She unscrewed it, removed the plate, and revealed the ancient mechanism within.

"What is that?" Killian asked.

"I don't know what my uncle was up to, but it looks like . . ." Genevieve was struck by a crazy notion. She slipped her necklace over her head and fitted her rusty Syrian key—the one she had worn for almost twenty years—into the lock.

Genevieve hesitated.

"Go on, then," said Killian in a quiet voice. "You're not seriously afraid, are you?"

She looked up. Met his gaze. Told the truth. "Yes."

He gave her a little smile, understanding shining in his eyes. "I'll be right by your side. If this is where the bodies are buried, I'll help you escape."

She gave a nervous laugh. *Why had her uncle sent her mother this key?* Was it merely a coincidence, or did it mean something? And why would he have disguised the lock with the wrong external plate?

She turned the key. The bolt was difficult to slide but finally gave way with a loud snick.

Genevieve blew out a long breath, then pulled open the door. She and Killian pointed their flashlights down into the hole.

A rusty ladder was bolted to one wall, leading down about six feet, then meeting up with a tunnel.

"Let me go first," said Killian, already launching himself through the hatch.

Genevieve put on her headlamp, slipped her necklace back on, and followed.

Chapter Fifty

"This is *craic*!" Killian exclaimed in a loud whisper.

Genevieve felt like whispering, too, as though they were entering a sacred space. It felt primordial, the pitch-black bowels of an ancient city that predated the Paris she had come to know. *L'empire de la mort*, the empire of the dead.

Tunnels led off in several directions. The air was stuffy, damp. Sepulchral.

"Which way?" Genevieve asked.

"Lady's choice. Where do ya fancy?"

She started down one passage. In about twenty feet they reached a dead end, retraced their steps, and tried a second. A big star had been scratched into the stone at the juncture: Killian and Genevieve both took note, not wanting to get lost. The dark passageways were disorienting, with no way to intuit in which direction one was walking.

Killian snapped a few photos, but so far they had seen nothing more interesting than dark, cramped stone tunnels. They had to squeeze past a crooked column made of chunks of concrete and stone, marked with a series of letters and numbers. Killian snapped more pictures.

"I've read about this: At one point buildings and roads started caving in on the tunnels, so workers braced them with columns. They left their information here, see? The codes tell which crew it was that completed the work."

A few feet farther down was an indentation in the wall. And a door.

"A storage closet?" Genevieve suggested.

"Maybe. Who knows? Could be anything. A

German bunker, maybe." He tried the knob. It was locked.

Killian looked at Genevieve in challenge, a tiny half smile on his face.

"You suppose you could open it?"

"We're not supposed to be down here at all, you know. Philippe told me the catacombs were *interdits*, except for the tourist part. And now you want me to break into a locked room?"

"You're already a criminal, you know, practicing locksmithing without a license," he said with a tsk. "Seriously, you're not curious? Besides, it's directly under Philippe's house, so it probably belongs to him. And he said you were welcome to look around, didn't he?"

"You're a bad influence," said Genevieve. "You're like the kid my mom told me not to hang around with."

But even as she said it, she knelt to look at the lock. Incredibly, it looked like a match to the one on the trapdoor: an ornate antique doorplate that didn't match the inner locking mechanism.

"What is it?" he asked.

"I think it's my uncle's work again."

"There, now. Practically an invitation to open it."

She unscrewed the plate and, once again, used the ancient key on her necklace to open the lock.

Killian started snapping pictures the moment the door swung open.

Inside was a small chamber with an iron-frame cot topped by a very sad looking mattress and a blanket. A pile of folded clothes sat atop these. There was a bottle of wine, and some sort of disgusting powdery substance that looked like it used to be bread. Tins of tuna fish and peaches and pâté, plus a can opener.

One entire wall held faint traces of a mural done in chalk: A Chagall-like painting of a man and woman floating among the stars, kissing.

Genevieve could hear Sylviane's voice: *"like the way love is supposed to feel."*

Killian let the camera fall on his chest and picked up a newspaper. "August 17, 1983. Front-page story of the day: the bombing of the Spanish embassy. I remember hearing about that . . . What do you suppose this place was? If it was a kids' hangout I'd expect to find old liquor bottles and signs of smoking, but this . . . ?"

"It looks like someone was hiding," Genevieve said. Her voice was trembling.

"You okay, Genevieve?"

She nodded. "I just . . . just the willies, I guess."

"Do you want to go? I'll walk you back to the entrance."

"No, it's okay. I'm good for a few more minutes. Finish up with your photos."

She wasn't ready to share with Killian what she

was only beginning to put together in her own mind. Not yet.

Genevieve picked up a book sitting beside the stack of clothing. Hemingway's *A Farewell to Arms*. She opened the cover and saw the stamp, in a bold, blocky script:

DAVE MACKENZIE
Under Lock and Key, Serrurier,
Rue Saint-Paul, Village Saint-Paul

Her heart started to thud loudly in her chest, the sound filling her ears. In the sepulchral quiet of the underground, she was surprised Killian couldn't hear it. But his attention was elsewhere, on taking photos of the mural.

Could this be where Angela and Xabier used to meet? Her (married) mother was so in love with another man that she agreed to see him here, in this stinking hole in the ground? Sweet, dutiful Angela Martin?

So much for the City of Lights. Chagall mural or no, this was no one's idea of a romantic getaway.

Genevieve felt sick at the thought of it. *How could she?*

"Hey," Killian's voice interrupted her thoughts. "I think we should get you out of here. I apologize, Genevieve. My enthusiasm for this sort of thing overcomes my good sense. I forget that not everyone shares my love of the decrepit."

"No, I . . . it's fascinating. But, yes, maybe I'm feeling a little claustrophobic."

"C'mon, then. I'll escort you back to the land of the living."

Chapter Fifty-one

Angela, 1983

"It's me," Angela manages, though her mouth is so dry she barely gets the words out. "Xabi?"

The arm around her neck is hot, scalding.

"Angel! I could have hurt you!" He releases her, falls back against the wall. His arm wraps around his stomach, as though holding himself in pain. "What are you doing here?"

She realizes she is crying. She feels dizzy, displaced. Is it the drugs, or is it being down here, in this cold, stinking warren to which her lover has run for safety, like an animal.

"I can't believe you are here, my angel. Are you all right? Sit, sit down, *mi alma*." My soul. He calls her his soul.

He leads her to the small cot, which squeaks loudly in protest when she half sits, half reclines on the pillow. He crouches before her, concern etched on his strong, handsome features. She studies him: He has grime and soot everywhere; it has settled into the tiny wrinkles at the corners of his eyes. He is wearing the same clothes he had on when last she saw him: the pale blue chambray shirt is torn, with large sections charred. She realizes he has not been treated in a hospital; instead he must have come directly down here after dropping her off at the emergency room.

His arm is still wrapped around his middle.

"Are you hurt?" she says. "You need a doctor."

He shakes his head. "This is not possible. I am okay."

She looks at him a long time and starts crying again. But this time she can hear herself whimpering, a strangely muffled keening sound that surges from her core.

"No, no, *mi alma*, please, don't cry," he whispers, leaning forward to wrap an arm around her. She can smell him; he hasn't showered. But it doesn't matter. The mere touch of him helps her settle; her flesh longs for his caress, for connection.

"Don't cry, Angel," he continues, his voice crooning, soft. "You are okay; you will be well. Does it hurt?"

"No, no, it's not that," she says into the shoulder of his shirt, her voice muffled. "What happened, Xabi? Did you really . . . ? People were hurt. Killed. Why did you do it?"

He releases her, sits back on a tiny footstool. He moves cautiously, as though worried about hurting her—or himself. He continues to stroke her head, pushing the hair out of her eyes, studying the place where his hand touched her head as though memorizing the sight, the sensation.

"Xabi?" she repeats, now wanting answers. Needing answers.

How could he?

He remains silent. He avoids her eyes, instead focusing his gaze on her mouth, her neck, the bandages on her arm.

Angela watches him watch her. Anger surges, along with nausea. The stench of this place washes over her; the scent of stale air and unwashed human and dampness. She barely is able to turn and lean over the side of the cot before she starts to retch, losing her breakfast right on the floor.

Par for the course, she thinks from some far-off, distant place. But she says, "Sorry, oh lord, I'm so sorry, so sorry," as Xabi clucks and tells her it is not a problem, he will take care of it, she should be in bed, taking care of herself, getting well— and forgetting all about him.

His voice, his velvet voice, comes from someplace distant, as though she is at the bottom of a coffee can and he is bustling about the kitchen, like the time they had *apero* at Philippe's house, before going out to the cabaret, that magical night with Dave and Pasquale, Philippe and Delphine—three couples in love and health and Paris and music so joyous it would never end.

• • •

When Angela awakens she is in Philippe's house. Alone.

How did he get her up here? Xabi is injured; she is sure of that. And she is no waif of a woman; she has always been strong, substantial.

He needs medical attention. Why hadn't he gone to Thibeaux? Or Pablo or Cyril or Michelle or Mario? One of the people sympathetic to his cause?

His "cause." The word sank, heavy and laden, into her heart. Xabi had been part of this, of hurting innocent people. Of instilling terror in minds and souls. How could he?

He had told her more about his life: His father had been imprisoned for decades. He grew up steeped in his mother's bitterness toward Franco and her disappointment when his ouster did not change things much; his mother died of a broken heart, he said, having lost not only her husband but her eldest son to the brutality of the state. He told her again and again about cradling his brother's bleeding form in his arms, of watching the light in his eyes fade, of the moment when Rémy had gone from beloved, overprotective older brother to . . . corpse.

Xabi told Angela she could never understand what it was like, to grow up that way. Perhaps he was right. Her complaints are trifling in comparison: a rural background, the lack of excitement, the tedium of life on the farm.

Images of home sweep over her. Of Jim and Nick, smiling and steady. The day-in, day-out caring for the animals. The scent of the morning damp, dew on the long grass wetting her legs as she makes her way out to the chicken coop, fresh eggs and buckwheat pancakes for breakfast, the aroma of real maple syrup heating atop the stove. Nick's serious face while he listens to Jim's unfailingly patient voice explaining the intelligent and stubborn nature of goats, how to approach them for milk.

Jim looking up at her, thanking her for breakfast, the trust and love unsaid between them and yet there in his expression. Always there. Constant. Warm. Safe.

And she had run away from that. How could she?

Suddenly she is awash in the knowledge that she wants (needs!) to go home. To Jim. He is a good man, reliable, dependable. He deserves better. So much better.

And to the warm embrace and sticky hands of her son. Her son, her dear Tricky Nicky. How she yearns for the slight metallic scent of his little-boy sweat, for the easygoing happiness in his big eyes.

Angela begins to laugh. She must look like a madwoman, she thinks, lying on a divan in a semiabandoned mansion, bandaged, strewn with cobwebs and underground grime, her laughter the only sound breaking the dusty silence.

But the laughter soon dissolves, overtaken by tears. Angela is racked with sobs, and another wave of nausea.

For the first time it dawns on her: It is morning sickness.

The next day, Angela returns to the room. Their tiny room in *les souterrains*. It is empty.

But he has left a letter:

Mi alma, my Angel,

Do you remember how I told you an American like you cannot understand? I think you heard that as an insult, but I do not mean this. I mean that if you are not grown up in a situation like mine, you cannot know what it feels like. This is why I think sometimes a radical solution is our only hope. At some point, it becomes the only form of self-defense.

I know you cannot understand. But I hope you can remember me as a man who loved you and cherished you beyond reason. A man who will love you for a thousand lifetimes, who adores you for exactly who you are. If things were different, I would have spent my life trying to make you happy. I would happily have died for you.

Please do not try to find me. It is too dangerous for everyone.

Believe this, please, Angela: Maite zaitut. I love you. Te amo. Je t'aime. And promise me: You will survive, you will be strong. You will be happy.

Yours, forever, Xabi

Angela goes to Pablo's restaurant and finds Michelle.

"He tried to stop it."

"What are you talking about?"

"Xabier tried to stop what was happening. But Thibeaux . . ." She blew out a stream of smoke, shook her head. "I don't know exactly what happened, but I know they fought. Thibeaux's in bad shape; he was hurt in the blast because of Xabi's interference. Believe me, Xabi won't be showing his face around here anymore."

So that's why Xabi didn't go to his friends for help, Angela thought. *They are no longer his friends.*

Pablo shows up, sees her. His eyes flicker down to her bandaged arm.

"Don't you think you've caused enough problems? Why are you here?"

"Xabi's hurt," she says. "He needs help."

"You know where he is?"

She catches her breath, shakes her head.

"If you know where he is, you tell us, we'll help him."

But if Michelle is telling the truth . . . they think

of him as a traitor now. They are ruthless enough to explode a bomb at the Spanish embassy. What would stop them from hurting Xabi?

Angela shakes her head and surprises herself with how easily the lies come: "He called me, when I was in the hospital. He told me he had been hurt, but he had a friend in the countryside who was going to pick him up and help him."

"Where in the countryside?"

"Somewhere in Provence. Or . . . Perpignan, I think?" she says, naming a town near the Spanish border. "I don't know any details."

Pablo bristles with suspicion and anger. When he speaks, his voice is low and threatening.

"You should run back to America, lady, where everything is happy."

She runs.

Back to America. Back to her husband. Back to her son.

Chapter Fifty-two

In the Village Saint-Paul, a pair of teenagers rode through the cobblestone courtyard on old bikes, their baskets full of baguettes and flowers. Several people milled around, poking their heads into La Terre Perdue and the other quaint shops that lined the village. Genevieve waved to Jacques across the way, but then closed the lace curtains.

She sat alone at the big table, spreading open the old newspaper, yellowed and crinkly with age. August 1983. That was, indeed, when Angela was here in Paris. Her "last hurrah," she used to call it. Genevieve always thought her mother had been here for a week or two, but from what Philippe said it was more like a couple of months. A long time to be away from your family.

"I love you, a bushel and a peck . . ."

Genevieve worked her way through the article with her French dictionary. The Spanish embassy had been bombed. Three people killed, ten wounded.

One of the casualties was an American woman who had been carried to the hospital by a man later sought in connection to the bombing. A Basque man named Xabier Etxepare. *"Xabier, with an X,"* Philippe had said.

Her mother's melted arm. *Paris.*

Genevieve checked her uncle's watch: In an hour she was supposed to meet up with Sylviane at Catharine's office for another attempt at a shopping makeover. She really wasn't in the mood, but it was too late to back out. And besides . . . she could try pumping her cousin for more information. Maybe she could jog Catharine's memory with a few specifics.

Jogging a memory . . . perhaps Pasquale would talk to her as well.

In the master bedroom, Genevieve pawed through Pasquale's scarf drawer until she unearthed the blue-and-yellow floral scarf Angela wore in the photo taken at the cabaret. She put her hair up and applied more makeup than she usually wore, approximating her mother's look in that picture.

And then she took the Métro to rue Blanche and went to visit Tante Pasquale.

Probably it was a rotten thing to do, to try to fool someone suffering from Alzheimer's, to allow them to think you are your own mother. But Genevieve felt desperate. She needed some answers. Catharine and Philippe claimed not to know the whole story. But perhaps Pasquale, who lived in the past much of the time anyway, did. Genevieve had nowhere else to turn.

Chapter Fifty-three

Pasquale

The woman looked so much like Angela. But . . . it wasn't Angela, was it?

Pasquale had been watching something on TV, but she couldn't remember what it was. A singing show? She liked music, always had. Dave with his record collection of American crooners, as he called them. They would dance in the living room;

sometimes he would distract her so long that she forgot what she was cooking, would burn the meal.

Dave laughing. His thick wrists, his pipe.

"Do you remember Angela, Pasquale?" said the woman.

Angela. Eyes bright, besotted, watching Xabi. The cabaret, music, wine, laughter. The singer climbing atop the table and singing directly to them; he could sense the passion as they all could, radiating off of the couple.

"Pasquale, can you tell me: Was it my mother, was she the American who was carried to the hospital? Is that how she hurt her arm?"

"Your mother?"

"Angela. Dave's sister. Do you remember?"

Pasquale's heart breaks for her sister-in-law. Angela is in an impossible situation: married to a good man (the father of her son) but in love with another. Who knows why some people bring out our passion, our life?

"Écoute-moi, Angela, listen to me," she tried to tell her: "You are not so much in love with the man, but with who you become when you are around him. In his arms. His lips upon yours. He has helped you to find yourself, but you must create this for yourself, not in relation to another. Écoute-moi, please listen to me."

Angela won't take the time to sit and listen, to think the words through. When first she arrived in

Paris she slept half the day away, but now they cannot keep her still for more than a few minutes; she flits this way and that. Angela says she is helping Delphine with the packing, but Pasquale knows that much of the time Angela disappears somewhere on the streets of Paris. It is easy to imagine with whom: Xabier.

They must hide it from Dave. But he is no fool; anger and sadness creep into those usually happy eyes. So upset with his sister. He cannot understand. And Angela, bless her, does not take pains to keep the adoration from her countenance. She is a woman in love. And a woman in love can be as deadly and unpredictable as a tornado. C'est tout. That's all.

At the cabaret, Xabi sat, brooding. His intensity, his smoldering silence, is seductive, sexy. Dangerously alluring. When he dances with Angela . . . the sparks fly off of them, a fireworks show right there on the dance floor.

In French, fireworks are called feu d'artifice. *Artificial fire. They are fake, manufactured. Yet more than dangerous enough to burn.*

"*Et le feu brûle.*"

"What did you say?" the woman asked. The hair looked like Angela's, but . . . was it really her?

"I said, fire burns."

The woman nodded. Pasquale tried to remember why she was talking about fire. She had been cooking and forgot the pan on the stove; it caught fire. This was why she lived in this place now, with the silk flowers and the acoustic tiles overhead. She wasn't in the Village Saint-Paul anymore. Not in her home. Never again.

They were walking in the garden. It was nice here. In the Village Saint-Paul they had only a few window boxes, no real garden. Still, Dave insisted on growing tomatoes in the window boxes, even though the neighbors would have preferred proper flowers. *He laughs:* "We will see who complains when they have fat ripe tomatoes for their salad!"

Dave always shares his tomatoes, as he does everything else. He loves his neighbors. Dave wants to help. He wants to do the right thing, no matter the cost. But after World War II, and then Algeria, he didn't want any more of that. Not with his in-laws, or his own sister.

"No more. Do you hear me? No more violence! What does it get any of us, Pasquale? Tell me that. What has it gotten anyone?"

He sends his sister the Syrian key. She had left it on his workbench when she went back to America; it was a silent apology, her leaving it behind. It is ancient, one of his favorites. But now he has used it to lock up her secrets, and then sent it to her. It is his way of saying he loves her, no matter what. Even after everything.

"Pasquale?" the woman asked. She had that hair like Angela. She spoke English, like Angela. "Do you have any advice for Angela, Pasquale?"

"For Angela?"

"My mother. I am Genevieve, Tante Pasquale. Your niece."

Pasquale studied the woman for a long time. She was crying, and Pasquale realized that she was crying, too.

But why? It would all be all right. Jim Martin was a good man. A safe man. Angela could tell him the truth. She *must* tell him the truth.

"*Écoute-moi*, Angela: It will be very hard, but you must tell Jim about the baby."

Chapter Fifty-four

*W*hat baby?

Genevieve hadn't been able to get any more information from her aunt. Pasquale became agitated, started crying in earnest. Pia fluttered out to the garden, frowning at Genevieve and clucking over Pasquale, offering to take her back to bed, to bring her a hot-water bottle.

Now Genevieve was left with yet more questions as she headed to Catharine's apartment, a ten-minute walk away.

What baby? Could Angela have been pregnant with Genevieve when she came to France? Had she been unsure about the pregnancy, wondering whether she wanted to have another child? It was the eighties; it wasn't as though Angela didn't have a choice. But then, it would be unusual for a happily married woman to want to terminate a pregnancy, wouldn't it?

But then . . . Angela hadn't been happily married.

"*Ça va*, Genevieve?" asked Sylviane when they met in front of Catharine's apartment building. "You are okay?"

"Yes. I was just visiting with my aunt."

"You look a little gray." Sylviane squeezed Genevieve's arm. "Your aunt, she is well?"

"Yes, thanks. She's fine. It's just . . . she told me something surprising. I want to ask Catharine about it."

"You want me to go away so you can talk alone?"

"No, no, of course not." *I've had about enough of secrets.*

But when Genevieve told her cousin what Pasquale had said about the baby, Catharine just shrugged.

"My mother is living a dream now," said Catharine. "Her whole life is a dream, I think, the reality mixing with memories, images, symbols we cannot understand. Things we are only vaguely aware of. Just as in a dream, we cannot understand the full meaning. Only she knows this."

"But what she said about the baby—did you know anything about that? What can you tell me about the time my mother came to visit?"

She blew out a long stream of smoke. "Angela—your mother—was lovely. She was not pregnant that I remember; I mean, she was not showing. She never said anything to me, but then, she probably wouldn't have. We did not have that kind of relationship."

"It takes many months to get fat with a baby," said Sylviane. "Maybe she was early."

"You know, to dream of a baby is, in general, a search for security," added Catharine. "But to dream of carrying an unborn baby might be about difficulties, having to work hard to face challenges, but in the end, to succeed. Perhaps my mother is thinking about facing the hard work of dealing with this disease, which will end, eventually, in her final rest."

As was so often the case when speaking with Catharine, Genevieve felt put off. But perhaps she was right. Was Pasquale's statement lucid, or merely the disjointed ramblings of an addled brain? After all, when Genevieve arrived, Pasquale had been talking about chewing bark, apparently dredging up memories from the war when she had nearly starved to death on a farm in the Franche-Comté.

Genevieve was roused by her thoughts when a man let himself into the apartment. He couldn't have been more than thirty; tall and rangy, with a full head of dark hair, longish and wild. Handsome, lanky, reminiscent of a poet. Adoration shone in his dark eyes, which were focused solely on Catharine.

He excused himself for interrupting, then whispered something in Catharine's ear, making her blush and smile.

Sylviane raised her eyebrows and looked over at Genevieve, whose eyes widened in response. They shared a smile.

After a brief discussion in hushed tones, the young man kissed Catharine on the lips, nodded to the other women, and left.

Catharine turned back to find Genevieve and Sylviane staring at her. "What?"

"He seems like a very nice . . . friend," said Sylviane.

Genevieve could barely believe her eyes, but Catharine's cheeks flushed even more.

"His name is Arturo."

"*Really* . . . and what is Arturo's story, exactly?" asked Sylviane.

"He is a very sweet boy."

"Apparently."

"Yes, he is my lover," Catharine said in clipped tones, raising her chin defiantly. "Is this what you're asking?"

"That is . . . most excellent."

Sylviane and Genevieve looked at each other and started to laugh. After a brief moment, Catharine joined in.

"I have an idea, Catharine," said Sylviane. "Perhaps you do not need my help after all. Maybe *I* need to learn *your* secrets! Let's all go out for *pastis*, and you will tell us all about this man Arturo."

Chapter Fifty-five

That night, after writing an epic, overwrought entry in her journal (her mind racing with the possibilities), Genevieve called her brother, Nick. First they traded pleasantries: Genevieve asked about the turkey hatchlings, and Nick asked about Paris.

Finally she addressed her real reason for calling: "You were old enough to know things when Mom came back from Paris. Did Mom . . . do you remember when Mom was pregnant with me?"

"Do you mean when she came back from France, pregnant?"

Genevieve's hand was wrapped so tightly around the phone she was glad it was an old-fashioned landline, the heavy kind that could take a squeezing.

"Are you saying that she wasn't pregnant when she *left* for France?"

There was a pause. "I don't know, Gen. I mean, not one hundred percent. I was just a kid myself. But Dad said a few things over the years. . . . He loved her, you know. To the day he died. And he loved you."

Genevieve's gaze rested on the piles of documents and bills on her uncle's desk. The paper effluvia of modern life that threatened to drown a person, but which, in the end, was meaningless.

Nick was still speaking.

"Listen, Gen, you always sort of idolized Mom. And I get that—you were just a kid when she died, after all. But she was . . . I don't think she was ever diagnosed or anything like that, but now when I look back on it, I think she might have had a problem with depression. Like, serious depression. Dad always said Mom wasn't really of this world, that she sort of existed on another plane."

Genevieve thought of all those times Angela seemed to be looking elsewhere, the times she couldn't get out of bed.

"And for some reason, she seemed to feel that she had to pay penance. I mean, she loved us; she was a good mother; we had some good times together. And I was one of the few who loved those sugarless carrot muffins she used to make. But I don't know—neither you nor she ever seemed particularly happy here, right?"

"I don't think I was cut out for farm life."

"Like everyone always said, I took after Dad; you took after Mom."

"So, just to be very clear: Are you saying that

maybe Dad . . . that maybe he wasn't my real dad?"

Another long pause. She could hear clucking sounds in the background and imagined Nick trying to keep the phone between his shoulder and his ear while he attended to his never-ending list of tasks: feeding animals, collecting eggs, tilling soil.

"I'm not saying that," Nick said finally. "I really don't know the absolute truth. I sort of figured *you* did, that maybe that's why you moved to France."

"How come you never said anything about any of this to me?" Genevieve asked, though she knew the answer. Nick wasn't like that, just like Jim; they didn't speculate. They didn't pry. They lived in the world in front of them, the here and now, and expected everyone around them to tend to their own business.

"What I *do* know is this," Nick said. "Dad was your father as much as he was mine. He loved you, Gen. He raised you. He did well by you. In my book, that's what makes a dad, no matter the details of biology."

After she hung up, Genevieve remained sitting at Dave's desk for a very long time.

Her dad—Jim Martin—had never made Genevieve feel as though she didn't belong. She had never felt less loved than Nick; there had been no favoritism. Genevieve had always felt like a misfit, but that was because of her own personality and dissatisfaction, not due to anything Jim had done, or *hadn't* done.

Details of biology. They seemed like pretty important details, all things considered. Still, Nick was right: Jim had raised her; he was her dad. And he was a good father. Quiet, undemonstrative, but as steady as a rock.

In fact, what struck her more profoundly was what Nick said about their mother. At eight years Genevieve's senior, Nick had been twenty-two when Angela died. He had experienced her as an adult, had been able to understand her in a way the young Genevieve hadn't.

All those years Genevieve thought she had failed at making her mom happy. But . . . maybe there *was* no making Angela happy. At least, nothing a little girl could have done.

Chapter Fifty-six

On the pretense of doing more work in Philippe's house, Genevieve returned to the basement and descended through the trapdoor to the catacombs. She made her way into the secret chamber, holding close her newfound knowledge about her mother and her suspicions about what had happened while she was in Paris.

She cast the flashlight beam around the little room, taking in the mural and the pile of clothes and the book from her uncle's collection.

Killian said he tried not to touch things when he crept around abandoned houses: His role was to photograph things just as they were. But Genevieve was not bound by such rules. Especially in this case.

She looked through the pile of clothes and spied the edge of an envelope sticking out from under a plaid shirt. She pulled it out.

There was a single name on the front: *Xabi.*

Genevieve perched on the side of the cot, taking a moment to turn the envelope over in shaking hands before ripping it open.

In the envelope was money—U.S. dollars and old French francs—and a note.

Dear Xabi,

You are right: I have to return to my husband, to my son. To America. My place is there, with them.

I want you to know that you gave me grace, and light, and warmth. Our love has brought me new breath, new life. I don't think I will ever understand how I could feel such things with you; and I know I will never forget them. Just as I will never forget you.

We will live together, forever, in my memories.

Your Angel

Genevieve folded the note and put it back in the envelope. Turned out her flashlight. Allowed the inky blackness to flow over and around her, the silence complete and total. In the absence of sensation, her mind came up with images: a young Angela, flushed with excitement, gilded with candlelight; her handsome lover leaning toward her, sharing a glass of wine.

A sudden sound at the door made her start. She jumped up and snapped on her light.

Killian.

"You scared me to death!" Genevieve said, hand over her pounding heart.

"Sorry about that. You gave me a bit of a fright as well, I gotta say."

"What are you doing here?"

"Philippe let me in on his way out. I found the trapdoor in the *cave* open, so I assumed you were down here. But then it was so dark I figured I was wrong. Hey . . . are you all right?"

Genevieve had stumbled back into the cramped chamber. The weight of the place was crashing in on her. Everything it might mean. Everything it *did* mean. She knew it in her soul.

"I'm just . . . I'm putting a few things together. About my mother. And . . . my father."

"Down here?"

"It's a little complicated."

The handsome terrorist, hiding from the authorities. Her wounded mother bringing him supplies.

The tears she would have shed. The betrayal she must have felt.

"You said you think she was unhappy when she came to Paris?" said Killian. "That she might have been thinking of leaving your father?"

His voice was very gentle, filling the space, pushing the ghosts away. Genevieve had not realized until just that moment how alone she had felt and how comforting it was to have him there, his presence at her side.

She nodded. "But there's more. Remember the newspaper we found down here? About the bombing? An American tourist was hurt."

"I don't understand. You think . . . was that your mother?"

She nodded.

"But what does this have to do with this room?"

"I think the man named in the paper, Xabier Etxepare, and my mother were lovers. Maybe she was trying to stop the bombing, something like that." It was too much to think that her mother, Angela Martin, could have actually been party to the crime, wasn't it? Impossible. She, who had gone to rallies at San Quentin to protest the death of a stranger; who thought it was wrong to kill, no matter what.

It took a moment for Genevieve to realize that Killian hadn't replied. She looked up to see his gaze, troubled, lingering on her.

"You're saying your mother was involved with a terrorist?"

"No, of course not. I think . . . maybe there's another explanation."

He was looking around the room now. Putting things together.

"So you're thinking they hid down here, afterward?"

"Maybe. He must have, anyway. Like I said, she was hurt in the explosion."

"Was she charged?"

"What? Of course not. She wasn't *involved* in the bombing; she was just in the wrong place at the wrong time. In fact . . . maybe she went there that day because she was trying to stop it."

A long pause. "Then who was helping him down here? Philippe?"

"No. He wasn't even in Paris at that time. My mother—Angela—was helping them pack up the house . . ."

"So your mother let him in? Helped him?"

"Why are you saying it like that? You didn't know her. She was the gentlest—"

"You told me yourself you have only a child's memories of her. Even terrorists can make caring parents, I imagine."

A dark veil of shame and anger and pain settled over her. Genevieve wanted to turn off all the lights, to remain here in the dark of the anonymous chamber, alone. After a long moment,

Killian let out a long breath that seemed to reverberate off the stone walls.

"I'm sorry, Genevieve. It's just . . . I'm Irish. The whole terrorism thing is a bit fraught for us. I had friends on both sides, and I know there are several sides to every story, but I've had enough of that crap to last more than a lifetime."

Genevieve remained perched on the side of the iron bed. She found herself wondering: Was this what happened? Had her mother—sweet, depressed, anguished Angela Martin—actually taken up with a terrorist while in Paris and had a relationship with him? A relationship that had produced a child?

Killian was staring at her, awaiting her response. Leaning up against the wall, arms crossed over his chest. *Not taking pictures now,* Genevieve thought. Finally, something to stop that incessant clicking.

"We're talking about my mother," she said, voice sounding hollow yet echoing off the walls. "Not some radical extremist. She couldn't have been involved in anything like that. She was from a little town in *Mississippi,*" she concluded, as though Angela's origin meant she must be an innocent in all of this.

"By way of California," Killian said. "The area you're from in California is known for some pretty radical politics, Berkeley and all that. Especially back in the day."

"Yes, but . . ." Genevieve thought of the faraway looks her mother would get when gazing out the kitchen window. Still, the idea of her mother taking part in something like this felt as unreal as Genevieve's own adolescent fantasies of returning from Paris a trained superhero.

But then again . . . would Genevieve ever have guessed that her biological father was anyone other than the silent, stoic Jim Martin?

Had Jim always been so somber? Or was it partly the result of the knowledge that his wife had had an affair in Paris, had become pregnant, and that his daughter was flesh of another man?

Pasquale had been saying as much, hadn't she?

Suddenly everything was falling into place. The strange, almost formal relationship between her parents—Angela and *Jim,* because Jim would always be her father no matter what. The argument between Dave and Angela, a disagreement so profound that it would lead to more than fourteen years of estrangement between beloved siblings. Her mother's secretive ways.

Had they all known about this?

Jim must have known. He must have. And Nick certainly hadn't seemed bowled over by her query, so he must have had an inkling, at least. Still, she was willing to bet neither man knew anything about Genevieve's biological father's involvement in a national incident.

Genevieve had wanted to know what Angela

was like, not as a mother, but as a *woman*. And now she had found out.

"Be careful what you wish for."

Killian broke into her reverie. "Listen, Genevieve, I didn't mean to say—"

"That's fine," Genevieve cut him off. "Please, would you mind leaving me alone now?"

"Genevieve—"

"Please don't say anything more. You don't know me, you didn't know my mother, and you have no right to be here. The catacombs are *interdits*."

"I—"

"*Go*. Please."

Genevieve remained in the tiny room for . . . how long was it? She lost track of time down in the dark. Breathing the musty, stale air. Imagining her mother coming to visit him here. At what point had her mother decided to return to the States? And how had she kept such a secret from Genevieve her whole life?

How *could* she?

Chapter Fifty-seven

Genevieve walked.

Raindrops fell, hours passed. Still, she didn't stop.

Finally she looked up to find herself at the foot of Montmartre. The rain was coming down now in earnest, in the way of Parisian rain: soaking, easily as plentiful as the feeble spray from the shower in Pasquale and Dave's place. Her hair fell across her face in wet locks. She was grateful for the storm; the streets were empty of tourists and even the heartiest of street performers, and her tears were camouflaged by the raindrops.

"I love you, a bushel and a peck . . ."

She couldn't get that damned song out of her head. Over and over, her mother's voice, haunting her. Genevieve let out an angry sob.

Was everything a lie? Just as Jason's affair had made Genevieve doubt all that had gone before in their relationship, finding this out about Angela made Genevieve second-guess everything she had known and thought about her mother. The absolute devotion Angela had apparently felt for her husband and children. The hundreds of cupcakes baked and lasagnas made; the warm, soft hugs; the scent she carried, of cinnamon and citrus and vanilla. The sensation of utter safety and unconditional love Genevieve had felt when the carpool let her out by the side of the road and she would head down the long dirt driveway and spot her mother weeding the carrot patch.

Angela would smile, let the hoe fall, and open her arms wide, so Genevieve could run and fling herself into her soft embrace.

All of it. Now she thought about the times when that faraway look came into her mother's eyes. Those mornings she couldn't get out of bed, when Jim would rouse Genevieve and tell her Angela had one of her sick headaches, that she would need to get her own breakfast. Even the protests at the prison: Were they due to deeply held moral beliefs, or simply the result of Angela thinking of her criminally inclined Parisian lover?

Genevieve's father. Her *father*.

No. Her dad was Jim Martin: steady, quiet Jim. She had railed against his stoicism, his lack of emotion, but now . . . Nick was right. She knew her brother was right: a real *father* is the man who raises a child, stands by her, cares for her, bakes nearly inedible, lopsided birthday cakes with bright blue frosting after her mother dies.

This was even truer if Jim knew about the circumstances of Genevieve's conception. He had to know. Surely. Genevieve had tried to piece the dates together, but she didn't have all the details. She supposed Angela could have been pregnant before she left for Paris, or that she could have told her husband that, anyway. A few weeks here or there; did men even notice such things when holding their newborn babies?

But surely Angela had told him the truth, had confessed to her affair. Surely she had enough regard for her husband, the father of her son, to tell him the truth. To allow him to decide for himself.

"A bushel and a peck and a hug around the neck . . ."

She started running up the steps of Montmartre. Shallow puddles splashed underfoot. The funicular was out of service since only an idiot would be out sightseeing in weather like this. So the only sound was the steady hiss of the rain, the squelch of her soles on the stone steps.

One flight of stairs; two. Genevieve gulped in air, couldn't get enough. Her thighs burned; the air started to sting in her lungs. Her temples began to throb. She welcomed the pain. When she couldn't run anymore she kept climbing, stubbornly; she wouldn't stop. Ignoring the nausea engulfing her, gasping for breath, then crying.

Her mother's singing voice kept repeating in her head. *"A bushel and a peck though you make my heart a wreck . . ."*

Genevieve let out the sobs in earnest as she mounted the steps. No one could hear. She was as alone at that moment as she had ever been in her life: the streets and sidewalks empty of tourists and locals, artists and street performers. No cars, no funicular. The Sacré-Coeur up in front of her, crowning the hill, gleaming like a white beacon in the storm.

One more flight. The final one, to the doors of the basilica.

She made a deal with herself: She would allow herself to wail and moan all the way there, screaming out her rage and pain and abandonment. And that would be the end of it. The *end*.

Her mother had lied to her. Her father and brother, too, probably. And, she supposed, Dave and Pasquale. Lie upon lie. Just like Notre-Dame, built stone by stone over a temple to Jupiter. Or Philippe's house, constructed and reconstructed according to the whims of fashion, each era meant to hide the last. Her whole life was built on prevarication and mendacity. No wonder she could never open up to truly share her heart with her husband; no wonder he had turned to another. She had no one, and nothing.

Even her damned, hard-to-spell, impossible-to-pronounce name was rooted in this; she knew that now. Her mother's "vacation" in Paris.

Finally the basilica doors loomed up in front of her. Bronze with a verdigris patina; lion's heads holding huge brass rings.

Nauseated, she couldn't breathe deeply enough, gulping in the wet air.

She turned to look out at the city laid out before her.

"I love you, a bushel and a peck . . ."

Genevieve sank onto the top step, every ounce of energy gone. She was probably still crying, but she couldn't even manage the sobs anymore. Just sniffling, face wet. Gulping for air.

After a moment, she felt a hand on her shoulder.

"Est-ce que je peux vous aider?"

Genevieve looked up to see a gray-haired, black-robed priest. He was asking if he could help her. Heedless of the rain that streamed down his face, he kept speaking in French that she couldn't completely understand, and didn't try to. His presence was enough.

"Ça va, mademoiselle?" Are you okay? he asked.

She nodded.

"Do you need a doctor, or spiritual help?"

She shook her head.

He sat down next to her, as if he were her only friend, looking out over the city. Even the gray veil of rain couldn't erase the panoramic view of the Eiffel Tower, the opera house, and Notre-Dame.

They sat side by side for several minutes in silence.

Finally, in French Genevieve didn't even realize she knew, she asked the priest: "Do you believe in ghosts, Father?"

He took a moment, as though considering her

query. Then he tapped his heart and said: *"Oui, dans le coeur."*

Yes, in the heart.

Genevieve had been carrying her mother's ghost with her. She had wanted to know the woman Angela was, and now she knew the truth: Her mother had been a woman capable of deep passion. She had loved, and loved deeply. She had also been unhappy and deeply flawed; disloyal, and torn between two worlds. And yet all of it—the distant looks and the vanilla-scented hugs, the crippling depression and the silly songs—contributed to the person she had been. She had made her own choices. That was how her story ended, as Catharine would say: as a wife and mother who had an affair in Paris, who had paid a heavy price, and who had returned to the little farm in Petaluma to do her best.

It had never been Genevieve's job to make her mother happy. Only Angela could do that.

And with that, Genevieve let go of her mother's ghost.

She fancied she could see it, like a figure from a Chagall painting, floating down the steps of Montmartre, taking a turn around the opera house, drifting toward the Seine, and finally disappearing amid the medieval spires of Notre-Dame, where, Genevieve supposed, it would commune with the gargoyles for some time to come.

Chapter Fifty-eight

Genevieve's new clothes fit into one of her uncle's heavy old suitcases. She chose a favorite lock and decided to keep the set of Victorian keys. She had packed up Dave's notes and the special locks and keys for his book and was leaving the packages with Sylviane, who had promised to send them to her.

With Catharine's permission, of course. "I am sorry you are not staying, my little cousin. But I think perhaps the dreams will lead you back one day. I hope so," she had said.

"You want me to just leave things locked up?"

"Yes, please take anything you want, and I will have one of the neighbors assess the rest to see if they can sell any of it. It will work itself out."

"Okay, good. I'm . . . I'm sorry about all this."

"Me, too. Very sorry. You know, the bureaucracy in France is difficult, but I'm sure we could figure out a way around it. Surely you could get certified—"

"It doesn't matter anymore," Genevieve had interrupted. "I'm going anyway."

"You are homesick I think?"

No. Homesick was about the last thing she was. Genevieve needed to go back at some point to deal with Jason and the divorce, true, but she

459

didn't have to move back for that. She was leaving because . . . because Paris was not her home. Not really. It was too painful now. She had no home. No real family, no real friends, nothing. But at least in the U.S. she spoke the language and she didn't worry about being arrested for working or deported for overstaying her visa. At the very least, there was that.

Besides . . . who becomes a locksmith in this day and age? It was an old-fashioned, antiquated occupation. And to try to become one in *France?* What had she been thinking?

She would sleep on Mary's couch for a little while, pick up a few copyediting projects, and try to figure out her next steps.

"This is stupid," said Sylviane, hugging a package of papers to her chest like a child with a beloved toy. "If you go back to no home, not even near movie stars, why you don't stay here in nice apartment in Paris?"

Genevieve let out a long sigh.

She had hoped to slip away undetected, but Sylviane had stopped by and, when Genevieve didn't answer the buzzer, had come around into the courtyard and spied her through the window, suitcase splayed open on the bed. After that, there was no stopping her.

"I think you are stupid," Sylviane repeated.

"Gee, thanks." Genevieve handed Sylviane the notices she had received, warning her against operating the business as a "foreign national." "What about those?"

Sylviane shrugged, hitched her hip up onto the open windowsill. Last night's storm had washed the city fresh, and the day dawned with a brilliant sun that warmed the wet streets and brought floods of customers out to the village's biannual antiques fair. The courtyard was packed with antiques of all kinds—rocking chairs and dolls and credenzas and kitchenware—along with display tables strewn with tchotchkes; dozens of people milled about, looking for bargains and soaking up the atmosphere.

"I tell you the secret of French bureaucracy, but you don't follow my advisements."

"I just . . ." Genevieve trailed off, wondering how she might try to explain everything to Sylviane, whether it was even worth the effort. She had given her the broad strokes of the story, but Sylviane didn't seem to grasp why she was so upset.

"I don't understand why it is such a great offense, what you tell me about your mother and this man. I mean, things were different then. It was the *eighties*. Do you remember seeing pictures of the *fashions?* Big hair, big makeup, everything very different back then."

"This isn't big hair, Sylviane. It's adultery, and me having a different father than I ever knew about."

"I was thinking, though, this means you are a true Parisienne," she said, waving her finger in the air as though she had just alighted upon the winning point. "Conceived here in Paris! Think about that! Perhaps you tell the bureaucrats that!"

"Really? You think informing the authorities that I'm the daughter of the man suspected of bombing the Spanish embassy is going to help my case?"

Sylviane shrugged again, sighed dramatically, and looked outside at the milling crowd.

Genevieve continued packing, trying to fit everything into her various bags. How had she managed to attain so much stuff when she'd been in Paris only a little more than a month?

Sylviane shouted something in French out the window. Genevieve looked up to see Marie-Claude, with Daniel on her heels. Behind them came their son, Luc, and Jacques. Soon there was a whole crowd around the window. Speaking in a mix of French and English, they conveyed their dismay that she was leaving, full of advice on how to deal with the authorities. An elderly neighbor named Madame Velain asked who would fix her door.

This is a nightmare, Genevieve thought as she tried to close her crammed suitcase. Her head still throbbed with the aftermath of the migraine she'd suffered all night long, and the last thing she wanted was to have to say good-bye to everyone, face-to-face. How could she possibly explain everything she was feeling? She checked her watch: The taxi was supposed to be here in fifteen minutes.

The shop buzzer sounded and Genevieve fought the Pavlovian response that made her want to answer it.

She steeled herself. *No more.* Paris would no longer be a dream; it was not her escape valve. She had to go back and face Real Life, as Jason would put it. Surely she could figure out some sort of win-win situation. Eventually.

What if that buzzer was the taxi? The driver was supposed to call the phone number when he pulled up, but what if he rang the buzzer instead?

She peeked into the shop. Her heart sank. Again.

It was Killian, holding a gift-wrapped package in one hand.

"Open the door, Genevieve, please," he said when she hesitated.

Why not? The whole neighborhood would be here soon, apparently. She let him in.

"Listen, I have to apologize—"

"No, you don't."

"I do. I sincerely apologize. I really put my foot in it down there, in the catacombs. So I brought you a peace offering." He held out the package, rather awkwardly wrapped in pink paper with an orange bow.

Genevieve focused on the present so she

didn't have to meet his eyes. "I don't really like presents," she said, her voice sounding hollow to her ears.

"Think of it as belated payment, then. For opening my door that first day."

Reluctantly, she took it from him, set it on the work counter, and opened it. It was a sepia-toned picture of Genevieve standing on the Love Locks Bridge. The solid bank of padlocks formed a low wall behind her; the edges of the photo were warped and out of focus, giving the photo an ethereal, other-timely cast. Wind blew her hair, and she was laughing as she reached up to push a lock out of her face.

Genevieve looked pretty, and happy. She looked like her mother.

Angela and Dave, atop Notre-Dame, the wind ruffling Angela's hair.

"It's . . . beautiful. Thank you."

"You're welcome. And I hope you accept my apology," he said, his tone husky. His eyes shifted over her shoulder. "What's going on?"

Through the open door they could see friends and neighbors crowding into the apartment. Sylviane would be calling in her five brothers soon, Genevieve imagined.

"It's nothing," Genevieve said to Killian. "It's the antiques fair today, and . . ."

Killian was already walking past her into the apartment. "What's with the suitcases?"

Genevieve opened her mouth to speak, but Sylviane beat her to it.

"She is going to sleep on friend's couch because is too much trouble to write forms for police."

"I'm sorry?" Killian said.

"The authorities have caught up with me, I'm afraid," Genevieve explained. "They won't give me a license to practice in France—"

"She did not try hard enough. You can't surrender to these people, I am telling her. But does she listen?"

There was a general hubbub among the neighbors. Everyone, it seemed, had an opinion on how to deal with the local bureaucrats.

"It really doesn't matter," Genevieve tried to explain over the general air of mayhem. "I'm leaving anyway. I—"

"You're *leaving?*" Killian demanded. "You mean, *leaving* leaving? Where are you going? Why?"

Genevieve tried using her old trick to keep herself from crying. She bit her tongue, imagined peppermint candy. But try as she might, she felt the hot prickle of tears stinging the back of her eyes.

Surely you're all cried out, aren't you? After yesterday's melodramatic, self-pity-and-tear-fueled sprint up Montmartre, Genevieve would have thought she'd be dried out. The migraine had blossomed before she even got home, and this morning she had awakened from fitful, locked-door dreams puffy-eyed and spent, feeling empty and hollow. And her thighs were killing her.

The buzzer rang again. That *damned* buzzer.

"I'll get it," said Killian. "You, stay here—don't go away."

Genevieve turned back to the crowd, wondering how to explain—in her mixed French and English and body language—how much they all meant to her, that their caring was not lost on her, that if only she could, she would have loved to have made this work, to have been their neighborhood locksmith and become an essential part of their community, like her uncle before her. But that it had never been realistic. Paris had been a dream . . . and the fantasy had died down in the dank, dark, secret catacombs. In the dizzying depths of the city.

But suddenly there was a rustling by the courtyard doorway, and the crowd parted like the Red Sea, allowing a dandily dressed man through.

"Who are you?" demanded Sylviane, jutting out her chin and physically positioning herself between Genevieve and the new arrival. Despite the situation, Genevieve had to smile at this: Apparently she now had a self-appointed, delicate-looking, bread-scented guardian.

"I am Monsieur Lambert," said the newcomer. "I am here to make the inspection of the shop of the *serrures*."

"Monsieur Lambert," Genevieve said, realization dawning on her. "I am so sorry, I completely forgot that I made the appointment for today. I'm really sorry I wasted your time. *Je suis désolée, pardonnez-moi.* I'm leaving anyway, so it won't be necessary."

"*This* is the man?" Sylviane asked before Lambert was able to say a word. "*Quel connard!* This is the little *bureaucrate* trying to chase Genevieve from Paris, *ça me fait chier.*"

The neighbors set upon him like buzzards on roadkill. Several women began poking fingers into Lambert's thin chest and making hand gestures that reminded Genevieve of the ones she had witnessed between drivers on her very first trip to Paris. She had a hard time keeping up with the French, but she understood snippets: her neighbors talking about the cultural tradition of the Village Saint-Paul, suggesting he grant an exception on the basis of heritage; several reminded him of the contributions of Americans to defeating the enemies in both world wars. Sylviane threw in the optimism and romance of American movies, sprinkling her language with a hefty dose of swearwords.

"Genevieve!" came a new voice from the direction of the shop. A cane tapped loudly on the tiled floor.

Genevieve turned to see the final nail in the coffin of her nightmare: Philippe.

"What is going on?" he asked. "You are having a party without me?"

"No, she say she is leaving," said Sylviane. "*C'est des conneries!*"

"But this is not possible. *Pourquoi*, Genevieve? Why do you leave us?"

"Look, everyone, thank you so much, really," said Genevieve. This situation was rapidly spiraling out of control; she had to rein it in. "Monsieur Lambert, I'm so sorry about all this, and you don't have to worry because I'm leaving anyway. I'm going back to California; the taxi will be here any minute to take me to the airport."

This last caused another roar of voices, everyone talking at once.

"Genevieve, *ma petite, pourquoi*?" Philippe asked her why in a heartbreakingly gentle voice.

She couldn't fight the tears anymore. She shook her head as they started to fall. "I'm sorry, Philippe. I—"

"You have friends here. Family, too." He nodded at the door, where Catharine now stood. Everyone started to greet her like the long-lost neighbor she was.

"He is right, Genevieve," said Catharine. "I came by to wish you farewell, but I see I am not the only one! Your neighbors who seem to love you. They never act like this when I try to leave!"

Laughter all around, people clapping one another on backs, already making plans for a

468

neighborhood dinner in the courtyard after the fair.

Marie-Claude came forward: "You know that I do not agree with Monsieur D'Artavel often. But in this, he is right, Genevieve. I think you are in your home, here."

"She is right," Philippe spoke again, taking Genevieve's hands in his. "Do not cry, *ma petite*. You are loved, you see? You are very loved. And you have very much work to do here. What about Madame Velain's door?"

Genevieve smiled, sniffled. "I'm not supposed to work anymore, remember? Even for free, it is not allowed."

At this Marie-Claude turned on Monsieur Lambert once again, and the crowd joined in. Finally he threw up his hands and said something in rapid French.

Sylviane smiled broadly and thrust the sheaf of papers toward him, insisting on his signature. He took a sleek fountain pen from his breast pocket and signed his name in several places, shaking his head and muttering the whole time.

"You see, Genevieve?" Sylviane said as she waved the papers in triumph. "What do I tell you? You cannot surrender to bureaucrats!"

She passed them to Genevieve, who saw that they now carried Monsieur Lambert's coveted signature.

"I still need the stamp."

Monsieur Lambert said something in rapid French.

"He say you will need to stand in line for that," translated Catharine. "Down at the employment offices. I will write down the address for you."

"We should go together," said Sylviane. "I know what we do! We go on my day off. It is not far from the rue du Commerce, we buy new dresses, have lunch."

"It's . . ." Genevieve let out a long, shaky breath. She studied the faces around her: Marie-Claude and Daniel and Jacques and Anna and other neighbors; Philippe and Catharine and Sylviane and Killian; even Monsieur Lambert and the numerous passersby who were now peeking in through the windows, trying to figure out the cause of the commotion. Did she want to leave them, to go back to her half-life in California? Wouldn't it be better to stay here, to dig in and work with her beloved locks and become part of a city and a neighborhood that made her feel more alive than she had in years? Time to move on from her past and free herself, now.

"Are you going to let yourself be defeated by a little lock? Remember, Genevieve: Love laughs at locksmiths! Trust your old uncle."

In the photo of her standing on the Love Locks Bridge, Genevieve looked a lot like her mother, but she was her own person. And she wouldn't repeat her mother's mistakes. Only she could make herself happy.

And she was happy in Paris, at Under Lock and Key in the Village Saint-Paul.

"I guess you know the secret to life in France by now, don't you, Genevieve?" Killian said in a low voice.

"*Ne te rends jamais*," Genevieve said with a nod, surrendering. "Never give up."

Chapter Fifty-nine

Genevieve had a dream in which she opened the door.

There were no dismembered bodies once she stepped through the doorway. Instead, it opened onto an octagonal room that looked like it was out of one of Killian's photographs of abandoned places. There was a queen-sized bed with an old-fashioned iron bedstead, covers neatly turned down; an old tricycle she had seen in Philippe's basement; a bookshelf of dusty tomes; a globe, a child's shoe, the christening outfit from Pasquale's closet she had packed up for Catharine. Papers strewn about the floor, everything covered in dust.

And at the center of the room was a table covered in keys: old-fashioned skeleton keys, the iron burglar's ring, modern blanks and various sets of modern house keys, and a few newfangled electronic models.

With a jolt Genevieve realized that the octagonal room had a door in each section of wall. *There were seven more doors to open.*

But rather than feeling frustrated or afraid, Genevieve stood in the middle of the room, turning around slowly to look at each door. Then she started to twirl faster, began to laugh. *She had all the keys!*

She awoke laughing. And wondering: What would Catharine make of *this?*

She checked Dave's watch. It was early, not even six in the morning. Perfect timing.

Genevieve brushed her teeth and splashed some water on her face in the tiny washroom. She made herself a cup of coffee, carried it over to her uncle's desk, picked up the heavy telephone receiver, and dialed an international number she knew by heart.

She caught Jason at a good time: It was evening there; he'd had a glass of wine with dinner. So he was well fed, relaxed. If Jason didn't eat and sleep regularly, he got cranky, like a toddler. This was a trait Genevieve had found charming when they first got together, but later it annoyed her no end. Now, when she thought about it, she was filled with a sense of fond acceptance that comes with having known someone for many years. Her anger toward Jason had started to mellow, transforming into feelings of vague regret and familial connection.

After they'd traded stories of "How's it going?" Genevieve closed her eyes, thought for a moment of what she needed to do in order to start her new life in Paris with her whole heart. And then she took a leap.

"I wanted to tell you that it wasn't just you," Genevieve blurted out. "I know you went outside our marriage, but . . . I was part of why you were looking for something else. You needed more. I see that now."

There was a long pause. Finally, he said, "I never meant to hurt you, Genie."

"I know. I never meant to hurt you, either. I know we care for each other, Jason, and I hope we always do. I mean that sincerely. But—"

"Uh-oh, here comes the 'but,'" he said in a lightly teasing voice.

She smiled, squeezed the heavy receiver. "Yes, here comes the 'but': I just don't think we're good for each other. I mean, we weren't terrible compared to a lot of people. I just . . . You and I want different things in life. I realize that now."

"You're saying we've grown apart?" he asked, humor no longer softening his tone.

"In some ways. In others, I just don't think we were well suited in the first place. But here's what I really wanted to say: It wasn't really your fault. I didn't know what I wanted myself, so how could you know? How could you have pleased a woman who didn't even know what she wanted?"

"And have you found what you wanted in Paris?"

"Not exactly, but I think I'm on my way to finding it. To creating it, maybe."

There was a long pause, and she heard ice cubes dropping into a glass. She could hardly blame him. It was tough to find the win-win in the death of a marriage, even when it was for the best. Reason enough to pour oneself a good, stiff drink.

"Have you ever read Simone de Beauvoir?" Genevieve asked.

"Please, Genie, I'm not sure I can deal with feminist theory right now."

"No, it's nothing like that. But I read something recently: She wrote that women often love to escape ourselves, rather than to find ourselves, and that because of that, loving a man can become a danger, rather than a source of life."

"Like I said, I'm not really up for philosophy."

"I know, I'm sorry. It just struck me, is all, because I think I did that: I was looking to you as a way to escape myself, somehow, when what I really needed to do was to *find* myself. My point is this: It wasn't just you. There were two of us in the marriage, and we both screwed up."

"But the upshot is: You're staying in Paris, and you want the divorce."

"Yes, yes, I am staying. And I do want the divorce."

She heard ice cubes tinkling, the sound of him swallowing. When he didn't say anything else, she continued: "I'll come back, if I need to, to resolve the paperwork. But we can probably do a lot of it by e-mail. I've got the name of a lawyer here who can give me some basic advice, but I don't want much. Just enough to cover the locksmith shop and expenses for a few months. I'll send some numbers by e-mail."

"Okay, I'll talk to a lawyer, get the ball rolling. Genie—thank you for calling. And for saying what you said."

"You deserved the truth. We all deserve the truth, at the very least. Oh, speaking of which— you'll be receiving a rather hefty bill from a Paris department store at the end of the month."

She heard him chuckle. "Paris really has gotten to you, hasn't it? You're not one to spend much on clothes."

"It was sort of a hostage situation with a very eager Parisian friend who is, I should hardly have to tell you, ever so much more put together than I am."

"I'll bet you look great."

"Thank you. I think I do, actually. Well, then . . . good night, Jason."

"Good night, Genie," he said.

But it was morning in Paris. And she was just waking up.

Chapter Sixty

The buzzer sounded just as Genevieve was putting the last of the tools she would need into her uncle's locksmith bag. Killian stood at the door, smiling.

"Ready?" he asked.

They were headed to Philippe's house, where Genevieve was to finish up with the last of the locks and Killian was to take a set of more formal photographs of the house, the basement, and the entrance to the catacombs. Philippe was going to meet them there with his daughter and her husband, who had decided to apply for a grant from the government that would help them to redo the grand old home into a school for children with special needs. Killian's photos would become part of the application.

Also, they had decided to close up the entrance to the catacombs for good, bricking it over.

When Genevieve mentioned the special lock on the trapdoor, Philippe said: "After your mother went back to America, Dave came and worked down in the *cave* for a while. He insisted on putting on new locks. Special locks. I don't really know why. You want to take it off, maybe put it in the book you are writing about locks? Okay!"

Genevieve felt somewhat sad that the home

would be converted into a public space, but as Philippe said, "Is for the best. The house, she is a relic of the past, like me! She must change with the times, do some good while she still can. And it will save her, ultimately, you see?"

Philippe had one other project he was working on: He had discovered that Marie-Claude and Daniel had an autistic grandson, as well. "We have more things in common than we know," he had declared, and he had invited them to help plan the new school. They had spent several late afternoons over *apero*, clarifying the past and planning for the future. "You see, Genevieve," Philippe had said with a wink, "it is never too late to heal old differences. We French, we are very dramatic, but this is okay! We must talk a lot, and it's always best over *apero*."

As they walked to Philippe's house, Killian said, "You mentioned you haven't seen much of the French countryside."

"Make that *any* of the French countryside."

"Well, it just so happens that I have a lead on an abandoned château in the Dordogne."

"You've moved on from the catacombs?"

Ironically, two days after they had discovered the entrance from Philippe's house, Killian finally succeeded in making contact with a group of full-fledged cataphiles, who maintained intricate maps of the tunnel system and who gave (slightly illegal) tours, for a price. After spending a few days tracking through the depths of the city, he seemed to have gotten his fill.

"When it comes right down to it, it's pretty much stone tunnel after stone tunnel," he said. "Loses its charm after a while—for me, anyway. Guess I didn't get bit by the catacomb bug like some of those lads; I prefer signs of people, of life. Best place I found down there was this old place that looked almost like an underground restaurant–slash–art gallery. Bunch of gorgeous graffiti, real works of art, and some tables with candles and old wine bottles and the like."

"Sounds kind of cool."

"Ah sure, 'twas. I'll take you there, if you like. But I'm thinkin' you might like this château best of all."

"How far is that from Château des Milandes, the castle owned by Josephine Baker?"

He smiled. "Not far at all. The whole river valley is full of châteaux . . . and plenty of them are abandoned. Also, the Basque country is an easy day's drive from there. We could go if you like, maybe track down some of the family."

"I . . . I'll think about it. Maybe. I think I need a little more time."

"I understand."

Killian had helped Genevieve do some Internet research into the events of August 1983. Not only was he better with computers and familiar with several databases, but he also read French fluently. It didn't take much digging to find the name—Xabier Etxepare—listed as a suspect wanted in conjunction with the bombing of the Spanish embassy. He had become a bit of a sensation, known as the *"terroriste amoureux"*— terrorist in love—who had risked being captured in order to run to the hospital with an American woman in his arms.

"That's something, anyway, then," Killian had said. "He risked himself to save her."

"Maybe," Genevieve mumbled. "Anything else?" *Was he still alive? Had he known about her?*

But Killian just shook his head. "It looks like he disappeared without a trace."

"A ghost, then."

"Aye, a ghost. But we're ghost hunters, you and I, aren't we?"

"We must plan the party for the, how do you say, when you open a store again?" Sylviane asked over espressos the next morning.

Genevieve, Sylviane, Catharine, Marie-Claude, Daniel, and Anna and her baby were seated around the little iron table in front of La Terre Perdue, sipping coffee and hot chocolate and snacking on croissants and small pieces of chocolate. The cobblestone courtyard of the village was quiet this chilly morning, with a few neighbors nodding hello as they prepared to open their storefronts for business.

"You mean the grand reopening?" suggested Genevieve.

"Is that it? It sounds so . . ."

"Obvious," said Catharine with a nod. "In English many words are like this."

"Hey," Genevieve said, feeling moved to defend her native tongue. "It's a perfectly good language. After all, we've stolen words from all the decent languages of the world."

They laughed and Marie-Claude offered everyone more espresso. Tomorrow Genevieve was going to venture to the government offices in pursuit of the necessary stamp on her paperwork. In what surely had to qualify as the oddest escort ever, she was to be accompanied by Marie-Claude and Catharine and Sylviane (who had offered to bring plenty of baked goods for the long line). With such French-speaking forces of nature at her side, Genevieve felt sure to prevail. Philippe had put her in touch with Dave's locksmith friend on the other side of town, and he had agreed to take Genevieve on as an (unpaid) apprentice for a few months. After completing her internship, Genevieve could take her certifying exam and become a full-fledged locksmith in Paris.

"Oh, Genevieve," said Daniel. "Almost I forget. Inside I have another lock for you. Also, there is a book for you, in English."

"Thank you, Daniel. How kind."

"It is a book about Jean-Paul Sartre," said

Marie-Claude as Daniel ducked into the store to retrieve the volume. "I have never been fond of him, but Philippe D'Artavel suggests we read about him and discuss his philosophies, as in days past when people did this. What do you think?"

"I want to be part of such a group!" said Sylviane, nudging Genevieve with her elbow. "It is like what you tell me about Gertrude Stein's salon. Maybe we make Village Saint-Paul famous for philosophical discussions, and this will attract interesting people to our neighborhood. Maybe interesting American men—who knows? And this is another reason to hurry with the grand reopening."

"Don't you think I should get certified as a locksmith before reopening the store?" Genevieve asked with a smile.

Sylviane waved her hand in a dismissive gesture. "What are you talking? It is not too early; how will you fail? This is impossible. And—"

"I know, I know: *'Impossible' n'est pas français.*"

After coffee, Genevieve swung by to fix the lock on old Madame Velain's door. It was an easy job—a simple rosette dead-bolt installation that took her only half an hour, so she made sure the back door lock and all the window latches were working properly, then took time to admire the photos of the Velain grandchildren. Madame

Velain invited her to stay for lunch, but Genevieve demurred. She had a lot to do: She still hadn't finished organizing her uncle's shop and had a lot of dusty old bins yet to work through.

Her uncle's old black leather locksmithing bag in one hand, umbrella in the other, Genevieve strolled down rue Saint-Paul, past the Red Wheelbarrow bookstore and several antiques stores; past the café with a cat in the window and the tiny shop specializing in vintage posters. It felt good. It felt like home.

Genevieve opened the door to Under Lock and Key and stepped inside. She breathed deeply the comforting aroma of oil and dust, heard the frenetic ticking of the clocks on the back wall, and felt the gossamer traces of her uncle Dave and *tante* Pasquale in every crack and crevice of the apartment. In the very grain of the wood and the rust on the locks, the tagine and the needlework and the old pipe. *These* ghosts she would gladly carry; she would keep them wrapped tightly around her like a favorite shawl.

Twice now, Dave and Pasquale—and Paris—had given her back her life, and her hope.

They had offered her the keys. Now all she had to do was open the doors and see what was on the other side.

The Paris Key

Juliet Blackwell

READERS GUIDE

A Conversation with Juliet Blackwell

Q.   What first inspired you to write The Paris Key?

A.   Like so many people before me, I fell in love with Paris the first time I visited (many years ago). I have returned several times since, and then two years ago I rented a rustic French farmhouse from a friend and spent a month in the countryside—near Bergerac—before heading to Paris. While there I discovered the Village Saint-Paul, a true fairy-tale-like neighborhood. I stumbled upon a dusty old locksmith shop and wound up having a fascinating talk with the elderly shopkeeper about the history of keys and locks. He fixed me a cup of tea, his granddaughter joined us, and neighbors dropped in! From that moment I knew I had to set a novel here, in this shop and this neighborhood and this city.

Q.   Did Genevieve's character surprise you in any unexpected ways as you wrote the book?

A.   I think Genevieve's bravery surprised me! I believe most of us have times when we feel like we'd like a do-over in life, but embracing change can be frightening. Genevieve is emboldened by her memories of being happy in Paris as a young teenager, but she's still taking a huge chance to move to a foreign country. And once there, Genevieve doesn't simply dwell in the past, but allows herself to shift her way of thinking, to experience the French approach to life. I remember thinking at one point, *Genevieve, are you going to get on this whole certification thing?* and she answered, *Yes, maybe after another glass of pastis.* She was embracing the Parisian pace of life! (And, yes, I do "talk" to my characters!)

Q. How much do you think suffering such a deep loss at an early age informed Genevieve's personality? And in what ways did it impact her outlook on life?

A.   I think she shut down certain parts of herself. I was a social worker for many years, and I learned that when we experience trauma at a young age, sometimes parts of us get "stuck" at that age. It makes it hard to move on, to achieve a mature outlook on life, such as opening up to new experiences and taking responsibility for our own happiness. The young Genevieve was hit hard by her mother's death, but also by what she felt was a second rejection when she was forced to leave Paris, and then by her father and brother's different manner of processing grief. The adult

Genevieve was given a rare chance to "know" certain aspects of her mother (and her uncle, and her father, Jim) that had been lost to her, and by facing them she was able to accept and open herself up to a fulfilling life.

Q.   Genevieve's cousin Catharine and her new friends, Sylviane and Philippe in particular, are such vibrant and unique characters. Did you have a favorite secondary character in the book?

A.   I would have to say Sylviane. I just love her energy and fun outlook on life. She has the straightforward, honest, yet sweet and caring style characteristic of many of the Frenchwomen I know. It can be rather startling at first to a Californian who is used to polite obfuscation, but ultimately I find it so charming! And after all, who wouldn't want a Parisian friend like Sylviane to take you to historic cemeteries and shopping and lunch—and to do a Parisian-style makeover?

Q.   Would you ever consider moving to Paris for a year? What about life there most appeals to you?

A.   Short answer: *Yes!* There are the obvious reasons: the wine, the food, the music and romance and art and architecture and history. But there's so much more. Even though Paris is a sophisticated, international city, things in Europe are still more old-fashioned than in much of the United States: There's an emphasis on family and long meals and conversation and taking time to relax and enjoy. I find this not only in France, but also in Italy and Spain and Mexico and Cuba. Even though I was born and raised in the area that became California's Silicon Valley, and even though I use computers every day to write and correspond and reach out to readers, I feel like some human part of us has been lost in the modern shuffle. I relish the slower pace, a chance to sit in parks and dream and read; and the knowledge that the time spent *not* working is easily as important as the time spent toiling away. And finally, I love to travel: I adore meeting new people and learning new languages and experiencing different ways of life. I think it opens up one's mind and soul and heart.

Q.   What do you think will be the biggest impact of Genevieve's decision to follow her heart? Do you think she will be more successful at opening herself up to those around her in Paris than she was back home?

A.   Oh yes, very much so. *The Paris Key* is about a moment of transition: not so much of an unhappy woman finding happiness, but more a shut-down person learning to open herself up to life: to new experiences and friends and love *and* even heartbreak—because you have to be willing to risk heartbreak in order to truly love. I imagine Genevieve will pursue her training as a locksmith, will continue to get to know her neighbors, and will take on her uncle's role as a cherished member of the community. Perhaps with Killian at her side, and perhaps not. Either way, I think she will make her decision based not on fear, but on what she wants and needs as a woman.

Q.   There's an undercurrent of mystery running throughout The Paris Key. *As a mystery author as well as an author of women's fiction novels, was that piece important to you?*

A.   I think all novels are mysteries at their base: Why did so-and-so do what they did? What happened? What was the motivation? What will happen in the future? How will the issues be resolved? As humans, we're hard-wired to be curious about other people's lives and experiences. We read in order to hear a story, to find out what happened or what the characters decide, and who they really are. I've always been drawn to stories about secrets—especially family secrets—and their long-reaching ramifications. Writing *The Paris Key* was different from my genre writing in that I was able to delve much more into the psyches of my characters and how the past affects them, rather than trying to uncover a murderer! It felt luxurious, somehow, to recount the sensory details of the Parisian surroundings and to explore the personal reflections and reactions of the characters. And in the end, to find out the whole mystery, since it was unraveled only as I wrote *The Paris Key*!

Questions for Discussion

1. Genevieve is sure that a drastic change of scene—moving to Paris—will make her happy. Do you believe in the geographical cure? What do you think about the possibility for new or different surroundings to bring out hidden aspects of someone's personality—or do they just make familiar problems worse?

2. When Genevieve moves to Paris, she leaves her comfort zone behind her. What do you feel is the hardest part about moving somewhere new? After reading *The Paris Key*, what do you think are the best and worst aspects of being forced out of one's comfort zone?

3. Genevieve finds life in Paris slower than in the United States, with a greater emphasis on seemingly old-fashioned pursuits such as reading, cooking, and spending time in parks and museums. Do you think you would enjoy that sort of lifestyle? How do you feel you would adjust to the slow pace of life in France? Do any potential drawbacks come to mind?

4. Do you think tourists see famous cities differently than the residents? In what ways? Will the novelty of Paris wear off for Genevieve, or will she find a permanent home there? What from the story makes you feel that way?

5. Genevieve often wishes she could have known her mother as an adult. Do you think women are destined to become some version of their mothers? In what ways do you think Genevieve became like hers, and in what ways did she follow a different path?

6. Did her Paris experiences transform Genevieve into someone new—or did it make her a "better" version of herself?

7. Are there parts of Genevieve's married life you can relate to? How about Angela's life on the farm in Petaluma?

8. Do you enjoy a novel more when the heroine is someone a lot like you or someone very unlike you?

9. Do you think what Angela did was unforgivable? How do you think it related to her struggles with depression?

10. Throughout the book, Sylviane encourages Genevieve and helps her adjust to living in Paris. Do you think Genevieve would have made the same choices without Sylviane's support? Do you have someone like this in your life? When have you been most grateful for his or her point of view?

11. Would you have gone down to explore the catacombs, despite the warnings to steer clear? Do you think the catacombs serve as a metaphor in the novel, and if so, in what ways?

12. Does it really matter who Genevieve's biological father was? Do you think Jim knew the truth? What about Dave? If Angela had lived, do you think she would have told Genevieve when she was old enough to understand?

13. What do you think are the most powerful uses of symbolism in *The Paris Key*? Do you agree with Catharine that the fable of "Fitcher's Bird" was relevant to Genevieve's experiences?

14. An important turning point in the book comes about when Genevieve has a realization: "Genevieve feared she kept her mother's

ghost alive, kept it strapped to her back like a proverbial monkey." Do you think Genevieve would have been able to release her mother's ghost if she hadn't come to Paris?

Juliet Blackwell was born and raised in the San Francisco Bay Area, the youngest child of a jet pilot and an editor. She graduated with a degree in Latin American studies from the University of California, Santa Cruz, and went on to earn master's degrees in anthropology and social work. While in graduate school, she published several articles based on her research with immigrant families from Mexico and Vietnam, as well as one full-length translation: Miguel León-Portilla's seminal work, *Endangered Cultures*. Juliet taught medical anthropology at SUNY-Albany, was producer for a BBC documentary, and worked as an elementary school social worker. Upon her return to California, she became a professional artist and ran her own decorative painting and design studio for more than a decade. In addition to mainstream novels, Juliet pens the *New York Times* bestselling Witchcraft Mysteries and the Haunted Home Renovation series. As Hailey Lind she wrote the Agatha Award–nominated Art Lover's Mystery series. She makes her home in northern California, but spends as much time as possible in Europe and Latin America.

Center Point Large Print
600 Brooks Road / PO Box 1
Thorndike, ME 04986-0001 USA

(207) 568-3717

US & Canada:
1 800 929-9108
www.centerpointlargeprint.com